D0231252

THE DARKEST DAY

Håkan Nesser is one of Sweden's most popular crime writers and has received numerous awards for his novels about Inspector Van Veeteren, including the European Crime Fiction Star Award (Ripper Award), the Swedish Crime Writers' Academy Prize (three times) and Scandinavia's Glass Key Award. His Van Veeteren series is published in over twenty-five countries and has sold over ten million copies worldwide. His standalone novel, *The Living and the Dead in Winsford*, was awarded the Rosenkrantz Prize for Best Thriller of the Year. *The Darkest Day* is the first novel in his Barbarotti series. He lives in Gotland with his wife, and spends part of each year in the UK.

Also by Håkan Nesser

THE LIVING AND THE DEAD
IN WINSFORD

The Van Veeteren series

THE MIND'S EYE

BORKMANN'S POINT

THE RETURN

WOMAN WITH A BIRTHMARK

THE INSPECTOR AND SILENCE

THE UNLUCKY LOTTERY

HOUR OF THE WOLF

THE WEEPING GIRL

THE STRANGLER'S HONEYMOON

THE G FILE

HÅKAN NESSER

THE DARKEST DAY

Translated from the Swedish by
Sarah Death

PAN BOOKS

First published 2017 by Mantle

First published in paperback 2017 by Mantle

This paperback edition first published 2018 by Pan Books
an imprint of Pan Macmillan
20 New Wharf Road, London N1 9RR
Associated companies throughout the world
www.panmacmillan.com

ISBN 978-1-5098-0934-9

Originally published in 2006 as *Människa utan hund*
by Albert Bonniers Förlag, Stockholm.

1 3 5 7 9 8 6 4 2

A CIP catalogue record for this book is available from the British Library.

Printed and bound by CPI Group (UK) Ltd, Croydon, CR0 4YY

Visit **www.panmacmillan.com** to read more about all our books
and to buy them. You will also find features, author interviews and
news of any author events, and you can sign up for e-newsletters
so that you're always first to hear about our new releases.

The town of Kymlinge does not exist in real life and Albert Bonniers Förlag has never published a volume of poetry entitled *The Fruiterer's Example*. Other than that, the contents of this book accord in all essentials with the known state of affairs.

ONE

DECEMBER

1

When Rosemarie Wunderlich Hermansson awoke on Sunday 18 December it was a few minutes to six and she had a very vivid image in her head.

She was standing in a doorway, looking out over an unfamiliar garden. It was summer, or early autumn. In particular, she was looking at two fat little birds; yellowy-green in colour, they were perched on a telephone wire ten to fifteen metres away and each had a speech bubble coming from its beak.

You've got to kill yourself, she read in one bubble.

You've got to kill Karl-Erik, she read in the other.

The messages were for her. She, Rosemarie Wunderlich Hermansson, was the one who had to kill herself. Or kill Karl-Erik. There was absolutely no doubt on that score.

Karl-Erik was her husband, and it took a few seconds for her to register that both of these absurd stipulations must of course have arisen from something she had dreamt – but it was a dream that swiftly faded, leaving only these two bizarre birds on a wire. Most peculiar.

For a little while she lay quite still on her right-hand side, stared out into the surrounding darkness in the direction of a fictitious dawn, which at that point had presumably progressed no further than the Urals, listened to Karl-Erik's invariably calm breathing and realized that the analysis in the vision was entirely correct. The birds had spread their stubby wings and flown off, but their statements still hung there, impossible to misinterpret.

Her or Karl-Erik. That was how it had to be. There had been an *or* between the speech bubbles, not an *and*. One precluded the other, and it also felt like a . . . like an absolutely imperative necessity for her to choose one or the other of these alternatives. Jesus Christ, she thought, swinging her legs over the side of the bed and sitting up. How could it have come to this? As if this family hasn't already had its fair share.

But as she straightened her back and felt the familiar morning aches around her third and fourth lumbar vertebrae, everyday thoughts came creeping in as well. A safe but rather tedious balm for the soul. She accepted them with a sort of listless gratitude, thrust her hands under her armpits and padded out to the bathroom. We're so defenceless first thing in the morning, she thought. So thin-skinned and vulnerable. A sixty-three-year-old needlework teacher doesn't murder her husband, it's completely out of the question.

Admittedly she had taught German as well, but that didn't appreciably alter their respective positions. Didn't make it more acceptable in any way; what on earth was the distinction between needlework and German in that context?

So presumably it is my own time in this vale of tears I will have to cut short, thought Rosemarie Wunderlich Hermansson. She switched on the light, regarded her large, smooth face in the mirror and noted that someone had stuck a smile on it.

Why am I smiling, she thought. There's nothing to smile about, is there? I've never felt worse in my life and Karl-Erik will be awake in half an hour. What was it the headmaster said? *The deeply resonant ore that . . . that what? . . . that provided the rising generation with its moral and intellectual sounding board?* Where the hell had he dredged that up from? What a chump. *Age group after age group, generation after generation, for forty years. Amassing growth rings like a pedagogical pine tree.*

Yes, Porky Bergson really had called Karl-Erik a pedagogical pine tree. Could there conceivably have been a hint of irony there?

Probably not, thought Rosemarie Wunderlich Hermansson, jabbing her electric toothbrush deep into her right cheek. Vera Ragnebjörk, her only teaching colleague in the almost extinct German language at Kymlingevik School, always used to say that Porky Bergson lacked the ironic dimension. That was why you could never talk to him as you did to other people, and it was presumably thanks to this unique deficiency that he had managed to remain the head of that school for more than thirty years.

Porky Bergson was only a year or two younger than Karl-Erik himself, but a good forty kilos heavier, and until that sad day nearly eight years ago, when his wife Berit died after falling out of a ski lift in Kitzbühel and breaking her neck, they had socialized quite a lot. All four of them. Bridge and so on. A trip to the theatre in Stockholm. A disastrous week in Crete. Rosemarie thought she missed Berit a bit, but she didn't miss Porky Bergson. Social contact with him, that is.

Why am I wasting my precious morning minutes on thoughts of that dimensionally challenged nonentity? she asked herself. Why don't I grab the chance of fifteen minutes' peace and quiet with the morning paper instead? I'm definitely losing control.

*

But no positive thoughts surfaced over her coffee and newspaper either. There were no bright spots. When she raised her eyes and looked at the kitchen clock – bought on impulse at the Kungens Kurva branch of IKEA for forty-nine kronor fifty as far back as autumn 1979 and presumably indestructible – it said twenty past six, so it would be at least seventeen hours until she was again granted clemency and allowed to snuggle up in her bed, putting another dismal day aside. To sleep, just sleep.

Today was Sunday. It was her second day as a happy pensioner, the final significant rite of passage before death, as some kindly soul had pointed out, and she told herself that if only she'd had access to a gun she would have acted on that wakening thought without delay. Shot a bullet into her brain before Karl-Erik had time to get to the kitchen in his striped pyjamas, thrust out his chest and declare that he'd slept like a baby. If those near-death descriptions she'd read about were right, it would be interesting to perch up there by the ceiling and watch his face when he found her slumped over the table with her head in a big, warm pool of blood.

But that's something you just don't do, either. Especially if you don't possess a decent gun and do have the children to think of. She took a gulp of coffee, burnt the tip of her tongue and put her everyday brain into gear. What was on the programme on this, her second day after a whole working life?

Clean the entire house. It was that simple. Children and grandchildren would be arriving in dribs and drabs tomorrow, and Tuesday was the big day.

The day that should have been the Day with a capital 'D', but had in some peculiar fashion shrunk into a kind of pompous anti-event because of Robert. That was exactly it. All through the autumn there had been talk of between 100 and 120 people; the only real upper limit had been imposed by the seating capacity of the Svea restaurant, but Karl-Erik had discussed the matter eight or possibly twelve times with Brundin – the manager – and if they went a little over the hundred it would be no problem at all.

Wouldn't have been. Robert's scandal had begun on 12 November. The venue had been booked for a very long time, but it hadn't been too late to cancel. Seventy or so invitations had already gone out and a score of positive replies had come in, but people were very understanding when it was explained to them that circumstances had led to a change of plan and a smaller family occasion.

Altogether very understanding. The programme had had almost two million viewers, and those who had not been watching had read all about it in the tabloids the next day.

WANKER ROB. The headline on the news-stands was seared into Rosemarie's maternal heart like the brand on a scabby sow, and she knew that ever after, for as long as she lived, she would never be able to think of Robert without adding that ghastly epithet. She had decided never again to read either *Aftonbladet* or *Expressen*, a promise she had not broken thus far, nor been remotely tempted to break.

So, it was to be a smallish family occasion. And it had been the same at school. The same discreet, charitable curtain had descended there, too. When Mr and Mrs Hermansson, with their combined total of sixty-six years' service, both retired from the bloodstained tiltyard of teaching at the very same moment, as some wit – it could scarcely have been Porky

Bergson – had put it, their presentation and leaving party amounted to nothing more than an extended staff meeting with cake, the appropriate number of red roses and a set of hammered-copper mulled wine cups – and Rosemarie, opening the parcel and catching a glimpse, could not help wondering whether Elonsson's hopeless Year 8s had been obliged to knock them together in the metalwork room in order to avoid a fail mark. Elonsson, unlike Porky Bergson, was possessed of a highly developed sense of irony.

Sixty-five plus forty. That was December's other big sum, and it came to 105. Rosemarie knew Karl-Erik was aggrieved that it hadn't come to a round hundred, but there was no fiddling with facts of that kind. Karl-Erik never fiddled any kind of fact. She tentatively stretched her back a couple of times without getting up from her chair and thought back to that night, forty years before, when she had managed not to bear down through two contractions, and thus delayed things until after midnight. Karl-Erik's poorly concealed joy had been unmistakable, and thank goodness, after all that effort. Their firstborn daughter had emerged from the womb on his own twenty-fifth birthday. There had always been an inordinately strong bond between Ebba and Karl-Erik, and Rosemarie knew that it had been forged at that moment. Right there in Örebro hospital at four minutes past midnight on 20 December 1965. The midwife was called Geraldine Tulpin, and that was a name that was hard to forget, too.

The family's Christmas celebrations had always suffered a certain distortion. Rosemarie had never put it into words – but a distortion was definitely the way to describe it. Ordinary people, Christian or otherwise, saw 24 December as the hub round which the winter darkness amassed, but for the Wunderlich Hermanssons, the twentieth was at least as important. Karl-Erik and Ebba's birthday; the day after the shortest of the year, the heart of darkness, and in some strange way Karl-Erik – without fiddling the facts, though he had come pretty close – had succeeded in shifting things by a day, to achieve a sort of triumvirate. His own birthday. Ebba's birthday. The return of light to the earth.

Ebba had always been her father's darling, the apple of his eye; from the very beginning, and ever since, he had invested his greatest hopes in her. He had never even tried to hide it: some children are of a higher carat than others, that's just the way it is in the genetic melting pot of biology, he had explained on one occasion when, unusually for him, he had enjoyed one cognac too many. Whether we like it or not. Rosemarie poured a second cup of coffee – a reliable cornerstone in stabilizing the wakeful state she relished so little – and thought, grimly and cynically, that the way things looked at the moment, he had undeniably backed the right horse.

Ebba was a rock. Robert had always been a black sheep and now he had put himself beyond the limits of acceptable behaviour; perhaps it came as less of a surprise than they were pretending. Kristina? Well, pretty much all you could say about Kristina was that she was the way she was; the baby had steadied her a bit and the last few years had brought slightly calmer sailing than those that went before, but Karl-Erik stubbornly insisted it was too soon to count their chickens, far too soon.

When did you last count any chickens, my wooden prince, Rosemarie had thought every time he said it, and she thought it again now in her dawn-less kitchen.

At that very moment, he came in.

'Good morning,' he said. 'It's odd. In spite of everything, I slept like a baby.'

'It all feels rather panicky to me,' she said.

'What does?' said Karl-Erik Hermansson, switching on the kettle. 'Where did you put my new tea?'

'Second shelf,' said Rosemarie. 'Selling the house and moving to that urbanization, of course. It feels ... well, as though we're panicking. Like I said. No, on the left.'

He clattered about with cups and caddies. 'Ur-ba-ni-za-ción,' he articulated, with genuine Spanish phonemes. 'I know you feel a bit dubious at the moment, but one day you'll thank me.'

'I doubt it,' said Rosemarie Wunderlich Hermansson. 'I doubt it to the tips of my toes. You need to trim your nose hairs.'

'Rosemarie,' said Karl-Erik, thrusting out his chest. 'I can't look people in the eye any more, here at home. A man has to be able to keep a straight back and hold his head high.'

'You have to be able to bend, too,' she retorted. 'This will pass. People will forget and get things back into reasonable proport—'

He interrupted her by slamming down his new tea caddy on the worktop. 'I think we've discussed all this enough. Lundgren promised we'd be able to sign the papers on Wednesday. I've had it with this town. *Basta*. All that's keeping us here is cowardice and inertia.'

'We've lived here for thirty-eight years,' said Rosemarie.

'Long enough,' said Karl-Erik. 'Have you had two cups of coffee already? Remember what I told you.'

'The idea of moving to a place that hasn't even got a name. They could at least have called it something.'

'It will get a name, as soon as the Spanish authorities decide on one. What's wrong with Estepona?'

'It's seven kilometres to Estepona. Four kilometres to the sea.'

He didn't answer. He poured boiling water on his health-promoting green tea leaves and got the sunflower loaf out of the bread bin. She sighed. They had discussed her breakfast habits for twenty-five years. They had discussed selling the house and moving to Spain for twenty-five days. Though discussed was hardly the right word, thought Rosemarie. Karl-Erik had made up his mind and then used his well-oiled democratic disposition to get her onto his side. That was the way it had always been. He never gave up. On any matter of importance, he was prepared to talk and talk and talk until she threw in the towel out of pure boredom and exhaustion. Classic filibustering. It could be the purchase of a car. It could be the wildly expensive bookshelves in the library – as he liked to call their shared study, where he spent forty hours a week and she four. It could be holidays to Ireland, Belarus or the Ruhr: this was expected, if you were the head of department for social sciences and geography.

And he had paid a deposit on that house between Estepona and Fuengirola without asking her. Entered into negotiations with Lundgren at the bank about selling their house without instituting the democratic process at home. He couldn't deny it, nor did he try to.

Though perhaps she ought to be grateful, really. It could just as well have been Finland or the Wuppertal. I've lived with that man all my adult life, she suddenly thought. I believed things might gradually mature between us, but it never happened. The thing was rotten from the word go and just got more rotten as the years passed.

And why was she so hopelessly lacking in independence that she had to blame her wasted life on him? Surely that was the ultimate sign of weakness?

'What are you brooding about, sitting there all quiet like that?' he said.

'Nothing,' she said.

'Within six months we'll have forgotten all this,' he said.

'Forgotten what? Our lives? Our children?'

'Don't talk rubbish. You know what I mean.'

'No, I don't. And incidentally, wouldn't it be better if Ebba and Leif stayed at the hotel? There are four of them. Four adults, it'll be a tight squeeze.'

He glared at her as if she were a pupil who had forgotten to hand in her homework for the third lesson in a row, and she knew she had only suggested it to annoy him. Of course, she was right that Ebba and Leif and two teenage sons took up more space than they could provide here at home, but Ebba was Ebba and Karl-Erik would rather sell his last tie than accommodate his favourite daughter anywhere but in the house, and the room, where she had grown up. Especially as it was the last time, the last time ever.

She felt a lump in her throat and swallowed down the rest of her lukewarm coffee. And Robert? Well, poor Robert would of course have to be hidden away from the eyes of the world as much as possible; they couldn't have him lounging about the hotel, where anybody at all could goggle and jeer at him. Wanker Rob from *Fucking Island*. The last time she spoke to him, the night before last, he had sounded almost on the verge of tears.

So it would be Kristina, Jakob and little Kelvin who had to check into the hotel. How could you christen a child Kelvin? The scientist associated with absolute zero, Karl-Erik had enlightened the new parents, but it had made no difference. Anyway, she was pretty sure they would see the hotel as a lucky draw; the emotional state Kristina had induced in Rosemarie ever since she grew up and left home was a triple-headed sensation of guilt, inferiority and failure. And for a brief but distinct moment, she became aware that the only one of her three children she really cared about and felt any compassion for was Robert. Was it because he was a boy? Was it that simple?

Though perhaps there would be some kind of opening with Kristina, sooner or later; for her, that is, hardly for Karl-Erik. He had always been the primary target of the girl's obstinance. Was there such a word? Obstinance? It had been like that ever since the day she reached puberty, but the pedagogical pine had remained unbending and bark-bound through an eternity of quarrels and arguments and disputes – displaying just the qualities one would expect from that sort of upright specimen. Stand your ground and never budge an inch.

I'm being unfair on him, she thought. But I'm so bloody sick and tired I feel like throwing up over the whole wretched thing.

As the seven o'clock radio news approached, Karl-Erik held forth, presenting a series of weighty and irrefutable arguments for letting Ebba and family stay in the house – and Rosemarie found herself thinking that what she actually wanted to do was go over to him, yank his tongue towards her and cut it off.

He had made his pedagogical contribution, so now it was time.

Followed by the automatic thought that she was being unfair again.

'All right, all right,' she said. 'It doesn't matter.'

'Fine,' he said. 'I'm glad we're in agreement. We'll have to try to treat Robert exactly as normal, that's all. I don't want us to mention that – thing. I'll discuss it with him in private, that'll have to do. What time did he say he was coming?'

'Late afternoon or early evening. He'll be driving. He didn't say anything more specific.'

Karl-Erik Hermansson nodded thoughtfully, opened his mouth wide and loaded in a heaped spoonful of natural yogurt with chunky muesli, untouched by human hand and enriched with thirty-two beneficial vitamins plus selenium.

She vacuumed upstairs. In a spirit of domestic solidarity, Karl-Erik had taken the shopping list and the car and gone off to the palatial Co-op superstore – which had opened a year before on the Billundsberg industrial estate – to buy five hundred kilos of birthday essentials and a Christmas tree. As Rosemarie dragged round the ancient Volta, bought at Eriksson Bros. Electric Machines, Home & Household back in the late winter of 1983 and presumably indestructible, she thought about the number of important decisions she had actually taken in her sixty-three years of life.

To marry Karl-Erik Pedagogue-Pine? Scarcely. They had met in their upper-secondary years at the Karolinska Grammar School (she an unassuming first year, he a stylish, besuited, ramrod-straight third year) and he had worn down her resistance in the same way he had continued to wear her down throughout the remainder of their life together. When he proposed, her initial *no* had been diluted via a second *maybe, but let's at least leave it until we've taken our exams* to a third *OK then, but we'll need somewhere to live first*. They had married in 1963, she had completed the textiles course at the Domestic Science College in June 1965 and Ebba had come into the world six months later. This, too, was not the result of any decision she had made.

She opted for a career as a needlework teacher because her best (and only) friend at upper-secondary school, Bodil Rönn, had already done so. They graduated together and Bodil got a permanent job in a school way up north in Boden, less than 500 metres from her boyfriend Sune's parental home, and as far as Rosemarie knew they still lived there. They had written each other letters and kept in touch for about fifteen years, but the last Christmas card had been seven or eight years ago.

Zero important decisions so far, she thought, dragging the monstrous Volta across the hall to start on the guest bedrooms. Or the former children's rooms, or whatever you wanted to call them. Ebba's room, Robert's room and Kristina's cramped little hole that wasn't really any bigger than a cupboard – but then it had never been their intention to have more than two children, especially in view of the fact that they had achieved one of each sex after only two attempts, but things had turned out the way they had. Life went its own sweet way and didn't always stick to the plan; Kristina was born in 1974, Rosemarie having come off the pill ten months earlier on her gynaecologist's advice, and if the disastrous Greek holiday with the Porky Bergsons had not given rise to any happier memories, it had at any rate begotten an unplanned daughter. Karl-Erik had forgotten to buy condoms and didn't get out in time. That was just the way it was, shit happens in this best of all possible worlds as it does everywhere else. What was this language in which her thoughts were clothing themselves, this bleak winter morning? God knows, something was out of kilter, that was for sure. What was the weather playing at? They still hadn't had so much as a centimetre of snow in this westerly part of Sweden and when she looked out of the window it seemed to her that the daylight, too, had given up and thrown in the towel. The air looked like porridge.

It was only when she had rolled up the long mat in the hall and started on the skirting boards with the vacuum-cleaner nozzle that she finally recalled one crucial decision. Hell, yes.

He was called Göran, went round in sandals without socks, and had been the stand-in school counsellor one autumn term. It was her third term at the school, five years after she had Kristina, and she simply couldn't get her head round the idea that a thirty-six-year-old mother-of-three really was what this beardy charmer needed, so as a consequence she had said no. And in all probability, it was this *no* that comprised the most important decision of her life. Turning down a broad-shouldered, freshly divorced school counsellor who had the hots for her. It had all happened on a staff training course held in the conference suite on board a ferry to Finland; the pedagogue pine had been ill for only the third time in his life (if you didn't count the congenital umbilical hernia), and the counsellor had sat in her cabin half the night, pouring out his passion. He had pleaded, he had begged. Offered her duty-free

Wolf's Paw cocktails. But no. Offered her duty-free cloudberry liqueur. But no.

She wondered what had happened to him; he had sun-tanned toes with interesting little tufts of hair and had presented an opportunity to change her life – but she had let him slip through her fingers. Just as well, perhaps; only one man had ever gained access to her most private regions, now desiccated and closed forever – but to be fair, as far as she knew, Karl-Erik's dick had never once strayed in their forty-two years, either. Before they got married he confessed that he was once together with a girl called Katarina at an all-night Saint Lucia party in the second year of upper secondary, but she wasn't really his type, a fact underlined a few years into the 1980s when she enjoyed brief notoriety as a hostage taker in the course of a bank raid in Säffle. Though why anyone would raid a bank in Säffle, of all insignificant places . . .

Anyway: the number of important decisions taken re-mained at the uncomfortable total of one. Rosemarie decided she'd done enough sucking up for now and wondered whether there was any justification for the optimistic thought that she might be strong enough for decision number two. The house was in both their names, she knew that. Without her signa-ture on the documents on Wednesday, the whole sale would fall through. The buyers were a couple called Singlöv, cur-rently living out in Rimminge; all she knew about them was that he was an electrician and they had two children.

But there was absolutely nothing she could do about the fact that a non-refundable down payment of a hundred thou-sand kronor had been made on a small house in Spain. Costa Geriatrica, wasn't that what they called it? For a painful second, another potential headline flashed into her mind's eye: WANKER ROB'S PARENTS FLEE TO COSTA GERIATRICA!

If only I weren't so dispirited, she thought, switching on the coffee machine again. If only everything didn't feel so horribly pointless. Where can I find strength to draw on?

A Needlework Teacher's Demise, she thought a minute later as she sank down at the kitchen table with her third cup of the day. That would make a pretty passable title for a book or a play, in her judgement, but being stuck in the middle of the action herself was no fun at all.

Humph, came a protest from some as yet unordered corner of her brain, I don't normally let myself get this overwhelmed by so many disconsolate thoughts. Could I possibly have had a little stroke this morning? If only I were a smoker, I would at least have the option of a quick drag.

What on earth is up with my brain today, thought Rose-marie Wunderlich Hermansson. It was only ten o'clock. There were still a good twelve hours to go before bedtime, and tomorrow children and grandchildren would come streaming in like . . . well, like what?

Press-ganged soldiers for a cancelled war?

O life, where is thy sting?

2

Kristoffer Grundt lay in his bed, wrestling with a curious wish.

He wanted to skip the next four days of his life.

Perhaps it wasn't such a curious wish for other people, he didn't know, but for him it was a first. He was fourteen years old, and he wondered if it was a sign that he was starting to grow up.

Of course, there were things he dreaded. Maths tests. PE lessons at the pool. Finding himself stuck in a quiet corner of the school with Oscar Sommarlath and Kenny Lythén from 9C.

But above all, the hardest thing of all to bear: his mother's look when she saw right into him and exposed what miserable stuff he was made of.

Not the same stuff as Henrik. Not by a long way. Something had gone wrong when it came to Kristoffer. They had the same genes, the same parents, the same brilliant inbuilt advantages; no, the problem was the tiny detail that was himself. Kristoffer Tobias Grundt and his backbone. No, wrong, Kristoffer Tobias Grundt and his lack of backbone. The hole he carried about with him at the centre of his soul where normal people had their character.

That was exactly it. That was how bad it was when you took a really close look.

But skipping four days? Deliberately shortening your life by ninety-six hours? Wasn't that an affront to the whole . . . concept?

The time was half past nine. It was Sunday. If it were Thursday tomorrow instead, it would be the twenty-second and two days to Christmas Eve. If he ever reached that point, he promised himself to break off and send a grateful thought back to now. To think backwards and remind himself that time, whatever else you might imagine, does move forward in spite of everything.

The problem was that it often passed so horribly slowly, and never skipped anything.

It wouldn't skip the unbearable car journey to Kymlinge.

It wouldn't skip Granny and Granddad and the other clueless relations.

It wouldn't skip the hundred-and-fifth birthday party and the equally unbearable car journey home.

And, thought Kristoffer, closing his eyes, above all it wouldn't skip the conversation with Mum.

'I realize,' she had said from the dark depths of the living-room sofa last night, just when he thought he'd crept in unseen and unheard. 'I realize that to you, this seems about the right time to get back. It's two in the morning. Come here and breathe on me.'

He'd gone over to her and blown a thin jet of air over her face. He hadn't been able to see her eyes in the dark, and she had offered no immediate comment. But he was under no illusion.

'Tomorrow morning,' she said. 'I expect an explanation. I'm tired, Kristoffer.'

He sighed, turned over in bed and transferred his thoughts to Linda Granberg.

It was Linda Granberg's fault he'd had six beers and a glass of red wine and smoked ten cigarettes last night. It was Linda Granberg's fault he'd decided to go to Jens&Måns's party at all. Jens&Måns were twins, fellow Year 8s but in a parallel class, and they had parents who were lax about their responsibilities. Who, just to take one example, went out to a party of their own in town and promised not to be back before three. Who admittedly wouldn't buy alcohol for their offspring, but who had quite generous supplies down in the basement and didn't do much stocktaking.

There were supposed to be eight of them, but Kristoffer counted at least fifteen. People came and went. He downed four beers within the first hour; Erik told him it had more effect if you got well stoked up to start with, and it had worked reasonably well. Linda looked to be keeping pace with him, and he had been bold enough to squeeze in beside her on the sofa and chat to her in a way he'd never brought himself to try before. She laughed at him and with him, and just before eleven she took his hand and said she liked him. Half an hour later, after another beer each, they started kissing, the very first time in his case, and she tasted so gloriously of beer and crisps and fresh tobacco and something soft and warm and delicious that was simply her. The very . . . what was it called? . . . essence? . . . of Linda Granberg. Lying there in bed ten hours later, he could still run his tongue round the inside of his mouth and detect lingering traces of the taste.

But it was a sad and swiftly evaporating memory. Mainly sad. After the kissing, they'd eaten pizza straight out of the box with their hands, one of the twins brought round acidic wine-box wine in plastic cups and then Linda started feeling sick. She stood up, swayed around a bit, and promised to be back soon. Staggered out in the direction of where you'd expect the toilet to be, and half an hour later he'd found her in a completely different room, sleeping in the arms of Krille Lundin from 9B. He'd begged a beer off Erik, smoked another three cigarettes and gone home. When he came to think of it, it wasn't just the next four days he felt like erasing from history, he rather wanted to include yesterday as well.

Linda Granberg, fuck you, he thought, but they were just empty words, because in the most literal sense that was exactly what he wanted to do. If he was being honest. And if he'd just played his cards a bit better, it could have been him and not Hockey-Krille Lundin lying there with his arms around her, he knew that. What a bloody lottery life could be, but of course a fifteen-year-old TV hockey jock had odds a thousand times better than a . . . well, what? Doughball? Mega-loser? Zero, nerd, nada? There were plenty of names to choose from.

He gave a start as he saw his mother at the door.

'We're just off to the shops. Perhaps you could make sure you get up and eat breakfast, and we'll have that talk when we get back.'

'Sure,' he said. He meant it to sound bright and accommodating, but the sound that issued from his throat had more in common with the cry of a very small animal that happens to get in the way of a lawnmower.

'Perhaps we could start by establishing who this conversation is going to be about?'

'It's about me,' said Kristoffer, trying to return his mother's steely blue gaze with a green-flecked one of his own. It didn't seem to go all that well.

'You Kristoffer, yes,' she said slowly, folding her hands in front of her on the kitchen table. It was just the two of them. The time was half past eleven. His father Leif had gone out on fresh commissions. Henrik had got home late yesterday evening after a demanding first term at university in Uppsala. Both doors were shut, and the dishwasher was grumbling to itself.

'Go ahead,' she said.

'We had an agreement,' said Kristoffer. 'I broke it.'

'Uh huh?'

'I should have been home at twelve. I didn't get back until two.'

'Ten minutes past.'

'Ten minutes past two.'

She leaned a little closer to him. Imagine if she gave me a hug, he thought. Right now. But he knew that he wouldn't get one until all this had been looked into. And it hadn't been looked into yet. Far from it.

'I don't like having to keep asking questions, Kristoffer. Is there anything else you want to tell me?'

He took a deep breath. 'I lied. Before, I mean.'

'I don't follow.'

'Before. I never planned to go to Jonas's.'

She indicated her surprise by raising one eyebrow by a couple of millimetres. But she didn't say anything.

'I said, didn't I, that Jonas and I were going to watch some films round at his place, but that was a lie.'

'Ah?'

'I was at the twins'.'

'Which twins?'

Why do you keep interrupting me with questions if you don't like asking them? he thought.

'Måns and Jens Pettersson.'

'I see. And why did you need to lie about that?'

'If I'd told the truth, you and Dad wouldn't have let me go.'

'Why wouldn't we have let you go?'

'Because it isn't . . . a good place to be on a Saturday night.'

'What would be wrong with going to the Petterssons' on a Saturday night?'

'They drink . . . we were drinking. There were ten or fifteen of us and we were drinking beer and smoking. I don't know why I went there, it was rubbish.'

She nodded and he could see he had caused her great pain. 'I don't really understand. Why did you go there, then? You must have had some reason.'

'I don't know.'

'So you're telling me you don't know why you do things, Kristoffer? That really worries me.' She looked concerned now, genuinely concerned. Give me a hug then, for Christ's sake, he thought. I'll never be good enough for you, whatever happens. Give me a hug and then let's forget this.

'I just wanted to see . . . I suppose.'

'See what?'

'What it was like.'

'What what was like?'

'Smoking and boozing, for heaven's sake! Can't you stop now, you can see I'm not up to it . . .'

The tears and feeling of hopelessness came welling up all of a sudden and much sooner than he had expected, and in a way he was grateful for that. It felt good to just give up. His head slumped to the table and he hid his face in his armpit and let the sobs come. But she didn't move, or say a word. The sobbing ebbed away after a minute or two and then he got up, went over to the draining board and tore off a generous length of kitchen towel. He blew his nose and came back to the table.

They sat in silence for a while longer, and it gradually dawned on him that she had no intention of hugging him.

'I want you to tell Dad about this as well, Kristoffer,' she said. 'And I want to know if you are planning to lie to us again, or if I can rely on you. Perhaps you'll decide to spend more time with the Pettersson twins in future? We're your family, Dad and I, and Henrik, but if you'd rather—'

'No, I—' he interrupted, but she interrupted him back.

'Choosing whether to go down the path of truth or lies is an important decision. You'd better spend a few days thinking it over.'

Then she got to her feet and left him sitting there.

Nope, not a single touch, he thought. She didn't even run her hand across my back.

And a feeling of mute rigidity, as new as it was paralysing, spread rapidly through his body. He left it a moment and then rushed out of the kitchen, upstairs and into his room. He could hear that Henrik was awake on the other side of the thin wall, and threw himself on the bed with a silent prayer that his big brother would decide to have a shower before he came in to say hello.

They'd swap me if they could, thought Kristoffer Grundt to himself. In fact, they would have swapped me for a different son long ago.

*

Leif Grundt gave his son a rather half-hearted hug after the short conversation he had with him before they sat down to dinner, noting not for the first time how different he and his wife were.

And that was putting it mildly. Ebba was a force to be reckoned with, but also a puzzle, that was exactly how he generally defined her, and what was more, a puzzle he had long since given up any prospect of solving. Ever. In the case of Kristoffer's debut with alcohol and tobacco – assuming it really was his debut, as he steadfastly maintained – the important thing, as far as his wife was concerned, was the lie. The betrayal inherent in not telling the truth, the conscious breach of their agreement.

For his part, Leif thought exactly the opposite. If the boy wanted to smoke and drink he sure as heck couldn't go round telling his parents about it in advance, could he? In the long term, he ran the risk of cirrhosis of the liver from the booze and lung cancer from the fags, but surely no one had ever died of a little lie?

Sooner a teetotal liar than a truthful alcoholic, in Leif Grundt's view. If one were to choose a future for one's children – not something that he imagined for a second would fall to his lot.

He couldn't deny that he did have a slightly dubious relationship with lies per se. If you really wanted to press the point – something else he would never contemplate doing, especially where his wife was concerned – you could say that the Grundt family's entire existence rested on a lie. Well, yes, it was only as a result of a crude and blatant bluff that the boys had been born at all.

If Leif Grundt had stuck to the truth, getting intimate with their mother would have been out of the question. Naturally. The idea of Ebba Hermansson allowing a butcher at the Co-op to pluck her cherished virginity was as unthinkable as . . . as the idea of Leif's stuttering half-brother Henry pulling off marriage to Pamela Anderson. Leif knew it and Ebba knew it, and Leif knew she would never admit this psychological fact even if faced with a firing squad. When he decided to pose as law student Leif von Grundt at the spring ball at the Östgöta student club in Uppsala in 1985 (having gatecrashed with a fake student ID), it was precisely that upgraded identity – not his utterly prosaic Co-op cock – that gained him access in her student lodgings at two the next morning to the wetlands of her virginity. Precisely that.

'You lied,' she observed two months later, when the resulting pregnancy could no longer be ignored.

'Yes,' he admitted. 'I wanted you and it was the only way to get you.'

'You're so prejudiced,' she said. 'I would have appreciated your honesty.'

'Quite possibly,' he said, 'but it wasn't your appreciation I was after.'

'I would have given myself to you anyway.'

'I doubt that,' said Leif Grundt. 'I doubt that very much indeed. So what are you going to do now?'

'Do?' said Ebba Hermansson. 'I'm going to marry you and have the baby, of course.'

And so she did.

It had cost her a year's interruption to her medical studies, but that was all. Pushing the limits of your paternity leave entitlement was pretty much obligatory if you were a Co-op employee in the mid-1980s, and when Kristoffer came into the world five years later it was a carefully planned step, just before Ebba embarked on her compulsory period as a junior doctor. Right on cue, their expected jackpot arrived: at Sundsvall Hospital further north, along with a tailor-made post as the manager of the Co-op store in Ymergatan in the same town. In due course, she was also able to complete her specialist training – and Ebba Hermansson Grundt became the living embodiment of having your cake and eating it when, as a thirty-eight-year-old mother of two, she took up her post as senior consultant in vascular surgery at the same hospital. The devil looks after his own, and in two days' time she would turn forty.

Thus ran Leif's thoughts, and he gave a wry inner smile. And the little matter of honesty versus dishonesty being a far more complicated story than people generally imagined, well, that was a truth he made sure to keep deep within himself. In a special store of worldly wisdom, you could say, into which he admittedly took a peek from time to time, but which he increasingly seldom invited his wife to visit. There was no reason to, somehow.

But the bloody boy had started smoking and drinking, and of course he would have to be rebuked. He needed to be shamed, to be made to feel wretched and worthless, that was the basic fact of the matter.

Content with his simple conclusion, Leif Grundt sat down at the table with his sons and wife. It was Sunday evening, and on the whole, the world was treating him well. Tomorrow they were off on their trip to Kymlinge and three days of real hell, he knew that, but tomorrow was tomorrow, and sufficient unto the day is the evil thereof.

3

At their very first, somewhat bewildered meeting a week after the scandal broke, Robert Hermansson had explained to his therapist that he felt suicidal.

But that was in answer to a direct question; he sensed it was the answer expected of him by the timid, slightly mouse-like man with the tinted glasses. He was expected to be suicidal and had therefore answered yes, and indeed, after what happened, he had found himself thinking along those lines several times.

Even to himself he could admit it would be a pretty logical conclusion to the whole sorry mess, and it would be lovely not to lie tossing and turning in his bed every single night, remembering his pathetic, wasted life. Lovely not to wake up in broad, mid-morning daylight in a cold sweat of anguish to face yet another meaningless day.

To finally give his self-contempt a kick up the arse, he thought, to step over the edge and vanish. Nobody, not one single person, would think it remotely strange for Robert Hermansson to take his own life.

And yet he sensed it wasn't going to happen. As per usual, he would lack the right resilience and resolve. As for how he would spend the remaining years of his life, he had no idea, but presumably it was a matter of getting through the next month and then moving abroad. He was signed off sick until the 26th; his temporary job at the newspaper ran until the end of the year and he was under no illusion that they would want him back in January.

A publishing company of the less serious kind had been in touch and offered to publish 'his version of events' as a book, promising an advance of 50,000 and a well-qualified ghost-writer. He told them he was not in need of a ghostwriter in any circumstances, and said he'd get back to them. Perhaps he should accept the offer? Why not? He could take the money, go to the Canaries or Thailand or any damn place he wanted. No, not Thailand again. Relax in a deckchair for two months, at any rate, with the typescript of his old novel, and give it a final tidy-up. *Man Without Dog*. Perhaps they'd take it on? Maybe it wasn't strictly speaking his version of events on the island that the shitty little publishing house was after, but just his name. Wanker Rob Hermansson.

And even if they then said no, wasn't it exactly what he needed, an escape? Concentrated work. Isolation and good weather. It was seven years since the last time he went through *Man Without Dog*, and maybe that period of time and his present situation were exactly what were needed for him to put a careful finishing touch to the text and get the novel published? Finally. The four biggest publishers in the country had had it for consideration – Bonniers twice – he had read three different readers' reports and had discussions with two editors. The man from Albert Bonniers Förlag had given grounds for hope. He had asked him almost insistently to go through the final six hundred and fifty pages one more time, try to cut out at least a hundred and fifty and then get back to them. In principle, they were willing to publish the book, there was no question about it.

But then, in September 1999, just when Seikka had clarified her intentions with regard to him, he had run out of steam. Run out of the steam to apply himself to his metaphors all over again, and who wouldn't have? He had two published volumes of poetry behind him. *The Stone Tree*, 1991, and *The Fruiterer's Example*, 1993. Both had had decent reviews; he was considered to be on a quest to find his own voice, and had taken part in a total of four readings and one poetry festival.

No, why should Robert Hermansson go hang himself? There was still hope.

Or at any rate, there were escape routes. The aforementioned. He asked no more.

He had never asked much of life, when he thought about it more intently. Life demanded more of him than he did of life, wasn't that right? By noon on Sunday 18 December he still had not got out of bed, but he had completed half the crossword in Friday's *Svenska Dagbladet* and gone back to sleep three times. The escape route, he thought. The symbol of my entire life?

That was certainly one way of seeing it. He had never been any good at sticking with anything, and anything he might possibly have learnt to stick with had not stuck with him. He was thirty-five years old and the only real activity in his life to date had been the search for something else. No bloody surprise, he thought, turning his pillow, that if you've grown up in the shadow of Ebba, you long to get out into the sunlight.

He had repeatedly chewed over that thought and it had long since lost its sweetness. There were certain things you could blame your family and big sister for, but not forever.

You could be a victim of external circumstances, but scarcely for all eternity. Not in the Swedish middle class of the late twentieth century. However much you delved into history and geography, it was hard to find people with prospects as good as Ebba, Robert and Kristina Hermansson. That was – as their father Karl-Erik would have put it – an incontrovertible fact.

And strictly speaking, it was only after he branched out on his own that things started to go awry. Robert had duly taken his final exams at his upper-secondary school back home in Kymlinge. It was 1988, and although he did not come top of the class, his marks were indisputably creditable. Not on a par with those achieved by Ebba a few years earlier, but then nobody had expected that. He was called up for his military service the same autumn, to be forged and hammered into a man over the course of ten months as a squad leader in the armoured infantry at Strängnäs. He detested every single day. Every single minute. In 1989, he moved to Lund and started his university course.

Humanities. His father advised against it and his big sister did the same, but he held his ground. He met Madeleine, who was beautiful and brave and on his side. They read philosophy and fucked. They read history of science and ideas and fucked. They drank red wine, smoked a bit of hash, read literary history and fucked. Sampled amphetamines, but stopped in time, read art history, fucked, published two collections of poetry (Robert) and had one refused (Madeleine). Read film studies, had a 650-page novel refused (Robert), fucked, got pregnant (Madeleine), gave up the hash but still had a miscarriage before twelve weeks, started getting a) panic attacks (Madeleine) and b) sick of Robert (Madeleine), and wasted no time moving back to her parents' in Växjö (Madeleine). Just sat there watching everything collapse around him (Robert).

Somehow, he had been able to maintain the illusion that he was taking his studies seriously, convincing both the student finance board and his family. But Madeleine's departure meant *finito*. He was twenty-four, miles from taking any exam, had an accumulated student debt of 350,000 kronor and some very bad drinking habits. His brave and beautiful fiancée had deserted him and his two well-received poetry collections had sold one hundred and twelve copies combined. It was high time for his family to intervene.

By the autumn of 1994, it was all sorted (except for the study debts that would presumably pursue him to the grave). With the help of his big sister's dry stick of a Co-operative husband up in the northern county of Medelpad, a relatively well-paid job at a district office in Jönköping was conjured up for him. Office work and three to four trips a month to Co-op stores in the region, i.e. northern Småland and Västergötland. Robert submitted to his fate and accepted. Make the best of a bad job, inner exile for his artist's soul, he simply had no choice. In the first week of September, he moved into a small-ish flat with a bit of a view over Lake Vättern, and on his third Saturday night at the third (and last) pub in town, he met Seikka. She worked at a day nursery and was taking evening classes in creativity at assorted adult education centres. Various sorts of creativity, from aromatherapy to feminist life drawing classes and transcendental self-defence. They moved in together in December and in November 1995 their daughter, Lena-Sofie, was born. Robert took up running at much the same time, in an attempt not to be blown apart by the pressure building up inside him. Initially ten to twelve kilometres every other evening, then working up to longer distances. In the course of 1996 he ran three marathons with times sub 2.50 (except the last one, which he had to abandon less than two kilometres from the finish because of acute stomach problems, but everything pointed to somewhere in the region of 2.46 and a half). He joined Vindarnas IF athletics club and found he had a real talent for track running. He ran his first 5K in an internal club competition and won with a 300-metre lead over the second-place runner. He then wrote to a well-known sports physiologist, who told him that long-distance runners often peaked after thirty and could benefit from postponing formal training until they were about twenty-five. Robert was then twenty-six, and could remember long-distance runner Evy Palm competing for Sweden when she was forty-six.

He enjoyed his heyday in the three seasons that followed. In 1997, he became district champion in both the 5K and the 10K, but it was when he decided, with no technical training, to enter a 3,000m steeplechase at Malmö stadium, that he found his true discipline. He came in third, after someone who ran for the national team and a renowned Polish athlete, in an impressive time of 8.58.6.

Lena-Sofie grew, and started at day nursery, while Seikka found new courses to attend. He neglected them, and went down to part-time at work so he could focus on his training. They made love once a month. They went to Finland over Christmas, to visit her parents in Lappenranta. Robert got into a fight with a brother-in-law and was left with a four-centimetre scar below his left ear. In 1998, he took part in his first Finland–Sweden athletics international. Fourth place, and second out of all the Swedish runners with 8.42.5. He improved on his personal best at the national championships in Umeå with 8.33.2 and won a silver medal. Seikka and Robert made love once a quarter. His parents-in-law came to visit them in Jönköping for a week, while they were in Sweden on holiday. No fights or irregularities occurred. While they were spending Christmas with Rosemarie and Karl-Erik at Allvädersgatan in Kymlinge, Lena-Sofie bit her grandfather on the lip, so there *was* a little bloodshed on that occasion. The next year turned out to be Robert's last in athletics. He found he couldn't improve on his personal best, and had to contend with a dodgy Achilles tendon that flared up from time to time, but still managed a fourth place in the Finland–Sweden athletics international, this time an away fixture in the Helsinki Olympic Stadium. His parents-in-law came to watch. All the way round the last bend and along the finishing straight, Robert battled step for step with a Finnish runner for third place, but had to concede in the final few metres. The Finns took first, second and third place. The tournament was held in August; he and Seikka had not made love since April and when he got home to his smallish flat with a bit of a view over Lake Vättern, she had emptied it of herself, her daughter and all their female possessions. On the kitchen table, he found a note in which she said that she didn't love him any more, that he didn't care in the slightest about either her or Lena-Sofie, and that she was now moving back to Finland and never wanted to see him again.

Robert realized that every word was totally true and decided once again to concede. But he still dialled his parents-in-law's number three times, though he hung up each time it started to ring.

This occurred late one Sunday evening, on 29 August 1999, and it was on Monday, 30 August that the accommodating editor from Albert Bonniers called and encouraged him to really get to grips with *Man Without Dog*. Robert did indeed put in a few hours on the voluminous manuscript on the Monday and Tuesday evenings, but he became increasingly aware of an inner void paralysing all artistic endeavour. He thrust the 650 pages into the claret-coloured, metal-edged box file where they were to remain untouched until December 2005.

Then he did another fortnight at the Co-op district office, and at the end of September he put his belongings into storage except for what he could fit into a rucksack, and moved to Australia.

The telephone rang, interrupting Robert's analysis of his life. It was his mother, informing him that his father wanted to know when to expect him.

'Don't *you* want to know?' he asked.

'Of course I do, Robert. Don't split hairs,' said Rosemarie Wunderlich Hermansson.

'All right, Mum. Tomorrow evening. Got a few things to do first, but I'll leave here between two and three.'

'Robert?'

'Yes.'

'How are you doing, honestly?'

'It is what it is.'

'I really wasn't trying to . . .'

She didn't complete the sentence and he didn't fill the silence for her.

'I know, Mum. See you tomorrow then.'

'It'll be really nice to see you, Robert. Drive carefully. You've got studded tyres, I hope?'

'Yes Mum. Bye Mum.'

'Bye love.'

He got out of bed. It was quarter past twelve. He went to the window and looked out over the city. It had started to snow for the first time that winter.

He thought about his mother.

Thought about Jeanette. No, didn't think. Tried to imagine her.

She'd called a week before. The previous Saturday.

'You don't remember me, of course,' she said.

'Not really,' Robert agreed.

'I'm a bit younger than you. But we went to the same schools. Malmen and upper secondary. Though I was a couple of years below you.'

'Right,' said Robert.

'Anyway, you must wonder why I'm ringing.'

'Kind of,' said Robert.

'I saw that TV programme.'

'A lot of people did.'

'I bet. But the thing is . . . er, I don't quite know how to put this. I like you, Robert.'

'Thanks.'

He thought of hanging up at that point, but there was something in her voice that appealed to him. A little bit gruff and earnest, somehow. She didn't sound like a stupid bimbo, even though what she had said so far might possibly indicate that she was one.

'The fact is, I've always liked you. You were part of that little gang of boys, there was always something special about them. If you only knew how often I went round thinking about you when I was in my teens. And . . .'

'Yes?'

'And you don't even know who I am. It's not very fair.'

'I'm sorry.'

'No need for you to be. Kids generally stick to their own year group at that age. They, like, don't look below them, it's only natural.'

Another pause, which he could very well have used to thank her and ring off. As if she were actually offering him that option, or that was how it seemed.

'Errm, so why *are* you ringing?'

'Sorry. Yes, well, I saw that programme and I realize the shit must really have hit the fan for you afterwards.'

'You're not wrong.'

'So I thought maybe you ought to know that there are people who still like you. Self-confidence and all that.'

'Thanks, but . . .'

'And then I heard you might be coming home, back here. For your father and sister's birthdays, I mean. Your dad was my form teacher, you know. So I thought, if you were going to be around for a few days . . .'

'Hmm,' said Robert.

'Yes, well, it was just a suggestion. But I haven't been in a relationship these last six months. I'd enjoy sharing a bottle of wine with you, and a chat about life. I live in Fabriksgatan, if you remember where that is?'

'I think so,' said Robert.

'No kids, not even a cat. Can't I give you my phone number, then you can ring if you feel like it. It might be quite nice to get away from the family for a little while?'

'Hang on, I'll get a pen,' said Robert Hermansson.

Her other name was Andersson, she told him before they ended the call.

Jeanette Andersson?

It was no good, he couldn't dredge her up from his memory. If he'd been able to look at a school photograph he would presumably have recognized her, but he hadn't kept any of the old school photo catalogues. Robert Hermansson wasn't the kind of person who hung on to that kind of relic.

But when his mother rang a few days later and nagged him again about coming to the 105th birthday party, it was Jeanette Andersson who tipped the balance. And he was honest enough to admit it.

But only just, and only to himself. Perhaps that was exactly how she had calculated it would be. He couldn't resist the temptation of going round to the house of an unknown woman, ringing at her door and being admitted.

Of course, Mummy dear. In that case, I'll come.

Studded tyres? Robert Hermansson?

His years in Australia had been both good and bad. He'd spent his first summer season on the move, up and down the east coast, working in an endless succession of tourist resorts. Waiter, cook, receptionist, steward, animal keeper (sick pandas who slept eighteen hours a day, and ate and crapped for the remaining six). Byron Bay. Noosa Heads. Airlie Beach. Bowling alley manager in Melbourne. None of the jobs lasted more than a couple of weeks. He celebrated the turn of the millennium at an Irish pub in Sydney, and it was in Sydney, too, that he met Paula and embarked on the third (and final?) substantial love affair of his life. Paula was from England and, like Robert, a refugee of sorts. She had run away from a brutal, alcoholic husband in Birmingham, had been in Sydney for two months when Robert met her, and was temporarily lodging with her sister and brother-in-law, both doctors. She had brought with her from England her four-and-a-half-year-old daughter, Judith. Paula, Judith and Robert moved in together in May 2000, after an acquaintance of less than six months. At the same time, they moved to the far side of the mighty continent and settled in Perth.

He loved her. He was hazier on the subject when he looked back on Madeleine and Seikka, but even in the rear-view mirror of hindsight he swore he had loved Paula. She possessed precisely the sort of gentle and forgiving temperament required for a woman to live with an alcoholic for six years, and Robert had the sense not to abuse that temperament. It felt as though they were growing together, and what was more, she was beautiful. Especially for an Englishwoman. Yes, he had loved Paula.

And Judith. As for his own daughter Lena-Sofie, who was five when he met Paula, he hadn't seen her for quite a few years. Seikka generally sent an email once every two or three months, which he answered in a friendly fashion, and he kept two photographs in his wallet. On some level, of course, Judith became a kind of surrogate and consolation.

It should have lasted, Robert thought, switching on the espresso machine. With Paula and Judith, it should have lasted.

Nor had his third (and final?) relatively serious attempt at living with a woman foundered on his own shortcomings. No, it was a double-edged sword of sudden violent death and sudden violent religiosity that had made Paula and Judith leave him. A ghastly concatenation of unfortunate circumstances, to be precise. Thus, in April 2003, after three happy years (he thought of them in exactly those terms, and with capital letters: My Happy Years), news arrived from England that Paula's father had been knocked down by an articulated lorry and killed. Paula travelled back to Birmingham with her sister and Judith for the funeral and to support her mother for a few weeks. Robert expected them home on 28 April. Next, he expected them on 5 May, and then on the twelfth. But on the eleventh, a long email arrived, in which Paula explained the improbable thing that had happened: the former wife beater and drinker had found God and been transformed into a good and responsible human being. Geoffrey was Judith's actual father, after all, and in the weeks she had spent in her old home country she had rediscovered her feelings for him. Besides which, her mother was shattered by her father's sudden death, and it didn't seem right to leave her all alone in life.

Robert resigned from the computer company where he had been working for the past eighteen months, crossed the continent again and spent just over six months on Manly Beach outside Sydney. As the antipodean summer slowly waned into autumn, he flew back home to Sweden. He landed at Stockholm's Arlanda airport on 15 March 2004, called his younger sister and asked if he could come and stay with her.

'Why don't you ring Ebba?' Kristina wanted to know.

'Don't be silly,' said Robert.

'For how long?'

'Just until I find a place of my own. A couple of weeks at most.'

'You do realize I'm about to have a baby?'

'If it's too awkward for you I'll find somewhere else.'

'All right, you bastard,' said Kristina.

He lived with Kristina and Jakob (and Kelvin, born in the first week of May) in their house at Old Enskede in south Stockholm until mid-June, when he was able to move into the more central, sublet apartment on Kungsholmen where he still lived today. At that point, he took a job as a barman in a trendy restaurant, reflecting that his life resembled nothing so much as a reed in the wind.

Or an insect buzzing round a light bulb. Coming too close and being pushed away, coming too close and being pushed away.

Coming too close and burning up? Too close to what?

Things were still pretty much as they'd been then – though in a different trendy restaurant and with a part-time job at the free newspaper *Metro* – when in May 2005 he read an advertisement in *Aftonbladet* and put himself forward for the TV programme *Prisoners of Koh Fuk*, the worst decision of his life, and ever to remain so.

Well, at least I've got an espresso machine, he thought, putting in the ground coffee for another cup. Most people on this planet haven't got an espresso machine.

He was spared further analysis of the traumatic maelstrom of October and November by the ring of the telephone. It was Kristina.

'How are you doing. Honestly?'

It was exactly the same question his mother had asked him and he gave exactly the same answer.

'It is what it is.'

'Sure you don't want to come with us? You know we've got room.'

'No thanks. I'll drive myself. Got a few things to do before I head off.'

'I can imagine.'

What did she mean by that? Were there things he ought to be getting down to? Things everyone else realized he needed to get done, but to which he was blind?

'Right then,' he said to round off the call. 'See you this evening.'

'Robert?'

'Yes?'

'Never mind, I'll tell you when we meet.'

'OK. See you.'

'See you. Bye.'

'Bye.'

It's what they're expecting, he suddenly thought as he ended the call. That I'll kill myself. The whole lot of them: Max at the paper; my therapist, that's why he wants me to pay after each session; even my sister.

4

Jakob Willnius pulled up the shutter of his cocktail cabinet and took out the Laphroaig.

'Want one?'

'Is Kelvin asleep?'

'Sleeping like a log.'

'Just a finger. What was that about Jefferson?'

Kristina leant back in the big Fogia sofa that curved like a banana and tried to work out if she was annoyed or just tired.

Or perhaps it was just a kind of anticipation of the major annoyance to come. Mentally charging up for the silent conflict that would inevitably colour the next few days. I've got to ignore it, she thought. It's ridiculous and unworthy of me, I'll leave my soul here and dance along. I'm a grown woman and it *is* just a one-off.

Jakob brought two glasses over to the table and sat down beside her.

'He rang from Oslo.'

'Jefferson?'

'Yes. He's going to make it to Stockholm after all. It'd be really useful if I could manage a couple of hours with him before Christmas.'

Her annoyance became actual, just for a second.

'What are you trying to tell me?'

Jakob regarded her as he twirled his glass in his hand. As inscrutable as a cat watching teletext, she thought. As usual. There was no detectable irony in his smile, which curved at exactly the same angle as the sofa, and no calculation in his pale-green eyes, in which she had wanted to walk barefoot, once upon a time, and of course it was the apparent lack of resistance that made it so hard to get the better of him. And that meant . . . she shifted her gaze from him and pondered . . . that meant the playing field for the imminent conflict was entirely within herself. It was unfair, deeply unfair: four years ago, she had fallen for this primitive elasticity of his, or whatever the hell you wanted to call it, and the paradoxical thought flashed through her mind that it was this very same quality which would make her leave him one day. It wasn't the first time. You'd work better in a film, Jakob Willnius, she thought. Much better.

'Cheers Kristina,' he said. 'What I'm trying to tell you is that if the Americans are willing to invest ten million in the Samson project, it would be pretty stupid to let it slip through my fingers just because I happen to be stuck at some abominable family dinner in Kymlinge. Abominable is a quotation from a well-informed and rational authority, maybe I didn't—'

'I get it. And exactly when is this Jefferson due to arrive?'

'Tuesday evening. And then he flies to Paris Wednesday lunchtime. But a breakfast meeting on Wednesday is within the realm of possibility.'

'Realm of possibility? We won't be home until Wednesday evening.'

'Quite right.' He was no longer looking her in the eye, but studying his nails instead, counting them or something? 'Kristina, you know I've agreed to make myself available for this extravaganza, but as far as I can see, I could drive up on Tuesday evening. Or overnight. You and Kelvin can either take the train home, or get a lift with Robert. He'll be driving back sometime on Wednesday in any case . . . great that he's coming, in spite of everything.'

Great, she thought. What the hell was there about Robert that was great? She knocked back her drink and regretted not having asked for two fingers. Or four.

'If I understand this right,' Jakob went on, 'there's no plan to make a night of it. We're staying at a hotel, after all, so they don't even have to know I'm pushing off a bit early. Don't you think?'

She took a deep breath and launched in. 'If Jefferson's that important, and you've already made up your mind, there's no need for you to discuss it with me, Jakob.'

She gave him a second in which to protest, but he merely sipped his whisky and gave an interested nod.

'How should I know what they've got planned? It's my sister's fortieth and my father's sixty-fifth. It's the first time you're meeting the family when they're all gathered together, and presumably the last, too, now they're selling the house and moving to the Costa Senilica. The family's scandalized; Dad's been striving all his life to be some kind of petit bourgeois pillar of the community and figure of respect, and then his only son decides to have a wank on television . . . so I've no idea what they've got in store for us down there, but if you've got to have breakfast with an American mogul, don't let this get in your way.'

He chose the easiest way out. Took her at her word, pretending not to pick up on the chasm of irony beneath. 'Good,' was his short, neutral response. 'I'd suggested nine on Wednesday, so I'll ring and confirm that.'

'And if the party doesn't end until midnight?'

'I'll drive straight there, however it turns out. It only takes three hours at night. Four or five hours' sleep, that's all I need.'

'Do as you like,' said Kristina. 'Who knows, perhaps Kelvin and I will come with you.'

'Nothing would give me greater pleasure,' said Jakob with another of his vapid smiles. 'Don't you want another finger? Delicious, this asses' milk.'

She woke at half past two in the morning and it took her an hour to get back to sleep. It wasn't usually a good time for positive reflections, and nor was it on this occasion.

This isn't going to work, she thought. There's no way Jakob and I can stick it out together. We're not acting in the same sort of play.

Our instruments aren't in tune . . . slowly and unresistingly, the arguments came streaming up to the surface . . . we're not in the same room, we don't speak the same language, oil and water, he never has a single thought that resembles what's going on in my mind. In five years' time . . . in five years' time I shall be a single mum at my first school parents' evening. And why on earth should I even bother to start looking for a new man? I give up.

I'm demanding too much, she thought, a minute later.

That's what Ebba would say. Marvellous sister Ebba. Don't be so bloody self-important, little sis. Be glad of what you've got; you could easily have ended up with much worse.

Not that Kristina would ever have taken it into her head to discuss the matter with Ebba.

But *if* she did. Unrealistic demands, you're asking too much. Why do you imagine that any human being – especially a man – would have anything to gain from wandering round in your confused feminist soul? Just look at those scripts you struggle with! Everyone else in the team just gets on with it and does the work according to the contract; it's only you who complicates everything and takes twice as long over the revisions. Rewriting and rewriting and rewriting. Your job is to produce rubbish, so learn to do what you're asked and then leave it! The world will never understand your genius anyway.

So Ebba could have said. If she'd had any idea how things stood.

A minute later came the inevitable weakness. When she imagined being on Ebba's side and subjected herself to punishing scrutiny. There's no genius lurking beneath that brow of yours, Kristina Hermansson! You haven't an ounce of originality. No genuine creative power. You're just a dissatisfied little bitch with delusions of grandeur. Always have been, and the only qualitative changes in your life will be turning first into a middle-aged bitch, then an old one.

She got up and drank some apple juice. Ate some crispbread and cheese. Stood in front of the bathroom mirror and looked at her body. It was the same old body as ever, which had been younger, but the breasts were of even size, the stomach was flat and the hips of the right fullness. No cellulite. She did actually look like a woman, and had she been a man she would presumably have appreciated what she saw.

But now she had signed herself up to the same male for the rest of her life, wasn't that true? And he preferred making love in the dark. Presumably because he didn't want her to see his bit of flab. So she was the only one who would occasionally look at this body, relatively well preserved so far. Thirty-one years old. Jakob was forty-three. If the twelve-year gap were applied in the other direction, it would mean she could get herself a nineteen-year-old. She felt a slight tingle between her thighs, but nothing more. Not yet.

Ludicrous, she thought. Good God, what ludicrous creatures we humans are. Why expend all this time and effort on contemplating ourselves and our supposed lives? Our self-obsessed course towards the grave.

I should find religion, she suddenly thought. At least start cultivating an interest in something. Whales or Afghan women or other oppressed species. My husband and my son? Surely that's the least that can be asked of me?

Maybe Robert, too. She knew she'd find it hard to forgive herself if he really did go off and kill himself.

But Jakob?

How could she induce herself?

He had flattered her from the word go. Said her manuscript really stood out amongst the twenty-four submissions, giving her feminine vanity a good old polish. He had promptly hired her, and although she was twenty-seven she had fallen like a teenager yearning for affirmation.

That was May 2001, in August they made love for the first time, and about ten minutes before they started he told her he was married and had twin fifteen-year-old daughters.

She fell for that frankness, too. And when he filed for divorce less than six months later, her friend Karen's gloomy predictions were disproved. (They'll never get divorced! How the hell can you be so stupid, haven't you ever read a psychology book? Amoebas like you should be sterilized!) It was only when she was pregnant, and their own marriage imminent, that she found out that Annica, the twins' mother, had been a year ahead of him in the new-partner game. It wasn't Jakob who revealed this but Liza, one of the two panther-like daughters. (Just so you don't think you cut our mum out of the picture in any way. She was waiting for someone like you to turn up!)

Under the leadership of the new alpha male, Jakob's former family moved to London around the time little Kelvin came into the world, and the memory of them seemed to fade like old photographs in bright sunlight. It was all very strange in fact, and something must have been seriously awry, but why go digging around in the compost of the past?

The house in Old Enskede cost a fortune. But Jakob Willnius had the money and the position; he was a senior commissioning editor, and also a sort of golden boy at the depersonalized, all-digital television centre, having outlived two notoriously difficult female bosses in a way no mere mortal had ever achieved. (Yes, there's something awfully special about him, I agree, Karen had admitted, but whether it's for the good in the long run, I couldn't possibly say.) He's acquired a woman twelve years his junior, Kristina thought in her more cynical moments. I'm his winning ticket in life and he'll never leave me of his own accord for as long as I let him fuck me twice a week. If I die of starvation one of these days, I've only myself to blame.

But the implacable gnawing of her everyday dissatisfaction had increased in recent months, it was undeniable. Her need to . . . well, what? She mulled it over as she left the bathroom. To punish him? That, too, was ludicrous, because what on earth did she have to gain from *punishing* Jakob? What were these treacherous words, lending themselves out to her thoughts?

But thought and feeling refused to align themselves with each other. They stabbed each other in the throat, and this was where it lay, she knew. The problem. This was its precise location.

I'm primitive, she thought as she slipped back into the double bed at a reassuring distance from him. But it's good that I understand my own motives. And there really is no more to life than this. *Bonjour tristesse.*

So what the hell shall I do? was her next thought. Or rather: What do I *want* to do?

What is it about my life that has suddenly become pretty much unbearable to me?

But before she had had time to try to straighten out those stubborn question marks, sleep finally claimed her. High time too, because in all likelihood she had less than three hours before Kelvin started making demands on her, in his understated way.

When the scandal was no more than a day old, her mother had phoned to ask whether Jakob could conceivably have had a finger in the pie when Robert was selected for *that programme.*

Kristina had dismissed the idea as absurd, but couldn't stop herself asking him about it that evening.

This, unusually, caused him to display signs of something reminiscent of anger. 'Kristina, what kind of insinuation is that? Christ, you know better than that. And you know what I think of Lindmanner and Krantze.'

'Sorry, it was my mother who asked. They seem pretty shaken at home, you know.'

'I'm not surprised,' Jakob observed. 'To be honest, I'm glad it happened. They're going to find it pretty hard to justify investments like that in the future.'

'So you think Robert's contribution could achieve something positive in the long run?'

'Why not? If people want more of that kind of thing, all they've got to do is climb a couple of steps down the scale and watch the porn channels. Don't you think?'

He was right, of course. But the scale itself annoyed her. One could see it – above the porn channels – in crude terms of three quality levels in the production industry of television entertainment. At the bottom were the reality TV formats, with *Fucking Island* as a kind of All-Time Low. In the middle were the soaps and the quiz shows. The TV sofas, the debates and ostensible social analysis. But enthroned at the top was revered old Drama – which admittedly didn't really exist any longer, or at any rate went by other titles these days, and basically rested to quite some extent on its laurels from the seventies and eighties – and this was Jakob's territory, where the top responsibilities were his. Not even viewing figures mattered very much there. Only quality and international prizes.

But anyway, though the scales could be discussed and modified from one point in time to another, it was indisputable that Robert Hermansson, her brother, was right at the very bottom. Hopefully it would be short-lived notoriety, but two million viewers were more than Jakob Willnius had achieved in his last half dozen productions.

Not counting yet another 'last film' about the hermit of

Fårö island, Ingmar Bergman. There was no way round it and the show must go on.

When she was on maternity leave, she had been quite certain she would not go back to the Factory, but when it came to the crunch she had no choice. One more year, she'd thought, I'll give it one more year.

The year had elapsed on the first of November. Now it was almost Christmas and she was still coming up with new ideas and writing scripts for a potential sequel to a much-disparaged drama series about a prime minister and a country in crisis. Plus a few other things of roughly the same calibre. From 20 January, she had two weeks booked in the Maldives; all right then, she thought, compromising, I'll give it till after that, and then call a halt. I've got to start something new in February.

'You're driving too fast,' Jakob said. 'We're not in any kind of hurry, are we?'

She slowed to 100 kilometres an hour. 'Do you want to stop for something to eat?'

He glanced at Kelvin. 'Wouldn't it be better to wait until our little crown prince wakes up?'

'OK. What are you thinking about, sitting there?'

His answer was a few seconds in coming. 'Your family, as a matter of fact. They'd make good material for a script.'

'Go to hell—'

'No, I'm serious. A sort of reality TV documentary; there have been plenty made in the States, but no one's tried it here. About what it does to a family when it happens—'

'Stop it, Jakob. If you say another word about it, I shall drive into the first rock face I can find.'

He put his hand on her arm for a moment and seemed to be thinking. 'Sorry,' he said eventually. 'I only meant that you're an interesting collection of people . . . and maybe a fairly typical one, too.'

'Typical of what?' she asked.

'Of our time,' he said. She waited for more, but nothing came. He carried on browsing through the evening paper. An interesting collection of people, she thought. Fine for *him* to say. An only child from an upper-class home in a posh suburb of Stockholm. His parents had died of cancer, different kinds and in different parts of the body, but within less than ten months of each other. That had been seven years ago. The only branches of Jakob's living family tree all grew upwards, and comprised him and the increasingly fading twins in Hampstead. Plus Kelvin. An old uncle had been on his death-bed in Gilleleje in Denmark for the past decade and was due to leave a considerable inheritance behind him when he finally departed this life. There was definitely every reason to question what lay behind his choice of the word *typical*. And *our time*.

'You're so right,' she said. 'I can see, when I think about it, that we offer pretty good entertainment value.'

This time he chose to notice the subtext. 'You don't even like any of them,' he retorted. 'I just don't get why you persist in defending them to me. I find it a bit childish.'

'It isn't entirely easy simply to amputate the body parts you happen not to like,' she explained patiently. 'Even though Jesus of Nazareth claims that one should. And anyway, I've never had anything against Robert . . . not until now, at any rate.'

He paused for thought again, folding up his newspaper and regarding her sideways.

'You've been furious with me for days now. Can't you just come out with whatever it is and give me a chance?'

But before she could answer, Kelvin woke with a hiccup and a little sob, and that was the end of the discussion.

5

The television programme *Prisoners of Koh Fuk* was the brain-child of two project-worker creatives at the top of their game – Torsten 'Bengal' Lindmanner and Rickard Krantze – and it was one of the country's production companies specializing in reality TV that actually made the wretched thing. The fundamental idea, if that wasn't a total misnomer in this context, was presumably to go the whole hog. To broadcast, over a number of weeks in the autumn, a series of reality TV shows so transparently awful that there need be no pretence of decency whatsoever. No more noble aim than showing people from the sleaziest, booziest and most naked angle.

The starting point was simple. Two groups – or teams – one male, the other female. Someone, or possibly a couple of people, would win a big pot of money. Initially, over the first two or three weeks, the teams would be kept apart, but only to the degree that left the television viewer, experienced in the ways of the world, in little doubt that transgressions were occurring. What was at stake – the point of the whole bloody shebang, as Krantze put it at the first and only press conference before they set off for the island in September – was to complete a very special assignment, but the form and content of that assignment were initially to be kept secret from participants and television viewers alike.

The five women were all attractive, with ages ranging between twenty-five and thirty-five. The common denominator was that they were all single and heterosexual, and that they had all at some point in their lives won a beauty contest of some kind. At the very least, they had been chosen for the leading role in the Saint Lucia celebrations at regional or city level. The island, Koh Fuk, lay a good hour away by long-tail boat from Trang in southern Thailand. The women's first task on the island was to acquire as becoming an all-over tan as they could; footage of their intensive sunbathing in bare flesh, silicon and string panties was transmitted each day to the male camp, which likewise contained five singles, aged twenty-six to thirty-eight. These gentlemen voted every evening on the best suntan, and awarded points for seven other feminine variables using a system devised by Lindmanner and Krantze, who also drew on expertise at one of the leading tabloids. The gentlemen, meanwhile, spent their days on a variety of trials of strength, including rope-climbing, long jump, handstands and arm wrestling, all conducted in the most basic attire: sunglasses and luridly coloured penis sheaths. Then every evening, in the company of the setting sun and a glass or two of champagne, the ladies, too, awarded points and made comments on the gentlemen's prowess, based on an equivalent system of variables.

The male team consisted – or was originally intended to consist – of a handful of celebrated, guaranteed-heterosexual elite sportsmen. The participants ultimately signed up by the production team heads had rather less star quality than the creators had hoped for, but what the heck? That was the line Krantze took in the aforementioned press conference. Life is a meatball.

The five were: an ice hockey player, veteran of sixteen years in the Swedish men's national hockey team and half a season in the Canadian National Hockey League; a wrestler who took bronze in the European Championships and two golds in the nationals; a skier with four medals in the relay and a third place in the big cross-country Vasaloppet race; a rower who'd reached an Olympic final and won a bronze at the Europeans; and Robert Hermansson, steeplechaser with two fourth places in successive Finland–Sweden athletics internationals.

The last of these, Robert, was unquestionably the least impressive of the pretty unimpressive collection, and got his place at the last minute as a substitute for a very famous footballer, who had unfortunately gone and got a girlfriend and cold feet just weeks before the group departure for Koh Fuk at the end of September.

After a little over a week (and in programme three), the scantily clad and becomingly tanned males and females were brought together for a beach party at which the alcohol flowed with positively Dionysian generosity, while a new phase of the contest began: tug of war, wife carrying, wrestling and leapfrog. Though the contestants and the television viewers (but not the tabloid press pack) were unaware of it, extra spice was provided by spiking the drinks with a mild dose of amphetamines, to heighten desire. After the competitions and the partying, the contestants were allowed to socialize freely on the beach under cover of darkness. With the aid of infrared techniques, no fewer than two full-on sexual encounters were filmed for the viewers' delectation. It was, however, impossible to make out who the participants were, leaving the field open for enjoyable speculation. Even at this early stage – the third programme – viewing figures were up to 1,223,650, a not unimportant total, because converted into kronor it constituted the first part of the promised prize money.

In programme four, two things were to be revealed: the final prize money (the 1,223,650 plus that evening's viewer figure, which amounted to a whacking 1,880,112, combining to make the grand total well over three million kronor); and the fundamental goal and purpose of *Prisoners of Koh Fuk*. And it was in the revelation of the latter that the true creative genius of Lindmanner–Krantze came to light.

The aim was impregnation. Nothing more and nothing less.

For some reason, the tabloids took Koh Fuk – or Fucking Island, as it almost instantly became known – to their hearts from the word go, each sending a permanent reporter plus photographer (with infrared technology) after the first programme. Maybe interest was piqued by a semi-verified story that two of the female beauty queens had both, at different times, kept company with a nationally notorious bank robber, which was considered to generate good synergy; maybe it was because the other reality TV series that autumn proved to be pretty mediocre offerings featuring rehashed conflicts, near-nudity and dull predictability; or maybe it was something else entirely. At any event, it soon became obvious that *Fucking Island* was the big TV hit of the season.

And almost everyone touchingly agreed that the central idea was a stroke of genius. Begetting a child.

And getting a million and a half for their trouble, too. Three million if they decided to stick together as a family. For the women, the crucial thing was to be first to have your pregnancy confirmed by the accompanying medical team. For the men: to be the one who had fertilized that woman's egg and to prove it by a DNA analysis of a sample taken from the amniotic fluid.

No more tugs of war. No more handstands or wife carrying. Very little competitive sunbathing.

In their place: indolence, dips in the sea, alcohol, and unlimited copulation wherever and whenever the opportunity presented itself.

And interviews. And lies. And breakdowns. And psychological counselling, copious mudslinging and yet more alcohol.

An avalanche of viewer reaction. Moral outrage. No fewer than three government ministers expressing their reservations on morning TV.

And nearly two million viewers for programme five, in which it was too early to confirm any pregnancies (naturally, and it was a masterful call in the clever art of deferred pleasure) – but in which it was possible to get odds on all five men and five women, individually or as couples. Amongst the women, a majorly silicon-enhanced, big-bosomed, brown-eyed girl from Skåne, who had been caught on film with two or possibly three of the men, had the lowest odds ratio – around 2.4 – while the virile rower was the bookies' favourite amongst the gents, offering the prospect of tripling your stake. Robert Hermansson languished somewhere between 15/1 and 25/1, and never came anywhere near the second least favourite, who was the skier and generally ranked somewhere between 8/1 and 12/1.

After the sixth programme, broadcast on 5 November, a double bet on Robert and a distinctly aggressive, semi-naked Saint Lucia queen from out in the sticks would have won you 158 times your stake, after a stinging slap round the face and some violent expletives from the latter, to the effect that if Robert so much as came near her she would bite off his balls.

Thus it was that in the next, and penultimate, programme (1,980,457 viewers) Miss Hälsingland 1995 was confirmed to be up the duff, with odds of 4.82. And it was in the same programme that former steeplechaser Robert Hermansson was revealed in all his drunken and pitiful frustration, howling at the moon and masturbating vigorously at the water's edge. The TV columnist of *Norrlandstidning* dubbed it a visual milestone.

Wanker Rob got headlines almost as big as Miss Hälsingland, but in the final programme (2,011,775) – in which the ice hockey player rather unexpectedly (single odds: 6.60; double odds: 21.33) emerged as the lucky stud and father of the child – he was not to be seen. He had left Fucking Island and was undergoing trauma therapy in a convalescent home at an undisclosed location in the Kingdom of Sweden.

Robert pulled his cap down over his eyes and put on the yellow-tinted glasses before he went into the petrol station to pay. He bought a coffee and some cigarettes, too; it suddenly struck him that it would be impossible to bear either his father or his big sister without a constant high dose of nicotine in his veins.

The time was quarter past four. It was Monday 19 December and he was less than an hour and a half's drive from Kymlinge. He walked round the perimeter of the petrol station forecourt four times to help pass the time. Smoked two cigarettes. He had promised to be there by seven at the latest. There was no reason for arriving at six or half past. When he crawled back into the car, it still felt way too early, but perhaps he could allow himself another stop? Buy some chewing gum and a Loka mineral water with lemon at another filling station and waste an extra ten minutes.

He rejoined the road and tried to conjure up the elusive image of Jeanette Andersson, who might turn out to be a saviour in his hour of need, but it was hard to lick her into any sort of shape, though the thought that she had been lusting after him even as a teenager was appealing, and more appealing the more he sucked on it. Fifteen to twenty years of repressed, pent-up sexual desire; what blossom of love might not flourish in such rich earth?

But it was hard to keep her in his mind; he had not been driving more than ten or fifteen minutes when he found himself engulfed by something he had never experienced before. A chafing yet paralysing discomfort, so intense and implacable that he had to pull into a lay-by, get out of the car and light another cigarette.

He looked about him. It was an extremely humdrum lay-by and no other cars had stopped there in the inhospitable grey chill of the dusky afternoon. The tarmac was glossy and free of snow. Not slippery, so presumably it was a few degrees above zero. Dense fir forest on both sides of the road, little traffic – roughly a car a minute in each direction – and the wind was light and from a northerly direction, if he was judging correctly.

But it wasn't the external world pushing in on him. The feeling that gradually spread inside him was both familiar and totally alien. It came from a spot somewhere between his stomach and his ribcage, possibly his solar plexus, and it grew slowly, and predominantly upwards, it seemed to him, turning everything in its path to ashes. Like an internal desert fire, or gangrene, impossible to fight against, it was just a question of waiting and accepting.

I'm going to die, thought Robert. Right here and now in this darkening lay-by, I'm finally going to die. I can't stop it, and I don't even need to step out in front of a car. I've had the seed of death inside me for a long time, it has been lurking there, growing and growing and biding its time, and now the moment has come. I can't move. I simply can't move, it's inexorable, this is the end of the road, and there'll never be a novel penned by my hand. Nobody will ever be able to read *Man Without Dog*.

He tried to raise his cigarette to his mouth, but his hand would not obey. He tried to open his fingers and drop the cigarette to the ground, but not the slightest tremor indicated that the signal had arrived from his brain. He tried to turn his head and look at the car rather than the dark forest and the restless sky, but nothing happened.

Nothing at all.

Not until the cigarette slipped from between his fingers almost without him noticing, and landed a few centimetres in front of his right foot. It smouldered gently for a few moments before going out; Robert could see it on the edge of his field of vision without lowering his eyes.

My God, thought Robert Hermansson. Am I dead now? Did I just die? Am I leaving . . . am I leaving my body this very instant and turning into something else?

But everything still seemed whole and indivisible. The ache in his chest was still griping, his breath came in short little bursts, the wind was still light and from the north and felt lethally cold to his damp brow, the lights of a vehicle dazzled him momentarily, went past and were gone. Light and sound. Light and sound.

An unknown number of vehicles passed by in the same way for an unknown number of minutes, an unknown number of events occurred or did not occur, out there in the world, and then he fell.

Straight ahead in a north-easterly direction with his hands at his sides; just before he hit the ground he managed to twist a little so his right shoulder took the impact. He remained prone, lying on his right side with arms and legs spreadeagled, and felt no pain, but was aware of his lower jaw starting to shiver. He tried to clench his hands without success and get his jaw to keep still before finally giving up and losing consciousness.

A short dream drifted in through the barred window of his sleep. He was only a child, four or five years old, and was standing before his father, having wet himself.

'You did it on purpose,' said his father.

'No,' he replied. 'I didn't do it on purpose. It just came.'

'Oh yes you did,' said his father. 'I know you, and you did it on purpose. You could have got to the toilet, but you wanted to torment your mother by making her wash your pissy clothes.'

'No, no,' he insisted, tears rising in his throat. 'It wasn't like that at all. It just came, and I can wash my pissy clothes myself.'

His father clenched his fists in anger.

'What's more, you're lying,' he said. 'You wet your trousers deliberately, you wear out your own mother and you tell lies. Why do you think we brought you into the world at all?'

'I don't know, I don't know,' he cried in desperation. 'I

couldn't help it, it's not at all like you say, Father, I love you all, let me live and I'll show you.'

But his father pulled out one of the drawers in the big desk where he was sitting and produced something. It was Kristina's head. It was bloody and horrible and severed from her body, and his father dangled it at arm's length, where it swung from right to left, from left to right above the desk. Kristina looked so sad and forlorn, and in the end he hurled her head straight at Robert, who was now wetting himself all over again, and just as he was trying to catch his beloved sister's head, at the very second he stretched out his hands towards it like a handball goalie trying to save a well-aimed shot, but before his fingertips made contact with her auburn hair, he woke up.

He scrambled hastily to his feet. Took three steps towards the edge of the forest, undid his flies and took a much-needed pee.

He crawled back into the car, shivering with cold, and was barely able to turn the ignition key and start the engine.

'No, wait,' said Ebba Hermansson Grundt, 'let's leave the audio book for later. We've got to have a thorough report from Henrik first. The first term at university is always a milestone in our personal development, whether we like it or not.'

Leif Grundt gave a sigh and turned off the CD player. For his part, he'd ended his personal development after two years majoring in business studies at upper secondary. Of course he took an interest in how his eldest son was getting on in Uppsala, for he performed his fatherly duties to the best of his ability and had himself grown up in Uppsala – in Salabacke, at a safe distance from the ivory towers, but even so. Henrik was Ebba's territory, a legal claim she had evidently staked and won when he was still in the womb, and that was just the way it was. Particularly now, with his law course, living in a hall of residence, part of the student-club culture, with parties, gentlemen's dinners, afternoon imbibing of Swedish punch, Latin drinking songs and all that stuff.

We'll see, thought Leif Grundt, but it could be the making of him in the end.

'It was fine,' said Henrik Grundt.

'Fine?' said his mother Ebba. 'You'll have to give us a bit more detail than that, I'm afraid. The end-of-term exams are in January, aren't they? I can't think why they have to extend the autumn term over Christmas and New Year, it wasn't like that in my day. Some little test, possibly, but a full set of exams? Oh well, at least it means you've got three weeks to revise, eh?'

'No worries,' said Henrik. 'There are four of us, we've been studying together all autumn. We'll start again on the second of January and cram for ten solid days.'

'But you've brought your books home with you, haven't you?' asked Ebba with a hint of maternal unease and concern in her voice.

'A couple,' said Henrik. 'You and Dad needn't worry about that.'

Leif started overtaking a German juggernaut in a dirty shade of yellow, and since Ebba Hermansson Grundt never spoke while overtaking was in progress, there were ten seconds of silence in the car. Kristoffer cast a quick glance at his brother, beside him in the back seat. *Needn't worry about that,* he thought. Was he just imagining it or was there a hidden meaning in what Henrik had just said? Was there something they actually ought to be worrying about? Something else?

It seemed very unlikely. Super Henrik had never given his parents anything to worry about. He made a success of all that he touched, and that applied to everything from school, sporting prowess and piano playing to Trivial Pursuit and fly fishing. It had always been like that. Once, when Henrik was eleven and was declared district champion in 'Ask Year 5', Dad had said Henrik only had one problem in life, and that was needing to decide whether to be a Nobel prize winner or prime minister. Mum had instantly declared that it would be no problem for Henrik to fit in both of those – and Kristoffer, who was six at the time, had gone to his room and sulked because, as usual, his big brother would grab all the plaudits and carry off both the trophies. Prime minister and Nobel prize winner. Blow you, Piss Henrik, he'd thought. I'll be king and then you'll see. I shall make you eat raw veg for the rest of your life until you choke.

But now – possibly, if he had interpreted that slight dissonance in his brother's voice correctly – there might be grounds for unease?

Fat chance, thought Kristoffer the Sinner, glowering mournfully at the salt-spattered juggernaut as it slowly slipped backwards outside the car window. Things like that simply don't happen in our family.

'And this girl?' asked Ebba, starting to file her nails, a task she only ever found time for if she was in a car but not driving herself, so she never missed the opportunity. 'You look out for each other, I hope?'

That means using a condom, Kristoffer translated silently

to himself. 'Yes,' replied Henrik. 'We look out for each other.'

'Jenny?' said Ebba.

'Yes, Jenny.'

'Medical student from Karlskoga?'

'Yes.'

'Does she sing in the student-club choir, too?'

'Yes, but we're not in the same one. I told you that already, didn't I?

Another brief silence followed. Fuck, thought Kristoffer. There really *is* something up.

'You seem a bit tired,' Leif put in. 'It's all that non-stop swotting and partying, I expect?'

'Leif,' said Ebba.

'Sorry, sorry,' said Leif Grundt, preparing to overtake another vehicle. 'But he seems a bit lethargic, don't you all think? Not in the same league as Kris and me, of course, but even so?'

Kristoffer smiled inwardly and thought about how much he loved his Co-op manager dad. 'How much further is it?' he asked.

'God and Mum willing, we'll be there for evening milking,' declared Leif Grundt, receiving an expressionless stare from his wife for his trouble.

'Thank goodness we're staying at the hotel,' said Kristina as they turned off the main road and the Gahn industrial area came into view, along with the church. 'It means I can pretend I don't belong here.'

It was a thought she would never have put into words if she hadn't been so tired, she knew that. When she was tired, almost anything could pop out of her mouth, unfortunately, and although it was true that she loathed all contact with the town of her childhood in the present age, there was no need to add fuel to Jakob's fire. No need at all.

'I've never really got the point of small towns at all,' he proclaimed. 'They're some kind of faulty link between the country and the proper towns, aren't they?' He waved to indicate a terrace of modern houses that they were just passing. A development designed for family living in the early seventies, the white brick showing signs of damp, with electric Advent candles shining from eight out of ten windows and small estate cars from south-east Asia on seven of the front drives. 'God must have had a real hangover when he created this lot.'

'There are people who think Stockholm isn't the centre of the universe, too,' Kristina said. She put the dummy in Kelvin's mouth, and he immediately spat it out again. 'I'm glad we've got here, anyway. So we'll check in and have a shower like we said, shall we?'

'Fine by me, if there's time.'

'It's only quarter to six. We don't have to be there until seven.'

'Your wish is my command,' said Jakob, stopping at a red light. 'Well look at that, they even have traffic lights now. Things are on the up.'

Shut up, you flabby Stockholmer with your sense of entitlement, thought Kristina, but although the fatigue hung like a ball of lead inside her, not a word passed her lips.

'Cock,' said Kelvin, unexpectedly.

6

Rosemarie Wunderlich Hermansson added the finishing touches to her seafood quiches, put them in the oven and stood up cautiously to stretch her back. It was six o'clock on Monday evening and no children or grandchildren had turned up, but within the hour, the house would be full. Ebba had called just after five to say they would be a bit late, but would still be there for seven of course, Mummy, no problem. Kristina had called in the last five minutes to say they had got to Kymlinge and checked in at the hotel. They were just going to freshen up and change little Kelvin's nappy.

Robert had not called.

A buffet of hot dishes with beer and schnapps was in prospect. Christmas root beer for the boys. Maybe Henrik, too, was grown-up enough for a proper beer. He was at university now, after all. But definitely no schnapps; Rosemarie and Karl-Erik were in complete agreement on that point.

Other than that, they were in disagreement on most things. Admittedly they'd scarcely spoken to one another all day, but that was the way it felt. And she felt it to the very marrow of her spine. It was a truth universally acknowledged that after forty years of marriage, words are no longer needed. It was simply in the nature of things – to the extent that she still had any power over her husband, that power was best exercised in the form of mute looks, and silences that spoke volumes. If she tried to use language as her weapon, she always fell short, something she had learnt at an early stage. Karl-Erik was possessed of a vocabulary that far outstripped the number of molecules in the universe, but to give him his due, he wasn't at all bad when it came to the pirouettes of silence, either – and which of them would actually claim the larger number of victories in the long run was anybody's guess.

Though perhaps it was worth bearing in mind what Vera Ragnebjörk once said: some duels had two losers. Perhaps they were the most usual kind, in fact. Long-drawn-out duels, so dreary and commonplace that you scarcely registered they were in progress.

She had allowed herself a mid-afternoon nap, just half an hour, and in the course of this well-earned repose she had once again dreamt that one of them had to die. They were on an island, surrounded by emerald-green water – presumably Robert's wretched Koh Fuk, as it had been on her mind – with the aim of survival. Him or her. Karl-Erik or Rosemarie. Some kind of trial of strength was approaching, a decisive battle in an old war with extremely hazy conditions and rules – and with weapons that went far beyond silences and looks – but everything was still at the preparatory stage, and she woke up before it was time to make the first thrust or parry the other's lunge.

But it meant the thought was still being kept alive in her. It was floating there, a diffuse and jellyfish-like plasma, in the semi-transparent layer between the perceptible and the imperceptible in the sea of her consciousness.

Eh, she asked herself in confusion, what? Was it really me who thought that?

Homemade meatballs. Smoked salmon. The dullest green salad ever, with some shop-bought French dressing. Two quiches. A big Jansson's Temptation. Halves of hard-boiled egg topped with red and black caviar.

God, what lack of imagination, she noted, surveying the spread. At least it would fill the kitchen table, especially once she added the bread and the big piece of cheddar. But it was Karl-Erik's menu preferences that counted here. On Monday evening and on Tuesday as well. He was the one turning sixty-five, not her. So, no laying of the dining table tonight, they'd save that for the big dinner tomorrow. The hot buffet could easily be consumed in armchairs and sofas in the living room. The informal family touch. Pleasant chat on topics great and small. The years gone by. The travails of the autumn. But not a TV supper, heaven forfend. A life seen in its context. Karl-Erik could reflect on his pedagogical achievements, now completed, with the help of illuminating and humorous anecdotes. Ellinor Bengtsson's unforgettable beetroot project in 1974. The fire in the church during the Saint Lucia celebration in 1969, when one of the candle-carrying girls in the procession ended up as bald as a coot. Assistant master Nilsson and his car deals – good God, she hoped he would at least keep Nilsson out of it. And indeed, Mr Grunderin the deputy head, and all that awkwardness over the nuclear power referendum in 1980.

And as she stood there, turning her eyes from the sad salad to the gloomy darkness outside the kitchen window, Robert popped into her head again as an even darker cloud and she suddenly wished that this, her whole life, was just one of those old films about the British upper crust, in which she could simply go upstairs to lie down, pleading a migraine or some other suitable indisposition, and stay there for as long as she felt like it.

Or she could run away to her sister's in Argentina and hide there for evermore. But she hadn't spoken to her in more than ten years. Rosemarie and Regina had come to Sweden along with their parents when they were seven and twelve respectively, four years after the war. The family had taken a chance when they left bomb-ravaged Hamburg, and had managed to put down roots in Sweden. First in Malmö, then moving up the country. Växjö, Jönköping, Örebro. But Regina had never really settled; she had left both her home and her country before she turned eighteen, and that was that. When their mother Bärbel died in 1980, they met at the funeral; when it was their father Heinrich's turn two years later, she didn't turn up.

She had been living in Buenos Aires for a decade, and Christmas cards arrived every year. No birthday greetings, just Christmas cards.

Buenos Aires, thought Rosemarie Wunderlich Hermansson. Could you conceive of anywhere more distant? Could you imagine a better place to hide?

It struck her that she was in fact following the same furrow that Karl-Erik had ploughed in the red earth of Spain, and she muttered angrily at her own thoughts.

And noted that she was muttering in German. It was because she'd been thinking about her family, no doubt. She had never formally trained as a language teacher; it was Karl-Erik who suggested she give it a try, when a vacancy arose in the mid-eighties and the school management was unable to attract any qualified applicants. She had been brought up in the language, after all.

So that was the way it was.

But not any longer, she reminded herself. They had reached the end of the road three days ago. What was it she had been thinking just now? Something important, wasn't it, or maybe just . . . ?

Karl-Erik came into the kitchen to inspect the arrangements.

'Looks good,' he deigned to say. 'Where are you going to put the beers?'

'On the kitchen worktop,' she said. 'But I assume we want them cold? So I haven't got them out yet.'

'Quite. I just wanted to know where you were going to put them.'

'Oh,' she said. 'Well, all right then.'

'Yes, fine, that was all I meant,' agreed her husband, now aged 64 years and 364 days, and went off to the bathroom to tie his tie.

Ebba arrived first. With her Co-op manager and her teenage boys. Rosemarie felt a sudden embarrassment at the rituals of greeting; the boys seemed so much more grown-up than she expected. But having hugged Ebba, she also hugged Kristoffer, who seemed shyer and more diffident than ever, and eventually Henrik and Leif, too. Henrik had overtaken his father in height, must be over a metre ninety by now. She hadn't seen the family for how long must it be? Eighteen months? Henrik had his mother's and Karl-Erik's eyes and nose, and Rosemarie's head swam for a moment as it struck her that he looked exactly as Karl-Erik had done when she met him for the first time at that school dance at the Karolinska almost half a century ago. A replay of Karl-Erik Hermansson? Good grief. It was a terrifying thought in so many ways, but fortunately there was no time to dwell on it. Karl-Erik the First was in the living room to receive them all in his turn; no hugs here, just good firm handshakes, as he ran an appraising eye over each member of the Hermansson-Grundt family. At arm's length, because he was too vain to wear glasses when he didn't really need to – and with his customary dogged smile. When he got to Kristoffer, Rosemarie could see he was on the point of bursting out 'Straighten that back, boy!', but he restrained himself; there is a time for everything, even the absence of pedagogy.

'So that's that,' declared Leif Grundt inscrutably. 'We're to take our bits and bobs and present ourselves on the top deck, I assume? Nice to have got here. Seven hundred kilometres is seven hundred kilometres, as it says in the Quran.'

'Was it icy?' Karl-Erik asked.

'Nope,' Leif replied.

'Much traffic?' Rosemarie asked.

'Yep,' Leif replied.

'Busy time on the surgical ward, I expect?' Karl-Erik said.

'It's a question of delegation,' said Ebba.

'Never a truer word spoken,' Leif Grundt agreed. 'I've delegated getting on for four tons of pig bums this past week, in fact.'

'Pig bums?' enquired Rosemarie, sensing that he needed someone to.

'Christmas hams,' Leif Grundt grinned genially.

'Excuse me, I've got to go to the bathroom,' whispered Kristoffer.

'Of course,' said Rosemarie, stepping in once more. 'Off to your rooms everybody. We've put you in your usual ones. I just hope Henrik hasn't grown out of his bed, that's all.'

'I'll be fine,' said Henrik with an engaging smile for his grandmother. 'I do bend in a few places.'

This elicited a hearty laugh from Karl-Erik, at least.

Kristina *et consortes* were next to arrive, about ten minutes later. Little Kelvin instantly turned his back on the assembled attention and clung to his mother's leg. Kristina was wearing a new, yellow – and very metropolitan-looking – wool coat, but looked tired; Rosemarie immediately made a mental note that she ought to have a little chat to her about anaemia, although she knew she would never get round to it, and didn't really want to anyway. Heart-to-heart conversations with Kristina had stopped sometime around the girl's twelfth birthday and perhaps (thought Rosemarie, revising her initial impression) it wasn't a matter of genuine tiredness. More like utter boredom, and she wondered if it was caused purely by the return visit to her parental home or whether there were other, underlying reasons.

Jakob Willnius was as skilfully charming as usual and sported a double-breasted overcoat that looked equally out of place in Kymlinge. He had brought his very own gift for the new retiree, too – and was careful to stress that this was not the actual present, which would be handed over tomorrow, of course – in the shape of a bottle of Otium, hah hah, that was to say, a single malt by the name of Laphroaig. Matured in oak casks since just after the birth of Christ. Every drop was the purest gold, and if consumed in moderation it ought to last six months, but if you had a bit too much you could fly, chortle chortle.

To show very clearly how much he appreciated this wonder from the capital city, Karl-Erik opened the bottle at once and offered it round; he poured a dram for all of them except the grandchildren (of whom the two Grundt boys were still settling into their rooms and Kelvin was sitting under the table, contemplating his right thumb) and they gave knowing ums and aaahs in appreciation of its characteristic smokiness – except Rosemarie, who brought out her usual comment about never really having got the whole whisky thing.

'Women are a mystery,' smiled Jakob Willnius.

'Isn't Robert here?' asked Kristina.

'No,' said her mother. 'But he rang yesterday and promised he'd be here around seven.'

'It's quarter past,' said Kristina.

'I know that,' said Rosemarie. 'Well now, I really must do a few things in the kitchen.'

'Would you like some help?' asked Ebba.

'No thank you,' said Rosemarie, and could hear for herself that it sounded more dismissive than she had intended. Was she already letting it get to her? Was she already finding it that hard to endure? It would be bad if her children noticed. 'But bring the boys down in fifteen minutes, anyway,' she said in a more conciliatory tone. 'We can't hang about getting ravenous just on Robert's account.'

'Wouldn't dream of it,' said Ebba.

'Hrrm,' said Jakob Willnius. 'So you're off to Spain, I hear?'

'Andalusia,' clarified Karl-Erik, confidingly shifting a few centimetres closer to his son-in-law. 'I don't know if you're aware of this, but there's an enormous wealth of history in those parts. Granada. Córdoba. Seville . . . not forgetting Ronda. The Moorish and Jewish elements; I actually thought I might go in for a bit of modest research. An inventory of the heritage of . . .'

The doorbell rang.

Wanker Rob had arrived and they were at full strength.

The brothers lounged on the two beds in their room, a space about twelve square metres. The wallpaper was dark green with thin vertical stripes in a paler shade of the same colour. There was a three-drawer chest, and on it stood two identical little lamps from Smögen, each with the name of the picturesque fishing village in ornate pokerwork on its wooden base. On the door of the fitted wardrobe hung a large 1988 calendar, sold to raise funds for Reimer, the local football team. Green jerseys, green shorts.

Kristoffer stared up at the ceiling, which was white, and thought about Linda Granberg. Henrik was composing a text message on his mobile phone. Gentle, freshly brewed rain spattered the window, sounding like a whisper from outer space or something.

'Who're you texting?' asked Kristoffer.

'A friend,' said Henrik.

'I get it,' said Kristoffer.

He closed his eyes. It was hard not to think of Linda. It was hard to bear altogether. It was hard not to come back to that idea of skipping a few days.

Two, at this moment, two would do. If it were Wednesday evening instead of Monday evening, he calculated, he'd be back in Sundsvall. Lying in his own bed in his own room instead of in this seedy dump. With Linda a bit closer to hand, living as she did only a couple of hundred metres from their house in Stockrosvägen. He could ring her and arrange to meet up. Why not? Say he wanted to give her a Christmas present.

Christ yes, why hadn't he thought of it earlier? Ring Linda, ask her to come to Birger's burger stand, give her some fucking irresistible present, and then they could have a burger and a walk and a cigarette each. Talk about life and start kissing; as soon as he got home he would damn well fix things with Linda. No doubt about it.

He cursed himself for having been careless enough to lose his mobile, wondering if he really would get a new one for Christmas – but maybe he could borrow Henrik's now, and text her?

'Can I borrow your phone when you've finished?'

'Mhm. What?'

'Can I borrow your mobile?'

'You know you're not allowed.'

'Why?'

'You know why.'

'Thanks. Who needs enemies when you've got brothers?'

No reply.

'I said "Who needs brothers when you've got enemies?"'

'I heard. But don't you mean the other way round?'

'What?'

'You said "Who needs brothers when you've got enemies?"'

'I did not.'

'Yes, you did.'

'Did not.'

Silence.

'Did not.'

Silence.

'Did not.'

'Kristoffer, I get so bloody sick of you sometimes. Can't you just shut up, so I can send this off?'

'Who're you texting?'

No reply.

'Who're you texting? Your girlfriend? Whatshername . . . is it that Jenny?

'Yes, imagine that. Can't you get a girl, Kristoffer, to give you something useful to do with your time?'

'Thanks for the tip. I'll think about it. Is she fit?'

'What?'

'Is she fit, this Jenny?'

'I don't want to discuss this with you.'

'Thanks. Brilliant. My only brother goes off to university and gets so cocky he won't even talk to me any more.'

'Cut it out, Kristoffer. Please just be quiet and let me finish this.'

'Can't you text and talk at the same time? I can.'

'That's because you never write anything important. And never say anything important.'

'Thanks again. With enemies like you, who needs brothers?'

'There, you did it again.'

'What?'

'Said it the wrong way round.'

'I definitely did not.'

Silence.

'I definitely did not.'

Silence.

This is the most hideous wallpaper I've ever seen, thought Kristoffer Grundt. The whole room, in fact. Even I must look good in here.

Maybe he could charge head first into one of the four walls and knock himself out cold for two days?

Karl-Erik Hermansson had never in his life consumed alcoholic beverages to excess – but having offered the rest of them a dram of the show-off whisky Jakob Willnius had brought, he was naturally obliged to do the same for Robert when he turned up about twenty past seven. It stuck in his craw, it really did, but in the absence of anything else you had to hold to custom and manners. Talk about the weather, which at the moment was freezing rain that could turn to snow if the temperature sank a degree or two – talk about how the weather had been all autumn in fact, he thought stoically, but he noticed it made his teeth ache to shake his only-begotten son by the hand and bid him welcome. Even if you could fool everybody else, he realized, you could never fool yourself.

And as he poured Robert the LaFrog or whatever the blessed stuff was called, he was naturally obliged to offer the others some more, as they had had time to drain their glasses. They all accepted, except Rosemarie – who repeated her litany that she had never understood the appeal of that renowned spirit and couldn't take much of it, anyway – and Kelvin, who was now lying on his tummy under the table, investigating the pattern of the rug.

And perhaps it was as a consequence of this initial overconsumption of the divine single malt that the evening turned out as it did.

Or perhaps there were other reasons. Psychologically muddled but mutually immediate and interacting factors, for example, of which none of those present had, or could be expected to have, a complete overview.

Or – of course – it was a combination of the two.

7

'One thing that really has surprised me in recent years,' said Jakob Willnius, 'is that more people don't opt to leave this country when they get the opportunity. I mean to say, who wants to wake up on a Tuesday morning in Tranås, when they could equally well be doing it in Seville? I completely understand your decision to go.'

'It takes a sufficient level of broad-mindedness,' pronounced Karl-Erik, looking as though he had devoted a fair amount of time to the general psychological aspect. 'Not everybody has that, nor can we expect them to.'

'When are you off?' asked Leif Grundt.

'We should get the keys on the first of March, or the fifteenth at the latest. The things we don't take with us are going into storage; we needn't start thinking about dividing up our estate yet.'

'Good God,' said Kristina. 'You can't think we'd ever—'

'There's nothing the matter with Spain,' said Leif Grundt. 'Forty million Spaniards can't be wrong.'

'Forty-two, actually,' said Karl-Erik. 'As at 1 January 2005. But they've got a demographic ageing bulge that almost rivals ours.'

'You moving there won't exactly help that, though?' said Kristina.

'I don't really see what you're driving at,' said Karl-Erik, cautiously sniffing his empty glass.

'That wasn't very nice,' said Ebba, pointing her fork at her little sister by way of warning. 'But you never talked about moving before, did you, Dad? I really hope this hasn't got anything to do with . . . the events of the autumn.'

'Of course not,' Rosemarie instantly exclaimed. 'I don't understand what you're talking about. Can't I persuade anyone to have some more quiche? We've scarcely started on the second one.'

'I'm on my way,' said Leif Grundt.

'I think I need another beer,' said Robert, heaving himself out of his armchair. 'But I can't manage any more quiche, if you don't mind, Mum.'

'Whatever you like, Robert,' said Rosemarie, and a slight look of melancholy, hard to interpret, came into her eyes.

'Balls,' said Kelvin, somewhat surprisingly, from down on the floor.

'We naturally don't intend to be part of any imbecilic colony of Swedish expats,' Karl-Erik went on, once he had put down his glass and given his wife a rapid glance. 'Remember that we only have to scrape the surface of Andalusia very lightly to find history and cultural riches virtually unparalleled in Europe. In the world. There were no Dark Ages there, and everywhere we find traces of a Jewish–Moorish–Christian coexistence that really are unique in time and space . . . yes, hah hah, I have to agree with Jakob. That's something entirely different from a Tuesday in Tranås.'

'Hrrm, yes,' said Jakob Willnius.

'Jakob isn't much of a one for small-town Sweden,' said Kristina. 'It's not just Tranås.'

'I hope the quiche wasn't too salty,' said Rosemarie Wunderlich Hermansson.

'The quiche was excellent, Mummy,' said Ebba Hermansson Grundt.

'Have you been able to sell the house?' asked Leif Grundt, returning with another heaped plate. 'It isn't that bloody easy these days.'

'Leif,' said Ebba.

'It hasn't quite gone through yet,' said Rosemarie. 'Salt is so complicated these days. There are so many different kinds.'

'We're signing the contract on Wednesday,' said her husband.

'Can I really not press anyone to some more ice cream and berries? There's loads left. Boys, how about you?'

Rosemarie Wunderlich Hermansson looked at her two grandsons unhappily. Henrik and Kristoffer shook their heads in unison.

'Maybe they're maturing into men,' Jakob Willnius suggested. 'Sooner or later there comes a time in a man's life when Gummy Raspberries and Bugg are things of the past.'

'Bugg?' queried Kristoffer, in spite of himself. 'What's bugg?'

'A brand of chewing gum,' explained a well-informed Leif Grundt. 'Still on the market, you know, though nobody buys it any more. Don't tell me you've forgotten "Four Buggs and a Coca-Cola?" Jolly good song.'

'Christ,' muttered Kristina.

'I know what Coca-Cola is,' said Kristoffer.

Karl-Erik cleared his throat and leapt in. 'There's a paradigmatic shift underway where our secondary cultural heritage is concerned, as perhaps you've noticed?'

'What?' said Kristoffer.

'Young people today have no idea who Hasse and Tage were. They've never heard of Gösta Knutsson, Lennart Hyland or Monica Zetterlund. I make an exception there for the students I taught myself, but taken overall there are a vanishingly small number of those. Yes, do please help your-selves to the dessert wine, it's Málaga; in a few months' time we'll have a cellar-load of the stuff.'

'Don't mind if I do,' said Leif Grundt. 'Really nice meal. But some things live for ever, don't they? Like Astrid Lind-gren's Emil, and the Co-op and all that. Here's to you, my dear wife. Just imagine you being forty tomorrow. To my eyes, you don't look a day over thirty-nine and a half.'

'Thanks,' said Ebba, not looking at her husband. 'As you've doubtless noticed, Leif's been to Co-operative charm school this autumn.'

'Hah hah, hrrm, well,' said Karl-Erik. He gnashed his teeth for a moment and then went back to his paradigmal shift. '*Fucking Åmål* is another amusing little example. Do you know what one of my students said when that film came out? "Well I know what fucking is, but what the hell is Åmål?"'

He chuckled with satisfaction and a muted merriment hov-ered momentarily over the assembled company in the living room. As if a mildly intoxicated angel of joy had accidentally got into the house, paused for a second and then realized his mistake before turning back. It was only Kristina who picked up Henrik's comment when he muttered under his breath: 'That story was all over the papers.'

I like Henrik, she thought. Yes, he's one person I really like.

★

'So you've really got a cellar to go with the house?' asked Leif. 'Thinking of the wine, I mean?'

'A sort of food cellar, in fact,' Karl-Erik elaborated with pleasure. 'Twelve to fifteen cubic metres, so we'll always have space for the liquid refreshments.'

'So shall I put the coffee on?' asked Rosemarie.

'Tea for me, Mummy,' said Ebba. 'I'll come and help you.'

Jakob Willnius came down the stairs.

'Finally!' exclaimed Kristina. 'What on earth have you been up to?'

'I've been getting our child to sleep, darling,' said Jakob Willnius unassumingly, and finished his glass of Málaga, which he'd parked on the oak sideboard next to a fragment of the Berlin wall set in glass. He sat himself down on the sofa, between Kristina and Henrik.

'It usually takes three minutes.'

'Well this time it took forty-five. What are you chatting about? Have I missed anything important?'

'Shouldn't think so,' said Kristina.

'Yes, can't imagine what,' said Robert. 'How soon can we go to bed without offending anybody?'

The room went quiet. Unusually quiet, considering there were no fewer than nine notionally adult individuals in it.

'Sorry,' said Robert. 'Think I had a bit too much wine. I apologize, Mum.'

'Haven't a clue what you're talking about,' Rosemarie said gaily. 'Nothing to say sorry for, is there? Right, time for tea and coffee.'

She went out to the kitchen, followed by her eldest and most well-behaved daughter.

'For heaven's sake, Robert,' ventured Kristina in a stage whisper. 'What was the point of that?'

Robert Hermansson shrugged, looking apologetic, and drained his glass of beer. Then for a moment he seemed on the verge of saying something, explaining a few things, but the opportunity slipped through his hands and it was another hour before he finally got to the point.

'I assume you're all waiting for some kind of explanation.' He put down the glass from which he had drained the next-to-last drops of the noble Laphroaig that was meant to last six months. But it had, at any rate, been distributed in quite a fraternal way between the various gentlemen. Not counting Henrik and Kristoffer. Kristina was drinking a glass of red wine. Ebba was still on the green tea. Rosemarie was washing up, Kelvin was asleep. It was half past eleven. It's time now, thought Kristina. All the preliminary skirmishing is out of the way.

'Or some kind of apology,' Robert added.

A long second of silence followed.

'No, really, we're not waiting for anything, Robert,' said Kristina. 'Yes, of course you can have a bit of my wine, Henrik.'

'No, we truly aren't, Robert,' Ebba insisted, but a little too late to sound convincing. 'Let bygones be bygones, for God's sake. The only thing we can learn from this is the art and importance of forgetting. And hope that others have mastered the art, too. Isn't that right?'

She looked round for support from the others, but all she got was a shrug from Jakob Willnius. She changed tack. 'Dad, are you sure there aren't going to be any birthday well-wishers dropping round tomorrow? Henrik, that's enough now.'

'Well I wouldn't exactly say sure,' muttered Karl-Erik. 'Rosemarie's laid in three extra gateaux and five kilos of coffee just in case. But anybody who does come will turn up in the morning. All you have to do is keep out of the way.'

'How can you know they'll come in the morning?' wondered Kristina.

'Because that was how I put it in the notice in the paper,' Karl-Erik explained with a yawn. 'No congratulations in person. Not at home after one o'clock.'

'Genius,' said Jakob, raising his glass with the very last drops of the precious whisky. 'If you've developed a taste for this, I recommend Gibraltar, anyway. Since you'll be in the neighbourhood. There's no cheaper booze in all Europe.'

'Is that so?' said Karl-Erik in a neutral tone. 'Well, we've got the twelve to fifteen cubic metres, as I say.'

'So nobody's sitting there waiting for an explanation, then?' resumed Robert, looking round the room. 'I'm sensing, like, some level of pressure.'

Kristina, one hand on Henrik's knee for support, got to her feet. 'Robert, come outside with me for a minute, will you?'

'Happy to,' said Robert. 'I need a fag.'

They went out and another sort of angel silently crossed the room. Karl-Erik yawned again and Leif Grundt scratched the back of his neck. 'I think the time has come,' declared Jakob Willnius. 'I'll go up and get Kelvin ready. Tomorrow's another day, after all.'

'What sort of standard is the hotel these days, by the way?' Ebba suddenly wanted to know. 'I remember what it used to be like.'

'You've never stayed at Kymlinge Hotel, have you?' asked Rosemarie, who had just come back into the room. 'Would anybody like a sandwich or some fruit?'

'No to both, thank you, Mummy,' said Ebba. 'But you know the hotel didn't have the best of reputations in my time.'

'It looked respectable enough when we checked in,' Jakob Willnius assured her. 'No prostitutes or cockroaches, as far as I could see. Though you never know quite how things will develop in the wee small hours.'

'Fruit?' repeated Rosemarie, as if sensing control was slipping away from her. 'A sandwich? Anyone?'

'Can't you hear they're all stuffed, my dove?' said her husband. 'Anyway, if you don't disapprove, it's time for the lost generation to retire to bed now. But sit up as long as you like.'

'Where have Robert and Kristina got to?' asked Rosemarie.

'They're outside, talking morality and smoking,' said Leif Grundt. 'Listen Ebbabebba, shouldn't we hit the hay as well? I've got to be up early tomorrow to sing for a fair lady I know.'

'Does Kristina smoke?' said Rosemarie. 'I'd never have—'

'No, she's doing the morality bit,' said Leif Grundt. 'Goodnight then, mortals.'

'No, Jakob. I really want to stay for a while. I want longer to talk to my family, surely there's nothing so odd about that?'

She had hoped he might at least show some sign of opposition to this, but he didn't. She realized he was relishing the chance of a tit-for-tat where Wednesday's breakfast meeting with the American magnate was concerned, and that she was in fact playing into his hands. It annoyed her. It would be better if he had to forge his own weapons, she thought.

'OK,' was all he said. 'I'll take a taxi with Kelvin. Come when you're ready.'

'An hour, maybe,' she said. 'I'll walk, it only takes ten minutes.'

'Don't underestimate those small-town dangers,' he said.

I never underestimate anything, thought Kristina. That's the whole problem.

By quarter past twelve the parental hosts, the lost generation, were settled in bed. Or at any rate, they were barricaded behind a closed bedroom door. Ebba Hermansson Grundt and Co-op manager Leif Grundt had also retired for the night. To the former's girlhood bedroom, behind another closed door.

Jakob and Kelvin Willnius had departed in a taxi for the Kymlinge Hotel in Drottninggatan.

On the ground floor in the Hermanssons' detached house at 4 Allvädersgatan, that left siblings Robert and Kristina, and brothers Henrik and Kristoffer. Kristina checked the time.

'Another half hour,' she announced. 'Otherwise I'll get a good bollocking from my big sister.'

'Nah,' said Henrik.

'Yes she will,' said Kristoffer, 'but it's the sort of thing you have to learn to take.'

'The wine rack in the kitchen looked a bit overloaded,' said Robert. 'I suggest we open another bottle.'

He left the room without waiting for their answer, returning ten seconds later with a Valpolicella.

'Tell me about Uppsala,' asked Kristina, leaning a little closer to Henrik.

It seemed an eminently harmless prompt, but to her surprise she saw the boy bite his lower lip, and for a moment, tears seemed to be welling in his eyes. Presumably neither his brother nor Robert noticed this state of affairs, but for her part, she was quite sure.

Her nephew was borne down by sorrow.

8

Kristoffer found his brother's mobile where he had hidden it. Under the pillow on his bed. Hah!

Why the hell am I thinking 'Hah!', he then wondered.

He felt a slight throb in his temples. It was just gone half past twelve; he had downed two glasses of wine, thought the others hadn't noticed, but now realized he was probably a bit drunk. That was no doubt why he was thinking something as nerdy as 'Hah!' on finding Henrik's phone.

The others were still down there. Kristina, Henrik and Robert. Kristina was great. She was his godmother; if his mother somehow died – lost her life, as you might say – it would be Kristina who stepped up in her place. Wow, he thought (more nerdspeak), imagine having Kristina as your mum!

Then a glowing red thought flamed up his brain. You couldn't go around thinking your parents ought to die. If God existed, that would be a black mark engraved permanently and forever against you in His records.

But Kristoffer didn't believe God was there. And, after all, they were sisters, his mother and Kristina; they had loads of genes and amino acids and stuff that were exactly the same, so there was no harm in just wishing they had more in common on the outside, too.

Robert had the same genes as well, of course. He looked a little bit like Kristina, too, come to think of it, but there was no denying he was a saddo. A real bloody loser. Wanking on TV!

Not that they'd talked about it much in the course of the evening. It was kind of a no go. A big juicy scandal that they all had to tiptoe round. Kristoffer hadn't seen the programme itself, of course; they didn't watch things like that in the Grundt household in Stockrosvägen in Sundsvall. But he had read about it in one of the papers, they'd talked about it at school – and thank goodness, yes, thank goodness, that from the word go he had obeyed his mother's orders and kept quiet about his uncle being a contestant on *Fucking Island*. Sometimes she was right in spite of everything, you had to give her credit for that.

The mobile was on. No password was required. Brilliant, thought Kristoffer. I've got a bit of Dutch courage now, and who would have imagined things turning out so conveniently in this skunk burrow? I'll fire off something naughty and irresistible to Linda. Yes, dammit, I will!

He formulated it in his head first. It took scarcely a moment, coming as easily and elegantly as running water.

Hi Linda. Feeling horny for you. Shall we give each other Christmas presents? Birger's burger stand, 9 on Thurs evening.

It sounded good. Irresistibly good. And then:

Don't reply for God's sake, this is my brother's phone. Just come. Kristoffer.

He smiled to himself. Was it going too far to say he felt horny? Heck no, that was the kind of thing chicks like Linda fell for. You had to stop being timid. He'd been far too timid all his life, that was his problem. If he carried on like that, he'd never find out how . . . how it felt to touch a woman *there*.

He pressed a key and the display lit up. *New message*, it said. New message to Henrik, in other words. Hmm, thought Kristoffer. Should he? Why not? *Read now?* All he had to do was press YES. Henrik would never find out. And he'd never find out Kristoffer had texted Linda, because he'd delete it straight away. It would only take a couple of seconds to read Henrik's message. Maybe it was from that Jenny? Maybe it was something risqué? He wondered if Henrik had screwed her. Of course he had; that was probably the only thing those students in halls of residence got up to in Uppsala. Went to student clubs and parties and screwed around. Did a couple of hours' study on a Sunday afternoon so they could keep up. Kristoffer hoped he'd be there before long, too. If only you could skip four or five years, then . . . no, not the skipping-over idea again. Enough of all that, he resolved; it was Linda Granberg who mattered. Here and now. Or Birger's burger stand on Thursday, at any rate. He looked at the display. It said *00.46*. *Read now?* He pressed YES.

Henrik, my prince. Missing you so badly. My arms around your body. Penetrating you in my dreams. J

He read the short message three times. What in hell's name, he thought. Penetrating you? What did that mean? Was it . . . was it just that she wanted to penetrate his dreams? No, couldn't be, it didn't say that. J must stand for Jenny. But what the heck did she mean when she said . . . ? Was this some utterly crucial variety of intercourse that had passed him by? Bloody hell, a woman couldn't penetrate a man, could she? Kristoffer hadn't seen many porn films in his four-teen years, but he wasn't exactly a virgin on that score. He was pretty well acquainted with what the female sexual organ looked like, in all its aspects and phases, but whatever else you could use it for, he didn't think you could penetrate anything with it. Just the reverse.

And what part of Henrik could anybody pen—?

Christ, he thought. It looks as though . . . I mean, this seems like . . .

For a second his mind went as blank as a new layer of water on an ice hockey rink. Then he realized what he had to do to be sure. Quick as a flash, almost before he had asked himself the question. He looked at the sender's number, memorized it and clicked his way to the address book. Started going through it from A. Henrik clearly did the same as him: used first names, didn't bother with surnames. He jumped straight to J and there, there he found it. He stared at the illuminated little display and couldn't believe his eyes.

Jens, it said.

Jens. The number tallied.

Well I'll be . . . thought Kristoffer Grundt.

There was no Jenny.

There was only a Jens. Henrik wasn't with some pretty female medical student from Karlskoga. He was with a guy. One whose name was Jens and who couldn't wait to stick his cock up Henrik's arse!

A host of contradictory impulses and thoughts started bombarding Kristoffer's mildly intoxicated brain, but once the storm had passed, he could scarcely contain his laughter.

His big brother was gay.

Super-Henrik did it with boys.

Or at the very least with one called Jens.

What . . . what a huge bloody advantage that gave him! That was exactly how it felt. It was the first word that popped into his head. *Advantage!* It wasn't an attractive thought, he knew that, but finally – for the first time ever – it was as if . . . as if he had some kind of a hold over that superman who was his brother. Thank you, o thank you, o great creator of the mobile phone, thought Kristoffer Grundt. This changes things, I'd say. Christ Almighty!

He wrote his text message to Linda, clicked it on its way and deleted it. Returned the phone to neutral and shoved it back under Henrik's pillow.

Jens! He switched off the Smögen lamp on his side of the chest of drawers but left Henrik's on. He turned to face the wall, contemplated one of the slightly paler green vertical stripes from close quarters and thought that this was going to age his mother and father ten years.

And for once, just for once, it wasn't him who was the problem.

Rosemarie Wunderlich Hermansson lay on her side with her knees drawn up and watched the red minutes of the clock radio. 01.12. Karl-Erik was flat on his back behind her, taking the same calm, faintly hissing breaths she had listened to for forty years. If I put a pillow over his mouth, she thought, would they stop? Was it that simple?

Presumably not. You can murder children and frail maidens that way, but not real men. He would wake up and start to defend himself. Besides, it was his birthday, and he would never forgive her if she tried to kill him on his sixty-fifth birthday.

She pushed the thought away. 01.13. Better to die herself, then. Though he would doubtless never forgive her for that, either. If she took her own life on the big day. Things were as they were. She had to get through the next twenty-four hours. Ebba's and Karl-Erik's big day. It should have been like a crest in the road, yet it felt more like a . . . what was it? . . . a sinkhole? Yes, it really did. But where was all this gloom coming from? Why was she prey to these morbid fantasies suddenly? Day after day, night after night. Was it just Robert's confounded TV programme or was Robert a catalyst for something else? She used not to think like this.

Or Spain? Was it Spain dragging her down into this muddy puddle of depression? 01.14. Or the fact that she had retired? Had she forfeited the aim and meaning of her life, simply because she no longer had a job to go to? Those blasted kids at Kymlingevik School?

The whole evening had been a walk through the valley of the shadow of death. A tightrope walk, at that; she had been a fraction of a second away from just throwing plates and cutlery to the devil and screaming out loud. Yet no one had noticed a thing. Mummy this and Mummy that, and your warm cloudberries are the best in the world, Mum. As if it took any sort of finesse to heat up some frozen cloudberries. She had served and cleared and washed up and delivered food-related lines from a script so old and dog-eared that nobody even noticed it was all a piece of theatre. She had fished into the depths of her soul for anything sensible to say – for warm feelings for any of her children (grandchildren and sons-in-law included) – but her hooks had dangled naked on limp lines, way down in the sinkhole. 01.15. Kelvin was a strange and introverted child, it made her wonder if he was quite all there. Autism perhaps, or Asperger's syndrome, though weren't they variants of the same thing? The monosyllabic sounds he uttered at long intervals always managed to peculiarly resemble words with sexual connotations. If I were twenty and had to choose one of the others to live on a desert island with, she thought – well, he'd have to be twenty as well, of course – I'm damned if I wouldn't go for Leif.

It was a slightly surprising conclusion, but at least Leif wasn't a wolf in sheep's clothing. Possibly a pig in a pigskin coat, but a kindly pig, and you never had to try too hard with him. Ebba's been lucky, she thought. She'll spend her whole life imagining she traded down, when in fact she drew the winning ticket. Arrogant goose, you should have been called Karl-Ebba! The thought hit her with a sudden flare of anger. She could almost smile at it in the darkness as she wondered whether there was essentially anything beyond a quarter century and differently shaped sexual organs to divide them. Father and daughter. Two peas in a pod, Lord help us! And the boys seemed down in the dumps, both of them. Especially little Kristoffer of course, but then he had had to grow up in the perpetual shadow of his big brother, the golden boy. Yes, Henrik was the third generation in a directly descending line. Karl-Erik, Karl-Ebba, Karl-Henrik. Imagine if it had been Henrik's birthday tomorrow as well. But when it came down to it, he was actually an unplanned human being, and she hoped that this simple fact might be the detail that proved his salvation.

And what Kristina saw – or had once seen – in Jakob Willnius was beyond her. Vigour, success, maturity. Charm and self-confidence, false as water. No, that was unfair, but there certainly was something about him that put her in mind of water. Transparency and adaptability, perhaps? Who bloody cares, thought Rosemarie. Why am I lying here analysing them, one after another? I don't give a damn about any of them.

But both Robert and Kristina are more me than Karl-Erik, anyway – her thoughts continued despite her, as if she no longer had the least control over them – that becomes more obvious with every year that passes. And maybe there *had* been a sort of warmth in Kristina's hug? An intimation, a silent message of collusion and reconciliation, after all. It was still too fragile for words and actions – 01.17 – but in time it could grow into something durable and useful. If she could only keep going, Kristina, and avoid falling apart along the way.

Like Robert. She dug her hands into the soft flesh above her kneecaps, then laced her fingers together and prayed to the god she occasionally believed in, but generally didn't, not to let Robert turn into an alcoholic. He had been blind drunk on that television programme, and he had drunk too much tonight as well. Dear God, she mouthed silently, protect my children – at least my youngest two, the eldest will be all right whatever happens – protect them from all the evil that awaits them on their path through life and protect me from myself. Let me at least sleep for a while now, and then hold it together for another day and a half. If I end up in hospital on Wednesday afternoon, it really doesn't matter – body or soul, it makes no difference, it would be rather lovely, actually. 01.18, I'll have to get up and take a sleeping pill after all, damn it, I should have realized, before my brain boils over. Before the sinkhole.

Before . . . I loathe these nights, truly I do, they've been almost worse than the days recently.

'I'm just going out for a bit,' said Robert. 'I need a walk and a couple of fags. Why the hell does it have to be so hard to handle this?'

'Handle what?' asked Kristina, refilling her own glass and Henrik's from the second bottle Robert had fetched from the kitchen. She spilled a few drops on the table. Christ, I'm drunk, she thought. I'll have to make this the last glass.

But actually, it felt rather good. When she thought about it, she hadn't been properly tipsy once since she found out she was expecting Kelvin. Two years, no, more, two and a half, no wonder there was that pleasant sense of novelty.

And so strange that it should happen this very evening.

'Coming home,' said Robert. 'It's the coming-home phenomenon I'm talking about. This whole goddamned slough of family despond . . . obviously I don't include you, Henrik. You know what I mean, Kristina?'

'Of course I do,' said Kristina. 'Don't you remember "My Family"?'

Robert gave a laugh. It was a classic. The year was 1983. Ebba was eighteen and in her final year at upper secondary. Robert was thirteen. Kristina was nine and in Year 3, and her homework was to write an essay entitled 'My Family'.

My family is like a prison. Dad is the prison governor. Mum is the cook. My sister Ebba, who has got really fat and doesn't fit into her jeans any more, is the prison guard, and my brother Robert and me are the prisoners. We are not gilty of the crimes they say we did but we have been locked away for life.

*Every day we get leave of absunse to go to another prison
nearby, it's called Kymlingevik School and there are loads of
other prisoners and guards. It's a bit more fun, not so strict.*

*Dad the prison governor is a mean devil and he always wears a
tie except on Sundays when he's unbutturned. Mum the cook is
scared of him and always does what he says. So do the rest of
us otherwise he hits us with a big club with nails in.*

*My sister the prison guard sucks up to him and is a mean devil
as well. Sometimes she can be kind to us prisoners but that's
always only because it's somebody's birthday.*

*As soon as Robert and me get big we're running away and
reporting our family to child welfare. And the King and Queen
Silvia who look after all badly treated children. The King will
ride out on his white donkey, shoot Mum, Dad and Ebba dead
and set Robert and me free. Then we will live happily ever after
until the end of time.*

True, true, true.

The essay created quite a commotion. It was the mid-
eighties; school psychologists and school counsellors were
busily going on courses to be told the Tale of Unreported
Cases. At least two cases of incest in every class, was the
candid assessment. At least three other serious causes for concern; it was just a matter of ferreting them out. The entire
Hermansson family was summoned to a meeting, which took
place in the counsellor's pastel-coloured room and was opened
by Kristina's form teacher – a solidly built lass of twenty-five
from down south near Landskrona, who later left teaching to
become Sweden's first female frogman – reading out Kristina's
composition.

Her mother, Rosemarie, fainted. Her father, Karl-Erik the Pedagogical Figure of Respect, went cross-eyed and started to stutter, but it was Ebba who saved the whole situation by bursting out laughing, hugging her little sister and saying that was the daftest thing she'd heard in her whole life.

Kristina admitted that at the time of writing she had been in a sulk because they wouldn't let her watch a TV programme about mass murderers and rapists in New York, and that this had made her lay it on a bit thick.

Robert was given no opportunity to say anything, but by the time Rosemarie regained consciousness, all was basically sweetness and light. The counsellor was happy, the director of studies was happy, and the frogwoman-to-be was as happy as she had the capacity to be, having a certain deficiency in that particular area. Karl-Erik's stutter also wore off, but his eyes stayed crossed for several days. There was speculation that he might in fact have suffered a slight cerebral haemorrhage.

'You really captured something there,' said Robert. 'I'm just popping out for a while, as I say. See you tomorrow, don't sit up too late.'

'I'll be off to bed soon,' said Kristina.

'Me too,' said Henrik.

It was five past one when he got down to the main square. Good, he thought. In this dump there isn't a soul about at this time of night. Nobody I need to hide my face from, if a man walk in the night he stumbleth . . . and so on.

Even so, a familiar feeling came creeping over him when he stopped in front of the dark entrance to the Royal cinema and looked about him. A wet blanket and suffocation. This corner of eternity had been the hub of his life for the first twenty years, no wonder he had been damaged by it. No wonder things had got screwed up.

He recognized the whiff of self-pity. Of course. Blaming the inward dreariness of your adult life on the outward ditto of your childhood was what mental wrecks had always indulged in, it was nothing new. Everybody had to be born somewhere. Raising yourself up was what everybody had to learn. He worked out that he hadn't been home for a year and a half, wondering simultaneously why he called it 'home'. A black hole that never seemed to lose its power of attraction, but perhaps that was how it was for everybody? You just had to beware of being sucked in. Had to keep your distance. He lit a cigarette and set off along Badhusgatan. What was it that had happened to him in that lay-by? *What?* You surely couldn't die of pure anxiety? Only of actions carried out under the influence of that anxiety. Or was it quite simply a physical collapse? Was that how such a thing felt? He had physically fainted. Could you feel so goddamned lousy that you just passed out? Not such a stupid defence mechanism if so. To sleep, sleep, as he had said, and forget both the world and his own putrid uselessness.

He hadn't looked his mother in the eye all evening. Nor many of the others, either, possibly only Kristina. She had found the right words when they were talking outside, no doubt about it: 'You're a fucking bastard, Robert, and I love you.' All the others had tried to position themselves on a convenient buoy somewhere between the bastard and the love, but only Kristina had the guts to embrace both extremes. And not give a shit about the space in between. It struck him that Paula had been that sort of woman. A woman who was intimate with both the grime and the grace. The dirty golden gleam of existence, the Madonna and the whore . . . the words were running riot in his head now, it was the whisky and wine of course; he got up as far as Norra Kungsvägen, stopped for a while and contemplated the attractive old water tower. Reddish-brown brick, perfectly round; just think if they could pull down every ugly water tower in this country and rebuild them all like this one. Dotted with small, friendly windows and crowned with a copper roof with a patina of verdigris; surely it ought not to have been so bloody remarkable? That would be a world to live in, thought Robert; in a world with round water towers of reddish-brown brick, I would be able to feel at home.

But a new Paula, then. That was what he needed, that would be his salvation. It probably wouldn't be impossible to find a new woman if he went and planted himself in the Canaries for three months. It was swarming with unattached women. He could fix up that brilliant old novel of his while finding his definitive Madonna-whore, yes, it was certainly high time. For both of those things. He lit another cigarette and started walking towards the church. Tomorrow I shall look my mother in the eye, he decided. Tell her not to cry over spilt semen (I mean milk, for Christ's sake, *milk*!) and that I've got a plan.

He had scarcely spared a thought for Jeanette Andersson all evening, but as he turned into Fabriksgatan he suddenly realized this was where she lived. Number 26, wasn't it?

Why not? thought Robert Hermanssson.

Admittedly it was twenty past one, but she wouldn't necessarily have to be up early for work the next day. He took out his wallet and found the scrap of paper with her phone number on it.

9

He's such a good-looking boy, thought Kristina. Hope he can stand up to his mother, that's all. But where does that sorrow come from?

'Are you happy, Henrik?' she asked.

It was the sort of question she could ask on the strength of who she was. His freedom auntie. He had been the one to come up with the phrase; quite a few years ago now, when they had spent a few summer weeks together in Skagen. Ebba and Leif had rented a huge house for an entire month, but Ebba had had conferences and surgical commitments that took up at least half that time and Kristina had been roped in as a kind of supplementary mother for the boys. Henrik had been twelve and Kristoffer seven. Kristina, do you know what you are, he had said one day when they were on the beach, building sandcastles and drinking Coca-Cola. You're my super yummy freedom auntie!

And he had hugged her with his bony, boyish body until she could hardly breathe, and then all three of them had wrestled so wildly that the sand went spraying up and the castle was reduced to ruins. With their combined strength, Henrik and Kristoffer managed to get their freedom auntie on her back, kiss her navel and gradually pack her into a thousand tons of sand, leaving only her head sticking out.

That must have been a good summer, she surprised herself by thinking. Or was it just memory's usual retouching that had come into play?

'I don't know,' he said. 'Well no, I don't think I'm particularly happy.'

'I've noticed. You know I'm listening, if there's anything you want to talk about.'

He sat there twirling his wineglass. Presumably he was a little tipsy, too, but that surely wasn't a state with which he was entirely unfamiliar? After a whole term in Uppsala. He's nineteen, she thought. Twelve years younger than her and not an especially desirable age, when she looked in her own rear-view mirror. But what was wrong? Was he short of friends? Were his studies going badly? Drugs? Or had he simply fallen out with that girl of his? Ebba had said he had a girlfriend who was reading medicine.

'Have you failed your exams?' she ventured, trying to help him get started.

He shook his head. 'Haven't had any. We have the one big exam in January.'

'So you've got a lot to do over the holidays?'

'Feels more like a cramming session than a holiday.'

'I see. But you think it's going all right? You've kept up in the autumn term, and so on?'

He nodded. It struck her that he might think she was stupid. That it was stupid of her to sit there and ask Super-Henrik how his studies were going.

'And you've chosen the right course?'

'I think so.'

OK, so that wasn't the problem. Have a bit more wine, nephew dear, she thought, so you feel bold enough to tell me what's troubling you. She raised her own glass playfully. Gave him a wink.

He took a gulp. Then shot her a look with a new kind of energy in it. He was weighing her up and seemed for a few seconds to be teetering on the brink of a decision. It was suddenly hard to think of him as only nineteen.

'There is one thing I don't think I can talk about,' he said finally. 'You'll have to excuse me, that's just the way it is.'

'Not even with me?' she asked. 'Not even in the middle of the night?'

He did not reply.

'Well, if it's something serious, I hope you've got someone else you can trust. Just don't go bottling it up inside.'

Bloody cod psychology, she thought. I sound like a school counsellor. She watched him. He had lowered his eyes. Folded his hands, his long, powerful, pianist's fingers, in front of him, and was sitting in silence again. His thick, dark fringe flopped forward, concealing his face. The intensity of his thoughts was almost palpable now. The decision was bubbling away in there, somewhere between his heart and his larynx, the words were all ready, it would be only a moment's work to voice them. She wondered if she truly could perceive this so clearly, or was just imagining it because she wanted it so much. But whatever the case, this was the crucial juncture; if he didn't tell her what was weighing on him now, he was not going to do it later, either. Tomorrow or next week or at any other time. I want to know, she thought. I really like this boy and I want him to open his heart to me. I will be able to help you, Henrik, don't you see that? I'm not your mum, I'm your freedom auntie. She contemplated putting her hand on his arm, but decided against it. The whole thing was balanced on a knife edge and too much pressure could tip his decision the wrong way.

She seized the bottle, still half full, and topped up their glasses again. Thirty seconds passed, maybe a minute; she had just decided how silly this all was, the red wine making her so daft and supersensitive and thin-skinned, when he straightened his back, took a gulp from his glass and looked at her with that special energy.

'I'm homosexual, Kristina,' he said. 'That's the problem.'

Already poised with his mobile phone in his hand, Robert was suddenly plagued with doubt.

Ringing up a woman who was a perfect stranger at half past one in the morning, would that be crazy? What if she had one leg and weighed a hundred and forty kilos? What if she was a toothless heroin addict?

Jeanette Andersson?

But on the other hand, what if she was to be his salvation? What if she was lying there waiting for him? His new Paula. She was clearly aware of the Hermanssons' 105th birthday, so she doubtless knew he was in town right now. That he had come back.

But even so. If only it were a Friday or Saturday night.

He opted for a compromise. A walk through Pampas to the sports ground and the railway, to be precise, keeping her at a slight distance. If he had not changed his mind in the ten minutes this would take him, he could call her – and if she actually answered and asked him to come, he still had ten minutes to think the better of it as he went back to Fabriksgatan.

Simple plan, thought Robert, lighting another cigarette as he gave a shiver. Smart. The cold air was raw and he was grateful at least that he had enough alcohol in his blood not to freeze. That was always something.

He threw back his shoulders and started to walk.

A stream of automatic and pretty divergent thoughts went through her head. She drank a little wine and made a conscious effort not to let any reaction show. Something told her it was important not to react the wrong way, and that same something informed her simultaneously that there were at least a hundred different wrong reactions to choose between. It surprised her that she could not find anything spontaneous to say. That no emotion presented itself which she could clothe in pure and truthful words. It was so obvious that Henrik was tormented. By both his sexual orientation and the fact that he had revealed it; she couldn't decide which of those two things weighed heaviest in his tense silence. He had leant back in the sofa, clasped his hands behind his neck and fixed his eyes on the ceiling. He evidently didn't want to look at her. She rapidly summoned – and discarded – the whole arsenal of politically correct platitudes: 'Why should that make you unhappy?' 'Everybody has a certain tendency in that direction.' 'Your sexuality isn't fully developed yet.' 'So what?' Instead, she tried to identify what she really felt and thought and believed; it really couldn't be that damned hard, if she only relaxed a bit . . .

Finally it came.

'You're really not,' she said.

'What?' he said.

'I said you're really not.'

He unclasped his hands from behind his neck and leant forward, elbows on knees.

'I heard. What kind of crap is that? Don't you think I know myself whether I'm—'

'No,' said Kristina. 'I don't think you actually do know.'

'And what makes you think you can claim that? I must admit, I'd expected a different reaction.'

A sudden sharpness in his tone. She looked him straight in the eye for a second before she answered.

'What sort?'

'Eh?'

'What sort of reaction did you expect?'

'I don't know. But not this one.'

'Does my reaction matter all that much?'

He shrugged and relaxed a little. 'I don't know. Yes . . . no, of course not. What the hell, now you know I'm gay, at any rate.'

She shook her head and smiled at him. Moved a bit closer on the sofa and ran her hand down his arm.

'Henrik, you listen to me. I've got at least half a dozen gay people in my circle of acquaintances. I know there are different kinds and that people turn out gay for different reasons. But I'm very sure that you don't fit into that gang. I'm sure you've had homoerotic experiences, but that doesn't automatically make you gay. I've had—' Here she stopped herself for a moment, but realized there was scope for being in two minds. 'I've been with women a couple of times in my life, and enjoyed it, but I realized pretty soon that I belonged in the other camp.'

'*You* were a lesbian?'

His amazement was wide-eyed and absolute.

'What I said was that I've had a couple of experiences of lesbian love. Just as you, I assume, have had experience of what it's like to be with a man.'

'My God,' said Henrik, and drank some of his wine. 'I'd never have thought it.'

'Didn't you have a girlfriend when you were at upper secondary, for example? Hanna, or whatever her name was.'

'I had two, actually,' Henrik admitted. 'But it never worked very well.'

'Did you sleep with them?'

'Yeah. Or something like that.'

He gave a laugh, self-mocking but somehow good-natured, too. She leant a little closer to him.

'And because it worked better with this guy who you presumably met in Uppsala, you conclude that you're homosexual?'

'Yeah, but—'

'Plenty of people are a bit bisexual, you know. They eventually choose one or the other, it really is no harder than that. It's like choosing a career . . . or a car, you simply don't need a Bugatti *and* a Rolls-Royce.'

'A Bugatti and a Rolls . . . ?'

He laughed again but it stuck in his throat, the sadness catching up with him again. He looked at her with a faintly wavering gaze, his face quite close to hers.

'Kristina, I *am* gay. Thanks for trying to pour balm into my wound, but it doesn't change the basic starting point.'

She held his eyes. Five seconds passed. Five dizzying seconds when something started to happen; it felt so strange to be gazing into her nephew's blue eyes like this, and at such close range. A few more seconds passed, the room around them somehow seemed to lose form and content, slowly arching into a glass bell jar, an incubator enclosing them, and suddenly all prior assumptions no longer applied.

No, she thought, this is just me, trying to gild this drunken state I'm in. Then she said:

'Put your hand on my breast, Henrik.'

He hesitated, not moving.

'Now, now, I'm not wearing a bra, you can see that. Go on.'

He did as she said. First outside her blouse, then under it. His hand was warm and careful. Her nipple instantly hardened.

'What are you feeling?'

He didn't answer. His hand trembled a little. Or perhaps it was her. Why should I put the brakes on now? she thought. Why make do with half measures? She put her hand on his crotch. Held it there and felt him swelling. *What am I doing?* a voice screamed inside her. *What the hell am I playing at?*

But she ignored it. 'I've got two breasts,' she whispered. 'Go on.'

He obeyed her again. She undid his jeans and put in her hand. Took hold of him.

'What are you feeling?'

He swallowed. His eyes did not leave hers. As if that were the illusory thread the whole thing depended on. He was caressing her breasts now. She got his underpants down under his balls and took a firmer hold. Cautiously moved him up and down a few times. He opened his mouth, breathing heavily.

'Christ Almighty,' he said, closing his eyes.

'Yes,' whispered Kristina. 'Christ Almighty indeed.'

★

Robert decided to do a whole circuit of the pitch-black sports ground before he got out his phone. One last circuit to give him time to opt out. Thin, diffuse drizzle had begun to fall; frosty precipitation that settled like a cold skin on his face and hair, but he still wasn't feeling chilled through. He hadn't seen a single person for the past fifteen minutes, just two passing cars and a stray cat that leapt out of a dark alley off Johannes Kyrkogata, right at his feet.

'It doesn't get much lonelier than this,' he mumbled to himself as he came back round to the main entrance – and that felt comforting, somehow. As if he had finally reached rock bottom. On a solitary amble round Kymlinge sports ground on a December night. He got out his phone. When he opened it, he saw the time had reached 01.51.

He stopped, took a deep breath and lit a cigarette. Felt with his fingers that there were only two more left in the packet and rang the number.

She answered after three rings.

'Yes, it's me.'

'Jeanette?'

'Yes.'

She didn't sound like someone just waking up, but he knew you couldn't always tell. Some people could virtually talk in their sleep and still sound sober and alert. Her voice had a certain rough quality with a slight sibilance to it. But it was warm, he liked it – and for one idiotic second a line ran through his head.

I'm your long-lost lover and there's snow in my hair.

He fought it back, having no time to ponder where on earth it had come from. 'Sorry,' he said instead. 'This is

Robert, Robert Hermansson. I know it's the middle of the night, but I'm having trouble sleeping, and if you still . . . ?'

'Come round,' she said simply. 'I'm waiting for you.'

'I didn't mean to—'

'Just come,' she said. 'I invited you, after all, and I wasn't asleep. You know where I live?'

'Yes,' said Robert. 'You told me. Twenty-six Fabriksgatan . . . is there a door code?'

'Nineteen fifty-eight,' she said. 'Where are you now?'

'The sports ground.'

'The sports ground? What are you doing at the sports ground in the middle of the night?'

'I went for a walk. And found myself thinking of you.'

'Good,' she said. 'You'll be here in ten minutes. I'll make some tea. Or would you rather have a glass of wine?'

'Tea'll be fine . . . I think.'

'All right. We can have both. I look forward to seeing you, Robert. Nineteen fifty-eight.'

She hung up. Her voice stayed in him, and he suddenly felt there was something vaguely familiar about it. He put his phone in his pocket, threw away his half-smoked cigarette and set off towards Fabriksgatan.

She was only wearing a dress and panties and could hardly have been more accessible, but once he had felt his way to her most erogenous spot, she interrupted proceedings.

'We've got to think, Henrik,' she whispered in his ear. 'We don't want other people to get hurt.'

'Mhm,' said Henrik.

'But if you want, I'm happy to go the whole way. You're duly noting that I'm a woman, I hope?'

'You are a woman,' he said huskily. 'You've got to let me carry on.'

She took her hands off him and pushed him away. Straightened her clothes. The wall clock struck two, its fragile chimes hanging in the room like an unmistakable reminder of external existence. The world did not consist of just this sofa and these two people. There was altogether, thought Kristina, an infinite number of paralysing relationships and circumstances to be taken into account. If one chose to.

'Tomorrow night,' she said. 'Jakob's going back to Stockholm in the late evening. If you want, I'll wait for you at the hotel.'

'But?' said Henrik. 'Is it really OK to . . . ?'

'Kelvin always sleeps like a log,' Kristina assured him. 'Yes, it really is OK. You needn't worry . . . and I'd very much like to teach you a bit about love before I'm done with you. About the very best bit.'

'God Almighty,' he repeated, staring at her. 'I can't take in . . .'

'Yes?'

'I can't take in the fact that you and I are sitting here like this, Kristina. What do you mean by the best bit?'

'The art of making it last,' she said. 'The sweet passion of deferred gratification. But we must go our separate ways now, I've a husband and kid to get home to.'

'Kristina, I . . .'

She put a finger to her lips and he stopped. She kissed him lightly on the palms of his hands and got to her feet. Swayed a little as the blood left her head, but recovered.

'No, don't come with me. See you tomorrow.'

The rain felt strange and dense, like a kind of soft, liquid moss, she thought, and it accompanied her for the whole dreary length of Järnvägsgatan. She was glad of it. Of its chill and persistence. Amongst the thousand thoughts and feelings tearing at her, there were two making their voices heard more loudly than all the rest.

We really are going to go the whole way tomorrow night.

It won't end well.

And as she crept along the corridor on the way to her first-floor room at Kymlinge Hotel – a third voice that was her own: *My nephew turns me on so much that I shall have to wake my husband and make love with him.*

It was twenty past two, but it didn't matter.

10

Karl-Erik Hermansson was woken at twenty to four by a distinct click inside his head.

That had never happened before. Neither thing. He didn't get clicks inside his skull, and he always slept like a log until quarter to seven. Be it a workday or a day of rest.

But, of course, now there weren't any more workdays. Only days of rest. That was a so-called indisputable fact. A condition of life one must learn to accept.

Never again to take his three-geared Crescent bicycle out of the garage and pedal the one thousand, one hundred and fifty metres to Kymlingevik School. Never again that single, elegant flourish as he fished his bunch of keys out of his jacket pocket, put the key in the lock and invited the sluggish horde to enter room 112. Never again to quote from memory Marcus Antonius's speech to the people on 15 March, 44 BC.

Nothing but days of rest. An eternity of mornings when he could stay in bed for as long as he chose and then devote his days to whatever took his fancy. His reward. The halcyon days after a whole life's moil and toil and new curricula. But why had he woken at twenty to four? Why had there been a click inside his head? There was also a faint background murmur he didn't think he recognized. Though that was probably just the radiator under the window on Rosemarie's side. She had probably turned it up on the sly, as usual.

But discounting that, something had still happened, it really felt that way, and there was a kind of anxiety hanging in his chest, something fluttering and slightly strained, wasn't there? He lay still and tried to focus on how he felt. And wasn't it . . . wasn't it at just this time – between three and four in the morning – that the majority of people died? The hour when life's candle was snuffed out while it was burning lowest. He was sure he had read that somewhere. Surely it couldn't be . . . ?

Karl-Erik Hermansson sat bolt upright in bed. His head swam for a few seconds before the blood was able to oxygenate his brain, but with that process complete, he was able to observe, thank goodness, that he felt as fit as a fiddle. Well, relatively fit, at any rate.

And it was only then, only then as he nimbly and vigorously swivelled his legs over the side of the bed and his feet found the fluffy softness of the bedside rug, that he remembered what day it was.

Their hundred-and-fifth birthday.

Sixty-five for him, forty for Ebba.

And that thought brought ten thousand other things whirling along in its slipstream. Estepona. Rosemarie. The cracking of his left heel. But to hell with all that, there were no cracked heels in Andalusia. *Muy bien*. Whisky. Whisky? Yes, that smoky show-off whisky Kristina's chap had brought along, he could still taste it on the roof of his mouth now. Lundgren at the bank, he popped up too, and that was all part of it. Part of the list of things he had to think about. The papers that had to be signed on Wednesday afternoon, tomorrow in fact, and the stuck-up family that was moving in here, he could swear neither the man nor the woman could name as many as three government ministers or two Swedish inventors of significance for industrial progress in the nineteenth and twentieth centuries. Cretins. It would be a relief to leave this history-less land. A real relief; though for the moment he couldn't remember the Stuck-Ups' real name. No matter, what else?

Robert.

Robert. No, begone.

Rosemarie, then. No comment. All right, back to the new crack that had opened up on his left foot, which would disappear as soon as he set it on the red earth of Spain . . . not the foot, that is, but the crack. Karl-Erik Hermansson had always been scrupulous about attributions, even in his thoughts . . . and then a jump back to Robert.

Gone. My thoughts have a different kind of structure at this hour of the day, Karl-Erik registered with slight surprise, and found himself unable to get beyond sitting there on the edge of the bed, looking at the painting of Örebro Castle that he had won in a crossword competition in 1977. Rosemarie hadn't wanted to hang it up, but once he had duly explained to her the important role the castle had played in Swedish history, she had naturally given way.

Robert again. Oh, very well. The prodigal son; he had decided to have the all-important conversation with him the previous evening – to get it over and done with – but it hadn't happened. Too many people and too many other factors, to put it simply. And whisky. Have to make sure he got round to it today, then. Preferably as early as possible. Before they sat down to the birthday dinner, at any event. There were some things that couldn't be sidestepped.

The conversation between the Father and the son. A large 'F' but a small 's', that was precisely how he saw it in front of him, clearly written in his head in block letters. Strange, but it certainly made the point. *Conversation* was the wrong word, however; a conversation was exactly what it would not be. To be precise, it was a matter of clarifying a position. The fact that – his thoughts skidded and idled for a few moments and then found purchase – that they had reached absolute zero.

Things could not be worse. That was exactly what he would say. *Absolute zero* was good. He hated the idea of even talking about the subject. The disgrace Robert had brought on the family was a life sentence . . . No, he didn't want to hear any apologies or explanations. What Robert had done was not open to any kind of relativization, and no again, we most certainly did *not* have any plans to leave the country, Mum and I, but the way things have turned out we have no other option. We see no alternative.

Shame, Robert, you've pushed us down into the swamp of shame, and we have to live with that, and now I don't want to say another word about the matter.

About this business? Should he say this business? No, *matter* was better. Business sounded too . . . well, he wasn't quite sure what.

He got up and went to the bathroom. Sat down on the toilet for a pee. For more than ten years now he had always taken his morning pee sitting down, he couldn't deny it. But only first thing in the morning. The dribble was even slower than usual today – maybe because of the unusual timing it hadn't had a chance to build up in its usual way – and he had time to go through his whole speech to Robert once more as he sat there.

He had had it in his head for over a month. The words, the formulations, the carefully weighed pauses. It was going to be a . . . a sort of pedagogical masterwork. The master reveals himself through his brevity. Robert would sit in silence. His father's words would bore into him, with implacable resolve. *Like ticks on a scabby hand*, he had read somewhere. Robert would understand what he had done. He would regret it bitterly, but that would not help. He would look at his father and he would realize that for something like this, one could not ask pardon. One could only wait for the mist of silence and amnesia to settle over what had been. Mist and balm. I only had one son, Robert, he would say – pause for effect – and I still only have one son. That is my lot. This hasn't been good for your mother, Robert, I've feared for her life, several times. No, *reason* was better. Feared for her reason. The shame should be yours and yours alone, Robert, but it also falls on your family. No, there's no need to say anything. Words are mere air after actions like these. I want you to know that our head, Mr Askbergson, actually wanted to relieve Mum and me of our duties for the rest of the term – out of consideration for us – but we stayed on. We kept a stiff upper lip as we went to work, we kept a stiff upper lip as we looked our colleagues in the eye. I want you to remember that, Robert. We shall be leaving this country in the spring, but we shall do it with heads held high. I want you to remember that.

He sat there chewing over his words, although the dribble had finished a good while before. Then he got to his feet, pulled up his pyjama trousers and flushed the toilet. He washed his hands and looked in the mirror. Something had happened to his right eye, hadn't it? He wasn't sure what, but it didn't look quite itself. The eyelid was drooping a millimetre lower than usual. Or was he just imagining it?

He splashed both eyes with cold water and checked again. It looked normal now.

There, see, just his imagination.

It was five to four. He returned to the bedroom and climbed back into bed beside his wife. The faint murmuring of the radiator was still audible. Örebro Castle hadn't moved.

Must try to get back to sleep, he thought. I've got a long day ahead of me.

First to arrive, at about nine, was a small deputation of relatives. It comprised Karl-Erik's two cousins from Gothenburg, one male and one female, with their respective other halves. They had just happened to be passing and had decided to look in for an hour on the big day.

They got through half a gateau and twelve cups of coffee. Neither Robert nor Leif nor the boys were up (or at any rate they had the presence of mind to stay upstairs); they all sat in the kitchen, the four passing travellers, the birthday boy and girl, Rosemarie and a boxer puppy named Silly who belonged to one of the cousins and left three puddles under the table.

The conversation went sluggishly and revolved mainly round another relative they had in common (Gunvald, 1947) who had emigrated to America, the current interest rate and all the lovely people you get to meet if you own a dog.

The TV programme *Prisoners of Koh Fuk* was accidentally mentioned *en passant*, but the subject was taken no further.

The family deputation, its mission accomplished, drove off in two almost identical little cars with metallic finishes, one white and one a silvery grey, at around quarter past ten. They left two presents behind them: one a largish framed work of art (100 x 70cm) comprising a seascape done in knotted wool, the other a smaller framed picture of a beach (70 x 40cm), also in knotted wool. The artist's name was Ingelund Sägebrandt, and Rosemarie was not sure if it was a man or a woman. In consultation with Ebba, they decided to store both pictures in the garage until further notice.

Once they had been duly stowed away, she went out and lifted the lid of the empty mailbox; it had started snowing and she could already feel the characteristic signs of incipient heartburn. This day is never going to end, she thought.

At eleven, eight colleagues from Kymlingevik School arrived. Leif had come down from upstairs, but not Robert or the boys. Nor was there any word from Kristina, Jakob and Kelvin; Rosemarie assumed they were treating themselves to a nice lie-in at the hotel, and on reflection she thought it was just as well.

Amongst the school colleagues was that hilarious joker Rigmor Petrén, who was the same age as Rosemarie and had undergone a double mastectomy, but was still going strong. Twenty-five years ago or thereabouts, she had taught Ebba mathematics (and one term of physics), and she had now composed a new and utterly hilarious song for Karl-Erik and his splendid daughter.

It had twenty-four verses and while it was being performed by eight voices, Rosemarie devoted her thoughts to two things. First, she imagined a marathon, run underwater and in the dark, and found it to be in some sense a new and interesting image of life; second, she wondered if there was something wrong with Karl-Erik's face. He didn't look quite the same as usual as he sat there very upright on a kitchen chair, smiling until his jaws went white with the strain.

Though perhaps that was simply the way to view everything, she thought. As a question of endurance. Rigmor Petrén was one of those teachers who always covered every single thing on the syllabus of every single course. Year after year. Even the cancer didn't dent her diligence. Her sense of humour turned everything in its path to ashes. Leif Grundt sneaked out to the toilet during verse seven and came back during verse nineteen.

When the song was over, they went into the living room and drank twenty-nine cups of coffee, polishing off the gateau the cousins had started on, plus two thirds of the next one. Co-op manager Grundt entertained them with an amusing comparative study of ham prices in the run-up to Christmas. Rosemarie's heartburn burst into full bloom.

Then assistant master Arne Barkman made an emotionally charged speech to Karl-Erik. About halfway through he was obliged to stop and blow his nose clear of the powerful feelings inevitably besetting him at such a moment. He and Karl-Erik had shared the same teachers' workroom for almost thirty years, and Arne was asking himself whether he would be able to return to his desk at Kymlingevik School in January at all. The vacuum left by Karl-Erik's departure could not be expressed in words, he claimed. So he did not intend to try. Thank you, Karl-Erik, that was all he wanted to say. Thank you for everything. Thank you, thank you, thank you.

'Thank *you*, Arne,' responded Karl-Erik right on cue, and gave his old comrade a thump on the back that brought the handkerchief out again.

Two bunches of flowers, a big one in shades of yellow and

another slightly smaller, redder-toned one, had been handed over on arrival, but now it was time for the presents. First a book by physician and comedian Rickard Fuchs for Ebba, who in her job must surely need a good laugh. Then seven gifts for Karl-Erik, the number symbolizing the muses or graces or virtues, or whatever set of seven one wanted to subscribe to, hah hah, and all with an unmistakable Iberian connection.

A bronze bull's head weighing a good kilo. A Rioja Gran Reserva 1972. A six-hundred-page picture book about the Alhambra. A tapas cookery book. A Spanish travelogue by Cees Nooteboom. A pair of hardwood castanets. A CD featuring guitarist José Muñoz Coca.

'I'm touched,' admitted Karl-Erik Hermansson.

'It's all too much,' said Rosemarie.

'Of course, they're a little bit for you as well, Rosemarie dear,' explained Ruth Immerström, social studies, RE and history. 'Yes, the two of you really will leave a gaping hole, just like Arne said.'

Their colleagues departed en masse, just before one o'clock. Rosemarie put all the presents on the oak sideboard, under the picture of the Battle of Gestilren (1210), and Ebba immediately went upstairs to get her two sons and brother moving.

'Robert isn't here,' she reported when she came down to the kitchen ten minutes later to help her mother with the washing up.

'Not here?' said Rosemarie. 'What do you mean, he's not here?'

'I mean he isn't here, of course,' said Ebba. 'He's made his bed, but he isn't up there. Or down here, either.'

'Who isn't here?' asked Kristina, choosing that moment to

arrive with her husband in his Armani suit and son in sailor
ditto.

'What a lovely dress you're wearing,' said Rosemarie. 'Red's
always suited you. Strange the way Ebba's so blue and you're
so red. One might almost think that—'

'Thank you, Mother dear,' said Kristina. 'Who isn't here?'

'Robert, of course,' said Ebba. 'But he's probably pushed
off for a walk and a smoke again. He's got a few things on his
mind. Did you all sleep well at the hotel?'

'Yes thanks, very well,' Jakob assured her, with Kelvin hanging in his arms like a rag doll. There's something seriously
wrong with that child, thought Rosemarie automatically.

'Actually, you look a bit tired Kristina,' she said, with the
same automatic response reflex. There was something about
her daughter's appearance that she could not but remark on.
'I thought you'd all had a decent lie-in.'

'I think I slept for too long,' said Kristina. 'Happy birthday,
Dad. Happy birthday, Ebba. What did you do with the presents, Jakob?'

'Damn and blast,' Jakob let slip. 'I left them in the car.'

'I'll get them later,' said Kristina. 'It's not time for them yet,
I don't suppose. Do you want to go and put Kelvin down for
a sleep upstairs?'

Jakob and Kelvin left the kitchen. Is she bossing him
around? thought Rosemarie. How come I didn't notice yesterday?

'Have you done something to your face, Dad,' asked Kristina. 'You don't look quite the same as usual.'

'It's his age,' put in Leif Grundt.

'Well, I don't really know,' said Karl-Erik, running his hands
down his cheeks. 'I woke up at half past three last night and

couldn't get back to sleep. Don't know why, but I do feel a bit tired, actually.'

'You need to trim your nose hair,' said Rosemarie.

'I think Dad should take a nap,' announced Ebba. 'There's been an awful lot going on at home this morning, for those of you who weren't here.'

It's not just that I can't locate my feelings for them, thought Rosemarie. They don't like each other, either. If I don't get a glass of Samarin for this heartburn soon, I shall self-combust.

The brothers Grundt appeared in the doorway, their hair tidy, and wearing collars and ties.

'Good morning, you two shirkers,' their father greeted them jovially. 'Hey, just a minute, what are those tinker's rags round your necks?'

'Why don't we have some coffee and a sandwich while we're all here?' said Rosemarie Wunderlich Hermansson.

11

In the course of the morning, the temperature fell by five degrees and the snow started coming down more heavily. Moreover, the south-westerly wind turned round to the north-west, and its speed increased from three to eight metres a second, but none of this did anything to prevent the next planned activity for the day: the walk round town.

For at least the past twenty-five years, Karl-Erik Hermansson had been doing this walk, which lasted a bare two hours, with the Year 8 pupils to whom he taught some of the more socially orientating subjects – to give the new generation at least some rudimentary knowledge of their own town and its sights – and there wasn't really that much difference between May and December.

The town hall. The cobblers' museum. The old water tower. The historical Hemmelberg House. Gahn Park and the well-preserved Rademacher Forge by the falls on the river Kymlinge. To name but a few of the sights.

Some of that day's participants had heard most of it before, but the new library had been formally opened just eight months earlier, and none of them had yet had a chance to see the newly restored painting above the altar in the church.

And anyway, it was nice to get out. They were all going, except for Rosemarie, who, in consultation with her friend and assistant cook Ester Brälldin, would stay at home to organize the approaching dinner, and Robert, who had still not been seen.

'It's just typical that he can't make an effort even today,' Ebba said to her sister, once their father had finished his historical account and numerous rounds of the cobblers' museum, and indicated to his troop that they could move on through the whirling snow up to Linnégatan.

'What do you mean, typical?' asked Kristina. 'He has the freedom to do what he wants, surely, just like everyone else?'

'Freedom?' said Ebba, throwing up her hands as if she couldn't really remember what this strange concept entailed. 'What on earth are you taking about?'

'I just mean we ought not to condemn him until we know his reasons,' said Kristina.

'I'd never dream of condemning anybody,' said Ebba. 'That's offensive to me, Kristina.'

'OK, I apologize,' said Kristina, wiping her son's snotty nose with a tissue. 'It's so easy to criticize Robert, that's all.'

'Hmph,' said Ebba, tucking her arm under her husband's.

'Right then, boys,' said Karl-Erik the Pedagogical Pine Tree to the brothers Grundt, 'can either of you tell me why this year is engraved above this gateway?'

'Eighteen forty-eight?' said Henrik thoughtfully, coming to a stop. 'The Communist Manifesto. Though I didn't know it was here in Kymlinge they wrote it.'

'Ho ho,' chuckled Karl-Erik, who had been able to snatch a fifteen-minute nap despite his busy schedule, and seemed to be back on slightly better form. 'Very good, lad. No, as far as I know, Marx and Engels never set foot in Kymlinge. But perhaps your mother can enlighten us?'

'The fire,' Ebba replied instantly. 'The whole of Kymlinge burnt down that year. Virtually all the buildings were wooden in those days, and this was the only one that survived. The story goes that there was a maidservant here on her own that night, and it was her piety and prayers that saved her and the house.'

'Precisely,' said Karl-Erik. 'And from 1850 onwards, the new town started being built. The Kymlinge we know. The new grid layout of the streets rather than the old medieval one. Two new squares, south and north. The town hall, as I told you . . . the covered market and—'

'Fair old snowstorm, this,' said Leif Grundt. 'Good job I fitted my winter soles. Did that whisky really run out yesterday?'

'Leif, please,' said Ebba, letting go of his arm.

'It somehow got polished off, yes,' observed Karl-Erik with a slightly worried expression. 'One really wonders where Robert can have got to.'

As if it had suddenly struck him that the two factors could be linked in some way, thought Kristina, and for the first time she felt a stab of anxiety on her brother's account. It was after four thirty and he hadn't been seen all day, which was surely a bit odd? Even for Robert.

Though he could be at home in the warm kitchen in Allvädersgatan, having a tipple with his mother and Ester Brälldin.

'Right, we'll take a brisk walk to the church and then I think it might be time to go home and start on all that lovely food,' continued Karl-Erik. He let down the ear flaps of the fur hat he had owned since the early sixties before he took command of his shivering troop.

*

'Ugh, what weather,' exclaimed Rosemarie Wunderlich Hermansson three quarters of an hour later, as everyone stamped their feet in the hall. 'Are you all back in one piece? No, where are . . . ?'

'Kristina and Henrik had to pop into the supermarket for something,' explained Ebba. 'Has Robert turned up?'

'No,' said Rosemarie, helping a comatose Kelvin out of the baby sling on his father's stomach. 'I can't understand where he's got to. But you must all be frozen through. Was it really necessary to drag them all out in this blizzard, Karl-Erik?'

'What drivel,' said Karl-Erik. 'I happen to be the oldest member of this gathering. If I haven't suffered any ill effects, I don't see why anyone else should have done. Now let's have some glögg in front of the living-room fire.'

'Of course we will,' his wife agreed. 'That will fit nicely, because we can take our seats at the table in about an hour. Els-Marie rang to wish you a happy birthday, by the way. Both of you, that is.'

'Thank you,' said Ebba.

'Thanks,' said Karl-Erik.

As it was not considered appropriate for young Kristoffer to drink glögg, it was not considered appropriate for Henrik either. Sibling solidarity was invoked. The brothers made the most of this and withdrew to their green-striped room for half an hour.

'Before I forget, can I ask you something?' said Henrik, once he had composed and sent a new text message.

'Mhm?' said Kristoffer with indifference from his bed.

'I – I need your help.'

What? thought Kristoffer. My help? Christ, the world must be coming to an end. Armageddon, or whatever it was called.

'Er . . . sure,' he said.

'Well not so much your help,' said Henrik, 'as your silence.'

'Oh yes?'

He noted that his heart was suddenly galloping in his chest, and hoped to God his brother wouldn't notice.

'Just your agreement to keep quiet, that is.'

'What about?' said Kristoffer, pretending to yawn.

Henrik just lay there for a few seconds, saying nothing, and seemed to be weighing something up in his mind. Kristoffer started to whistle lazily.

'I'm thinking of going out for a couple of hours tonight.'

'What?'

'I said I'm thinking of going out for a couple of hours tonight.'

'What for?'

'And I want you to keep quiet about it.'

'Got it . . . but why are you going out?'

Henrik hesitated again.

'I don't think you need to know. I just don't want you to let on to Mum . . . or anyone else.'

Kristoffer whistled a few more notes. 'Stairway to Heaven', it sounded like. 'If I'm going to keep quiet, I think I've got the right to know what you'll be doing.'

'Well, I don't.'

Kristoffer thought about this.

'Maybe, but in that case, well . . .'

Henrik sat up on the edge of the bed.

'All right then,' he said. 'I'm going to meet an old friend.'

'A friend? Here in Kymlinge?'

'Yes. What's so strange about that? They moved here a few years ago.'

You're bloody well lying, brother, thought Kristoffer. And you're doing it badly. But what the heck shall I say?

'Is it a girl?' he asked. It came almost automatically, without him thinking it first, but the moment the words were out of his mouth he realized it was exactly the right question to ask. In the circumstances. *All* the circumstances. Three seconds went by.

'Yes,' said Henrik. 'It's a girl.'

Kristoffer could feel the excitement ticking inside him, and had to simulate another yawn to camouflage it. Oh boy, he thought, you're as bad at lying as a trotting horse is at shitting. Might that girl happen to be called Jens?

But how on earth could Jens be in Kymlinge? Didn't Jens live in . . . ?

No, of course, yes, thought Kristoffer. It was Jenny who lived in Karlskoga, and the thing about Jenny was that she apparently didn't exist.

'Well?' said Henrik.

'Er . . . fine,' said Kristoffer. 'I'll keep quiet. Not a word shall pass my lips.'

'Good,' said Henrik. 'Well, I'm not entirely sure I'll be going, but if.'

'But if,' repeated Kristoffer. 'I get it.'

Or not, he added in his head. Not really.

Although, thinking about it, there was no reason why Jens's parents' house shouldn't be somewhere near Kymlinge. Or even in the town itself. No reason at all, even though it did seem a bit unlikely.

Oh well, thought Kristoffer, this has undeniably turned out to be an interesting trip. Better than expected, I have to admit.

'I don't understand what you mean,' said Karl-Erik in irritation. 'What are you driving at?'

'It can't be that hard to understand,' said Rosemarie. They were out in the laundry room, into which Rosemarie had unceremoniously bundled her husband. 'Robert hasn't come back.'

'I had noted that,' said Karl-Erik. 'But the fact is, the table's laid, the first course is ready, Ester says, and everybody's sitting there waiting. Are you saying we should let that damned rascal ruin the entire—'

'He's your son,' Rosemarie interrupted. 'Consider what you're saying.'

'Bah,' said Karl-Erik. 'I've considered every word I've uttered for the past fifty years. I've had enough now. Can't you get that into your skull?'

Good heavens, whatever is up with him? Rosemarie had time to think before the Robert cloud descended again and cast its darkness over her mind.

'Calm down,' she said. 'Actually, I've discovered something.'

'Well, well. And what is it you've discovered? It's almost half past six, we really can't wait any longer. It isn't only me who's losing patience.'

'What I've discovered,' said Rosemarie, forcing herself to speak slowly, 'is that he didn't sleep in his bed at all last night.'

'Rubbish. Of course he did. Where else would he have slept? And his car's parked outside.'

'I know his car's still outside,' said Rosemarie, taking a step closer to her husband, so she was speaking very close to his face. It didn't feel normal, but there was no better way of finding out how many glöggs he'd consumed. 'Now you listen to me, Karl-Erik,' she said. 'Robert didn't sleep in his bed. I put one of his old pairs of pyjamas and a towel under his pillow, and they're folded up there just where I put them. Robert must have gone off during the night. He never went to bed.'

A nervous look flashed into Karl-Erik's eyes, but she could only detect a reasonable concentration of glögg fumes on his breath. 'Did you say anything to – to Kristina and the others?' he asked. 'I think he sat up with the others – whichever of them it was – who stayed up after you and I went to bed.'

'I haven't told anybody,' said Rosemarie, stepping away again. 'I only discovered this five minutes ago.'

Karl-Erik thrust out his chest and looked grim.

'We'll have to ask them, of course. Perhaps he said something . . . You think it looks as though he went out late last night, then?'

'What do *you* think?' responded Rosemarie. 'It doesn't feel very nice to sit down to dinner, anyway.'

'His mobile!' said Karl-Erik, seizing on the idea. 'We can ring his mobile, of course.'

'I've already tried,' said Rosemarie. 'Six or seven times this afternoon. It seems to be switched off, it goes straight to voicemail.'

Karl-Erik gave a sigh. 'His bag? Presumably he had a bag with him yesterday?'

'Still in his room,' said Rosemarie. 'Karl-Erik?'

'Yes?'

'You don't suppose anything could have happened to him, do you?'

Karl-Erik cleared his throat at exaggerated volume while attempting to laugh and shake his head at the same time. It made him look and sound like a sick dog. 'Don't talk nonsense. What could happen to Robert here in Kymlinge? Let's have dinner. He'll probably turn up, and if he doesn't, we'll ask the others after the meal. There are more important things to consider at the moment, don't you agree, Rosemarie dear?'

'All right,' said Rosemarie with a gloomy nod. 'I suppose we'll have to, then.'

In the doorway en route to the waiting dining table, Karl-Erik checked himself for a moment, as if suddenly remembering the lie of the land and wanting to underline the fact. 'Let me tell you one thing, Rosemarie,' he said. 'Just at the moment, I'm pretty damn tired of Robert. If it turned out he'd run away to Australia again, nobody would be more grateful than I.'

'I realize that, Karl-Erik,' replied Rosemarie, and went off to the kitchen to tell Ester Brälldin she could serve the blinis with red onion, steamed asparagus and two kinds of lumpfish caviar.

There were speeches.

With the blinis and Riesling, the senior guest of honour welcomed the whole football team (evidently including himself, the absent Robert, and Ester Brälldin out in the kitchen, or they would scarcely have made it to eleven). This was a big day, he announced. For him and for Ebba. Turning forty meant you were still in mid-leap, and had ten years to go until you reached the midday high point of fifty. Turning sixty-five meant that you had not only landed, but also reached the goal. Figuratively, that was, and if you chose to continue along the route of sporting metaphor.

The last sentence was a bit tricky and Karl-Erik stumbled slightly over the words, causing his wife to wonder again how he really was. He wasn't entirely himself, was he, the assiduous pedagogical pine tree?

At any event, he then launched himself into a twenty-minute survey of compulsory education in Sweden since the start of the current system in 1968, then proposed a proper herring for (that should surely have been 'hearing', thought Rosemarie), and a toast to, 'good old Knowledge with a capital K, which is an end in itself and ought not to sell out to avaricious market sybarites and passing fads,' and ended by bidding them all very welcome once more.

After that came saddle of venison with early season vegetables, glazed onions, blackcurrant jelly and pommes duchesse, and before the plates were cleared it was Leif Grundt's turn. His contribution fell into three parts. First, he told an obscure story about a big-busted deli counter assistant at a Co-op store in Gällivare, then he praised his wife's virtues for twenty seconds, and finally he said that, personally, he'd never have guessed his father-in-law was a day over sixty-four and a half.

During the cheese course, Rosemarie suddenly burst into tears. She was obliged to leave the table, explaining on her return that this outburst of emotion was the result of feeling so moved. What with (nearly) everybody gathered together and everything.

At that moment, to everyone's surprise (except possibly Ebba's), Henrik got to his feet and sang a cappella – some sort of Italian serenade, it seemed to be – a bravura performance that was met with rousing applause and considerably heightened the mood.

Then it was pears topped with caramelized almonds and

served with brandy cream, and Jakob made a sophisticated but slightly impersonal speech (which might be because he had delivered it about twenty times before in assorted contexts, noted his wife), thanking the hosts for the meal. At this point, even Ester Brälldin was dragged out of the kitchen and plied with a glass of the popular Málaga dessert wine.

Finally, it was time for coffee, cake and presents. The main event for Ebba was a new set of everyday china of a well-known English make: plates, dishes, saucers, coffee and tea cups, serving plates, bowls and a soup tureen – but she also received a couple of so-called 'experience gifts'. A Japanese hot-stone massage and dining package at Yasuragi in Hasse-ludden, and a day – including body splash – at the Selma Lagerlöf Spa in Sunne (where she had already been twice, but who could keep track of such things?).

For Karl-Erik, the haul was rather more mixed: books of various kinds, a dressing gown, a walking stick with a silver handle, five silk ties (most likely purchased by Robert at Bang-kok airport), a digital camera and an old lithograph of the autumn battle at Baldkirchenerheim in 1622.

It was only after they had ticked this item off the day's agenda that the question of Robert's whereabouts came up for discussion. It was now almost eleven, and the 105th birth-day celebrations had, one might say, reached their formal end. It was time to air the skeletons in the closet, as Leif Grundt rather clumsily put it, earning a mild rebuke from his exactly forty-year-old wife.

'He went out for a walk and a cigarette,' said Kristina. 'I didn't check the time, but it must have been about half past twelve.'

'How did he seem?' asked Rosemarie.

'I don't know,' said Kristina. 'Much the same as usual, I suppose.'

'Why are you asking how he seemed, Mum?' asked Ebba.

'It's a natural question in the circumstances, surely?' Rosemarie said.

'Sure,' said Leif Grundt. 'I daresay he's found a woman, that's all. It seems to be what he needs.'

'Leif,' said Ebba sharply. 'That's quite enough.'

'Yeah, yeah,' said Leif. 'It's just a theory. Have any of you got one of your own?'

'I think it was a bit later than half past twelve,' Kristoffer put in tentatively. 'I went to bed at twenty to one and he was still here. I said goodnight to him.'

'All right,' said Karl-Erik. 'Ten minutes either way makes very little difference. Have we really nothing else to talk about?'

'I'm sure we have, Karl-Erik,' said his wife. 'But quite a few of us are a bit worried about Robert. Even if you don't seem to be.'

Karl-Erik drained his coffee cup and stood up.

'I've got to go to the toilet,' he said.

'Shit happens,' said Leif Grundt.

'But seriously Kristina, how did he seem to you? The two of you had that private chat outside, after all. Was he drunk when he left?'

Kristina regarded her mother's anxious face and tried to weigh her words. What should she say? Had Robert behaved strangely in any way? Drunk? Well he clearly hadn't been sober.

Nor had she. Most assuredly not. But truth to tell, her attention had been focused elsewhere. Good God, you could say that again, especially *after* Robert left.

And today Henrik had told her he definitely intended to meet her at the hotel. If she had imagined that, on reflection, the idea of him would grow sickly and pale, she could not have been more mistaken.

'I'll come to you tonight, Kristina,' he had declared when, as if by prior agreement, they both slipped into the little supermarket after the town walk. 'You haven't changed your mind, have you?'

She had shaken her head. No, she hadn't changed her mind. Not unless he had.

After that they had hardly exchanged a word all evening. Avoided looking at each other, and maybe it was only to be expected. And all through the long banquet she had felt a strange arousal, reminiscent of . . . well, of when she was fourteen or fifteen, full of raging hormones and fixated on one pimply teenage boy after another. As Henrik was singing his song, her heart had pounded dangerously.

But at the same time: if Ebba had had any suspicion of what was going on between her son and her sister, she wouldn't have hesitated for an instant to kill her. Kristina knew this with a conviction as powerful as – as the one felt by a small animal when it suddenly comes eye to eye with a lioness determined to protect her offspring. Yes, that wasn't a bad image for the whole scenario.

But Robert? No, she really had no idea what Robert might be up to.

'Say something, Kristina,' urged her mother. 'Don't just stand there thinking.' They were out in the study, each with a small glass of Baileys. Rosemarie had manoeuvred them in there and Kristina realized her mother imagined her to possess some kind of secret information on the subject.

'I'm sorry, Mum,' she said, 'but I honestly don't know. Obviously, Robert hasn't been feeling great, but if you think he went out and killed himself, I'm pretty sure you're wrong.'

'But I never said—' began Rosemarie, but then interrupted herself by stamping on the floor. Then she stared at her foot in surprise and seemed close to tears again.

Kristina stood there mutely for a few moments, watching her mother. She suddenly felt infinitely sorry for her and was seized by an unexpected urge to give her a hug. But before she could so much as put a hand on her mother's arm, Jakob appeared in the doorway.

'Kristina?'

'Yes?'

There was no need for him to say more. She knew. He had been drinking mineral water all evening and was near to breaking point. It was unmistakable to someone who knew how to interpret the signs. He couldn't wait to get away from there. Couldn't wait to dump his wife and son at the hotel and get into the car in solitary majesty. To drive home to Stockholm on the empty night-time roads, listening to a Dexter Gordon CD. This was a different sort of situation, and she felt she understood him to a degree.

And that sudden flaring of tenderness for her mother faded and died.

'All right, Jakob,' she said. 'Yes, maybe it's time now.'

'You're not going already?' Rosemarie exclaimed. 'I mean, we haven't even . . .'

But she couldn't find any words for the fictional obligations remaining to be fulfilled. 'I'm so worried about Robert, that's all,' she said instead.

'I'm sure there's a perfectly natural explanation,' said Jakob. 'He's bound to turn up any minute.'

'Do you really think so?' said Rosemarie, gazing artlessly at her son-in-law. As if Jakob Willnius, by dint of being cosmopolitan and employed in a top position in Swedish television, also possessed the clairvoyant ability to give his opinion on prodigal sons who had wandered off into the winter night out in the sticks and lost their way.

'I'm sure,' he repeated. 'Perhaps he just felt all the pressure was getting too much for him. Of course, it would be entirely understandable if that were the case. Don't you agree?'

'May – maybe so,' stammered Rosemarie Wunderlich Hermansson. 'Well, I hope that you're right. And that nothing's happened to him. It's just so . . .' Her gaze flickered between her daughter and the daughter's gently smiling husband a few times, but she could find nothing else to say.

For one second, she thought, for one second I got the idea Kristina was going to hug me. But I expect I just imagined it.

'I'll go up and get Kelvin ready, shall I?' said Jakob.

'Yes of course,' Kristina nodded. 'You do that. Thanks, Mum, it was a very nice party.'

'But so soon, are you really . . . ?' Rosemarie ventured, but even to her own ears it sounded so jarring that for the third or fourth time in swift succession she cut herself short and lapsed into silence.

What's the matter with me? she thought. I can't even talk normally any more.

12

Altogether, there were eighteen pictures of the house in Spain, and once Kristina, Jakob and Kelvin had gone off to the hotel in their Mercedes, these were brought out.

'Who took them?' asked Ebba.

'I did, of course,' said Karl-Erik.

'So you two have been there?'

'Only me,' Karl-Erik explained. 'I went down one weekend. The first weekend in Advent, in fact. It was twenty-three in the shade, though there was hardly any shade, hah hah. Sky as blue as a real Swedish summer's day.'

The photographs were passed round. Eighteen slightly out-of-focus pictures of a flat-roofed, whitewashed house in a large cluster of other flat-roofed, whitewashed houses. Bare mountains in the background. A bougainvillea or two. The odd cypress. A small swimming pool with white plastic chairs and light blue water.

In a couple of the shots you could see the sea in the distance. It appeared to be a number of kilometres away, with a network of modern roads leading down to it.

'No pictures of the inside?' asked Leif Grundt.

'The present incumbents were at home,' explained Karl-Erik. 'They move out in February. I naturally didn't want to intrude.'

'I see,' said Ebba.

'I only had my old system camera,' he added apologetically. 'It isn't working properly, the light meter's unreliable. That was why I asked for this digital one. We'll be able to send you pictures every week. Via the internet.'

'We'll look forward to that,' said Leif Grundt.

'How many pixels?' asked Kristoffer.

'Lots,' said Karl-Erik.

It all went quiet for a moment and the wall clock took the opportunity of striking twelve.

'I really hope you're both agreed on this and you know what you're letting yourselves in for,' said Ebba.

'Have you ever been to Granada, Ebba, my dear girl?' asked Karl-Erik, his voice taking on a mildly reproving tone. 'Have you ever stood on the Puente Nuevo bridge in Ronda and looked down into the ravine? Have you ever—'

'Dad, I'm not saying it's wrong to move there, I just hope you haven't rushed into the decision.'

Karl-Erik gathered up the photographs and put them back in the envelope where he kept them. 'Ebba, let's not discuss this now,' he said doggedly. 'I don't have to remind you what happened this autumn. There are situations in life that call for decisive action.'

'But you don't mind me asking?' said Ebba.

'Would anyone like a sandwich before bed?' asked Rose-marie, coming in from the kitchen. 'Or some fruit?'

'Are you mad, Mum?' said Ebba. 'We've been eating for five hours solid.'

'I . . .'

But her voice cracked, so she took a deep breath and tried again.

'I wonder whether we . . . whether we ought to ring the police.'

'Out of the question,' declared Karl-Erik to his wife once they were alone in the bedroom, fifteen minutes later. 'Whatever you do, you're not to contact the police. I forbid it.'

'Forbid?'

'Yes, forbid.'

His face was a colour Rosemarie could not remember seeing before. Well, on plums and other over-ripe fruit perhaps, but never on her husband.

'But Karl-Erik dear,' she said tentatively. 'I was only thinking that—'

'You weren't thinking at all,' he broke in angrily. 'Don't you see what havoc you would cause? As if what's already happened isn't enough! How can he have the gall to come here and disappear on top of everything else, damn him, I can't bear to think about it . . . Wanker Rob vanishes into thin air in Kymlinge! Can you see the news-stands, Rosemarie? This is your son we're talking about.'

Rosemarie swallowed and sank down onto the edge of the bed. She had never seen him so incensed before. Not in forty-five years. If I contradict him now, thrombosis will do for him, she thought.

'Don't say that word, please,' she said meekly, and he went off to the bathroom muttering and cursing under his breath.

In a way he was right of course, she could see that. She dared not think what the papers would write and what people would say, if it came out that Robert really had disappeared. Here in Kymlinge. On the occasion of a birthday party at his parents' house!

And if she rang the police, you could be sure it would come

out. Half of what you read in the papers and half of all radio and TV coverage was to do with the police. One way or another.

O Lord, what shall I do? thought Rosemarie Wunderlich Hermansson, putting her hands together in her lap – but the only answer that came was an image projected onto her mind's eye: it showed Robert, forsaken and frozen to death in a snowdrift. O Lord, help me, she tried again, I can't go on much longer.

And she remembered that dream she'd had. About the birds with the strange speech bubbles in their beaks. Saying it was her life or Karl-Erik's. Let him live, she thought. Take me away instead. If I don't have to wake up tomorrow morning, I'll feel nothing but enormous gratitude.

'Sure you don't want to come?' asked Jakob Willnius, as he pulled up in front of the faint red shimmer of the entrance to Kymlinge Hotel.

'I don't think so,' said Kristina.

'It'd only take quarter of an hour to run up and pack your things, you know,' he said.

Kristina gave a vague nod. His own suitcase was already in the boot, a detail he had taken care of when they left the hotel that morning. With typical Jakob Willnius efficiency. He always thought of everything; tiny details that might lie hours – or days – in the future, but that could usefully be dealt with in advance.

Does he really want me to come with him? she wondered. Or is he just pretending? To be polite. Domestic political correctness?

'Is it this Robert thing that's stopping you?'

'Amongst others. It would feel a bit rotten just pushing off. And if he doesn't turn up, Mum's certainly going to need . . . well, someone to talk to apart from Ebba.'

What an incredibly convenient excuse, she thought. Talk about ennobling your base motives. But he bought it, of course.

'OK,' he said. 'I can see that. But how will you two get back, if good old Robert doesn't show up?'

'There are trains,' said Kristina. 'But actually, I won't feel I can simply leave if it turns out he genuinely has gone missing. I mean, in that case something must have happened to him. He can't have *planned* this.'

She unfastened Kelvin from his child seat. Jakob got out of the car and went round to the passenger side. 'No need for you to come up,' said Kristina. 'I'll carry Kelvin on one side and my bag on the other. I'll be fine.'

'The child seat?' said Jakob. 'If you get a lift from Robert you might need . . . ?'

'Oh, we can sit in the back, if so. I really don't fancy lugging it on the train with me.'

She stood up and heaved Kelvin onto her arm. The boy woke up and looked at his parents with his usual melancholy air. Then he rested his head on Kristina's shoulder and went back to sleep. Jakob stroked the back of his hand gently down the boy's cheek, looking at his son and then at his wife.

'Kristina,' he said, 'I love you. Don't forget that. I thought it was so nice when you got back yesterday.'

She gave him a quick, guilty smile. 'So did I. And I love you too, Jakob. I'm sorry if I don't show it enough.'

She stood on tiptoe and kissed him. 'Right then, off you go.

We'll ring you tomorrow. Good luck with your American, but first, drive carefully.'

'I promise,' said Jakob Willnius, brushing her cheek in the same way as he had his son's. 'Lucky it's stopped snowing, I'm sure they'll have cleared most of it.'

Then he got into the car and drove away.

When she got up to her room, it was twenty past twelve. She settled Kelvin in the extra bed in the alcove without disturbing him, got undressed and went for a shower.

What am I doing, she asked herself. What's driving me to this? Shouldn't – shouldn't Jakob's love be enough? But now I'm washing away his last touch and preparing myself for someone else.

It's shameful, there's no other word for it.

Such thoughts were justified, of course, but she also knew that however much she reproached herself, whatever blame she threw in her own direction, it would all just be part of a rhetorical game.

It's at moments like this, when people have choices like this, that they ruin their lives, she reflected.

And the strange thing is that it's so profoundly human.

But it was still – at one level – about helping Henrik find his sexuality. That was what had set all this in motion. At any rate, that was what she wanted to persuade herself, and if – *if* it all ended well, because it actually might, it really *ought* to – then perhaps they, he and she, nephew and aunt, might laugh at it all one day in the future and think back on it as a good memory. A delicious secret that they shared and could keep hidden in their hearts for the rest of their lives. To take out for inspection at brief and carefully chosen moments.

I must have read that in three novels and five magazines this past year, she thought, stepping out of the shower and starting to dry herself with the hotel's bright-red bath towel.

Then she looked at her naked body in the mirror in the same neutral, mildly accepting way she had done in her own bathroom in Old Enskede the other evening.

She tried to imagine what it would feel like to have nineteen-year-old Henrik pressing his lanky body against her. Pushing his way into her.

In an hour's time, perhaps. An hour and a half?

She took her mobile and slipped between the pleasantly cool hotel sheets, naked. They had not been changed since yesterday, she noted. She and Jakob had made violent, almost brutal love in this very bed, on this very bed linen, less than twenty-four hours ago. And now . . .

Her fingers played over the device's tiny keys, but something held her back. Voices called out inside for her to change her mind. She decided to leave it ten minutes and consider; to try simulating at least some sort of reflection.

Two things surfaced from the jumble of conflicting feelings. The first was that image of Ebba as a lioness defending her young to the last breath. With the blood trickling between her teeth.

The other was something else, something she could say with certainty that she had not thought about for quite some years. It was something Jakob's daughter Liza had said, that time she rang from London.

That Jakob could be violent. *He isn't as sophisticated and cool-as-a-cucumber as you think, just so you know and don't get caught out.*

Jakob, violent? She hadn't believed it then, and there had never been the slightest indication since. Besides, the twins despised both Jakob and herself, they'd made no secret of that. They wouldn't be above sowing a few false fears.

So why had it come to mind now?

The lioness and the violent cucumber?

Kristina gave a laugh. She had no intention of leaving herself vulnerable to either. But the laugh caught in her throat and died. She weighed her mobile in her hand. They hadn't made an arrangement, but she had his mobile number. Perhaps he was waiting for the go-ahead.

I daren't, she thought suddenly.

But her fingers on the tiny keys seemed to be controlling things. Once she had brought up the number, five little keystrokes were all it would take.

Come.

And then *Send. Yes* or *No*?

She deleted it. Let it be up to him.

13

Kristoffer Grundt had hardly spared a thought for Linda Granberg all day, but when he looked down at his cock as he took a pee before he went to bed in the WUR (World's Ugliest Room, as the brothers had decided to call it), he found that he was.

He wondered how that fitted together. The fact that he happened to think of Linda as he stood there with his cock in his hand.

But rather than trekking any further along this Freudian track (oh yes, Kristoffer Grundt knew what sort of character Sigmund Freud was, even at fourteen), he stashed away Little Willy (as his mother had always called his magnificent organ when he was younger) in his underpants and thought what a wimp he was. A nerd, a fool, a clown with an inflated opinion of himself, you name it. Linda Granberg would never encounter Little Willy and it was just as well, really. She'd probably laugh herself to death.

But when he was in bed, five minutes later, there she was in his head again, and it was only then it struck him that she must have replied in some way to the cheeky text he'd sent yesterday.

He wished he knew how she'd done it. He also wished he hadn't just said she should turn up to Birger's burger stall, but had the sense to ask her to get in touch with him somehow. But how? Again, *how*?

Maybe he could send her another text? Ask straight out if he could borrow Henrik's mobile; their relative positions had shifted a bit since yesterday, after all. Maybe Henrik would say yes? Even if he didn't yet realize the full extent of their new positions.

He sighed. It was bloody annoying that he'd lost his mobile. Living without a phone in this day and age was like being a dinosaur in the Stone Age, thought Kristoffer Grundt. Doomed to extinction.

On the other hand, he wasn't entirely sure he wanted to know. What if Linda was pissed off with him and wanted him to go to hell? In that case, he'd rather wait a couple of days to find out about it.

And on further consideration, it seemed stupid to put pressure on Henrik. Stupid to be cocky and hint you were holding an undreamt-of trump card. There was bound to be a better time to make use of it later on. If Linda happened to answer a follow-up text, say, he would really need his brother's mobile. And that was asking a lot. It was half past twelve; if she got a text from him now, she might not answer until the morning. And even if the answer arrived during the night, he could hardly expect Henrik to leave his phone behind when he was off to meet Jens.

Jens? Presumably it *was* him?

Who else could it be? Kristoffer surreptitiously watched his brother, who was just coming into the WUR, and wondered if he was hiding anything else. Perhaps it really was just an old friend he was meeting, after all, and he'd said it was a girl to wind him up? It wasn't impossible.

I couldn't care less, Kristoffer decided. And I couldn't care less about his phone, either.

But he regretted that he hadn't asked to borrow it earlier in the day. Or somebody else's. His mum and dad had both left theirs at home; Leif because he hated mobile phones (even if he accepted that he had to have one for work), Ebba because she wanted to escape the ten calls a day from colleagues in urgent need of advice before they went into the operating theatre.

Because it would have been great to lie here and imagine Linda missing him, thought Kristoffer. Really great.

Henrik got into bed in a T-shirt, keeping his pants and socks on.

'So, when are you off?' Kristoffer asked him.

'Don't worry about that,' said Henrik. 'The main thing is for you to keep quiet. And who knows, I might not even be going.'

'How will you find out whether you're going?'

'Kristoffer, please. Go to sleep and think about something else. If I do go, it won't be for half an hour or more.'

Kristoffer switched off his lamp and thought for a while.

'OK bro,' he said. 'Have a good time, anyway. You can rely on me.'

'Thanks, I'll remember that,' said Henrik, and switched off his light, too.

It felt good, thought Kristoffer. Henrik thanking him. That rarely happened – and to be honest, it was because he rarely had cause to. Now, I must stay awake without him realizing and check whether he goes or not, thought Kristoffer, turning over the ridiculously large and hard pillow.

But when Henrik Grundt tiptoed carefully out of the

room, twenty minutes later, Kristoffer was already asleep, dreaming he was out for a tandem ride with Linda Granberg. She was in front, with him behind; her naked bum wobbled and danced before his eyes and it was wonderful to be alive.

'There's something up with Henrik,' said Ebba. 'I can sense it.'

'Henrik?' mumbled Leif from his cramped half of the bed. 'Don't you mean Kristoffer?'

'No,' said Ebba. 'When I say Henrik, I mean Henrik.'

'Correct,' said Leif. 'So what do you think it is, then?'

'I don't know. But something isn't right. He's not himself. I wonder whether something happened in Uppsala that he's not telling us about. Haven't you noticed . . . well, that something's going on?'

'No,' said Leif truthfully. 'It's passed me by, I'm afraid. But I did notice that Robert's fallen off his perch.'

This was met with silence, and Leif briefly wondered whether it was worth putting a hand on her hip. He didn't think so. She was almost entirely sober, and irritated to boot. As for him, he was a bit drunk and a bit tired.

And they'd already made love once this December.

'Shall we put the light on,' he asked, without knowing why he was making the suggestion. To shed some light on Henrik, perhaps? Or on Robert, or on everything?

'Why would we want to put the light on? It's almost one o'clock.'

'I know,' said Leif Grundt. 'I take back the suggestion. So where do you think Robert's got to, then?'

It was a few seconds before Ebba replied.

'I think you were right there,' she said.

'Eh?' said Leif in genuine surprise. 'You've lost me now.'

'A woman,' sighed Ebba. 'You had a theory that he'd met a woman. I agree with you, it seems pretty likely. I'm sure he's got some old flame in this town, too.'

'Hmm,' said Leif Grundt, placing his right hand cautiously on her hip.

But it proved just as futile as he had predicted.

Two correct theories in one day then, he thought happily, and gave a little titter in the darkness.

'What are you laughing at?' demanded Ebba. 'If there's anything to laugh about in all these problems, I'd love you to share it with me.'

'A problem shared is a problem halved,' said Leif and turned his back on her. 'No, it was nothing, just a tickle in my nose. Let's sleep on it.'

I'm married to an idiot, thought Ebba Hermansson Grundt. But I chose him myself.

Or did I?

The roads proved not to be as easily passable as Jakob Willnius had expected, and it took him over an hour to do the first seventy kilometres. He met two oncoming snowploughs and overtook one going in his direction.

Not that it really mattered much. He liked being alone in the car, especially at night; the Mercedes purred like a cat and he had a Thelonious Monk album spinning in the CD player. He thought of Kristina, and realized he had been a bit concerned about their relationship recently, but it felt good now. It had been a few weeks since they'd last made love, but she'd had her period and he knew it wasn't anything to worry about. And their embraces last night had been wonderful. Why am I using an archaic word like 'embraces', he wondered, although, a rose by any other name would smell as sweet. She had focused on her own satisfaction in a way he hadn't seen since before Kelvin was born. And what's more, on leaving her outside the hotel, he had felt that she would have been happy to do it all over again tonight.

And she had said that she loved him – in that way that meant she really did.

You're a lucky man, Jakob Willnius, he thought. Bloody lucky, you just remember that.

He knew it to be so. He had indisputably been lucky. Far luckier than he deserved. Things could have ended disastrously with Annica, they really could, but he had escaped unscathed. The worst-case scenario would have been a court case and a scandal, but mercifully he had had money. Annica and her lawyer had accepted a financial settlement, on condition that she had custody of both daughters and never had to see him again.

But Annica was a different story, he thought, that had been acted out in a different chapter of his life. He had learnt that much.

Though he did still have dreams about her, nightmares as well as the opposite; hot, arousing dreams that were sometimes so real he thought he could detect the smell of her when he woke.

But now it was the smell of Kristina lingering in his nostrils. Damn, he thought, I really miss her, crave her. He wished she had come with him. If that bloody Robert hadn't gone and vanished, she could have been beside him in the car now; they would have travelled together through the night and he would only have had to reach out a hand to . . .

The bleep of his phone interrupted his fantasies.

It's her, he thought. It's Kristina.

But it wasn't. It was Jefferson.

'Jakob, I'm terribly, terribly sorry,' he began.

Then he apologized for calling in the middle of the night, but that wasn't what he was so sorry about. No, things had gone and got infernally complicated in Oslo. *Infernally complicated.* Were they always so impossible to deal with, the Norwegians? Not really used to the negotiating table, was that it? And state regulations left, right and centre? But what the hell, Jakob could no doubt enlighten him on that another time. The thing now was that he'd had to stay on for an extra day in Oslo, and then fly direct to Paris on Thursday. The meeting they had arranged simply couldn't be squeezed in. Could they possibly make it the start of January instead? In Stockholm, of course. He just had to pop across the Atlantic to celebrate Christmas and New Year in Vermont first – but then, around 5–6 January, what did Jakob reckon to that?

Arrogant Harvard poof, thought Jakob.

'Sure,' he said. 'I can't see any problem with that.'

Jefferson thanked him, reiterated that he was terribly, terribly sorry, wished him a Happy Christmas and hung up.

Jakob Willnius swore and checked the time. It was a quarter to two. He put his mobile back in the breast pocket of his jacket. Glanced at the fuel gauge and saw that he had a bare quarter of a tank left.

He had another three hours' driving ahead of him to get to Stockholm, probably three and a half in view of the road conditions. He suddenly felt tired.

If he turned back, he could be snuggling into bed with his wife in just over an hour.

Just as he was thinking that – and before he had made up his mind – an all-night petrol station came into view. He turned into the forecourt. At any event, he needed to think and get a cup of coffee down him.

I'll call her and see what she thinks, he thought. If she's like she was yesterday, she won't say no.

But as he dipped into his breast pocket for his phone, his fingers made contact with his hotel key, which he had forgotten to leave at reception at Kymlinge Hotel. Why not surprise her, he thought.

He got out of the car and started filling the tank with highly potent 98-octane fuel.

Well, why not? Creep in quietly like a thief in the night, peel off his clothes and slip in behind her warm back.

'Fuck you, Mr Bigmouth Shit-talking Jefferson,' muttered Jakob Willnius when the pump had finished ticking. He went into the shop, paid for his petrol and got a double espresso from the machine. He took it back to the car and set off for Kymlinge.

14

When Rosemarie Wunderlich Hermansson woke up on 21 December, it was twenty to six and she had two distinct thoughts in her head.

Robert's dead.

We're losing the house this afternoon.

But no birds. And no speech bubbles. She stayed there in bed for a while, staring out into the surrounding darkness and listening to Karl-Erik's regular breathing as she tried to weigh the two thoughts. Judge the level of truth in them. The first of them she dared not keep in her consciousness for more than brief, abysmal moments. *Robert dead?* It came and she pushed it away; it came back, and was rebuffed again. Perhaps he was upstairs in bed? Perhaps he had come back overnight? She decided not to go and check. Because if he wasn't there, if he really had been gone for two nights and one day, it could only mean . . . no, it was too much.

The other thought, then. The house. This afternoon at four o'clock they would be sitting in Lundgren's room at the bank. So there it was. They would sit on his birch-veneer office chairs and sell their lives. She and Karl-Erik. For thirty-eight years they had lived in this house. Ebba was two when they moved in, and Robert and Kristina had been born here. They had lived in Kymlinge for almost forty years. This is where I had my existence, she thought. This is where I felt at home. What's to become of me now? Shall I never again sit out in the arbour and enjoy the first new potatoes of the season? Shall I never again see the plum tree we planted six years ago bear fruit? Shall I . . . shall I sit on a white plastic chair on a bare mountain and meet death? Beneath the red-hot Spanish sun? Is that what it's all been for? Was this the fate this desolate god carved out for me?

And what did He envisage I would take with me? My sixty-three wasted, crumbling years? My distance course in Flemish embroidery? My address book, so I can send weekly postcards to my three . . . *wellll*, four then . . . women friends and tell them about the blue pool water and the blue seawater and the white plastic chairs?

No, thought Rosemarie Wunderlich Hermansson. I don't want to.

But it sounded so faint inside her, that 'No'. So hopelessly faint and pitiful. How was she to find the strength to go against Karl-Erik on this? And where? *Where* should she pitch the tent of her resistance?

Tent of her resistance? What in heaven's name was that? There was surely no such phrase . . . But if Robert was dead, they couldn't trot off to the bank and sign away their lives in those circ—?

She got out of bed. All at once she felt angry with herself. Why should Robert be dead? Why was she surrendering to such ludicrous, crow-black prophecies? And it was so chronically typical of her, wasn't it? When the children were little she had been constantly haunted by thoughts of them dying. Being run over by buses, falling through the ice or getting bitten by rabid dogs. Robert was thirty-five years old, he could look after himself. And hadn't he in fact absented himself for most of his life, anyway? That was his speciality, in truth. Now he was keeping out of the way for a few days again, for some reason or another, and what was so odd about that?

But why should she go and take her seat opposite Chalk-stripe Lundgren and write off her life like some stupid goose? Why not . . . why not tell her tyrannical pedagogue pine that he could pack his bag and move to Andalusia on his own? Or wherever he liked, for that matter. Simple as that.

But as for her, she fully intended to stay where she belonged. In Allvädersgatan in Kymlinge, Sweden. You take yourself off to the Costa Geriatrica and imagine yourself a cut above all those other sun-fried oldies! Research on Moorish and Jewish heritage? What rubbish, thought Rosemarie Wunderlich Hermansson. What crap, Karl-Erik Telegraph Pole!

She went out to the kitchen and put the coffee on. And as she sat there with her elbows rubbing on the kitchen table and waited for the coffee machine to finish gurgling, her courage and drive sank in her like a stone in a well.

As usual. Exactly as usual.

I'm nothing but a timid goose, she thought. A fool of a woman, sixty-three years old and with no purpose in life.

Other than to worry. To dwell on dismal day-to-day prophecies and wait for the next disappointment.

Misfortunes small and large. Misfortune with a capital 'M' today, perhaps. Robert? Was he the doom-laden prophecy that was about to be fulfilled?

Death? Yes, it really did feel as if that was the dark figure lurking in the reeds this time. Nothing more or less.

But not her own death. She wasn't worrying about that at all. I'm far too insignificant for Death to care about me, she thought with resignation. I shall live like a shrinking ball of fluff until the end of time.

Her coffee was ready.

The house was still asleep. The small misfortunes were not yet awake.

Nor the large.

'No honestly, Mummy dear,' said Ebba Hermansson Grundt, 'we don't need lunch before we leave as well. We've got over 650 kilometres to go, so we'll stop for a bite to eat on the way. A normal breakfast is all that's necessary.'

'Yes, but I think—' Rosemarie tried to object.

'I'll wake the boys and Leif in half an hour. What a gift men have for sleep, don't you think, Mum?'

'I heard that,' said her father, who was at the kitchen work-top blending his morning muesli. 'What a prejudiced view, sweetie. Remember the alarm clock was invented by a man. Oscar William Willingstone the Elder.'

'Because he couldn't wake up of his own accord, Daddy dear,' said Ebba. 'Now, what about Robert? Is he back?'

'I don't know,' said Rosemarie.

'Don't know? What do you mean?'

'I mean that I don't know, of course,' said Rosemarie. 'I haven't been up to check.'

Ebba regarded her mother with a worried frown creasing her brow. She looked as if she were about to offer some mild reproof, too, a simple rebuke from daughter to mother, but whatever it was, she kept it to herself.

'Any more operations to do before Christmas?' enquired Karl-Erik, sitting down at the table with his bowl.

'Eight,' said Ebba in a neutral tone, 'though not especially complicated ones. Five tomorrow, three on Friday. But after that I get a few days off for Christmas. All right Mum, I'll go up and check.'

She got to her feet and went out. Rosemarie looked at the clock. It was a few minutes after seven-thirty. She wondered whether to have her third cup of coffee but decided on a glass of Samarin instead. A stitch in time . . . Karl-Erik was browsing through the newspaper. Is he really as unconcerned as he seems, she asked herself. Or is he just trying to give that impression? He would certainly be astonished if she stabbed him between the shoulder blades with the big carving knife. Would he manage to get a word out, or would he just crumple and hit the floor like a sack of potatoes, she wondered.

Perhaps he wouldn't even have time to be surprised?

I will never know, she thought wearily. She stirred the Samarin into a glass of water. Downed it in three deep draughts and started unloading the dishwasher. Karl-Erik sat in silence. She wondered how many times she had done precisely this. Unloaded everything from the dishwasher. This was their third one. It had been working faultlessly for . . . what was it now? Four years? No, more, at least five . . . she tried to work it out as she dried off the saucepans with a tea towel – that was the only function she found slightly less than satisfactory, the drying – yes, it was almost six years in fact. Once, sometimes even twice a day for six years, what did that add up to? A lot, though Karl-Erik did occasionally lend a hand, she had to give him that . . .

'Are they coming round for breakfast?'

'What?'

'Kristina and that lot. They'll drop in for a sandwich before they head off, won't they?'

'I don't know,' was Rosemarie's honest reply. 'Er, yes, I think that's what we agreed.'

'You think?' said Karl-Erik.

'I don't remember,' said Rosemarie. 'With all this Robert business, it's hard to keep track . . . of other things.'

Karl-Erik did not reply. He carried on reading the paper.

In three days' time it's meant to be Christmas Eve, thought Rosemarie jadedly. And in three months' time I'm meant to find my way to a supermercado whenever I want to go shopping. What are the dishwashers like in Spain? If Ebba comes back and tells me Robert's upstairs in bed, she suddenly thought, I promise to go with Karl-Erik without a single grumble. To the bank *and* to Spain.

What strange sort of deal was that? she then wondered. That was the right word, wasn't it? The English word *deal*? Horse-trading, as it used to be known, and that was a word she felt she could relate to. They called it *Kuhhandel* in German. But why should she need to trade Robert for Spain? What were these idiotic voices inside her, asserting that she had to choose one or the other? Making out that it was some kind of equation of hope: Robert's life or the house in Kymlinge. That it would be presumptuous to imagine both could be sorted out. That she had to . . .

Ebba returned.

'Nix,' she said. 'Little brother isn't back home today, either.'

Everything started to go black and for one brief second Rosemarie was sure she would faint.

But she hung on tight to the worktop and recovered. She closed the front of the dishwasher, even though she hadn't completely emptied it. Straightened up and looked at her daughter and husband, both sitting there at the kitchen table, safely nestled in their hundred and five years, in their innate hereditary concord – not appearing the least bit anxious. She took a deep breath.

'The police,' she said. 'Will you please now go and ring the police, Karl-Erik Hermansson?'

'Certainly not,' replied Karl-Erik, not even raising his eyes from the newspaper. 'And I also forbid you to do it. As discussed.'

'Dad, I really think you ought to listen to Mum in this case,' said Ebba.

Kristoffer woke up and stared into a dark wall.

Where am I? was his first thought.

It took him a few seconds to realize. A weird dream about hyenas quickly receded and vanished into his subconscious. Hyenas running around laughing scornfully in something that looked like an old quarry. Why was he dreaming about hyenas? He'd never even seen one, had he? Not in real life, anyway.

Nor that many quarries, either.

He looked at the luminous face of his watch. It was quarter to eight. He turned over and put on the light. The green stripes of the wallpaper returned. Henrik was already up. Damn it, thought Kristoffer. I must have slept like a log last night. I didn't notice whether he went out or not.

Oh well, he thought, switching the lamp off again. Suppose I'll have to ask him how it went. I'll just lie here for a bit. He might be in the bathroom, in which case he'll be back any minute.

Or had their mother already come in to wake them? He tried to remember the sequence of events, but it felt futile. She had woken him so many times, so many mornings in so many different tones of voice, that it was impossible to distinguish one from another. Maybe she'd been in, maybe not.

Today was Wednesday at any rate, he remembered. This evening he'd be back home in Sundsvall. And tomorrow . . .

Linda Granberg. Birger's burger stall. Kristoffer turned over and switched on the light for a second time. Pointless to lie there when he was so wide awake. And a bit hungry, actually, though he wasn't normally in the mornings. Might as well get up, he decided. Have a shower and go down for some breakfast.

Standing in the cramped shower cubicle as the water gushed over him, he thought about Henrik. What a transformation! What a complete turnaround had taken place in just a few days. From the perfect, infallible Super Henrik to the . . . what was the word? Promiscuous? . . . to the promiscuous Henrik, who had hooked up with a guy called Jens and went cruising about in secret in the middle of the night, for shady assignations.

Assuming Henrik really had gone out last night. He couldn't be sure. But in some way he felt this had brought him and his brother closer. Even though Henrik still didn't know that he knew. Because Henrik wasn't unblemished, that was the novelty of it. He had his dark sides, just like anybody else. Like Kristoffer himself. He was . . . well, human, quite simply.

Good news, thought Kristoffer. Exceedingly good news.

Then he turned the heat up a degree and moved on to reflect on Uncle Robert. In his case, the promiscuity (difficult word, thought Kristoffer, but good) was well-documented, and had been for a long time. He'd been the black sheep of the family long before he beat all records on *Fucking Island*. He'd never been amongst the favoured topics of conversation round the dinner table in Stockrosvägen up in Sundsvall.

And now he'd gone missing. Or had he come back during the night? Kristoffer caught himself wishing he hadn't. It was cool just to vanish into thin air like that. Several of the others, especially Granny, seemed worried about him, but not Kristoffer. It was probably just as Dad said. Robert had found a woman, and instead of enduring the agony of an exceptionally tedious birthday party, he'd decided to spend the time with her. He didn't give a shit what people thought and said. Kristoffer hoped he could aspire to that state one day. A state in which you decided your own fate and actions, and weren't dependent on . . . on your mum, to put it bluntly.

Because that was the way it was. It wasn't on Dad's account Henrik had asked him to keep quiet about his nocturnal escapades, that was obvious. Leif had reacted to Kristoffer's transgressions last Saturday exactly the way a good dad should react. By being bloody furious with him and telling him to damn well pull his socks up and think about what he was doing – but not burdening him with a load of guilt. That was the way it should be between parents and children. Straightforward and simple, not all that beating about the bush. A good dressing down and then everything was all right again.

But how would he react if he found out Henrik was homosexual? Well, that would be a different kettle of fish, as he would put it. A completely different kettle of fish, thought Kristoffer, turning off the shower. He heard a knocking on the door.

'Henrik?'

It was Mum.

'No it's me, Kristoffer.'

'I'm glad you're up. Come down and have some breakfast when you're ready.'

'Sure,' replied Kristoffer, and started to inspect his face in the mirror.

No more than four or five spots; bearing in mind the way he'd stuffed himself with chocolate these past few days, he had every reason to feel satisfied. If he restrained himself today, he should be pretty presentable at Birger's burger stall in . . . in about thirty-seven hours' time.

'Rosemarie, you've got to try to be a bit realistic here,' said Karl-Erik at that slow, emphatic, pedantic, schoolmasterly pace which meant he did not intend to repeat what he was about to say. 'There's nothing to point to anything having happened to Robert. You and I – and Ebba – know his character. There's no need for me to give examples. He evidently felt somewhat under pressure, being here – perhaps he felt ashamed, to put it plainly – and he had every reason to. So he rang up some old contact here in town. Rud . . . what was that schoolfriend of his called? Rudström?'

'Rundström,' said Rosemarie. 'He moved to Gotland some years back. But why didn't he let us know? That's what makes me uneasy, Karl-Erik. Surely Robert wouldn't just . . . ?'

'Because he feels ashamed,' her husband said firmly, as if that settled it. 'As I said. And he hasn't got any particularly acceptable reason for staying away. What would he say to us?'

'So why did he bother coming at all, then? And his car's still parked here – completely covered in snow.'

'He doesn't need the car,' Karl-Erik explained patiently. 'My guess is that he'll come and get it this afternoon, when he knows everyone else has gone home. I just don't understand why you have to make such a mountain out of this molehill, I really don't, Rosemarie. Robert doesn't deserve your attention.'

Kristoffer came into the kitchen and politely wished them a good morning. Karl-Erik broke off and seemed to be in two minds about whether the bad boy was an appropriate topic for fourteen-year-old ears. He apparently decided he was, for he went on.

'So you explain to me, Rosemarie, what it is you think has happened to our prodigal son?'

Kristoffer sat down at the table. Rosemarie looked at Ebba for some sort of continuing support, but could not really tell if it was being offered or not. And Ebba was Karl-Erik's daughter, after all, she reminded herself. She shouldn't forget that in her eagerness.

'All I want,' she said finally, 'is for you to ring the police station – and the hospital – to check.'

'So you think they wouldn't tell us if he'd ended up at one of those?'

'Not if he—'

'Even Robert must have some form of ID on him,' Karl-Erik ploughed on. 'And if he hasn't, well, it's pretty likely they'd recognize him anyway, don't you think?'

Rosemarie said nothing. Ebba cleared her throat and stepped in to mediate.

'I suggest you leave it a bit longer. It's not as if you want the police to go straight out and start looking for him, is it, Mummy? In that case it would be sure to be in the paper tomorrow. And you don't want them coming out here to interrogate us; that wouldn't be very nice either, would it?'

The telephone rang. Rosemarie took the opportunity of going into the bedroom to answer.

'Where's Henrik?' asked Ebba.

Kristoffer shrugged and poured some fruit yogurt into a bowl. 'Don't know.'

Ebba looked at the clock. 'We ought to leave in an hour's time. Do you know whether Dad's in the shower?'

'I think he is,' said Kristoffer.

Karl-Erik folded up his newspaper and regarded his nephew for a moment. He seemed to be considering giving him some piece of advice or other – a nugget of worldly wisdom – to take back up to Sundsvall, but evidently failed to find the right one amongst the many thousand conceivable alternatives, and got up from the table instead. He went to the window, pushed back the curtain and peered out at the thermometer.

'Minus twelve,' he reported. 'Well, let's hope you've topped up the anti-freeze, anyway.'

'Of course we did, Dad,' said Ebba. 'Though I'm not so sure about Robert's snow heap.'

'A decent blanket of snow actually provides good insulation,' said Karl-Erik Hermansson. 'I thought you would know that.'

'And so I do, Daddy dear,' said Ebba.

Rosemarie returned just as Leif Grundt put in an appearance, fresh from the shower and wide awake. 'Good morning Christian folk,' he said. 'I don't know if you've noticed, but a new day has dawned.'

'Yes, we know,' said Ebba. 'Who was on the phone, Mum? You look a bit worried.'

'No, I'm fine,' said Rosemarie with a fleeting smile. 'It was only Jakob. They're not coming in for breakfast, some meeting's come up in Stockholm and he's got to get back. The coffee's over here, Leif. Shall I pour you a cup?'

'Thank you, fair Mother-in-law,' said Leif Grundt. 'Yes, probably best to tuck in now, so we can keep going. Now that we're heading north again. Has our leading TV personality turned up, then?'

'Leif,' said Ebba with a warning edge to her voice.

Rosemarie gave a deep sigh and went out of the room. Kristoffer put two slices of bread in the toaster and thought about what a talent his father had for saying the wrong thing. The question was whether he did it on purpose or not; in either case, it was rather wonderful.

'Thanks for a delicious breakfast, Daddy dear,' said Ebba. 'I'll go up and start packing, and tell Henrik to get a move on. Can I help you with anything before we go, Dad?'

This was presumably an invitation to consult a medically trained daughter about any aches and pains, old or new, even Karl-Erik realized that, but he merely shook his head and folded his arms on his chest.

The only symptom he was aware of was the vague whooshing in his head that had started after yesterday morning's click, assuming it wasn't the radiators, and he had no intention of discussing that with anyone. Particularly not with people who might possibly be in possession of some unpalatable explanation.

'I've never felt better in my life, sweetie,' he said, thrusting out his chest. 'And I slept like a baby.'

15

Kristoffer was lying on his bed in the WUR again.

It was half past eleven and they were over an hour late leaving.

'Go and wait in your room, Kristoffer,' his mother had instructed. 'I'll come up and see you in a while, but we grown-ups need to talk this through first.'

This meant Henrik. After a good deal of confusion and numerous questions and witness statements – from all of those present in the Hermansson's detached house in Allväders-gatan, Kymlinge: Mum, Dad, Granny Rosemarie, Granddad Karl-Erik and Kristoffer himself – it had gradually emerged that Henrik really wasn't there. Nobody seemed to have bumped into him all morning; each of them thought he had had breakfast with someone else, thought they had heard someone say they'd met him on the stairs, heard him in the bathroom, spoken to him – but once all the information had been methodically sifted through under the competent leader-ship of Ebba, all these suppositions proved to be incorrect.

No one had seen Henrik all morning, that was the fact of the matter.

A hint of suspicion had come into Kristoffer's mind almost straight away, so he had had plenty of time to decide on the line he would take. It wasn't particularly difficult.

'No Mum, I haven't seen him either. He was already up when I woke up.'

There hadn't even been any need to lie, in fact. Henrik *had* been up when he woke up. Kristoffer had *not* seen him all morning.

Keeping quiet about a little piece of information that nobody expressly asked for? No, he couldn't really be blamed for that. Not yet, at any rate.

Though, in ten to fifteen minutes' time, positions would doubtless shift a fair bit. Things would come into sharper focus. His mum would come upstairs and instigate a more thorough cross-examination. This was the trial he was now bracing himself for.

Are you aware of anything that could explain where Henrik has got to? She would want to know that, for example, and then he would be obliged to come out with a pure lie. Cross a boundary. The very boundary that had been under discussion on Sunday, when he was the one in the naughty corner.

Not that it really bothered him. Not much, anyway, he realized as he examined the situation a little more closely. Protecting Henrik – the new, promiscuous Henrik – was non-negotiable. That was the deal they had made. It was Henrik in a hole this time, not Kristoffer, and it was hard not to feel a certain satisfaction about this simple but unusual state of affairs.

And Henrik would take the whole rap himself when he showed up, of course. It would never come out that his younger brother had concealed information. Kristoffer would get off scot-free; he was not running the slightest risk in lying to his mother. On the contrary, it was his duty to keep to the agreement he and Henrik had made.

Brothers in arms.

But it certainly showed an unusual lack of finesse, he couldn't help but observe. He found this surprising. Henrik had clearly slipped out for his secret assignation some time during the night and then . . . well, Kristoffer didn't really want to think in any detail about what he might have got up to, but then, when all the nameless stuff was over, he and the other person, whoever it was, had presumably crashed out – and overslept! How monumentally stupid, thought Kristoffer. And what kind of whopper would he tell when he got back?

He had apparently turned off his mobile. They'd tried to reach him countless times in the last hour, but only got through to his voicemail. It wasn't like Henrik not to have his mobile on, not like him at all. Kristoffer couldn't work out what the adults were really thinking; Leif had come up with the idea that Henrik had gone for a ski, a theory he had to modify to a jog to take into account the lack of any suitable skiing equipment in the house, and then abandon altogether in view of the snow conditions.

Nobody seemed particularly worried so far, but perhaps it was bubbling away beneath the surface. Kristoffer didn't really feel able to judge the current situation. Though the fact that they had sent him up to the WUR so they could talk things over undisturbed did of course show how seriously they were taking the whole thing. What was more, it was rather weird that there were now two people missing, not just one. Even though Kristoffer hadn't actually heard any of the adults utter a word about any connection. But perhaps it was just a matter of time; after all, they didn't yet know what he knew.

You're fucking stupid, brother, muttered Kristoffer to himself, realizing the same instant that this was the most disparaging thing he had ever thought about Henrik. The very idea that he would find himself lying to his mother's face for his elder brother's sake! He would scarcely have believed it a couple of days ago.

But he was going to keep a stiff upper lip, and right until the last drop of sweat, let nobody think otherwise. His mind was made up. But that didn't stop him wondering what in hell's name Henrik was doing – and having lain there and done that in his green cell for a while, he started to get a distinctly uncomfortable feeling in his stomach.

A bit scary and a bit – well, sad, he supposed. What's happening to you, brother Henrik? thought Kristoffer.

He stared into the wallpaper, but as expected he found no answer written there.

'Kristoffer, we've got to get to the bottom of this, I'm sure we're both agreed on that?'

'Yes,' said Kristoffer.

'Henrik isn't here and we don't know where he is.'

Kristoffer attempted to nod and shake his head at the same time, hoping to appear as accommodating as possible.

'He seems to have gone off very early this morning, or . . . ?'

Kristoffer did not supply the missing words.

'. . . sometime during the night,' said Ebba.

'I don't know,' said Kristoffer. 'I didn't notice anything, either last night or first thing this morning. I must have been fast asleep, I'm afraid.'

His mother tried to penetrate him with her steely blueness, but it seemed to him that he withstood her gaze pretty well.

He wasn't in the dock this time, and that made things easier. Considerably easier.

'He didn't say anything to you?'

'About what?'

'I don't know, Kristoffer. If he planned to pop out for a few hours, for example?'

'No,' said Kristoffer. 'He didn't say anything like that.'

'Are you sure?'

'Yes, I'm sure.'

'But I must say that you—'

'Yes?'

'You don't seem surprised that he isn't here.'

'What?'

'You don't seem surprised and that's a bit odd, I think – I'm trying to work out what it could mean.'

It was an exaggeratedly insinuating attack and he parried it in the only possible way. 'Not surprised? I don't know what you're talking about, Mum. I've got no idea where Henrik's gone and I'm as surprised as everybody else.'

She hesitated for a moment, and then yielded. 'All right, Kristoffer. I believe you. But if you think back, was there really nothing he said – or just hinted – that could explain where he's got to? The two of you must have chatted about all sorts of things.'

Kristoffer bit his bottom lip, simulating deep thought for a moment. 'No,' he said. 'No, Mum, and I can't think of anything relevant he said.'

'Do you think Henrik's been himself these past few days? I mean to say, you've scarcely seen each other all autumn. Hasn't it felt to you as if . . . well, as if something about him has changed?'

Bingo, Mother dear, thought Kristoffer. If you only knew how changed your golden boy is, you'd start shitting bricks and have a haemorrhage. And just once, continued his train of thought, I wish that, just once, I could say these things out loud instead of only thinking them.

'Mmm, no . . .' he said. 'I don't think so. But he'll soon be back to explain everything. Maybe he thought we were off around lunchtime so . . . maybe he's out buying Christmas presents?'

Ebba appeared to give this suggestion serious consideration before she deemed him in need of another dip in her bath of blue acid. But he didn't give an inch.

'What did the pair of you talk about last night?'

That's none of your business, Madam prosecutor, ran the formulation in his head. 'Nothing in particular,' his mouth said. 'He told me a bit about Uppsala and so on.'

'Oh yes? What did he tell you about Uppsala then?'

'That it was fun studying there. But really hard work.'

'Did he tell you anything about Jenny?'

Kristoffer thought about this.

'He mentioned her, I'm pretty sure. But only *en pessant*.'

'*Passant*.'

'Eh?'

'*Passant*. You said *pessant*.'

'Sorry.'

'Well, it doesn't matter. Anything else?'

'That we talked about?'

'Yes.'

'We talked a bit about Uncle Robert.'

'Oh really? And what conclusion did you reach?'

'None really,' said Kristoffer. 'Except that he seems a bit strange.'

'Did you indeed?' muttered Ebba. 'Well, just at the moment, I'm not particularly interested in how you two see my brother. But if you think of anything else about Henrik, then we – Dad and I . . . and Granny and Granddad – don't want you to keep quiet about it.'

'Why would I keep quiet about it?' asked Kristoffer with an indignation that felt almost genuine. 'I want to get away from here, too. If I knew anything, I'd have spat it out straight away, for sure.'

She paused one last time.

'Good, Kristoffer,' she said eventually. 'I'm relying on you.'

Then she left the room.

Stupid Henrik, thought Kristoffer once she had closed the door. Where the hell are you?

He checked the time. It was one minute to twelve.

By two o'clock, snow was falling again, and in the Hermansson household, they had finished lunch. Smoked sausage and potatoes in white sauce; normally Karl-Erik's absolute favourite, but today it felt completely out of place. No one had much appetite, and the tense silence hanging over the dining table went with them to the coffee and crullers in the living room. Kristoffer didn't drink coffee, but he had a Christmas root beer, and while he was drinking it he surreptitiously studied the mute expressions on the adults' faces: his mother and father; his grandmother and grandfather. He wondered what was going on inside their skulls. A lot, he assumed. Irritation, anxiety. Apprehension, frustration, you name it. All the questions that could be asked had already been asked, and nobody seemed willing to repeat them. All conceivable guesses had been guessed and all speculations speculated on. The car was packed and ready to go on the drive; there was just that little detail of a missing passenger.

The thing nobody had really put into words yet, thought Kristoffer, was the fear, of course. The lid still seemed to be on the really blackest fears, and here he was beginning to feel the head start he had on the others rapidly shrinking. Admittedly, he knew what he knew: Henrik had slipped out to a secret assignation sometime during the night – possibly with an unknown lover named Jens (though Kristoffer was increasingly having his doubts about that) – but why on earth he hadn't come back first thing, or in the course of the morning, was a question that loomed ever larger with each passing minute.

Henrik had vanished. Robert had vanished. This is the weirdest bloody thing I've ever experienced, thought Kristoffer Grundt.

'It's five past two,' said Rosemarie Wunderlich Hermansson, as if this announcement might shed light on something. But the only thing it achieved was to make a vein in Karl-Erik's temple start squirming like a maggot. It had done the same at various points during the day; Kristoffer had had his eye on it and knew it meant that his grandfather was annoyed or upset about something. There was a strange look to one of his eyelids, too. It drooped over his eye and made him look a bit tipsy, thought Kristoffer. He was pretty sure that this wasn't actually the case.

As for his dad, both Leif's eyelids were drooping, and Kristoffer guessed he was falling asleep. He had been unusually quiet for the past half hour; it had been obvious from the look of him that he was nowhere near producing any more convincing theory as to where his splendid – and hitherto almost infallible – son had got to.

His mother, Ebba, looked resolute, as if she were concentrating in preparation for an operation that promised to be too complicated by far. Or as if she were working away in her head at the new and paradoxical Henrik equation, and couldn't get so much as a sniff of the solution, though she would normally have solved it long ago.

Kristoffer sighed and took another cruller, although he was stuffed already. The potatoes in white sauce felt like a slowly swelling coat of glue inside him and he wondered whether he ought simply to drag himself upstairs and take a nap in the WUR while awaiting his brother's return. Or perhaps it would be best to stay put and keep himself *au fait* – was that the phrase? – with what was happening. Or not happening.

What in fact happened, at that exact moment, was that Granddad hauled himself out of his armchair and went over to the window. Thrust his hands into his trouser pockets and rocked back and forth on his feet a few times. He cleared his throat loudly, still with his back to the others. He struck up with a 'Hrrm. Now it's like this: at four o'clock, Rosemarie and I have to be at the bank. We'll have to see whether you folk have got on your way by then or not.'

'Well of course they—' started Rosemarie, but the thought changed direction halfway and took on a different significance. 'Whatever are you saying, Karl-Erik? We can't go off to the bank, now that—'

'Now that what?' Karl-Erik demanded, turning round. 'We've got an appointment. Lundgren is expecting us and the Singlövs will have come all the way from Rimminge.'

'That's thirty kilometres at most,' said Rosemarie. 'They

can easily go back home. You must realize we can't leave Ebba and Leif in the lurch now that . . . and Kristoffer . . . no, we must stay here, and you'll have to ring and cancel the meeting.'

'I'm damned if I—' began Karl-Erik, an as-yet-unseen vein bulging in his other temple, but before he could get any further in his argument, Ebba stopped him.

'Please, Dad, not now,' she said. 'And Mum, you really needn't cancel for our sake. It's ridiculous. What is the point of five people sitting here waiting when three are more than enough, and what's more . . . no, I don't know – don't know what I was going to say . . .'

And with that, Ebba started to cry

Initially, Kristoffer didn't realize what was happening. Perhaps it was because he had never seen his mother cry before. At least not that he could remember. But it was a peculiar sort of crying, too, reminiscent of some kind of machine that wouldn't start, like a little engine, in fact; her shoulders moved up and down and she exhaled and inhaled in small, panting gasps. Her head wobbled to and fro in time with her shoulders, and that was where the problem lay, thought Kristoffer; an engine coughing and spluttering and coughing again but the cylinders, no matter how many there were, could not work together to create any real propulsion.

As if she had never cried in her life and didn't really know how to do it.

The others presumably didn't realize what was going on either, because it took his grandmother a while to start clumsily stroking her daughter's back and arms to console her. Leif stepped in to relieve her a few moments later and patted his wife on the head, while Karl-Erik just stood there in the middle of the room, looking like a male boxer dog that had trapped his paw in a lift door.

At any rate, that was how it looked to Kristoffer, not that it occurred to him to lend his weeping mother a hand, either. She was his mother, he knew that, but he was convinced it would require a considerably better touch than he could provide. Yet it made him very uncomfortable to see her like this, so unexpectedly helpless, and when he glanced in Granddad's direction he could see the same confusion and frustration in those eyes as he could feel revolving in his own mind.

Damn, damn, damn, thought Kristoffer, as he clenched his teeth so he wouldn't start sobbing as well. Mum's crying, this is really serious. Get yourself back here Henrik, you fucker. This isn't funny any more.

A short while later, the tears had subsided and they had reached an agreement. Rosemarie and Karl-Erik would go and see Chalk-stripe Lundgren at the bank as arranged. The paperwork would only take an hour at most, and if the situation was unchanged when they got back to Allvädersgatan, the police would immediately be informed.

That was the way they left it. There was no reason to be over-hasty.

Kristoffer was never given the chance to voice his opinion on this plan of action, but having returned once again to his bed in the World's Ugliest Room, he gloomily had to admit that if he had been, he would still have had no objections.

The snow went on falling and the hours passed. Rosemarie and Karl-Erik Hermansson drove to the bank and returned with their business accomplished. At that point, Kristoffer had slept for three quarters of an hour and lain awake for at least double that length of time; he came down the stairs just as

Granny and Granddad were coming through the front door. He did not know how his mother and father had spent the afternoon, but they also presented themselves in the kitchen a minute later.

Granny looked at Ebba and Ebba shook her head. Her eyes were red-rimmed. Kristoffer realized she had been crying again and this gave him a sense of helplessness he didn't think he had ever experienced before. A sort of ice-bound panic, yes, that was more or less what it felt like.

After a short discussion, it fell to Karl-Erik's lot to take on the agreed task.

As he stood there with the receiver in his hand, waiting for an answer, the wall clock in the dining room struck twice, indicating that it was half past six. It was Wednesday 21 December, and Robert Hermansson and Henrik Grundt were more missing than ever.

16

Detective Inspector Gunnar Barbarotti could just as easily have been called Giuseppe Larsson.

When he came into the world on 21 February 1960, his father, Giuseppe Barbarotti, and his mother, Maria Larsson, were entirely in agreement on one thing. They would never have anything to do with one another again.

They disagreed on everything else. Such as a name for their new baby boy (weight 3,880 grams, length 54 centimetres). Giuseppe thought it ought to sound Italian, Swedish being the language of peasants and yokels, and if they wanted to give the boy a good start in life, it was vital for him to have a suitable name.

His mother, Maria, had no truck with such emotional, southern-European drivel. Their son should bear a healthy, ancient Nordic name; coming to school with a macaroni-and-greasy-charmer of a name would put him at the bottom of the pecking order from the very start. Giuseppe could wax his moustache and shove off to warmer climes; the boy's name was none of his business.

Giuseppe made it clear that this was a matter of such importance that if Maria intended to continue with her obstructions, he would seriously have to consider marrying her so he could exert legitimate influence over the naming of his first-born son. And other things as well.

In the end they compromised, on the wise advice of Maria's elder sister Inger, who single-handedly owned and ran a hot-dog stall in Katrineholm. The Italian language was not to be despised, she thought, and if elements could be combined, the result often proved better than any fixation with one of the parts. Hot dogs with bread rolls were generally to be preferred to hot dogs with hot dogs. Or bread with bread.

So they opted for *Gunnar*, after the sisters' late and much lamented elder brother, and *Barbarotti*, after the child's father – who, while its mother was still in the maternity hospital, was busily packing his possessions to move back home to Bologna. Both parties declared themselves to be at least semi-satisfied with the proposed solution, and neither of them thought Giuseppe Larsson sounded anything but daft.

Which meant, if you wanted to split hairs, that there were actually two things they agreed on.

It was when Gunnar Barbarotti was abandoned by his wife Helena – four years ago, when he was forty-one – that he made his deal with God.

The nub of the matter was the existence of the latter. As for his own existence, Gunnar Barbarotti was all too painfully aware of it. He and Helena had been married for fifteen years; they had three children, and suddenly to discover – pretty much overnight – that you were part of SB, the Superannuated Brigade, had made him doubt everything. God's presence or absence was admittedly not very high on the agenda – that was monopolized by questions about the point of ploughing on at all, about what he had done wrong, why she hadn't said anything earlier, how the hell he was going to spend his evenings when he couldn't work overtime, and whether it wouldn't perhaps be best to change job entirely. But a month after the blow fell, when he had already moved into his doleful little flat on Baldersgatan in Kymlinge, God popped up in the middle of the night, during a long succession of sleepless nights.

Perhaps it was Gunnar himself who summoned Him. Projected Him up from his martyred soul to call Him to account – but be that as it may, they had a long and fruitful conversation, resulting in the aforementioned deal.

There were so many pitiably useless proofs that God existed, Gunnar Barbarotti and Our Lord were in total agreement on that. One after another, ephemeral circumstances or theological quibbles were cited as evidence that unequivocally settled the matter. Anselm. Descartes. Thomas Aquinas. What Gunnar was looking for – and God professed all the sympathy in the world for his quest – was something more concrete. A simple, rational method that could decide the question once and for all. It could be allowed to take its time, in God's view. Certainly, but not *too* much time, said Gunnar, who had to take account of his own limited lifespan; he very much wanted to find out how things really stood while he still had some time on this earth left to him, and God listened and conceded to even this condition without any unnecessary palaver.

Finally – it was getting on for five in the morning by then, and a snowplough conjured up by the Devil had started sending out sparks as it scraped the tarmac outside Gunnar Barbarotti's bedroom window – they agreed on the following model of proof:

If God actually did exist, then one of His principal tasks ought to be listening to the prayers of the unfortunate human race, and granting them to the extent that He considered them justified. He was of course right to reject immediately all those that were unseemly or self-interested. Gunnar Barbarotti could not for his part remember a single instance in his entire life when his prayers had been heeded. God countered with scepticism. And how many prayers have you ever sent me from a pure and earnest heart, you agnostic scoundrel? To his shame, Barbarotti had not kept track of this, though of course it could scarcely have been many – but that was all water under the bridge and from this point on he was prepared to give the whole thing a fair chance.

All right, said God. *We have a deal*, said Gunnar, in English, as if a marginal language such as Swedish were not really capable of expressing or embracing an agreement of this calibre.

The external timeframe was set at ten years. In this time, Gunnar Barbarotti would test the supposed existence of Our Lord by sending up prayers to Him as often as seemed appropriate and legitimate, and then – in a special notebook acquired for the purpose – note whether they were answered or not.

Now naturally, this did not apply to just any foolish prayer – winning a fortune on the racing or the lottery, beautiful nymphs materializing out of thin air with no greater desire than bedding the inspector, and other such egoistic notions – but only to the altruistic, reasonable kind. The kind which could plausibly come to pass if you just had a bit of luck, and which had no ill effects on anyone else. A prayer for a good night's sleep. For nice weather for a fishing trip. For his daughter, Sara, to sort out her differences with her best friend, Louise, in a satisfactory way.

Gunnar Barbarotti had gradually (in consultation with God, of course) developed a points system to deal with how great the likelihood for a favourable outcome was judged to be. If Gunnar's prayer was not answered, God always got a minus point – but if it was, Our Lord could win one, two or even three plus points.

Twelve months after the divorce, God didn't exist. He had scraped together a total of eighteen plus points and a whopping thirty-nine minus points, coming to minus twenty-one on aggregate.

Things went a little better in the second year, and the balance was adjusted to minus fifteen. In the third year, He regressed to minus eighteen, but it was in the fourth – and current – year that the tide began to turn. As early as May, the score was even, and by mid-July, God actually existed by a very decent margin of six points, a lead that was however eaten up by a rather dismal and soggy week's holiday in Scotland, an ear infection and an autumn packed with onerous and largely unproductive police work.

Today, Thursday 22 December, God was two points below the existence line – with nine days to go before the end of the year. Admittedly, the marathon as a whole still had six years to run, but it would have been nice to see in the New Year in the pious hope that there was a benign higher power to turn to in one's hour of need.

So thought Gunnar Barbarotti. Maybe that was also why he had sent up a desperate three-point prayer late last night – and if only God had the sense to put it into effect, He would take the lead again, as it were. Only by one measly point, it was true, but in a postscript to his prayer, sent off a few minutes after he woke up this morning – less than an hour ago, in other words – Gunnar had promised the potentially existent Almighty that if his prayer were heeded this time, he would make no more requests until they were into the New Year. God could look forward to being left to exist in peace and quiet for at least ten days. Right through the change of year, in fact, so wouldn't that be a feather in His hat?

God replied that he wasn't in the habit of wearing headgear of any kind, but that He would devote Himself to the task in hand with His customary goodwill and impartiality.

It was a bit urgent, Gunnar pointed out. The train was due to leave at 13.25 and if nothing had happened by then, all would be lost. To put it bluntly.

I see, said God, switching to English.

Good, said Gunnar Barbarotti.

The matter at stake was Christmas.

Ever since the sudden breach with Helena – between Christmas and New Year four years before – Gunnar Barbarotti had found it hard to get into the proper, authentic Christmas spirit. Nor had the former husband and wife adopted the idea of celebrating the festival together for the sake of the children, a solution that was more the rule than the exception amongst their circle of acquaintances. They operated an every-other-year system: all three children with Helena the first Christmas, all three with Gunnar the second, and so on. This year it was to have been Gunnar's turn to welcome Lars and Martin to his little flat in Kymlinge; the eldest child, their daughter Sara, who was eighteen and in her second year at upper secondary, already lived with her father – a decision that she had taken at the time of the divorce, rendering him astonished and delighted in equal measure.

But Lars and Martin – now nine and eleven – lived with their mum in Södertälje.

With their mum and their replacement dad, Fredrik, to be

precise. Until recently, at least. Fredrik Fyrhage had arrived on the scene suspiciously soon after the separation, but Barbarotti had managed to resist the temptation to look into the matter more closely. Sometimes dignity was more important than knowledge. It had cost him some sleepless nights, but he had done it.

At any event, this Fredrik had proved himself from the word go to be a real wonder man, possessing pretty much without exception all the important qualities and virtues that Barbarotti himself lacked – right up until September this year, when he left Helena, Lars and Martin without explanation for a dark-skinned belly dancer from the Ivory Coast.

Hearing of this, Barbarotti attempted to console his ex-wife. At least the man didn't seem to be a racist.

But Helena had had a nervous breakdown, even so – and to crown it all, her father up in the mining town of Malmberget suffered his first stroke at about the same time. He was relatively fortunate, emerging from it alive, though with marked impairment down his left side, an ironically fitting after-effect, Gunnar Barbarotti thought, for an old miner who had been a Communist all his life. These two things – the black belly dancer and the stroke-afflicted mine worker – coming together, however, made Barbarotti weaken. After a couple of tearful phone calls he had agreed to take Sara up north to the pit for the celebration of a proper family Christmas beneath the Pole Star. Granny and Granddad. Gunnar and Helena. The three children.

Having made this promise in mid-October, he had regretted it every day since. If there was one set of people Gunnar Barbarotti couldn't stand in this world, it was his former in-laws.

Hence his prayer.

O Lord, You who for the time being do not exist, although perhaps You do after all, throw a real spanner in the works of this damn trip. Let me off, let Sara off, grant me and my daughter a quiet Christmas here in our home in Kymlinge with pasta and lobster and Trivial Pursuit and some good books – and an early-morning Christmas service if we manage to get up in time – instead of this wretched family funeral for seven people in a cramped, frost-damaged four-room asbestos prefab and endless darkness and deep-frozen relationships and a perverse old Communist with left-side paralysis and his aggrieved wife. O Lord, do anything, but let no one come to harm or dishonour, and just a tip, I could imagine myself slipping on a patch of ice and breaking some minor bone in my body, or having a heavy icicle fall off a roof onto my head, I'm prepared to go that far, but You know best O Lord, and there are three points at stake as You know, Amen.

Gunnar Barbarotti looked at the clock. It was twenty past nine. He had eaten half a breakfast in bed and read a whole newspaper; it was time to get up and make coffee. Stand in the shower and await a miracle.

On the way to the bathroom he passed Sara's room, debated for a moment whether to give her an initial wake-up call, but decided to leave it. She could well afford to sleep for another hour; if he knew her, she would have packed her bag the previous evening, and she was generally a marvel of efficiency in the mornings.

In fact, she was a marvel all round, he thought as he stood under the shower, and not just in the mornings. He had read somewhere (Klimke, presumably) that of all the joys a man could experience here on earth, there was nothing to match the joy that a good and wise daughter could bestow.

Quite right, observed Gunnar Barbarotti, applying shampoo to his thinning hair, and what could beat some tranquil Christmas time together, and five days off work spent with such a daughter.

Absolutely nothing, O Lord, so hear my prayer.

The miracle that secured God's existence over the Christmas break came in two parts, and occurred between quarter and five to ten. First, Chief Inspector Asunander rang.

Asunander was head of the CID with the Kymlinge police and Barbarotti's immediate boss. He was bloody sorry to impose, he said, and if Gunnar Barbarotti couldn't field the ball himself, he could pass it to Backman.

Barbarotti chose to let this initial football metaphor pass without comment. Eva Backman was his colleague and good friend, and had also been able to arrange some days off over Christmas. She needed them, too, Gunnar knew, because her marriage seemed to have reached the point where it could very easily hit the rocks – but there was still a clear glimmer of hope. Eva's husband was a certain Wilhelm, generally known as Willy, and founder, chairman and coach of KUT, the Kymlinge Unihockey Tigers. The couple had three sons of fourteen, twelve and ten, who all played unihockey and were seen as genuine budding talents. Over the past twelve months, Eva Backman had slowly but implacably started to loathe the sport and everything about it, after maintaining a neutral stance for many long years. She had confided to Barbarotti that she even came out in a rash in the crooks of her arms and round her neck whenever she was obliged to watch a match, which she normally had to do twice a week. She had confided this to her husband, too, and Barbarotti gathered he had not taken it the right way.

But Eva loved her husband and she loved her kids. She didn't want everything to go to pot because of some stupid sporting activity. Or because of her own unreasonable stance; Barbarotti and Backman had talked it over just a couple of days before, so he knew how things stood. Being required to work over the holiday period rather than spending Christmas with the family (with not so much as a training session scheduled for the red-letter days) could well have disastrous consequences for Eva Backman.

But either Barbarotti or Backman had to take on the case, said the Chief Inspector, making it clear that there were no other options. Backman was actually the more obvious choice, being closer, but there was the matter of Backman's domestic circumstances . . . not something one liked to bring into the equation, but the way things were looking, perhaps she could use a few days in the bosom of her family? What did Barbarotti think?

Barbarotti agreed. In principle. And if even Asunander was aware of Backman's situation, things must be pretty serious. What were the particulars of the case he had called about?

Chief Inspector Asunander cleared his throat in the long-winded fashion for which only thirty years' assiduous pipe smoking could pave the way, and explained that it concerned a missing person.

Correction, two missing persons.

Then he paused and adjusted his false teeth. They always slipped sideways when he talked too much. It was his job's fault that he had them at all. Barely ten years before, when called out in the course of his duties, he had encountered a pumped-up bodybuilder armed with a baseball bat; the blow hit Asunander squarely in the mouth and he lost twenty-six teeth in half a second, which was quite possibly a world record but also led to a year or more of extensive jaw operations with not very successful outcomes. His dentures simply refused to fit snugly, and the perpetual need to readjust them meant that he often expressed himself as briefly as possible. Particularly if his hands were full and he was obliged to keep his pipe clamped in the corner of his mouth. Sometimes he sounded like an old-fashioned telegram, especially if he had already suffered some slippage. He tended to omit little things if they were not vital for comprehension.

'Odd biz,' he said. 'Only report by phone so far – last night and this morn.'

'I see,' said Gunnar Barbarotti.

'Def time to get over there. Check in more detail. Right now. You take it?'

'Give me fifteen minutes,' said Gunnar Barbarotti. 'I've got a train north at one thirty. A lot of arrangements to cancel if I'm taking it on.'

'Got you,' said the chief inspector. 'Ring me in ten. Merry Chris.'

He had just come off the phone when Sara staggered into the kitchen.

He stared at her. Something was wrong. Her lovely auburn hair looked as if someone had peed in it. Her eyes were glassy and red-rimmed, she was breathing heavily through an open mouth and her full-length nightshirt had taken on the look of a grubby shroud – a sudarium. She stopped, propped against the fridge.

'Dad,' she said feebly.

Gunnar Barbarotti resisted the impulse to rush over to his daughter and lift her in his arms. 'Sara, love,' he said instead. 'What's the matter?'

'I . . . think . . . I'm . . . ill.'

The words found their way singly over her cracked lips and barely had the strength to reach his eardrums.

'Sit down, Sara.'

He pulled out a kitchen chair and she sank into it. He put a hand to her forehead. It was burning hot. She looked at him with an empty gaze and half-closed eyes.

'I don't . . . think . . . I'm up to . . .'

'Have you taken your temperature?'

'No.'

'Sara, go back to bed. I'll bring you a drink and a thermometer. You really don't look well.'

'But Mum . . . and Malmberget . . . ?'

'That's cancelled,' said Gunnar Barbarotti. 'I've got to put in some hours at work as well. We'll stay and have our Christmas here in Kymlinge, you and me.'

'But—'

'No buts. Shall I help you back to bed?'

She got to her feet and swayed, and he held her up by putting one arm round her waist.

'Thanks Dad, but I can walk by myself. Need to pee as well . . . but if you could bring . . . bring me something to drink . . . that would be great.'

'Of course I will, love,' said Gunnar Barbarotti. He fished out two fresh pillows with clean pillowcases. Opened the window to briefly air the room, tucked his daughter up in bed, put two glasses on the bedside table – one of water, the other of cranberry juice – stood over her while she took her temperature, 39.2, and as soon as he could see she had dozed off again, tiptoed gently out of her room.

He made two phone calls.

The first to Chief Inspector Asunander, to agree to take on the two missing person cases.

The second to his ex-wife, to say he was sorry, but something had come up. Sara was in bed with a sky-high temperature and could hardly even stand on her own two feet.

Once that was out of the way, he went over to the living room window and cast a glance up at the greyish-mauve December sky.

'My humble thanks,' he murmured. 'I'll be back in touch in January.'

Then he got out his little black book and made a note.

17

Before setting off to number 4 Allvädersgatan, the point in Kymlinge where by all accounts the disappearances had originated, he dropped in at the station for a briefing from Sorrysen.

Sorrysen was really called Borgsen, Gerald by forename and Norwegian by birth. He had worked in the district for five years and had – as Barbarotti generally put it – a remarkably strong sense of integrity. He was about thirty-five and lived a bit outside town at Vinge with his wife and two children. He never participated in any voluntary activities with his colleagues, never went out with them for a beer; he did not seem to have any particular interests and he almost always – hence the nickname – gave a slightly sorrowful impression.

But he was beyond all question an honest and competent policeman.

The briefing took ten minutes. Sorrysen had written a summary on two pages of A4, and he delivered the whole thing orally as well.

Two people had been reported missing by the same informant, a certain Karl-Erik Hermansson, aged sixty-five, former upper-secondary teacher at Kymlingevik School and very recently retired. The two missing persons were (1) his son Robert Hermansson, aged thirty-five, who had disappeared while on a visit to his parents in Allvädersgatan some time during the night between Monday 19 and Tuesday 20 December and (2) the informant's grandson Henrik Grundt, aged nineteen, who had disappeared at some time during the following night, i.e. between 20 and 21 December. Both Robert and Henrik had been in Kymlinge on the occasion of a double celebration on the twentieth: Karl-Erik Hermansson's sixty-fifth birthday, and his daughter Ebba's fortieth (she being Henrik's mother).

Robert Hermansson was ordinarily resident in Stockholm. Henrik Grundt was officially registered at his parents' home in Sundsvall, but also had a room in student accommodation in Uppsala, where he had just completed his first term of law studies. Or would complete it in January, to be precise, as the exams were held in the new year.

The informant, Karl-Erik Hermansson, could offer absolutely no suggestion about what could have happened to either of the missing persons, nor could he say whether the two disappearances were linked in any way.

A general alert had gone out at ten the previous evening, but no sightings had yet been reported.

One detail, which was not provided by the informant himself but which eventually emerged, was that the first to go missing, Robert Hermansson, was identical with the briefly infamous contestant of the same name in the so-called reality TV series *Prisoners of Koh Fuk*.

'Wanker Rob?' Barbarotti asked.

Sorrysen had refrained from using the term himself, but he nodded in confirmation.

As he left the station, he thought about Asunander's description of the situation: *Odd business.*

The chief inspector was not known for exaggerating, nor had he done so on this occasion, thought Gunnar Barbarotti as he got into his car and set off for Allvädersgatan in the western part of the town.

A double disappearance on the darkest day of the year? Well, 'odd' hardly covered it.

Karl-Erik Hermansson looked pale but collected, his wife Rosemarie pale and torn in several directions. Barbarotti had considered for a moment how strictly he ought to apply the basic rule of always speaking to the informants one at a time, but had decided not to follow it this time.

Not to start with, at any rate. If more thorough questioning proved necessary, he would have to take them individually when the time came. They were sitting in the living room, rather over-furnished to Inspector Barbarotti's mind – with the heterogeneity of styles and colours that bore witness to a long life shared by two residents who were none too troubled by the costly lodestar known as good taste. The suite was of dark brown leather and must date from the seventies, while the cream-coloured, glass-fronted display unit with dimmed lighting was of a considerably later vintage. On the walls hung a motley collection of pictures in frames that sucked the life out of the subject matter, and the wallpaper was pale yellow and blue with a claret-coloured border of floral garlands. On the solid pine table, Rosemarie Hermansson had laid out a spread of coffee, a ginger cake and four sorts of biscuits. The china was white with a blue floral motif and the paper serviettes were a festive red and green, but what the heck, thought Gunnar Barbarotti, he wasn't here to write a feature on interior design.

'Right then, my name is Inspector Barbarotti,' he began. 'I'll be looking after this case, and trying to solve it to everybody's satisfaction.'

'Case?' said Rosemarie Hermansson, dropping some ginger cake in her lap.

'We hope so,' said her husband.

'Let's start by running through the facts,' suggested Gunnar Barbarotti, opening his notebook. 'So you'd gathered the family together for a little party to mark . . . ?'

'To mark the fact that Ebba and I happen to have been born on the same day,' Karl-Erik Hermansson jumped in to explain, adjusting his shiny tie in mottled shades of green. 'They happened to be landmark birthdays for us both this year. I was sixty-five, Ebba forty.'

'Which day?' asked Barbarotti.

'Tuesday the twentieth. The day before yesterday, that is. Well, it was just a modest little family affair. We've never been ones for anything grand or over the top, my wife and I. Have we, Rosemarie?'

'No, yes,' agreed Rosemarie Hermansson.

'So it was our three children and their families. Ten of us in all . . . one of them just eighteen months old, our youngest grandchild. Yes, they all arrived on the Monday, and the party itself was the day after . . . on Tuesday, as I said.'

'But by then, one person was already missing?' asked Barbarotti, sampling his coffee cautiously. To his surprise it was strong and just how he liked it. I'm prejudiced, he thought. At every possible level.

'That's right, yes,' said Karl-Erik Hermansson, nodding thoughtfully. 'Though none of us actually realized the seriousness of it at that point, I'm afraid.'

'Why not?'

'Pardon?'

'Why didn't you realize the seriousness? Had your son . . . it was your son, wasn't it, who disappeared between Monday and Tuesday?'

'Yes, it was Robert,' affirmed Rosemarie Hermansson.

Gunnar Barbarotti gave her an encouraging smile but then turned back to her husband.

'You say none of you saw it as serious. Does that mean Robert had some reason to stay away . . . that you perhaps thought you knew where he had gone?'

'Absolutely not,' insisted Karl-Erik Hermansson. 'This . . . er, this perhaps calls for a little explanation. My son . . . I mean *our* son, of course . . . hasn't been himself recently.'

Interesting way of putting it, thought Gunnar Barbarotti. But fine, if you went and masturbated on television, you were presumably not quite yourself. He noted that Rosemarie Hermansson was shredding her red and green serviette in her lap and he had a distinct sense that she was not far from breaking point.

'I am aware of that television programme,' he said. 'But I didn't see it myself. I don't watch much television at all, in fact. So you saw a link between his disappearance and . . . well, how he was feeling?'

Karl-Erik Hermansson seemed to be hesitating. He glanced at his wife and fingered his tie again. It was silk, unless Gunnar Barbarotti's eyes deceived him. Thai silk, if he were to venture an educated guess. Perhaps he had had it as a present on the big day.

'I don't really know,' said Karl-Erik Hermansson, finally. 'I didn't have time to discuss it with him properly. I was going to, but I didn't get the chance. Things don't always turn out quite as planned . . .'

Once he had said it, he appeared to shrink a little. As if he had admitted something he had not been intending to admit, thought Barbarotti – and that left the space for his wife to say something.

'Robert arrived around seven on Monday evening,' she explained. 'So did the others. We had a bite to eat, nothing very special, and some of them stayed up talking for a while after Karl-Erik and I went to bed . . . and it's like Karl-Erik said, there wasn't really time for any individual conversations that evening.'

'But Robert was one of those who stayed up a bit longer?'

'Yes. I think it was him and Kristina, our daughter. They've . . . well, they've always been close. Ebba and Leif's sons stayed up too, I think.'

'And then Robert vanished?'

Rosemarie exchanged a look with her husband, as if to get his confirmation that she could continue. 'Yes,' she said, shrugging her shoulders dejectedly. 'He apparently went out for a walk and a cigarette. That's what Kristina says, anyway . . .'

'What time was that?'

'About half past twelve, perhaps a bit later.'

'And who was still up at that point, I mean when Robert went out?'

'I think it must just have been Kristina and Henrik. Kristoffer says—'

'Just a moment. Who's Kristoffer?'

'Ebba and Leif's younger son. Well, you'll get a chance to meet them all later . . .'

'I see. So what does Kristoffer say?'

'He says he went up to bed just after half past twelve. And Robert, Kristina and Henrik were still there . . . well, here in the living room.'

Gunnar Barbarotti nodded and jotted something in his notebook.

'And Kristina?'

'They went back to Stockholm yesterday.'

'What time yesterday?'

'Early in the morning.'

'But you discussed Robert's disappearance with her on Tuesday?'

'Yes of course. Though it took us a while to notice he was gone. And it was the big day, as well. People coming round with presents and so on . . .'

'When did you notice he was missing? Robert, that is.'

Mr and Mrs Hermansson looked at each other. Karl-Erik's brow furrowed and then smoothed out again.

'Around lunchtime, maybe . . .'

'At first, we assumed he'd gone out for a walk during the morning,' his wife added. 'It was later in the afternoon that I discovered he hadn't slept in his bed at all.'

Gunnar Barbarotti made some more notes. Drank some more coffee. 'All right,' he said. 'We might have to go into all this in slightly more detail eventually. First I must try to get an overview of what happened.'

'It's incomprehensible,' said Karl-Erik Hermansson with a heavy sigh. 'Completely and utterly incomprehensible.'

Gunnar Barbarotti made no comment, but inside he was starting to feel that this was an interpretation he could certainly subscribe to. At least for the time being.

Completely and utterly incomprehensible.

'I shall talk to the Grundt family afterwards, of course,' he said. 'But first I'd like to hear what you two can tell me about Henrik.'

It took twenty-five minutes for the Hermanssons to tell the inspector about Henrik Grundt and his disappearance. In Gunnar Barbarotti's notebook, however, it amounted to just six lines.

The nineteen-year-old boy had – for some unknown reason – left his bed and his room during the night between Tuesday 20 and Wednesday 21 December. Probably not before 1 a.m. – when his brother Kristoffer, who was sharing the room, went to sleep – and definitely not after 6.15 a.m., when Rosemarie Hermansson got up and would have heard anyone moving around upstairs.

Why? Well, neither his grandmother nor his grandfather had any idea. It would be best to ask the boy's parents and brother about that. For their part, they just felt desperate and very confused.

Inspector Barbarotti said he entirely appreciated their feelings, but they should still not give up hope of a positive outcome. Before rounding off his conversation with Mr and Mrs Hermansson, he asked them if either could see any kind of link between the two strange disappearances.

None at all, they said. On that point, husband and wife were touchingly unanimous.

'My parents have taken this very hard, I hope you understand that.'

Ebba Hermansson Grundt had asked to speak to him alone.

He knew she was a senior surgical consultant, but she was also the sister of one of the missing and the mother of the other. It was rather odd for her to start by referring to her parents.

'I do understand that,' said Gunnar Barbarotti. 'I've just been talking to them.'

'Especially Mum, as I'm sure you noticed. She hasn't slept all night. I tried to get her to take a sleeping pill last night, but she refused . . . she's pretty close to going over the edge. But perhaps you could see that?'

'It's a very normal reaction in situations like this, isn't it?' said Gunnar Barbarotti. 'How are you feeling yourself?'

Ebba Hermansson Grundt sat bolt upright in her chair and breathed in slowly through flared nostrils a few times before answering. As if she had to run a check on herself before she could deliver the correct reply. 'I feel the same,' she said. 'But it would be much worse if I lost control.'

'You're used to keeping it?'

She studied him, perhaps looking for signs of criticism or irony. Evidently, she found none, because she replied: 'I'm not unfeeling, if that's what you think. But for Mum *and* Dad's sake – and for Kristoffer's – I'm trying to hang on to some optimism.'

'And your husband?'

She hesitated for a moment. 'For his sake, too.'

Gunnar Barbarotti nodded. That wasn't really what he had asked. He found himself feeling a bit sorry for the well-balanced, well-toned woman sitting opposite him. She was forty years old, had two children and was a senior consultant. A very onerous job; it must have taken its toll, but even so, his guess would have been more like thirty-five.

'I do understand,' he reiterated. 'But I'm sure you realize I have to subject you to a few questions nonetheless.'

'Go ahead, Chief Inspector.'

'Inspector. I'm only a detective inspector.'

'Sorry.'

'Please don't apologize. Anyway, first of all I'd like to know whether you see any kind of connection between these two disappearances. Is there anything to indicate that they're linked in any way?'

She shook her head. 'I've been thinking about that non-stop for twenty-four hours,' she said, 'but I can't come up with anything. I mean, it's strange enough for one person to go missing, but for . . . well, for both of them to vanish into thin air . . . no, it's utterly incomprehensible.

'Even to me,' she said after a momentary pause. As if things that were incomprehensible to her mother or husband did not necessarily prove incomprehensible to Ebba Hermansson Grundt herself.

In this case, however, they were.

'If you're convinced of that, then I suggest we discuss them one at a time,' said Gunnar Barbarotti, turning the pages of his notebook. 'Robert first, perhaps? What have you got to say about him?'

'What have I got to say about Robert?'

'Yes please.'

'In general, or as regards his disappearance?'

'Both, perhaps?' suggested Gunnar Barbarotti tentatively. 'Can you see any motive he might have had for going off, for example? If we completely exclude your son from considera-tion for now.'

Ebba Hermansson Grundt sat in silence for a few seconds,

but did not seem to be searching for an answer to the question. It was more a case of deciding what she would and would not tell him, guessed Inspector Barbarotti.

'OK,' she said eventually. 'To be completely honest, I thought from the outset that he'd simply gone off to hide.'

'Gone off to hide?'

'Or however you want to put it. Robert's quite a spineless person. If a situation gets too uncomfortable, he might very well run away. You no doubt know what he got up to this autumn?'

'You mean that television programme?'

'Yes. That more or less says it all, doesn't it? He's presumably not been feeling all that great recently, and it wouldn't be particularly surprising if this family get-together was too much for him. Suddenly having to face up to your closest family, and . . . well.'

'You think he's somewhere here in Kymlinge?'

She shrugged. 'I don't know. But his car is still parked outside. He grew up in this town. I'm sure he has a few old acquaintances he could take refuge with.'

'Women?'

'Why not? But this is all speculation. It could be completely wrong. He must realize how terribly he's worrying Mum, and I didn't really expect that of him.'

'Did you talk to him much on Monday night?'

'Scarcely at all. We only had a few hours and it was a full house, so to speak. And besides, my husband and I went to bed fairly early.'

'How did he seem?'

'Robert?'

'Yes.'

She paused before she answered. 'As one might have expected, I suppose. A mixture of arrogance and insecurity. Of course, he has to try to put a brave face on it, but inside he must have been feeling pretty awful. Dad asked us not to mention that wretched programme, and we didn't.'

'But you didn't speak to him alone at any point?'

'No.'

'Did anybody else?'

'I think my sister Kristina did. They've always . . .'

'Yes?'

'They've always been a bit closer than Robert and I have.'

Gunnar Barbarotti wrote *Kristina* on his notepad and underlined it twice.

'Rather too much time has passed,' he said.

'Pardon?'

'You indicated that Robert could possibly have decided to stay away of his own volition. But he disappeared on Monday night. Today's Thursday. Don't you think—'

'I know,' she interrupted. 'And yes, I agree. A few hours or a day, perhaps, but not this long. Something must – something must have happened to him.'

Her voice quavered slightly and he realized this last conclusion could also have implications for her son. He turned a page in his notepad and decided to move on to disappearance number two.

'Henrik,' he said. 'Let's talk about your son for a while instead.'

'Sorry,' said Ebba Hermansson Grundt. 'Just give me two minutes.'

Her voice was far from steady. She got up and hurried out of the room. Gunnar Barbarotti leant back and looked out of the window. A few flakes of snow had begun to fall. From somewhere in the house came the sound of a radio, a news bulletin. But the doors of the living room had been carefully closed; he had no notion of what the other members of the stricken family were doing to help the minutes pass. And the hours. Poor devils, he thought involuntarily. This can't be easy.

Then he poured himself some more coffee and tried to get some glimmer of a sense of the direction this case might be heading in.

None came.

18

'No, I've no idea where Henrik is. Can't even hazard a guess. It defies all reason.'

She was composed again, but he assumed she had been crying. The two minutes had turned into five and her face looked as if she had just washed it.

'Does Henrik know anybody here in Kymlinge besides his grandparents?'

'No.' She shook her head, but no more than a centimetre in each direction. 'None at all. Henrik has only been here seven or eight times in his life, at most. Never for more than a few days. He doesn't know a soul in this town.'

'Can you be sure of that?'

'As sure as it's possible to be.'

'So Henrik is nineteen. He's been studying law at Uppsala for a term. Is that right?'

'Yes.'

'Can you tell me a bit about him?'

'What do you want to know?'

'I just want to get a general picture. Is he conscientious? Calm or nervous? Interests? Do you get on well with each other?'

She swallowed and nodded. Wiped something from the outer corner of her eye with the knuckle of her little finger.

'We've always got on well, Henrik and I. He's conscientious and clever. Things come easily to him . . . whatever they are. Studies, sport, music . . .'

'Friends?'

'Has he got friends, do you mean?'

'Yes.'

'He's got lots of good friends, and he's always been honest with me. I'm – I'm proud of my son, I want you to understand that, Chief Inspector.'

Gunnar Barbarotti didn't bother to correct her. He closed his notebook and put it down beside him on the sofa. He put his pen in his breast pocket and clasped his hands round his right knee. It was a practised gesture for creating intimacy, and as usual he felt a slight sense of shame as he performed it.

'There's one thing I don't really understand,' he said.

'What's that?'

'He must have gone out during the night.'

'Yes, I assume so.'

Something in her eye irritated her again and he gave her time to wipe it away.

'Can you think of any plausible – or at any rate conceivable – reason why your son would have got out of bed and left his room – and the house – in the middle of the night?'

'No, I . . .' she said uncertainly.

'Is he a sleep walker?'

'No. Henrik has never walked in his sleep.'

'Does he have a mobile phone?'

'Yes, of course he's got a mobile. We've been ringing him ever since . . . well, ever since he went missing.'

'No reply?'

'No, no reply. Why are you asking about this? You presumably know it already?'

Gunnar Barbarotti paused briefly. 'I ask because I can see two conceivable alternatives in front of me.'

'Two?'

'Yes, two. Either your son left his room because somebody rang him. Or he had already decided to do it when he went to bed.'

'I . . .'

'Which do you think the most likely?'

She thought for a few seconds.

'I think them both equally unlikely.'

'Can you think of anything else, that is to say, a third alternative?'

She frowned and gave a slow shake of the head. A wider movement this time, but still controlled, as if she was very conscious of what she was doing, even at this level.

'To my mind, there can be only one other explanation,' declared Gunnar Barbarotti, clasping his hand round his left knee for variety.

'And what . . . what could that be?'

'That someone came and abducted him.'

'That's the most idiotic idea I've ever heard,' snorted Ebba Hermansson Grundt. 'How on earth could anyone abduct a grown—'

'All right,' interrupted Barbarotti. 'I just wanted to exclude the possibility. I agree with you that it's unlikely to have happened that way. How were things for him in Uppsala?'

The question seemed to catch her unawares.

'In Uppsala? Fine . . . they were fine. Naturally the first

term at university is a bit overwhelming, but it's like that for everybody.'

'What do you mean by that?'

'By what?'

'I sensed you were hinting something wasn't quite as one might have hoped.'

She looked at him for a second, her mouth fixed in an irritated line. 'No, I wasn't doing that at all,' she said at length. 'But, of course, I don't have insight into everything he may or may not have done in Uppsala. Student life has its ups and downs, that's all I meant to imply. But perhaps you didn't—'

'I spent eight terms at Lund,' Gunnar Barbarotti informed her, and received a swift and slightly surprised glance in return. 'Has he got a girlfriend, Henrik?'

She hesitated again. 'Well, he certainly seems to have met a girl in the course of the term – she's called Jenny. But she's never visited us in Sundsvall, so I don't know how serious it is.'

'Have you ever spoken to her on the phone?'

'Why would I have done that? Henrik only came home twice, all term. Law is a pretty demanding subject, so . . .'

'I know,' said Gunnar Barbarotti. 'I did a law degree myself, in Lund.'

'Did you? And then you . . . joined the police?'

'Exactly,' he remarked. 'And then I joined the police.'

She had no further comment to offer on this, but he could see she was struggling to balance the equation. And if there was one message he had picked up from their conversation so far, it was that Ebba Hermansson Grundt liked equations to balance.

'Do you know whether Henrik received any calls while he was here in Kymlinge?' he asked.

She thought about it and then gave a shrug.

'I can't answer that. I can't remember seeing him on the phone at all. But I didn't have my eye on him very much. Perhaps Kristoffer could tell you. They were sharing a room, after all, so he should have noticed if Henrik rang anybody or received any calls.'

'I will be talking to Kristoffer and your husband about this,' Gunnar Barbarotti assured her. He was silent for a few seconds while he watched a little fly come in to land on the green and red tablecloth, evidently unaware that it was December and that it had woken up far too soon. Or too late.

Then he leant back on the sofa and picked up his notepad again.

'What did he take with him?' he asked.

'Pardon?'

'Have you checked what he took with him when he went off? Outdoor clothes? Toothbrush? Phone?'

'Oh yes, of course, sorry, I didn't understand what you meant. Yes, that's right, his jacket, scarf, gloves and hat are gone. His phone and wallet, too.'

'But his toothbrush is still here?'

'Yes.'

'Was his bed made?'

'No.'

'What do you think that points to?'

'It . . . I suppose it means he intended to come back, of course. Good God, Chief Inspector, it sounds as if you . . . as if you're interrogating me here. I really hadn't expected . . .'

'Do excuse me,' said Gunnar Barbarotti. 'But I'm rather

interested in the conclusions you draw yourself. I mean, you're his mother and you probably know Henrik better than anybody else. It would be arrogant of me if I thought I could be clear on the way things stand before you are. Wouldn't it?'

'I don't think—'

'If I provoke you a bit, you might think of something important, whereas we don't get anywhere if I sit here feeling sorry for you.'

'I see,' she said curtly, but he could tell she agreed with him. Naturally, he thought. Appealing to her maternal feelings and her intellect, he could hardly go wrong.

'So what does it point to?' he repeated.

She gave it due consideration this time. Leant her head a little to one side, and he suddenly remembered that a Finnish skier whose name he had forgotten used to do the same in the closing phase of races.

'I understand what you're saying,' she resumed. 'He went off because he had some reason to do so, that has to be it. Possibly he was going to meet someone . . . someone who rang him, perhaps.'

'It doesn't happen to be the case that this girl . . .' He had to leaf back through his notepad. '. . . Jenny. That she happens to live somewhere in these parts?'

He could see the thought had never occurred to her. 'Jenny?' she exclaimed. 'No, I think . . . I have the idea she comes from Karlskoga. And why should she . . . ?'

'I agree it sounds a bit far-fetched,' agreed Gunnar Barbarotti. 'But it needn't necessarily have been her. It could have been some fellow student, for example. When I was studying in Lund, we came from literally all over Sweden.'

'Hmm,' said Ebba Hermansson Grundt, looking suddenly quite critical. 'No, I have to say I don't buy this.'

Nor me, Gunnar Barbarotti thought gloomily. Nor me. But the question is what to buy otherwise.

He conducted his conversation with Leif and Kristoffer Grundt straight after their wife and mother had left the room, and afterwards he asked himself if he should have taken a little break and a breath of fresh air first. Neither of them had much to add to what he had already learnt from the three previous informants, but after more than two hours on the sofa in the Hermanssons' house, he was starting to lose focus a little. If there were things to detect between, or beneath, the words that were actually spoken, he was far from certain that he would be capable of picking them up.

At least his powers were not so blunted that he could not see his powers were blunted, and with that small comfort in mind, he decided to let it go.

Anyway, he thought it most unlikely that Leif Grundt was keeping anything to himself that could shed light on the situation. He was a big, powerful man who came across completely differently from his wife and exuded a kind of phlegmatism – or good-naturedness, at any rate. But perhaps that was a conscious ploy: a strategy and modus vivendi. He assumed it was of no significance for the disappearance, but still found himself wondering about the respective roles and balance of power in the Grundt family. It seemed beyond all doubt that the mother, Ebba, was the one in control of things.

How would he deal with a woman like Ebba himself, thought the inspector, then shook his head, aware of having strayed beyond the bounds of relevance.

Kristoffer turned out to be a fairly quiet boy. He was four-teen, and Barbarotti could sense that he had grown up largely in the shadow of his brother, five years his senior. Henrik was plainly one of those richly gifted young people who succeeded at everything they did, that had been made unmistakably clear to him – whereas Kristoffer seemed to be, well, what? Certainly not a youngster going astray, but an extremely average fourteen-year-old.

He had shared a room with Henrik during the stay at their grandparents' house; Gunnar Barbarotti had been upstairs to see it, a cramped little galley with two beds, a chest of drawers and wallpaper so revolting that he wondered whether people who hung that sort of thing on their walls could really be in full possession of their faculties.

On the subject of his brother's disappearance, Kristoffer had little to add. He had fallen asleep just after half past twelve on the night in question, and at that point Henrik was still lying in his bed. He hadn't noticed him get up and leave the room, he hadn't heard a phone ring; when he got up the next morning he had assumed his brother had woken first and was in the bathroom or down in the kitchen.

No, he couldn't remember Henrik speaking on his mobile at any time in their Kymlinge visit. He might have sent a text or two, but he couldn't even swear to that.

They had chatted a bit, of course, but not a great deal. A bit about what it was like being in Uppsala, a bit about Uncle Robert, but nothing had been said to offer any kind of clue about the disappearance. Either of them.

Barbarotti got a general sense that father and son enjoyed a good and easy-going relationship; the boy was tense of course, but as far as he could judge, this had nothing to do with his father's presence during the conversation. But he still decided, as they were talking, that he ought to have a session with Kristoffer on his own in the next day or two, for another, slightly more probing interview.

Partly because of the weariness he had detected in himself, partly because it couldn't hurt.

Unless, of course, things resolved themselves happily soon. Leif announced that they had no intention of going back up to Sundsvall until Henrik turned up.

Just in case anyone was imagining otherwise.

By the time Gunnar Barbarotti was standing in the hall with all five family members in front of him, it was half past five and he was searching in vain for something optimistic – or comforting, at least – to say as he left, but here, too, his own fatigue, exacerbated by an impending headache, threw a spanner in the works. All he could think of was:

'We'll keep on working on this and see how things go.'

Well, he thought in the car on the way home, I certainly didn't promise too much there.

Sara didn't seem any better. She was asleep in bed when Gunnar Barbarotti peeped cautiously into her room; she was breathing heavily and wheezily through her open mouth, and for a moment he felt terror grip him.

What if this were the price? God had heard his prayer, but demanded a sacrifice: his daughter's life. It was all some malevolent Old Testament story.

He held on tight to the door frame, watching her and feeling his headache grow into a pulsating cloud under the top of his skull. I'm insane, he thought. I've got to stop playing with the higher powers; this sort of bargaining just isn't on, talk about hubris.

But before anything else . . . before anything else I've got to get a couple of paracetamol down me before my head splits open.

His time with the Hermansson family had sent his spirits to a really low ebb, there was no doubt about it. The flat smelt dank and dirty. There was a sickroom stuffiness in Sara's bedroom and the kitchen was littered with dirty dishes. He hadn't done any food shopping or thought about checking in with a doctor. In Barbarotti's world, you took to your bed if you got ill. Slept yourself better and had plenty of fluids. That was all. But what if it was more serious than that, what if she needed some kind of medicine? What sort of father was he?

He went over and sat down on the edge of the bed. He pushed back his daughter's matted hair where it was plastered to her face, and laid his hand on her forehead.

Sticky, as he already knew. But not as hot as this morning, he reckoned. She opened her eyes, looked at him for a moment and then closed them again.

'How are you?' he asked.

'Tired,' she whispered.

'Well, you just sleep, love,' he said. 'Have you had plenty to drink?'

He had put two fresh glasses beside her bed before he left around two – water and grape juice – and she had drunk about half of each. She moved her head slightly, perhaps giving a sort of nod.

'I'll just pop and get some shopping from the Co-op. Be back in half an hour. Is that OK?'

Another head movement. He stroked her cheek clumsily and left her.

Simple domestic chores – with the emphasis naturally on

looking after a sick daughter – kept him occupied for the rest of the evening. He found some candleholders and lit candles here and there, he played Mercedes Sosa over and over on the CD player; there weren't many albums in the flat that they both liked, but Mercedes Sosa was one of them. He made an omelette with steamed vegetables, and Sara took two mouthfuls and said it was lovely. He took her temperature, which had gone down to 38.5. He asked about her symptoms and she said her throat hurt. She felt sort of weak and achy. Just wanted to sleep.

He let her do so, once he had changed the bed and aired the place a little. Then he left the door of her room ajar, creating at least the illusion of being together – but as to that warm cocoon of settling in as darkness descends, and quietly anticipating Christmas with a bit of making and wrapping and some nuts and home-made toffee, they came nowhere near. Not remotely near. That was partly because the ingredients were lacking, of course: not just the nuts and the toffee but also the wherewithal to make and wrap. And anyone with the enthusiasm for that sort of activity; some things were simply better from a distance and in the imagination.

But Mercedes Sosa and the candlelight did what they could. And the paracetamol had worked; his headache was gone. At around nine, Helena rang from up in Malmberget and reported a little tartly (but not as tartly as he had expected) that they were missed but that everyone was fine; the snow was two metres deep, it was minus twenty-five and her father seemed to be taking the situation in his stride. Gunnar Barbarotti had a word with each of his sons, five minutes each, and was told that Granny had made a gingerbread house that was as wonky as anything, and that they were going to ski down Dundret Mountain tomorrow. He said he was sorry he couldn't be with them but they would get their presents at New Year instead of Christmas.

After the call, he checked to see how things were with Sara. She was sleeping like a log. He took a beer out of the fridge and sat down at the kitchen table. He started reading through the notes of his conversations with the Hermansson family, and tried to visualize what had actually happened.

It really wasn't easy. Two people had vanished without trace from the same address at an interval of around twenty-four hours. None of those he had talked to had any idea where they could be.

In the middle of the night, they had gone off somewhere. To the same place, perhaps? Could that be it?

He found it hard to believe. All the information he had received seemed to point to Robert Hermansson and Henrik Grundt having very little to do with each other. They happened to be related, that was all; uncle and nephew, but none of the other family members were able to recall them so much as talking to one another on the Monday night, while they were still at the house in Allvädersgatan.

Though both had sat up late, he reminded himself. If he had understood correctly, a quartet of them had stayed up longer, after the others retired for the night. Siblings Robert and Kristina, and siblings Kristoffer and Henrik Grundt. Then Robert Hermansson had gone out for a smoke and vanished.

And the next night, Henrik Grundt had left his bed and vanished.

That was how it appeared.

Why? Gunnar Barbarotti shook his head in frustration and

took a gulp of beer. It was a peculiar case all right. He felt there weren't even any sensible questions to be asked.

But hopefully, he thought, hopefully it would be possible to sketch out a plan of action, even so . . . How he would set about trying to get somewhere with all this.

The missing persons alert was the first possibility, of course – an action that had already been taken; their pictures would be in the paper tomorrow and perhaps some insomniac local would have seen something. A glimpse of one or the other on their way to something as yet unknown in Kymlinge.

It wasn't entirely impossible, at any rate. One could always hope. But what would he himself, lead investigator Barbarotti – and thus far the only police officer (except perhaps Sorrysen) involved – do next?

Loyal to his notebook and his usual procedures, Gunnar Barbarotti started drawing up a list.

Ten minutes later he had come up with four points, all of which could be tackled the following day.

1) Make phone contact with those present at Allväders-gatan who had not yet been questioned: Jakob Willnius and Kristina Hermansson. Especially the latter. Decide poss. time to meet in person at a later date.

2) People Robert Hermansson knows in Kymlinge? Which old friends might he still be in touch with? Talk to them.

3) Interview Kristoffer Grundt again. If there's anyone keeping quiet about something (consciously or unconsciously), it has to be him. The brothers shared a room and must have talked to each other quite a lot.

4) Look into mobile phone traffic.

That was it. And Sorrysen had presumably already started work on point four. Mobile phone traffic was Sorrysen's area, that had become standard practice for some reason, but of course he would have to check his colleague was shouldering the task in this case, too.

Because both Robert Hermansson and Henrik Grundt were equipped with mobiles. Naturally. Gunnar Barbarotti had read somewhere that there were more mobiles than people in the country. Fifteen years ago, there were more wolves than mobiles. It was what it was, there was a time for everything.

He drank up his beer and checked the time. Twenty past ten. He got a clean tea towel out of the cupboard, wet it under cold running water, went in to see Sara and wiped her face with it. She woke with a start.

'Dad, whatever are you doing?'

'I'm helping my dear daughter with her evening ablutions,' he explained kindly.

'Oh my God,' she groaned. 'Give me some water to drink, don't throw it in my face.'

'How are you feeling?'

'Tired,' said Sara. 'I had a dream about you.'

'What?' said Gunnar Barbarotti. 'Haven't you got anything better to dream about?'

'Not at the moment,' said Sara. 'But it wasn't very nice. You went out to buy something, and then you disappeared. I don't like the idea of you disappearing.'

'But I'm sitting right here,' said Gunnar Barbarotti.

'I can see that,' said Sara with a wan smile. 'And I'm grateful. And I'd be even more grateful if you brought me that water and let me get back to sleep.'

'Right away, love,' replied Gunnar Barbarotti. 'Right away.'

19

The day before Christmas Eve, heavy snow fell on Kymlinge and surrounding areas.

Gunnar Barbarotti woke early and looked out of the bedroom window in amazement at a landscape that could just as easily have been Malmberget. Or Murmansk. A thick layer of white snow beneath a grey-black sky. Between the two, a whirl of movement. But still a sort of deathly stillness.

He got up to fetch the newspaper from the hall. Popped his head round Sara's door and saw that she was asleep and had drunk a whole glass of water and half her grape juice. He got himself a bowl of yogurt and a glass of juice from the kitchen and snuggled back into bed. He started to leaf through the newspaper.

The piece about Robert Hermansson and Henrik Grundt was on page six. Two columns, with photos of both the men who had disappeared. The headline was short and sweet: **MISSING**.

There was only a single line about one of them having appeared in the not unfamiliar television series *Prisoners of Koh Fuk*, and the piece said the police had no suspicions as yet that foul play lay behind either of the disappearances.

Gunnar Barbarotti had not spoken to any journalists himself, and he wondered who had. Sorrysen or Asunander, presumably. And he wondered how long it would take for the tabloid evening newspapers to get hold of the story. Not very long, if they adopted their usual working methods. And then the headline would not stop at **MISSING**, he felt pretty certain of that. Mrs Hermansson in particular had tried insistently to enlist his help on this, but of course he had not been able to offer her any guarantees. The whole point of going to the press was to get the public involved, and if the public got involved, it was naturally impossible to exclude the tabloid press.

Impossible, and perhaps not entirely desirable either, he had tried to explain. Normally, that was. However you looked at it, it was difficult not to allow that the mass media per se had a certain right to exist. For better or worse.

So Gunnar Barbarotti had said. Mrs Hermansson had had to concede, and her husband had done the same, and Barbarotti hoped that at any rate those wretched reality TV commentators in the royal capital would not use the same epithet for Robert as they had done last time he was on the agenda. He also hoped they would consider themselves above having to come out to the sticks the day before Christmas Eve. Seeing as they now had vintage Christmas TV presenter Arne Weise and the whole holiday viewing schedule to analyse.

But he knew full well it was no more than a pious hope. Come to that, hadn't Arne Weise retired a few years ago? Or died? In some areas, Inspector Barbarotti was aware that he was painfully out-of-date. More wolf than mobile phone, you might say.

He finished reading the paper and started planning his day. What should he do? He looked through the list he had written the night before, and decided to postpone his return visit to Allvädersgatan until the afternoon. Better to give them a little time and try to establish contact with the sister in Stockholm, to whom he had not yet spoken. And ring the station to assure himself they weren't forgetting to let him know if any tip-offs came in. They ought to be well aware of that anyway, of course, but you never knew. If it was Jonsson on phone duty, there could be a delay of hours or even days, he knew from experience. Particularly with Christmas and suchlike in the offing.

He got through to Sorrysen. No, no tip-offs had come in yet. Not even from old Hörtnagel, who was notorious for phoning in, whatever the subject. During that Soviet submarine scare in Hårsfjärden he had rung in several times to report periscopes in the River Kymlinge, and whenever there was an escaped prisoner on the loose anywhere in the land, Hörtnagel would generally have spotted him. He was Austrian and considered himself to have a considerably better overview of things than could be expected from simple Swedes with sluggish old peasant blood in their veins.

'Maybe he died this autumn?' suggested Gunnar Barbarotti. It was on the tip of his tongue to ask whether Sorrysen might also know if Arne Weise was still alive, but he kept it to himself.

'I don't think so,' said Sorrysen, keeping his voice flat. 'He had his eighty-seventh birthday last week, and I saw him on skis in the town park an hour ago.'

Barbarotti looked out of the window again. Perhaps going out for a ski wouldn't be a bad idea for me, either, he thought. All that oxygen in the air and so on. 'It would be good to know straight away, if anything does come in,' he said.

Sorrysen promised to see to it. He also promised to deal with the mobile phone traffic, having, as expected, already noted both the relevant numbers, and they ended the call. Gunnar Barbarotti stayed in bed a while longer and tried to remember whether he still owned a pair of skis these days, but he came to no conclusion. He assumed they'd disappeared at the time of his separation from Helena. Along with so much else.

He got up and went into the shower. It was high time to get started on his day's work.

'Kristina Hermansson?'

'Yes.'

'My name is Gunnar Barbarotti. I'm a detective inspector in Kymlinge.'

'I see.'

'It's about your brother and nephew going missing. Have you got time to talk at the moment?'

'Yes . . . yes of course.'

She sounded muted and mournful. Her voice was quite faint and he assumed she was talking on a cordless handset quite a long way from its base unit. Or perhaps it was just that his own ears had had enough. News of his faraway Italian father was that he had been stone deaf for the past five years, so perhaps his son was also predisposed that way.

'I'll need to see you in person, too, for a more thorough talk. You and your husband. Is there a convenient time in the next few days?'

'Of course. We're spending Christmas here in Stockholm. How do you want . . . ?'

'Let's come back to that. But for now, I've got a few questions that you might be able to help me with.'

He could hear her drinking something. Or maybe it was just interference from the meanders of his own ear canals.

'Of course. I naturally want to do all I can to – to help shed light on this. It's truly awful, I don't understand what could have happened. Have you any idea where they've gone?'

'Not at the moment,' said Gunnar Barbarotti.

'No. I spoke to Mum late last night. She told me you came round, sir, and talked to . . . er, all the others.'

'No need to be formal, if you don't want to.'

'Sorry. Well yes, good.'

He thought he could detect that she was not far from tears.

'If we start with Monday night,' he suggested. 'I understand you sat up talking to the two missing persons after the others had gone to bed. Is that correct?'

'Yes, that's right. It was me, Robert and Henrik . . . and Kristoffer. The others went to bed a bit earlier.'

'Your husband?'

'Jakob took Kelvin – he's our son – back to the hotel.'

'You were staying at Kymlinge Hotel?

'Yes. There wasn't room for us all at Mum and Dad's. We opted to stay at the hotel to make things easier.'

'Yes, I know about that,' said Gunnar Barbarotti. 'But you decided to stay and talk to your brother and nephews, rather than going back to the hotel.'

'Yes.'

He wondered briefly whether it would be worth digging a bit deeper on this point. Had Kristina and her husband fallen out? Possibly, but he decided to postpone the question until he met her face to face.

'I see,' he said. 'And why did you stay?'

'Because I wanted to talk to them, of course. It was a long time since I'd seen Robert or Henrik . . . or Kristoffer.'

'And what did you talk about?'

'All sorts of things. The sort of things family members talk about when they meet after a long break, I suppose.'

'Such as?'

'Pardon?'

'Can you give me any examples of those topics of conversation?'

I'm going in too hard, he thought. Why does it always turn into a cross-examination when I've been going for a few minutes? She isn't suspected of anything; I'm only trying to get information out of her.

'Well . . .' She hesitated. 'We talked about various things. You know about Robert, I assume . . . that television programme he was on?'

'I know about that,' Gunnar Barbarotti confirmed.

'He was in a pretty bad state, actually. We talked about that quite a lot, just the two of us. We've always been pretty close, Robert and I. He felt ashamed, of course, but he had a bit too much to drink, I suppose he was trying to take the edge off the anxiety . . . well, you know?'

'Was Robert drunk that evening?'

'No, not drunk. Well, you might say he was tipsy.'

'What time was it when he went out?'

'He said he was going out for a cigarette and a walk. I think it was just after half past twelve.'

'And that was the last you saw of him?'

'Yes.'

'And he was a bit drunk.'

'Yes, OK, he was a bit drunk.'

'What had you all been drinking?'

'Beer and wine with the meal. A bit of whisky . . .'

'Were you drunk, too?'

'No, not particularly.'

'But a touch?'

'Yes, perhaps. Is that illegal?'

'Not at all. But you're the one who talked to Robert most. You were outside for a while, just you and him, so your mother told me. What did you talk about then?'

She paused before she answered.

'He was . . . well, he was pretty down. He'd been a bit rude to Mum, as well.'

'Rude? In what way?'

'It was nothing really. He was tactless, that's all. There was a sort of agreement that nobody would say anything about him overstepping the mark in that TV programme, and he thought it felt weird, everybody pretending nothing had happened. He said something a bit coarse.'

'And you talked to him about that when you were outside, just the two of you?'

'Yes.'

'Told him to calm down?'

'No, it was . . . it was nothing as serious as that. But I felt sorry for him. Felt he needed a bit of a chat.'

Gunnar Barbarotti pondered. He reflected that while the telephone was a very practical device in many ways, it also concealed a good deal. Of the person you were talking to. He wished he were sitting at a cafe table with Kristina Hermansson instead.

'Ah,' he said. 'Is there anything in whatever you and Robert talked about that could offer any hint of where he's gone?'

There was a deep intake of breath, followed by a heavy sigh. The telephone was able to convey that much, at any rate.

'No,' she said. 'I've been going over every single word we said, for three or four days now, and there's nothing, believe me, not a thing, to . . . well, to shed any light on what's happened. I'm devastated about this, you – you have to understand that . . . both of them . . . Robert and Henrik . . . it . . . it's . . .'

She started to cry.

'I'm sorry.' She was gone for a short while. Gunnar Barbarotti stared out at the falling snow and thought of nothing. Or possibly of wolves. There was something about wolves and snow that went together, somehow.

She was back. 'I'm sorry. I find – I find it so hard to deal with this. So there's nothing new to report, then?'

'I'm afraid not. But we were called in rather late. Robert disappeared on Monday night, and you didn't contact the police until Wednesday evening, by which time a second person had gone missing. What made you wait so long?'

'I don't know. I suppose everybody thought Robert . . . well, that he was deliberately staying away. That he'd gone round to see someone he used to know in Kymlinge, and decided he just couldn't face the family get-together. That would be . . . understandable, at the very least.'

'And you thought that, too?'

'I guess so.'

'Do you know of any old acquaintances of Robert's in Kymlinge?'

'No, I don't. Mum and I talked about it, but neither of us

could come up with any likely candidates . . . and it's been almost four whole days now.'

'We shall be looking into all this more closely,' Gunnar Barbarotti promised. 'But as you say, why should he stay away so long?'

'I don't know,' replied Kristina Hermansson with a sob. 'I really don't know.'

'If we move on to Henrik, your nephew,' he hastened to say, to divert her from another descent into tears. 'What did the two of you talk about?'

'All sorts of things.'

Brilliant answer, he thought.

'Such as?'

'What leaving home felt like, amongst other things. Henrik's started a course in Uppsala, you know – we talked about student life and that sort of stuff.'

'Do you have a good relationship with your nephews?'

'Yes, I think so. We've always liked each other.'

'Do you include Kristoffer in that?'

'Of course.'

'But it was mostly Henrik you were talking to?'

'Well, Kristoffer went up to bed at . . . er, about quarter to one, it must have been.'

'So that left just you and Henrik?'

'Yes, though we can't have stayed chatting for more than another fifteen minutes. Then I went back to the hotel.'

'But you were talking to Henrik on his own for fifteen minutes?'

'Roughly that. I didn't look at the time, but it wasn't all that long.'

'Right. And you didn't talk about anything in particular during that time?'

'No . . . his studies . . . a few old memories. When he and Kristoffer were little . . . that sort of thing.'

'Thank you. So this was on Monday. How about Tuesday, did you talk to Henrik much?'

'Hardly at all. That was the actual birthday – Dad and Ebba's big day – no, I don't think I exchanged many words with Henrik, actually.'

'How was he?'

'Pardon?'

'How was Henrik? Was he happy? Fed up?'

'He was fine, I think. He thought it was nice to get away from home – seemed to like it in Uppsala.'

'Did he mention a girlfriend?'

'No, I don't think so. Ebba, my sister, said something about a girl called Jenny, but I'm pretty sure he didn't mention her. Maybe it wasn't particularly serious.'

'But he wasn't depressed?'

'Depressed? No, I don't think so. Earnest . . . he was earnest, but he always has been. Why are you asking whether—'

'And he didn't say anything that could explain why he's gone missing?'

'No.'

'Or tell you about any special plans?'

She gave another sigh.

'Oh please, I've thought about this day and night. If anything had occurred to me, I would have told you right away. But it's as incomprehensible to me as to everybody else. I've scarcely slept a wink for two nights now, and—'

'When did you and your husband go back to Stockholm?'

'What? When did we . . . er, we went back on Wednesday. First thing, my husband had to get to a meeting, so we left about eight.'

'And at that point you didn't know Henrik was missing?'

'No, we didn't. Mum rang just after lunch to tell me. I couldn't believe it was true.'

Hmm, thought Gunnar Barbarotti, that was an opinion with which he could certainly concur. It really was a bit difficult to believe this whole thing was true.

'Well, thank you very much for this information,' he said. 'But I would still like to meet you in person. And talk to your husband as well. When do you think that might be possible?'

They batted dates and times to and fro for a while, and then agreed on the third day of Christmas. Tuesday.

Unless there had been any developments by then, of course; he was careful to underline that.

He had asked for a list of Robert Hermansson's potential contacts in Kymlinge, and when he got back to Allvädersgatan just after two o'clock, Rosemarie Hermansson had one ready.

It comprised four names.

> Inga Jörgensen
> Rolf-Gunnar Edelvik
> Hans Pettersson
> Kerstin Wallander

The two women were former girlfriends, the two men former schoolmates, explained Mrs Hermansson. But they all still lived in the town, so if you think there's any point, Inspector . . . ?

He didn't, not really, but he said nothing on that score, only that they would naturally look into the matter. To help him further in his quest, she gave him a class list out of a school catalogue from Robert's time at upper secondary, so there was nothing for it but to start sorting through and weeding out.

He took both lists and put them in his briefcase. He realized he already had tasks enough to occupy two or three colleagues for two to three weeks, if it came to it, but decided to refer the matter to Asunander. It was not up to Gunnar Barbarotti to decide on workload distribution. He thanked Mrs Hermansson and asked to speak to Kristoffer Grundt. One or two questions had come up as a result of yesterday's conversations, and he didn't want to miss anything.

It was important not to miss anything, Rosemarie Hermansson agreed. Would they mind being upstairs? A friend of hers had dropped round and the Grundts were still with them, so they would probably prefer to be somewhere quieter.

Of course, Gunnar Barbarotti assured her. Upstairs would be fine.

Kristoffer Grundt looked like a normal fourteen-year-old today, too. Not that Gunnar Barbarotti was entirely sure how normality manifested itself at that age. Not just at the moment, anyway; it was some years since his time with the police youth task force, and his daughter had turned eighteen. But still. He had read somewhere that fourteen was the most moral of all ages, the time in your life when you could most clearly see what was right and wrong – not that you necessarily acted accordingly, but you had the clear-sightedness. Subsequently, the older you grew, the more obscure things got. They became muddier and harder to determine.

Don't believe a damn word of it, thought Gunnar Barbarotti, his eyes on the bony youth sitting opposite him.

'How are you doing?' he asked.

'I didn't sleep very well,' said Kristoffer Grundt.

'I can imagine,' said Gunnar Barbarotti. 'You don't much like it here in Kymlinge, do you?'

'Not much,' admitted Kristoffer Grundt. 'But as long as Henrik turns up, then . . .'

'We'll do what we can,' promised Gunnar Barbarotti. 'That's why I need to ask you a couple more things. About Henrik, that is. Never mind your uncle for now.'

'Sure,' said Kristoffer.

He's not stupid, thought Gunnar Barbarotti. I must remember that. 'Well, the way I see it is this,' he said. 'When all is said and done, your brother must have left here of his own volition on Tuesday night. We don't think anyone came and abducted him. So, what's your take on it, did some idea just pop into his head and make him plunge off into the dark?'

Kristoffer thought for a moment.

'No,' he said. 'I don't think that, of course.'

'So he must have been planning to go,' went on Gunnar Barbarotti. 'Or he got a phone call from somebody, asking him to go somewhere.'

'We talked about this yesterday, though.'

'I know. But things sometimes occur to people afterwards, too. Are you sure you didn't hear the phone after you went to sleep on Tuesday night?'

'I didn't hear a thing.'

'Even in your sleep, a sound like that can . . . find its way through, so to speak.'

'Oh? Yes, but I don't remember hearing anything.'

'Would you recognize Henrik's ringtone?'

Kristoffer Grundt thought about it.

'No, I don't think I would, actually. I know what he had at

home in Sundsvall, but he's probably changed . . . and he's got a new phone, too.'

'And you've never heard his mobile ring?'

'Oh yes, hang on, it did ring once on the way here . . . Mum and Dad haven't brought their mobiles, but Granddad – or Granny – rang him once. But I don't remember the ringtone.'

'Quite a standard one, then?'

'Yes.'

'Not one of those with horses neighing or a church organ or anything like that?'

'No, I would have remembered it in that case.'

'All right. We'll leave that there for now. Let's imagine instead that Henrik knows he's planning to go out during the night. Maybe he's lying there waiting for you to drop off. Do you follow me?'

'Yes.'

'What I've been asking myself is why you didn't know about it.'

'What? Why would he have said anything to me?'

'I didn't say he must have said something to you. But you should have noticed something.'

'Why?'

'Because you were sharing the same room. You must have been with each other almost all the time. You must have talked a lot . . . so, I think you really ought to have something to give me.'

'But I haven't anything to give you.'

'I don't mean you knew about it in advance. But if you think back, was there really nothing Henrik said or did that might give us some hint of what his plans were?'

'No.'

'Not even some tiny detail?'

'No.'

'Have you been thinking about this?'

'I've thought about it a lot.'

'Did he mention the name of anyone here in Kymlinge?'

'No.'

'Are you aware of him knowing anyone here except your grandparents?'

'I don't think he knows a soul. Why would he? We've hardly ever been here. I don't know anybody.'

Gunnar Barbarotti paused briefly. He felt a fleeting sense of powerlessness and it left its mark on his soul. 'But there has to be something,' he said with slow emphasis. 'I'm sure you agree with me on that? Henrik must have had some sort of plan, and I find it odd that you didn't notice a single little thing . . . You do understand, don't you, that all I'm looking for is some tiny hunch.'

He waited another few seconds to give the boy a chance to confirm his suppositions. But Kristoffer just looked down and bit his lip.

'Something that might sound wholly insignificant when one first hears it, but that might in retrospect turn out to contain a crucial lead. You understand what I'm talking about, don't you?'

Kristoffer Grundt nodded. Then he slumped over the table slightly, his empty eyes staring straight ahead. Gunnar Barbarotti leant back and observed him. The most moral of all ages, he wondered again. Either we'll get something here, or we won't.

'Of course I understand what you're talking about,' said

Kristoffer Grundt finally. 'But I still can't think of a single thing.'

So that was that, thought Inspector Barbarotti with a tired sigh.

20

The Christmas bank holidays came and went.

Sara gradually improved. Father and daughter spent Christmas Eve largely in front of the television. The presenter had changed gender and skin colour and was called Blossom. Sara had a comfortable bed on the sofa, while he nested in the armchair or dashed out to the kitchen and back with little treats to keep hunger from the door. Sushi. Black olives. Blinis with sour cream and caviar. He had bought it all in half an hour at the deli stalls in the indoor market, and he periodically offered up grateful thoughts to the existent God while trying to imagine what was being consumed up in Malmberget. He had experienced it once and felt nauseous at the very memory of gnawing on a pig's trotter for half an hour. After the ritual watching of the Disney cartoons he rang to wish them a Happy Christmas, and heard that Martin had hurt his wrist skiing on Dundret that morning in temperatures of minus twenty-two, but that everything was OK otherwise.

Apart from that, they read the books they'd had for Christmas presents. For Sara that meant Moa Martinson and Kafka, hand in hand in some inscrutable fashion; some school project must presumably be behind it, but he didn't enquire. And for him, just what he had asked for: *Train* by Pete Dexter.

The missing persons case was at a standstill. On the surface, at least. Both evening tabloids had covered the story, but in some merciful way it managed to drown in the general Christmas excess. Or perhaps the reality televisionites had such a short half-life that they were forgotten after two months. Was that a blessing to quietly pray for, wondered Gunnar Barbarotti. He had been in touch with Allvädersgatan and had been told that a couple of journalists had rung, and a photographer had been outside, apparently taking shots of the house, but that was all.

He hadn't discovered anything else useful. The Grundt family stayed on and spent Christmas in the parental home; it would have felt wrong in every way to go up to Sundsvall without Henrik, his mother declared. But sooner or later, if there was still nothing happening, they would of course be obliged to take that step as well.

Gunnar Barbarotti said he thought they were sensible to stay on for now, and offered his assurances that the police were mobilizing all available resources to get to the bottom of what had happened.

That was a modified version of the truth, of course. What was actually happening was that they were waiting for tip-offs from Detective General Public and for telephone-traffic data from the mobile phone operators – Christmas had apparently held up that detail too; it was generally quicker – and that Sorrysen, assisted by Lindström and Hegel, was busily going through the lists of conceivable acquaintances of Robert Hermansson. Late on the afternoon of Christmas Day, Gunnar Barbarotti received a report on progress with the latter, and it was as unambiguous as it was negative. None of the thirteen people interviewed to date (the four labelled 'close' plus nine from the class list – all still living in the locality and proving easy to contact) had had any idea Robert had been visiting Kymlinge. That was what they claimed, at any rate, and Sorrysen said he hadn't the slightest reason to doubt their statements.

So that was that. Gunnar Barbarotti also asked Rosemarie Hermansson if they had said anything at all about Robert and Henrik coming to stay in the run-up to Christmas – told any non-family members, that was to say. She conferred briefly with her husband and then came back on the line to say neither she nor Karl-Erik had advertised their plans widely. Certainly not. But people naturally came to know about them anyway, somehow.

At school, for example. She assumed. News always tended to float up to the surface there, sooner or later. Bad news especially.

But had they kept a low profile where Robert was concerned, Gunnar Barbarotti wanted to know. Yes, admitted Mrs Hermansson, they had kept a low profile with Robert.

He thanked her and rang off. He didn't feel he had learnt anything, but he was used to that. He took the remaining piece of sushi and went back to Pete Dexter.

On Boxing Day, Sara felt well enough to get dressed, clean her room and go out for a walk with a friend, and Gunnar Barbarotti decided to give Eva Backman a call. His colleague had now had four whole days in the bosom of her family and might be in need of a change. Even if she had not been exposed to a constant diet of unihockey.

An hour and a cup of coffee at the Stork, for example? There was a case on which he'd be very glad of Backman's opinion.

Eva Backman accepted immediately. Willy and the kids

were off to the cinema anyway, she said, so she needn't even feel guilty. Gunnar Barbarotti couldn't decide whether she was lying or not, but his need to talk to somebody with a bit of sense about the events at Alllvädersgatan was so pressing that he pushed aside any misgivings.

They sat over their coffee for an hour and three quarters at Cafe Stork. He laid out the facts of the case and Inspector Backman listened with her hands folded and her eyelids characteristically half-closed; they had been working together for almost eight years now and he knew this did not mean his colleague had fallen asleep. On the contrary, the hazy look in her eyes meant she was paying very close attention.

'Freaky as hell,' she said when he had finished.

'You reckon?' said Gunnar Barbarotti.

'Yeah. It's the weirdest thing I've ever heard. Any ideas?'

'Gunnar Barbarotti shook his head. 'That's the trouble. I haven't any ideas.'

'None at all?'

'None at all.'

Eva Backman applied herself for a while to collecting crumbs from the cake plate with a dampened forefinger. 'How do they seem?'

'Who?'

'The family. The whole gang. I mean, you get the sense . . .'
She stopped short.

'What is it you get the sense of, Eva?'

Eva Backman said nothing but took out a cigarette packet.

'You've started smoking again?'

'No, that's a misconception. I just look at the packet for a while, and anyway, you can't smoke indoors any more and I've no intention of going out into the gale on that balcony.'

'Sorry. Well, what was it you got a sense of?'

'It's like this,' said Eva Backman, lowering her voice and leaning across the table. 'If we find a woman murdered, we check whether she was married. If it turns out she is, we bring in the husband. In eight cases out of ten, he did it. Don't look in your neighbour's garden when you can smell the rat in your own. It's all in the family. That's all I'm saying.'

'Do you think I'm an idiot?' said Gunnar Barbarotti. 'Do you think this hasn't occurred to me?'

'Good, but I was a bit worried.' She leant back, took a cigarette out of the packet and sniffed it.

'Hmm,' said Barbarotti.

'Looking and smelling,' said Eva Backman. 'That's not harmful. What were you saying?'

'I can't really remember,' said Barbarotti with slight irritation. 'But I think I was trying to explain that it's a bit hard to sew this together into a family matter.'

'Why?'

'Would Rosemarie Hermansson kill her own son and grandson and bury them out in the garage, is that what you're trying to say? She's a retired needlework teacher, for heaven's sake, Eva. Needlework teachers don't go around murdering their nearest and dearest.'

'She taught German, too. I had her for two years.'

'That doesn't make a scrap of bloody difference. Focus now, or you'll have to pay for your own coffee.'

'All right,' said Eva Backman, putting away her cigarettes. 'But I didn't say Mrs Hermansson was behind this. I just pointed out that it could be worthwhile trying to unpick these family relationships a bit. That's not worth arguing about, now is it?'

Barbarotti gave a snort.

'Do you seriously think one of the others abducted Robert *and* Henrik? If so, why? How?'

Eva Backman shrugged. 'OK, I don't know,' she admitted. 'Just trying to be a bit constructive. What do *you* think, then?'

Gunnar Barbarotti sighed and threw up his hands in resignation. 'I told you. I don't think anything.'

'Oh?' said Eva Backman, and for a moment a gentle look came into her eyes, as if she wanted to console him. It was soon gone. 'But you've at least got a plan of action, I suppose? Even when we don't know what to do, we have to come up with something. Otherwise we just get dozy and lethargic.'

'It's always so uplifting to talk to you,' said Gunnar Barbarotti. 'But yes, of course I've got a plan of action.'

'Mhm?'

'Does that mean you want to hear what it is?'

'I'm sitting here, aren't I? Well?'

'The sister. Kristina.'

'Got you.'

'I'm off to Stockholm tomorrow. Robert's flat, too, I thought.'

'Good.'

'Well, it can't hurt to take a look. Erm, and then I'll go on to Uppsala and try to make my entrée into student life.'

'Bound to be lots going on in student life between Christmas and New Year,' said Eva Backman with an indulgent smile.

'Bound to be. I'm really looking forward to it.'

'Thanks for the coffee,' said Eva Backman. 'Well, have a good trip.'

'Haven't been to Stockholm for a year,' said Gunnar Barbarotti.

The detached house where Kristina Hermansson lived with her husband and son was in Musseronvägen in Old Enskede. It was a big old wooden villa, built in the 1920s or 1930s at a guess, thought Gunnar Barbarotti, and probably worth five million or more. A rapid calculation told him that his own flat in Kymlinge would fit beneath the rust-red tiles of the mansard roof five times.

The husband, Jakob Willnius, still wasn't home, but ought to be there within the hour, Kristina Hermansson informed him. He had asked to have a word with him as well, and the man had had no objection. Their son Kelvin was three houses along the street, with the childminder he shared with various other children, but as he was not yet two, Gunnar Barbarotti decided to forego the questions in his case.

They sat down in a large, glazed verandah with infrared heating, looking out over the garden. Kristina Hermansson was around thirty, with dark brown hair in a pageboy cut and, he thought, attractive. He couldn't ever aspire to a wife and a set-up like this, he noted soberly. He had never come anywhere near, and he wondered why this lower-class perspective was presenting itself just now; he was not in the habit of falling into emotional trenches, but there was something about the blue dusk falling swiftly over the old fruit trees out there in the garden, about the creak of the basket chairs, about the exquisite, delicate cups she served the tea in – Meissen china, if he was not mistaken – that made him feel like a country bumpkin.

'Here you are,' she said. 'Maybe I should have made you a sandwich, too, but . . .'

He shook his head. 'I had something on the train, it's fine.'

'. . . it's really taken it out of me, all that's happened. It feels so unreal.'

She rubbed a little mark off the table with her thumb; it was an unconscious gesture, but it suddenly struck him that Kristina Hermansson was actually as much of a fish out of water in this setting as he was. The difference was that she had had a few years to get used to it.

'You've got a beautiful home,' he said. 'How long have you lived here?'

She calculated. 'Four years . . . yes, it'll be four years in April, in fact.'

'Can you tell me about Henrik and Robert?'

'Yes . . . what do you want to know?'

He clasped his hands and regarded her gravely. 'Anything at all that you feel might be important,' he said.

She sipped her tea but said nothing.

'There must be a reason for their disappearance,' he elaborated. 'Possibly there are two reasons, entirely different, but it's too early to make any judgement on that yet. I'm not particularly keen on coincidences. There's an explanation – or it could be two – and if I knew what they were thinking and how they were feeling in the hours before they went missing, well, then presumably I'd also comprehend where they've gone. Or at least have a vague idea. Do you see?'

She nodded.

'Of the people who were there at your parents' house, you must be the one who was closest to Robert. That's my impression, anyway. Do you agree?'

'I . . . yes, you're right,' she said, sitting up a little straighter. 'We've always liked each other, Robert and I. I know most people consider him an idiot, but I don't care about that. He is as he is, but it's always worked between the two of us, somehow. He lived here with us for a while, actually.'

'Oh?'

'Yes. He came home after a few years in Australia and needed somewhere to crash. It was just for a few months.'

'And Henrik?'

'What?'

'What sort of relationship did you have with Henrik?'

'I've always liked him, too. Him and Kristoffer. There was a period of a few years when I would step in as a kind of reserve mum for them occasionally; my sister has a capacity for devoting a bit too much of her time to her job. Though of course we haven't seen that much of each other recently.'

'And what are relations like between Robert and Henrik?'

She thought about it, but only for a moment. 'Non-existent. No, I don't think they've ever been at all close. Are you asking this because you imagine there could be a link between . . . well, their disappearances?'

'What do *you* think?'

'No,' she said, without hesitation. 'I don't believe there's any link. Though that just means two mysteries instead of one, so I don't really know . . .'

'Let's try to confine ourselves to observations rather than speculation,' he suggested. 'And let's start with Monday evening – you stayed up talking to Robert and Henrik, isn't that so?'

'Yes, that's right.'

'And you went outside and had a serious talk to Robert after he insulted your mother?'

'I don't know that we . . . well yes, we did, of course.'

'What did the two of you say, exactly?'

'Not that much. He said he felt awful and almost couldn't bear being in the house. Said he felt ashamed. I told him to pull himself together and try to play along. It's worked before. I asked him if he had any plans for the future, and he said he thought he'd go away somewhere and finish writing his novel.'

'His novel?'

'Robert's had this novel on the go for . . . well, I don't really know when the project started. Ten years ago, perhaps. I suppose he thought it would be a convenient time for sitting alone in some corner of the world and getting the book finished.'

'I see. He never said anything about taking his own life?'

She shook her head. 'No, he didn't. I've wondered about that, of course, but I don't think he was suicidal . . . or is. He's not the type, although one can never know. But he's been through quite a lot, Robert, and I don't remember him ever talking along those lines. Or being afraid that he might do it. He knows . . .'

'Yes?'

She gave a laugh. 'I think he knows I'd be absolutely furious with him if he took the coward's way out. That I'd come and haunt him in the kingdom of the dead and hold him to account and so on.'

'Your mother said she thought he'd been in therapy after that TV business. Do you know if that's correct?'

'I think he went to see a psychologist a few times.'

'You don't happen to have his or her name?'

'No, sorry.'

Gunnar Barbarotti nodded. 'And Henrik?'

'You mean was Henrik . . . was Henrik likely to take his own life?'

'Yes.'

'No, why should he be? Of course, I've thought about that, too, but it seems totally absurd. If Robert or Henrik – or both – had killed themselves, why haven't they been found? Bodies can't vanish into thin air, can they?'

'A person could jump into Kymlinge River,' suggested Gunnar Barbarotti tentatively. 'But we haven't started dragging it yet. We think we need some kind of reason first. So what I'd like to know now, if you don't mind, is what you and Henrik talked about on Monday evening. And how he seemed. Have you thought any more about it since our phone call?'

'I've done little else,' said Kristina Hermansson. 'But I'm getting nowhere. Like I said, we mostly talked about things we remembered from when he and Kristoffer were younger; I was with them quite a lot back then. A bit about how he was finding Uppsala, too, but not that much . . . and, er, he might have mentioned a girl, I think her name's Jenny, but I didn't get the impression it was anything very serious. I'm – I'm sorry, but I can't invent things that don't exist.'

'And on the Tuesday?'

'We didn't talk much on Tuesday. And never just the two of us on our own. It was Dad and Ebba's big day, lots going on, and loads of people there all the time. I didn't really think about Henrik very much – though he did sing for us at dinner. He's got a lovely voice, Henrik.'

'What time did you and your husband go back to the hotel, roughly? You all went together that evening, didn't you?'

'Yes, we did. It must have been soon after half past eleven.'

'Did you say goodbye to Henrik?'

'Yes – yes, of course I did.'

'And you didn't notice anything in particular?'

'About Henrik?'

'Yes.'

'No, why would I have? There was nothing unusual about him. We were all busy talking about where Robert had got to, of course. We'd sort of ignored it during dinner, so as not to spoil things for Dad and Ebba. But once we left the table we started discussing where he could be. I think Mum was the most anxious.'

'And how about you?'

'Well of course I wondered. But like I said, I thought he'd bottled out, basically. Found some old friend, and I expected him to turn up the next day.'

'I see. And then you went to the hotel and the next morning you all drove up to Stockholm?'

'Yes. We'd vaguely planned to drop in at Mum and Dad's for breakfast, but it turned out Jakob had to get back for a meeting around twelve o'clock, so we had to leave earlier.'

'And when did you find out Henrik had gone missing?'

'Not until we got home. Mum rang and told us . . . that is, she said they didn't know where he was. It didn't sound all that serious to start with . . .'

'But Robert was still missing. Surely they must have . . . ?'

'Yes, yes of course. Mum was pretty shaken, but I think she was trying to act more calmly than she actually felt.'

'But it wasn't until Wednesday evening that your father contacted the police. Can you explain why he waited so long?'

'Yes,' sighed Kristina Hermansson. 'I'm afraid there's a very simple explanation. It hit Dad terribly hard, that business with Robert and the television programme. He really didn't want Robert in the spotlight again. I think the others had a job persuading him to ring at all.'

'Ah, I see,' said Gunnar Barbarotti. 'Yes, well, perhaps that doesn't sound so odd, in the circumstances.'

He shifted in the basket chair. Drank some tea. Although, he thought, that just makes the rest of it seem all the more peculiar. I'm getting no further forward with this.

Not a centimetre.

His conversation with Jakob Willnius took half an hour. He stayed put in the same basket chair and looked out of the same mullioned window. Jakob Willnius had a glass of white wine, while Barbarotti stuck to the tea.

The pickings were sparse. Very sparse. Television producer Willnius confirmed his wife's account of what had happened during their stay in Kymlinge on every point, and as expected he had no insight whatsoever into the characters of the two missing individuals. He had never even met Henrik before – and had scarcely exchanged more than ten words with him on this occasion. As for Robert, he had had him to stay in the house for a month or so, a couple of years ago, but they hadn't really got into any deep conversations, Jakob Willnius explained with an apologetic shrug of the shoulders. Robert was Kristina's *raison d'être*, not his.

Gunnar Barbarotti reflected for a moment on his use of that particular French phrase – misuse, actually, in Barbarotti's opinion – but he didn't query it. It was some kind of class marker, he presumed. On the whole, Jakob Willnius came across as calm, urbane and well-balanced; he had married into the Hermansson family, and while this did not fill him with great joy, he at least seemed to have peace of mind enough to take it with equanimity.

And why shouldn't he, wondered Gunnar Barbarotti when he had taken leave of the couple and was on his way to the underground station. Considering he had got himself a wife like Kristina.

As for Gunnar Barbarotti, he had stayed away from women entirely after his divorce from Helena. Until a month ago, that was. Her name was Charlotte and she was a fellow police officer; he had met her at a conference in Gothenburg. They both had a bit too much to drink and then got good value out of each other in her hotel room for most of the night.

The problem was, she was married. To another policeman. They lived in Falkenberg and had two children aged ten and seven. She had informed him of this the following morning, over breakfast; but after all, he had had the chance to ask her about it the night before, and had not done so.

They hadn't met since, but they had spoken on the phone a couple of times. She sounded as embarrassed as he felt, and they had agreed not to have any more to do with each other for the time being. But to be in touch towards the summer, possibly. Gunnar Barbarotti didn't really know how he felt about the situation – nor what state Charlotte's marriage was in – but his heart was racing throughout the two phone calls, and the night in Gothenburg had without a doubt been his most memorable for a number of years.

But getting off with a colleague's wife, even if you didn't know him, was definitely not a thing to be proud of, and he was relieved they had put a lid on it for now. Yet the sense of regret and the faint sweetness of unspoken hope were not to be sniffed at, either.

Robert Hermansson's flat was in a block dating from the 1930s, in Inedalsgatan in the Kungsholmen area. Fourth floor; a brass plate on the door said Renstierna, but there was a handwritten scrap of paper with the name Hermansson above the letter box. Gunnar Barbarotti spent an hour poking around two small rooms plus an even smaller kitchen, looking for any indication of what might have befallen the missing tenant. A PC Rasmussen from the Stockholm force kept him company, mainly by going outside to smoke on the diminutive balcony overlooking the inner courtyard.

When they left the flat and locked the door behind them – with the assistance of a rather grumpy caretaker – Gunnar Barbarotti had two items in his briefcase. One was an address book he had found behind a packet of spaghetti and a teapot on a kitchen shelf, and the other a kind of notepad that was beside the phone on the bedside table in the bedroom. Both the impounded objects contained a mess of scribbled names and telephone numbers, and he did not look forward to sitting down and starting to go through them. Barbarotti had come across the manuscript of the novel he had been told about – *Man Without Dog* seemed to be its working title – in two piles on a cluttered desk. He had glanced at it and decided to leave it in peace for the time being. Six hundred and fifty pages were six hundred and fifty pages, when all was said and done . . .

It was quarter to seven by the time he was back in his room at Hotel Terminus, and once he had called home to check Sara was all right, he decided to work for exactly two hours, not a minute more. Then he would cross Vasagatan, have two dark beers at the pub in the central railway station, and digest the day's impressions.

And that was exactly what he did.

21

While Barbarotti was having breakfast, Sorrysen rang.

'He made a call in the night.'

'Who?'

'We've got the mobile phone records. Robert Hermansson made a call at 01.51 on Monday night.'

'Who to?'

'We don't know.'

'Of course you know. I mean, the number must be—'

'He rang another pay-as-you-go mobile. We've got the number but we don't know who it belongs to. You know how it is.'

'Damn.'

'You could say that.'

'And Henrik? Henrik had a mobile too, didn't he?'

'We haven't got those records in yet. It's a different operator. I expect they'll turn up during the day.'

'Fine,' said Gunnar Barbarotti. 'So, Robert Hermansson made a call in the middle of the night, before he vanished. Now we know. Anything else?'

'Not for the moment,' said Gerald Borgsen.

Hmm, he thought, slipping his mobile back in his jacket pocket. What conclusions can we draw from that, then?

None at all, that was the fact of the matter. Hypotheses,

then? Well, possibly. There was one very plausible guess, at any rate: Robert Hermansson had decided to pay somebody in Kymlinge a visit. He had rung up the person in question – in the middle of the night – and asked if it was all right to come round. And then . . . ?

Well then he had either gone there, or gone somewhere else. Take your pick.

But on the other hand, continued Barbarotti, sharp as a knife in his deduction work as he decapitated his four-minute egg in one well-aimed swipe, on the other hand, he could just as well have rung up a former girlfriend in Stockholm. Why not? Just for a chat and to wish her Merry Christmas while he happened to be rather the worse for drink. Was it possible to localize the recipient of the call as well, nowadays? Roughly, at any rate? Or did that only apply to outgoing calls?

It was only quarter to nine in the morning, but he could already feel the weariness creeping over him. Not physical fatigue; he would happily have run eight or ten kilometres – twelve if he were beside the sea – but a sort of persistent, hopeless pressure, a state that was hard to describe. A feeling of . . . well, of inadequacy in the face of a superior force. The villain of the piece was the flow of information, he was quite clear on that point. The condition of the modern age was the fact that you suddenly found yourself with any amount of data – potential and actual information by the ton. That was the way with modern police work; it was not a matter of hunting down information, that most readily captured of prey – what mattered was being able to sift through it.

They could, for example, talk to all the seventy-seven or one hundred and eleven people Henrik Grundt had called or been called by in the past two months, once they had his phone records in their hands. They could interview all his fellow students and all his teachers in the faculty of law, they could widen it out to the student-club choir and his old circle from upper secondary in Sundsvall and then send the whole lot to *Guinness World Records*, thought Barbarotti gloomily. 'The world's largest and least successful police investigation', huh, there was plenty of competition for that title, no doubt. As for Henrik's uncle Robert, Barbarotti had spent three hours last night (one of them on his return from the pub) poring over the scrawls on the man's notepad, trying to sort out what wasn't important; the problem was that there was no method for that kind of weeding out, or none that worked particularly well, anyway, for the simple reason that he didn't know what he was looking for.

And if he put the work into the hands of others, they wouldn't know what they were looking for, either. He remembered having read somewhere about this sort of information overload in the old East Germany. With one in four citizens being a Stasi informer, and each informer's foremost task being to inform, they simply received such a volume of reports that they scarcely had time to skim through them, let alone read them in depth and evaluate the content.

Never mind acting on it.

And how was he to know which phone number or hastily scribbled name was crucial for the case? Or which of the 172 ink-shitting young lawyers up in Uppsala actually had their fingers on any pulses? It was just like with new technology: the haystacks grew and grew, but the needles didn't get a millimetre bigger. Why not go and check out Robert's fellow contestants on the reality TV show, for that matter? Perhaps the whole thing was some kind of grudge match originating on Koh Fuk? That would be worth a headline or two in due course, if he was right.

Another variant was that Robert Hermansson had simply wearied of all the attention and other crap, and had gone to ground with some old flame. Was lying low somewhere. Considering the overall situation – and bearing in mind that his nephew had also gone missing, and in the latter's case without having any particular cause to lie low – this solution did not seem altogether plausible. But even so, he could feel the haystack weighing on him. Or haystacks, plural, if he was looking for two needles.

Backman had a good model, he remembered. First you decided what to do. Then you did it. If that didn't solve the case, you had to decide on another step to take.

Backman's as smart as a killer whale, thought Gunnar Barbarotti. I'll go and get myself another cup of coffee, I think, so at least I stay awake.

He did achieve one thing that afternoon, as it turned out. He located the psychologist whom Robert Hermansson seemed to have consulted after his breakdown on *Fucking Island*. His name was Eugen Sventander, he had consulting rooms in Skånegatan in the Söder part of the city, and his recorded message informed callers he was away for Christmas and New Year and would be back on 9 January. Sventander was one of a group of psychologists and therapists at various addresses in Stockholm who were specialists in this field: taking on burnt-out reality TV participants and building them back up into viable citizens again. They usually managed it in six to eight months, with two sessions a week, reducing to one towards the end; quite often it was the relevant television channel that paid for the treatment.

Satisfied with this clear and unambiguous briefing from one of Sventander's colleagues in the group, Gunnar Barbarotti got on the train and continued north to Uppsala. Henrik's accommodation was in the student housing area of Rackar-berget, known as the Triangle. It contained five rooms, each with its own toilet and shower. There was a communal kitchen, decorated with a Che Guevara poster, a semi-naked black woman and a dartboard. Gunnar Barbarotti asked himself if there had been any progress at all since he sat drinking warm beer out of a can in student accommodation in Lund, twenty-five years earlier.

The girl who let him in was called Linda Markovic and one of the rooms was hers. She was small and slender. She was studying maths, and her parents lived in Uppsala, but she preferred to spend the time between Christmas and New Year in her own little place in the Triangle. She had to study and for that she needed peace and quiet. The occupants of the other four rooms weren't there, she told him, and they wouldn't be back for a few days.

She asked if he wanted coffee. He accepted, and sat down at the kitchen table with its indestructible laminated top, probably originating in the same era as Señor Guevara.

'Henrik,' he started. 'As I said, it's about Henrik Grundt. The reason I'm here is that he seems to have disappeared.'

'Disappeared? There's only instant. Is that OK?'

'That's OK. Your rooms are wall to wall with each other, aren't they?'

'Yes. I've been here three terms. Henrik's is a sublet; it's almost impossible to get your own room when you're a fresher. Anyway, he moved in here in September.'

'Do you know him well?'

She shook her head. She had a strange, old-fashioned hairstyle, he thought. Short, dark brown corkscrew curls, and cut short at the back of her neck. Or maybe he was the old-fashioned one, that was always a possibility. She poured hot water into two purple mugs, pushed the instant coffee across to him and opened a packet of Singoalla biscuits.

'Not much to offer you, I'm afraid,' she explained. 'But I hardly suppose you've come here expecting a slap-up meal.'

'Correct,' he said. 'So you don't know Henrik all that well, then?'

'No,' she said, taking a biscuit. 'I can't really say I do. We don't socialize very much at all in this flat; they do vary. We see each other at breakfast time, and over tea in the evening. That's it.'

'But you have chatted to him a bit?'

She shrugged. 'Yes, of course.'

'What impression do you get of him?'

'Fine, I'd say. Not cocky like some of the guys can be – no, he seems reliable, I'd say. Calm. What's he got himself into?'

'We don't know yet. All we know is that he's missing.'

'How can . . . I mean, he's just vanished?'

'Yes.'

'Sounds horrible.'

'Yes. Though some people choose to disappear, of course. Or to stay away for some reason. That's precisely what I've got to try to find out.'

'About Henrik . . . ?'

She stopped herself and looked at him in slight confusion. He met her eye and had no trouble interpreting her look.

'I can see what you're thinking. Yes, some do kill themselves as well. There's nothing to indicate Henrik's done that, but one never knows.'

'I can't imagine he would . . .'

She left the sentence unfinished. Gunnar Barbarotti tried his coffee and burnt his top lip.

'Is there anyone in the flat Henrik has a bit more to do with?'

Another shake of the head. Her corkscrews danced. 'No. He and Per went out to the same student club together at the start of term, but it was only the once. Per . . . Per's a bloody pest. When he's drunk, I should say, which he is from time to time.'

'Has Henrik got a girlfriend?'

'In Uppsala?'

'Yes. Or anywhere else?'

'Shouldn't think so.'

'What does that mean?'

'That I don't think he's got a girlfriend, of course.'

Gunnar Barbarotti thought quickly and decided to rely on his intuition.

'I got the feeling it meant something else.'

'I don't follow. What do you mean?'

But he could see she was flushing. She tried to hide it by biting into another biscuit, and suddenly seemed nervous. She had hinted at something, and now she wasn't prepared to back herself up. What in hell's name? thought Gunnar Barbarotti.

'Linda, I'm pretty used to reading what people say and don't say,' he said slowly, trying to nail her with his look. 'And what they say without really being aware of it. When you said, "I shouldn't think so", you were really saying something else as well, weren't you?'

A bit pompous, he thought, but she fell for it. She hesitated for a second or two, bit her lip and tugged at one of her corkscrews.

'I only meant I wouldn't be surprised if Henrik's gay.'

'Oh yes?'

'But that's only my own private guess, remember that. I've never asked any of the others and it doesn't bother me a bit. Sometimes you just get that impression, that's all . . . well, I expect you know?'

He nodded.

'Not one of those really camp gays, of course, and I could be totally wrong. It's not something I've thought much about.'

'I understand,' said Gunnar Barbarotti. 'Does he often have friends round – or fellow students – male or female?'

She thought about it. 'I think they came round for a study session a few times. Four or five of them, all law students, er, two boys and two girls, I'd say.'

'Does he go out partying much?'

'No. He goes to the student club now and then, I guess – the Norrland club, in his case. I think he sings in their choir as well. And Jonte's cafe, of course, all the law students hang out there. But I've never seen him really drunk, he's pretty moderate, actually.'

'Which can't be said for everybody?'

'No, it can't be said for everybody.'

Barbarotti leant back. Homosexual? He hadn't heard that from anyone else.

'Jenny?' he asked. 'Have you met any friend of Henrik's called Jenny?'

'Never.'

'Sure?'

'If I have, we've never been introduced. But one girl in three seems to be called Jenny these days.'

'All right,' said Gunnar Barbarotti. 'That'll probably do for the moment. You've got spare keys to each other's rooms, you said? Could you possibly let me into his?'

She seemed unsure. 'Have you got permission for this?' she said. 'Shouldn't you show me that in writing first?'

He nodded and took out the search warrant. She glanced at it, got up and opened one of the drawers by the cooker. And suddenly, as she bent over momentarily, he saw a breast and a nipple. Her maroon top was cut low under the arms and within it her right breast was hard to ignore.

'We had these keys cut voluntarily,' she said. 'Except Ersan; he doesn't trust anyone, but then nor would I if I had his background.'

Gunnar Barbarotti swallowed and accepted a key. He decided not to go into where Ersan came from. 'Thanks for the coffee,' he said instead. 'I won't disturb you any more. I'll let you know when I'm through.'

'That's quite OK,' said Linda Markovic. 'There are thirteen days to go to the exams, I've got all the time in the world.'

'I remember what it was like,' said Gunnar Barbarotti, realizing he didn't envy her in the slightest.

But that breast refused to leave his retina of its own volition.

He spent the afternoon and evening meeting a choir leader, a cousin of Leif Grundt's and a study adviser in the law faculty. The choir leader was called Kenneth and was able to contribute his verdict on Henrik's baritone. It was very fine, he maintained, although in the choir he was merely one amongst many, of course, but with the right sort of ambition, he could certainly develop into a soloist.

A Jenny? No, none that he had heard of.

The cousin was called Berit, and Henrik had stayed with her for the first two weeks of term, before he found the room in Karlsrogatan. They had met only once since Henrik moved out, but her impression was that he was an extremely conscientious and pleasant young man.

Jenny? No, she didn't know anything about any girls.

The study adviser was called Gertzén, and knew that Henrik was registered at, and studying in, his faculty. He knew no more than that, but there were a lot of students to keep track of, and it could be difficult, especially at the beginning, to have an opinion on each and every one.

Jenny? Inspector Barbarotti didn't even bother to ask the question.

It was 8.30 by the time he retired to Hotel Hörnan in its attractive position beside the frozen Fyris River, which still had a small patch of open water to which the ducks were flocking. He could see them from his window, and a little further to the north he could glimpse the multi-screen cinema and the Norrland student club, where Henrik had apparently taken his first faltering steps in student life. Where he had sung in the choir, and where he had potentially also . . . no, Barbarotti was tired of speculating. He looked back to the ducks down in the black water and wondered whether he felt more dejected, or less, than he had done this morning, travelling up on the train to this grove of Academe.

Hard to decide. Henrik's room had not yielded much, anyway. No letters. No notes. Not even an address book; he belonged to the young and rational generation, which entered all its important data into its mobile phones or computers. He had not got into the computer – a PC that looked very new and flashy – and the mobile was presumably in the same place as its owner.

That was to say, *location unknown*. There had not been anything compromising in the room at all. No erotic literature on the shelves (not even a porn mag) to offer a clue to the occupant's sexual preferences. It had all been neat and tidy, just as he had expected. He felt he ought to be getting to know Henrik Grundt a bit by now. Always the same impression: well-behaved, quiet and careful. The idea of his potential homosexuality had, up to now, only found nourishment in a young female student's very private and extremely vague observations; the fact that Gunnar Barbarotti could not really let the thought of it go was presumably first and foremost because there was not much else to which said thought could be attached.

He closed the heavy curtains and switched on his mobile, which had been off during his last interview of the day, with study advisor Gertzén. It was still in his hand when there was a bleep to announce that he had voicemail messages to retrieve.

Well one, at any rate. It was from Sorrysen. He said Henrik Grundt's mobile phone records had come in that afternoon, and there were a few things of interest. If Barbarotti happened to hear this before nine, he could ring him at home.

He checked the time. It was five to.

'Don't say a word, I know. Henrik called the same number as Robert, exactly twenty-four hours later?'

'Not exactly,' said Sorrysen. 'No, Henrik didn't ring anyone on either the Monday or the Tuesday. And he only received one call – from his grandparents when the Grundts were on

their way down from Sundsvall. But there was some SMS traffic that might be of interest.'

'I'm all ears,' said Gunnar Barbarotti.

'Nothing that bears directly on him running away, mind.
The last one he received came at 22.35 on the Tuesday evening; the last he sent was ten minutes later. Same number.
Apart from that, he had a total of seven text messages over
the four days, even on Christmas Eve, but didn't answer any
of them. The texts have been deleted, unfortunately, they're
only stored for seventy-two hours max, but still.'

'I see,' said Gunnar Barbarotti, suddenly feeling something
cold and disquieting turn a page inside him. It wasn't hard to
paint the picture behind the information Sorrysen had just
delivered. And a pretty dark one it was.

'From the same number?'

'Five of them.'

'And is it the same one as—'

'Yes. If we just look at the past week, that is from the seven-
teenth of December up to and including the twenty-fourth,
the same number sent twenty-two texts and Henrik answered
fourteen times.'

'And?'

'What's your own view?'

It was so rare for Sorrysen to go in for this sort of dramatic
tension that he didn't know what to think.

'Pay-as-you-go cards can't be traced?' he said automatically.

'Wrong,' said Sorrysen. 'We've got the subscriber's name.'

'Excellent,' said Gunnar Barbarotti. 'Out with it then, or do
you want me to kiss you first? In which case, it'll have to wait
until the day after tomorrow.'

It was a stupid comment, but Sorrysen received it as if it were a poor second serve.

'The name is Jens Lindewall. The address is 5 Prästgårdsgatan, in Uppsala, if you happen to be passing.'

'Well I'll be . . . wait, can you say that again so I can write it down?'

'I'll text it to you,' said Sorrysen. 'Then you'll have the number, too. Bye then.'

Well I'll be damned, Gunnar Barbarotti completed his unfinished response inside his head. Sometimes things *do* fall into place, one mustn't forget that.

The text containing Jens Lindewall's details arrived a minute later, and it took him another five to decide what to do. In that short space of time he wondered above all whether to ring Eva Backman to talk it over with her just a bit, but he quickly realized that he knew very well what advice his colleague would offer him.

And almost as quickly, he decided he ought to follow that advice.

He pulled the curtains back before he rang the number. The sky was that mauve shade you get with snow, and the ducks down on the river looked frozen into the ice.

He let it ring six times. Then once more, with that unmistakable little drop in tone. Then the voicemail message.

'*Hi, you're through to Jens. I've gone to Borneo, leaving this tyrant of a mobile phone in a desk drawer. I'm back on 12 January. I wish everybody a really Happy New Year. If you want to wish me one back, you can do it after the beep. Bye.*'

No thank you, my friend, thought Gunnar Barbarotti furiously, and switched it off. But you bloody well make sure you get yourself back here pronto, or we'll set the Bornean cops on you, and they're no laughing matter!

He pulled the curtains shut for a second time and regretted having promised to remain prayer-less for three more days.

And as he put out the light, the image of Linda Markovic's breast reappeared. It's pitiful, thought Gunnar Barbarotti. My love life is at such a low ebb I'm reduced to dreaming of split-second nipples on student girls I don't even know.

And God claims He exists?

TWO

JANUARY

22

Gunnar Barbarotti did not like flying.

Charter flights were the worst of all, and domestic flights weren't far behind. But when the domestic schedules couldn't cope with their routes, they were almost worse than the charter flights. If you bought a package holiday to Fuerteventura, you could be pretty sure of landing in Fuerteventura eventually. If you took a domestic flight they could turf you out anywhere. Depending on circumstances. Apparently.

Like now. He had left home hours before dawn cracked, boarded a plane from Gothenburg Landvetter and landed at Stockholm Arlanda fifty minutes late, around nine. He had been re-booked onto a later plane to Sundsvall – because his original one had already flapped off – and finally touched down at Östersund airport on the island of Frösön at quarter past one, because of fog at Midlanda airport between Sundsvall and Härnösand. He had seen it for himself through the cabin window; it was a dazzling winter's day throughout Sweden, except above this badly placed runway, which the weather gods had swathed in fog as thick as semolina pudding.

But he had not prayed to Our Lord for a safe landing, so there was no question of any plus or minus points on the existence scale.

From Östersund he was sent on a two-and-a-half hour

coach ride to Sundsvall, and when he got out at the bus station in this metropolis of Medelpad – in the very middle of Sweden, according to local lore – it was exactly 4 p.m. His total delay amounted to four hours and fifty-five minutes.

But never mind; if nothing else untoward occurred, he still had an hour for his talk with Kristoffer Grundt, after which he would have to take a taxi in order to catch the last flight back down to Stockholm.

So things had not quite reached the point of throwing up his hands or writing indignantly to the newspapers, and on the other side of the street, outside the 7-Eleven convenience store – just as they had finally arranged, making allowances for all the delays – young Mr Grundt was shifting nervously from one foot to the other in the slushy snow. For the first time in ages, Gunnar Barbarotti had a sense that something might be about to happen in this Sisyphean task, as Eva Backman had started calling the whole wretched business. Not a break-through. Not the hope of a prompt and definitive solution, that would be asking too much – but perhaps a small step in something that possibly, eventually and without any pretensions, might be perceived as the right direction.

That little opening.

He didn't know how many working hours had been spent, but he knew that all the sweat and toil had hitherto produced no results. Nothing had emerged to shed light on what had happened to Robert Hermansson and Henrik Grundt, who had had the bad taste and poor judgement to vanish from 4 Allvädersgatan in Kymlinge in the middle of all the Christmas bustle. Three weeks had now passed, and Gunnar Barbarotti and his colleagues were all too aware of the old police rule of thumb that the cases you solve are solved in the first few days after the crime.

Or not at all.

And nobody was in any doubt that what lay behind the course of events in Allvädersgatan must be some sort of crime. Neither Barbarotti nor Backman nor Sorrysen. This was the troika that was in charge of the investigation, taking collaborative decisions, giving collective orders and then checking all the empty hooks on the lines they had speculatively cast out – and being called in at regular intervals to Chief Inspector Asunander on the second floor, to account for themselves.

Asunander's rheumy eyes had started to yellow and glare more and more since they had passed the year's end and entered January. Put at its simplest – if one did not mind stooping to broad generalizations – it meant that in a less civilized and less regulated society he would have preferred to throw all three of them to the wolves and replace them with police officers with a bit more gumption and brainpower. Come up with a suggestion yourself then, bigmouth, was Backman's usual response. Just for bloody once, come up with something constructive, you impotent, deskbound buffoon!

She did not deliver these tips in open court, but wisely kept them as something to chew on over the beers that two thirds of the troika, from force of habit and congenital disposition, but never more than once or twice a week, would consume in moderation at the Elk on Norra torg, at the end of a hard working day. That leopard won't change his spots, was Barbarotti's usual riposte. Or lay a golden egg. That fellow's got a wasteland between his ears, and his internal landscape is as sterile as . . . well, as a wasteland.

And that would make Backman laugh.

And after all, their efforts had not been entirely without result. Not really as unfruitful as the chief desk inspector's inner domains. There were some dead ends that had taken them a little further than the rest.

The mobile phone jungle, for a start. Here they had already found their way to Jens Lindewall, with whom they had admittedly not yet been able to establish contact, he having opted to spend Christmas and New Year in another jungle – in the Sabah province of Borneo – but tomorrow morning he and his plane would drop in at Arlanda, and even if no one else was going to greet him with a bouquet, Gunnar Barbarotti certainly intended to do so. Though without the foliage, just with a few well-chosen questions.

Unless his plane from Midlanda this evening decided to carry him off in the wrong direction, of course. He had learnt not to count his chickens.

In the other disappearance case, too, they had fought their way a bit further through the thicket before they had to stop. The fact that Robert Hermansson had used his mobile to call someone at 01.51 the night he disappeared had been revealed to them almost immediately via the operators' lists, though of course it was a curse that he had called someone on pay-as-you-go. But all was not lost. The recipient of the call had been traced to Kymlinge, so it was not a matter of some old flame at the far end of the country, as Barbarotti had feared. Robert had actually rung a person who, at least on the night in question, had been in Kymlinge, and naturally they had also pounced on this pay-as-you-go number and investigated it a little more closely. The pickings were thin, unfortunately. Apart from the Robert call, the phone number in question had been used only four times in December, all of them between the fifth and the fifteenth, all of them outgoing calls.

Once to Robert Hermansson in Stockholm, twice to a pizzeria in Kymlinge, once to a women's hairdresser's in Kymlinge. The troika had spoken to both the pizzeria and the hair salon: at the former, their guess was that it was someone ordering pizza; at the latter, their guess was that it was someone making a hair appointment. The combined clientele of these two public institutions was estimated to be between 1,200 and 1,800. Eva Backman devoted quite a long time to working out what size the combined clientele must actually be, mathematically and in terms of probability, and over a Thursday beer she had rather surprisingly (at least for Gunnar Barbarotti, who had only achieved an averagely competent grade in school maths in his time) presented the fairly precise figure of 433.

'How the hell did you get to that?' the over-critical Barbarotti insensitively asked.

'Don't worry your little head about that,' was Eva Einstein's riposte. 'Robert Hermansson rang one of 433 women in Kymlinge. She's potentially linked to that damn hairdresser's.'

Einstein-Backman then spent two days drawing up a list of everyone who had had an appointment at Maggie's Hairdresser's between 5 and 23 December (not that they had the names of them all, but plenty they did), which came to the pleasingly low total of 362, and just as she was finishing that task, the proprietress of that fashionable establishment called to say that they had been obliged to turn away just as many. Backman-Numbskull swore to herself, applied a dose of extremely restrained rounding, and once again arrived fairly exactly at the figure 433.

'You see?'

'I see, o master,' Gunnar Barbarotti admitted, but at the same time he had felt mental exhaustion come creeping over him again, like a consumptive fog.

But still, he had to admit, it had been an unusually long and hopeful dead end.

But the fact that Kristoffer Grundt had rung him the previous evening and said he had something important to tell him – something he claimed to have been keeping quiet until now – had to be considered the most interesting feature of the investigation to date.

Didn't Backman agree?

Hell yes, was Backman's view. You bet.

'I've only got an hour, can we go into this place, and I'll record whatever you've got to tell me?'

Kristoffer Grundt nodded.

The boy had a Coke, while he went for a double espresso. Just as well to be wide awake, in case some bit of shit didn't come out on the tape. It seemed to be that sort of day. They found a corner behind a stone-dead jukebox and an artificial fig tree, and sat down.

'Well?' began Gunnar Barbarotti, pressing record. 'What was it you wanted to say?'

'I'd prefer it if you didn't tell Mum and Dad about this,' said Kristoffer.

'I can't guarantee anything,' said Barbarotti. 'But I promise to keep it quiet if possible.

'You don't know . . . Has anything happened?'

'What do you mean?'

'You don't know any more about where Henrik's gone?'

Kristoffer Grundt was in torment, that much was clear. He

had presumably been so for some time, Barbarotti thought. The boy couldn't keep his eyes still, his hands moved restlessly between his glass, the Coke bottle and the table edge – yes, something was weighing on him and presumably had been for far too long. He had dark rings under his eyes, too, although he was only fourteen, and his complexion was the colour of a dirty sheet.

Though probably most people in this country look like that at this godforsaken time of year, when you came to think of it.

'No,' he said. 'We still don't know anything about what's happened to your brother. Now tell me what it is you've been keeping quiet about.'

The boy shot him a shy glance.

'Well, the thing is . . .' He was groping for the words. 'I'm sorry I didn't say anything sooner, but I'd promised him . . .'

'Henrik?'

'Yes.'

'You promised him something? OK, go on. What did you promise?'

'I promised Henrik not to tell. But now . . . well, now I realize that maybe . . .'

He stopped. Gunnar Barbarotti decided to help him onto the right track. 'You're not bound by that promise any longer, Kristoffer,' he said in as kindly a way as he could. 'If Henrik could, he would release you from it. We've got to do everything we can to get him back, I'm sure you think the same?'

'Do you . . . do you think he's alive?'

There was a faint ray of hope in his voice, very faint. He's making the same judgement as I am, thought Gunnar Barbarotti. He isn't stupid.

'I don't know,' he said. 'Neither you nor I can know that. But we can hope and we can do our best to find out what has happened. Can't we?'

Kristoffer Grundt nodded. 'Well, the thing is, that he – that he went out that night. I mean he planned to go out.'

'Right, I see,' said Barbarotti. 'Go on.'

'That's it, really. He told me he was going out that night to meet somebody, and he asked me to keep quiet about it.'

'And then he went?'

'Yes, he must have done. But I don't know when, because I fell asleep.'

'You fell asleep before he left the house?'

'Yes.'

'Who was he going to meet?'

'I don't know.'

'Don't know?'

'No. He said he was going to meet an old friend and I asked if it was a girl.'

'Yes?'

'And he said that it was.'

'A girl?'

'Yes.'

'Hmm,' said Gunnar Barbarotti, and reduced his espresso to a single. Kristoffer Grundt drank a little of his Coke. A few seconds went by, the boy stared down at the tabletop, and Barbarotti had a fleeting vision of how it must feel to be a Catholic priest and hear confession.

'There's something else, isn't there?' he said. 'You haven't told me all you know?'

Kristoffer Grundt nodded.

'There's a bit more,' he mumbled.

'You think your brother lied to you?'

Kristoffer Grundt gave a start. 'How . . . how do you know that?'

Gunnar Barbarotti leant back. 'I've been doing this for quite a few years now. You learn to pick up on things. So what else have you got to tell me?'

'I don't think he was going to meet a girl.'

'Ah. Why not?'

'Because I – because Henrik's gay.'

'Gay? What makes you think that?'

'Because I borrowed his mobile and happened to see it.'

'Can you see from a person's mobile whether they're gay? You're joking, right?'

'No, of course you can't.' Kristoffer Grundt laughed, against his will. 'I borrowed Henrik's mobile to send a text. And then I happened to read a message that had come in. And what the message said was pretty . . .'

'Clear?'

'Clear, yes. It was from a guy who – well, I found this bit out from his address book – from a guy called Jens. So I don't think Henrik was going to meet a girl.'

'And who do you think he was actually going to meet?'

'I don't know.'

Gunnar Barbarotti had expected no other answer, but he still felt a faint stab of disappointment that Kristoffer couldn't squeeze out a little surprise on this point.

'But if you were to guess?'

The boy thought for a moment. 'No idea, honestly. Perhaps it was that Jens, who happened to be in Kymlinge – though it definitely seemed . . . No, I didn't know what to think. It was . . .'

'Yes?'

'It was, like, too much all in one go. I'd just found out Henrik was gay, and then he was off out in the middle of the night. Henrik, who's always been so good and conscientious. It was hard to take it in properly.'

'I can imagine,' said Gunnar Barbarotti. 'And Henrik's homosexuality, nobody knew about it?'

'No.'

'And you didn't tell him you knew about it?'

'I didn't have time to. And anyway, I'd borrowed his mobile without permission, so I didn't want to say anything.'

'I get it. So he had a plan then, Henrik? When did he tell you about it?'

'That evening. An hour or so before we went to bed, no more.'

'Can you repeat to me exactly what he said?'

'I don't really remember. But I'm sure it was just that he'd be out for a couple of hours during the night and I was to pretend I knew nothing about it. I asked why and he just said he was going to meet someone. And then, er, then I asked that thing about the girl. That was it.'

'Why did you ask if it was a girl, if you knew he wasn't interested in girls?'

'No idea. I just blurted it out. I mean, he'd invented that Jenny in Uppsala, so he probably didn't want us to know about it – that is, I assume she doesn't really exist.'

'All right. Have you told anyone else about this? Your mum and dad, for example?'

'Of course I haven't. I don't want them to find out about . . .'

'About your brother being gay?'

'Yes. Not that it's a bad thing, I mean, it doesn't bother me, but I'm sure they'd be pretty upset – or sad – on top of him going missing and everything. No, I don't want them to know about this. That's why I kept quiet about it, it's not only because I'd promised.'

'I understand. And you didn't find out any more about this Jens?'

'No, how could I . . . ?'

'That's fine. And I can tell you that you were right about it not being him Henrik went out to meet that night.'

'But how – how can you know that?'

'Because we've checked Jens out. He's got an alibi. He was almost a thousand kilometres from Kymlinge on the night of the twentieth of December.'

Kristoffer Grundt's jaw dropped. Literally. He just sat there with his mouth hanging open and stared at Detective Inspector Barbarotti.

'So you knew . . . ? You've known about . . . ?'

Gunnar Barbarotti fished his mobile out of the breast pocket of his jacket. 'Let me give you some advice, young man,' he said. 'If ever in your life you're thinking of committing a criminal act, and you want to be sure of getting caught for what you've done, make sure you use one of these.'

'What?' gaped Kristoffer Grundt.

'Now, of course we don't tap the phones of ordinary, honest citizens,' Barbarotti went on. 'But we know who's ringing who. When they do it, how often they do it, and where they are when they make each individual call. Let's say, for example, there were two young men in Uppsala who rang and texted each other more than ninety times over a period of two weeks – then, well, we'd draw our conclusions.'

'I see,' said Kristoffer Grundt.

'Good,' said Inspector Barbarotti.

But again, that gets us no further forward, damn it, he thought an hour later as he sank into a window seat on the pleasantly half-empty plane to Arlanda. And what was more, it looked as though it was going to take off on schedule. We're just jogging on the spot. We're – we're worse than our domestic airline.

The thing that felt most ironic of all, considering what he had advised young Mr Grundt towards the end of their conversation at the Charm Cafe, was that Henrik, of course, had *not* used his mobile. He had *not* rung the person he was planning to visit, he had *not* sent a text to announce 'I'll be there in half an hour'; and as Detective Inspector Barbarotti stared out of the minimal cabin window and listened to the de-icing sprays, it seemed to him that this very factor – this absent factor – was the strangest thing in this whole strange case.

Because what did it mean? If Henrik really had arranged to meet someone during the night, he must have had some method of making that arrangement. *How*, in short. The police had got into his computer in Karlsrogatan in Uppsala and been through his personal emails with a fine-tooth comb – and in them it was made pretty explicit that he had had homosexual experiences between the end of November and the start of December – but had found nothing about arrangements for a nocturnal encounter down in Kymlinge. Henrik Grundt had not telephoned, at any rate not from his grandparents' phone; the only thing left, as far as Gunnar Barbarotti could interpret things, was that he had met the person in question and that they had sorted it out face to face, as it were.

But *when*? When had they reached their agreement, in that case?

And of course, the billion-dollar question – *who*? Who the hell was Henrik Grundt to have met in Kymlinge? It was just as his younger brother had pointed out: he didn't know a soul there. Could it have been someone he knew from Uppsala? Someone who was down in that neck of the woods for Christmas?

Another male partner who was not Jens Lindewall?

Still seemed bloody unlikely. And did it really have some connection to Robert's disappearance the night before? If two people went missing from the same address in a town of scarcely 70,000 inhabitants, just twenty-four hours apart, couldn't any underachieving lumpfish work out that there must be a link?

I get so tired of all this, noted Gunnar Barbarotti as he took the little box of juice and plastic-wrapped sandwich proffered by the air stewardess. It's possible to think of an innumerable number of variants in this affair. But none that seem the least bit credible, and none that have anything to do with facts. Like . . . well, like imaginary maps of an unknown continent, that was how it felt.

What? His thoughts were in confusion. *Imaginary maps of an unknown continent*? But it was a rather good image of the whole thing, actually. He'd have to remember to use it to shoot down Eva Backman at some convenient juncture: Now you're just drawing imaginary maps of unknown continents, dear!

Not bad.

But surely they ought to get something, at least something,

out of that damned elusive Lindewall when he dropped out of the skies from the jungles of Borneo tomorrow morning?

They had a right to demand it, in fact.

Content with these intelligent summations, Inspector Barbarotti opened the little carton and spilt juice on his trousers.

23

Typical, thought Gunnar Barbarotti as he checked in at the Radisson at Arlanda SkyCity. When you get a chance to stay at a decent hotel for once, you arrive at ten in the evening and have to be up before six. I could just as well have crashed on a sofa.

When he had slipped between the cool, freshly mangled sheets and put out the light, he prayed an existence prayer.

O great God, if you really exist – which at this moment you actually do, though not by much, I'd just like to remind you – make the plane from Bangkok tomorrow be about four or five hours late, so a poor, hard-working plainclothes cop has time for a proper hotel breakfast this one time in his dull life! I naturally can't offer more than one point for such a trifle, but I would still be more grateful than you, even you, o great God, can imagine. Good night, good night, I've asked for an alarm call at quarter to six, and I shall check with arrivals the minute I open my eyes.

The plane from Bangkok landed five minutes ahead of schedule.

Detective Inspector Barbarotti had time for a shower and a cup of coffee, that was all. He sat waiting with cup number two on the table in front of him in one of the airport police interview rooms. He had the feeling that if Jens Lindewall didn't have the sense to behave, he would chop off his ears and lock him up for an indefinite stretch.

Next to Barbarotti sat a blonde female police assistant, filing her nails. If Lindewall didn't show up within the next two minutes, Barbarotti felt he would snatch the file out of her hand, throw it to perdition and tell her that manicures were outlawed in police interview rooms according to the Swedish Penal Code, chapter four, paragraph seven, section three, subsection four.

He also had the feeling he was being a bit too touchy.

Jens Lindewall looked tanned and healthy. If a little anxious. He was tall, blond and well-toned, and was wearing khaki, with heavy boots and a rucksack. More or less as you might expect a younger brother of Bruce Chatwin to look, after a month at the equator. Two-day stubble. A twisted blue scarf tied round his neck. Gunnar Barbarotti registered, reluctantly and with a slight feeling of queasiness, that this young man could readily find someone of either sex to share his bed with very little effort.

'Sit down,' he said. 'My name is Detective Inspector Gunnar Barbarotti. Welcome home.'

The young man stared at him and a muscle in one of his cheeks twitched a couple of times. But no words came out of his mouth. He put down his rucksack, pulled out a chair and sat down. Barbarotti regarded him evenly. The assistant put away her nail file.

'What's this all about?' said Jens Lindewall eventually.

'Is it correct that you have had a sexual relationship with a young man named Henrik Grundt?'

'Henrik . . . ?' said Jens Lindewall.

'Henrik Grundt, yes. You had a relationship in December;

we've been trying to get hold of you since Christmas. Henrik Grundt is missing.'

'Missing?'

'Just so. Why have you been keeping out of the way?'

'I haven't . . .' He loosened the knot of his scarf and crossed his arms on his chest. He seemed to be deciding not to take this lying down. 'I haven't been keeping out of the way. Or . . . well, maybe I have. But it's what I usually do: go away for a few weeks each winter and stay incommunicado; I didn't know it was against the law. It's part of my life cycle; you experience everything where you are much more intensely that way, Inspector, if you get what I mean.'

'I can imagine,' said Gunnar Barbarotti. 'And if your parents happen to get run over by a timber lorry while you're away, they can just go ahead and bury each other? That's right lad, scruples are for Mr and Mrs Average and lowlifes like them.'

Having delivered this inventive retort, he felt very clearly that his sadistic streak had had enough of an airing for one misbegotten morning. 'Now, please be so good as to answer my questions and stop faffing about,' he couldn't help adding.

'Yes . . . sure. But what is it you . . . ?'

'You had a relationship with Henrik Grundt from November to December. Do you admit that?'

'Yes.'

'In Uppsala?'

'Yes, I live in Uppsala.'

'We know. And you flew to south-east Asia on the evening of twenty-second December?'

'Er . . . yes, that's right. But Henrik's missing, you say? Is that why you're—'

'For more than three weeks now, yes. You spent the days immediately prior to your departure at your parents' in Hammerdal?'

'That's right, but how . . . ?'

'Your itinerary took you via Bangkok to Kuala Lumpur, then on to Kota Kinabalu and to Sandakan on the north-east side of Borneo. And the same route back. Is that right?'

'How can you know all that . . . ?'

'I just know. Doesn't matter how I found out. Well?'

Jens Lindewall sighed. 'Yeah, it was like you said. I set off from Sandakan . . . it must be forty-eight hours ago. So I'm actually a bit tired, you'll have to excuse me.'

'I've been in the air a fair bit myself these past few days,' countered Gunnar Barbarotti. 'Can you tell me something about your relationship?'

'Mine and Henrik's?'

'Spot on. Let's leave your others aside for now.'

'What is it you want to know?'

'I want to know everything,' said Gunnar Barbarotti.

He didn't, of course – and mercifully he didn't have to – but when he let the young man leave the interview room forty-five minutes later, he still felt he had found out more than enough.

Jens Lindewall was twenty-six years old. He worked for an advertising company in Uppsala and had been gay for as long as he had been sexual, basically. He had been in a long-lasting relationship (eleven months) that had ended last autumn, in September, and it was in the wake of that shipwreck that Henrik Grundt had come floating up. They met at the Katalin music pub behind the main station one Friday in November, ended up at the same table and started to talk.

Henrik Grundt was not really aware of his own sexual orientation, but that all changed that night – to cut a short story even shorter. Then they were together for about a month, and they always met in Jens's little flat on Prästgårdsgatan, never in Henrik's student room in the Triangle. Jens confessed unashamedly to having fallen instantly and fiercely in love with the young law student, and he got the impression it was mutual. But he admitted that Henrik Grundt had had some difficulty when it came to accepting his homosexuality; he had had a few pretty desultory experiences of the opposite sex previously, the way he described it, and if Jens were to venture an estimate, he would say Henrik stood at around 65–35 on the homo–hetero rating scale – which, if Barbarotti understood correctly, meant that in an ideal world, one sexual encounter in three would be with a woman, the rest with men. It was the first time Barbarotti had ever come across such a scale, but he nonetheless entered it carefully in his notebook. You learn something new every day, he thought.

The last time Jens and Henrik met was 17 December, the day before they were both off to their parents' homes in Hammerdal and Sundsvall respectively. They had spoken on the phone a few times after that date, and exchanged a number of texts. Jens Lindewall's last four messages, sent on 21 and 22 December, had gone unanswered. Gunnar Barbarotti could not help asking how his love life had been while he was away, and Jens Lindewall said, very frankly, that it had been good.

'So you weren't a couple, as it were, you and Henrik?'

'We gave each other freedom,' replied Jens Lindewall. 'That's the greatest of gifts.'

When Barbarotti asked if he wasn't concerned about Henrik's disappearance, the answer came that of course he was, but that he would be bound to turn up. People just needed to be alone sometimes, especially young people, Jens Lindewall had learnt that from experience.

After his interview with the good-looking young globe-trotter, Detective Inspector Barbarotti hurried back to the breakfast buffet at the Radisson; he had an hour and a half before his flight left for Landvetter and he was as hungry as a wolf.

The plane was only half an hour late, but he still had plenty of time to sum up the case in his head. Or *cases*. He still could not decide whether they were dealing with one or two, but as the investigation had not, however you looked at it, made more than tiny advances on either track, it didn't really matter.

At any event, neither of his sessions with Kristoffer Grundt and Jens Lindewall had shed much light on anything. What had happened in the course of those twenty-four hours in Allvädersgatan remained a mystery. When Henrik went out into the night on 20 December, it seemed to have been a highly conscious and pre-planned act – he had asked his brother to keep quiet about it – but why he left his grandparents' house, and where he was going, well, they had not learnt a single jot about that.

And Jens Lindewall had merely confirmed what they had already concluded. No more and no less. He and Henrik Grundt had had a relationship lasting a few weeks in November and December. Henrik had vanished, Jens had gone off to south-east Asia, and these two things had nothing to do with each other.

As for Robert, they had reached a similar impasse. Gunnar Barbarotti had lost count of the number of people they had talked to in Kymlinge these past weeks – it must have been getting on for two hundred – but he knew all too well what the result was.

Zilch. When Robert Hermansson left the town of his childhood fifteen to sixteen years ago, he also seemed to have cut all ties. Not a single one of those asked so far had been in touch with the missing reality TV personality even once in the course of the past decade. Or so they claimed.

We're stuck, thought Inspector Barbarotti. We're as stuck as hell.

And like some kind of inverted confirmation of his statement, at that moment an air hostess came by and pointed out that he had forgotten to fasten his safety belt.

Rosemarie Wunderlich Hermansson battled her way up Hagendalsvägen. The wind was blowing straight at her, coming from the north-west, it was minus twelve and if she didn't get indoors soon, she thought she would die.

Perhaps not such a bad way to go, all things considered. Sinking to the icy pavement between the housing association office and Bellis the florist's and taking her last breath on a dark and freezing January afternoon. It was hard to say what it was that had kept her clinging to life this past month, really hard. Ever since that terrible Christmas week she had felt as though she didn't really exist, as if her soul had been sucked out of her body leaving only a shell, this brittle, scraggy, decrepit ghost of skin and bones that was now struggling the last few metres to Maggie's Hairdresser's up at the corner of Kungsgatan – not comprehending why on earth she hadn't phoned to cancel her appointment, which she had made as the usual matter of course on her last visit.

But never mind, she didn't comprehend much of anything else that carried on happening either: not why she got up in the mornings, nor why she went out shopping for food for lunch and dinner, nor why she spent an hour doing a Spanish course with Karl-Erik every evening between nine and ten – the items of vocabulary went fluttering through her head like strange birds, in one ear, out of the other, not to mention the verb forms. Before going to bed she took a sleeping tablet that made her sleep for precisely five hours; she woke between four and half past, trying to prolong those absolutely blank seconds after waking, when her mind was still wiped clean. When she did not remember what had happened, scarcely even knew who she was, but the seconds were never more than seconds, and sometimes even less.

And then she would lie there on her side with her hands thrust between her knees – turned away from her husband and from her entire life – while she stared over at the window and the sighing radiator and the sad curtains, waiting for a dawn that felt as distant as the answer to the question of what had happened to her son and her grandson on those dreadful days in December, when her soul had been sucked out of her body leaving this decrepit ghost of . . . and that was how the thoughts flapped round and round in her head like birds of a different feather, exhausted birds who came and went, came and went, and how could one possibly tell the difference between one morning and the next, tell one awakening from the first, or the eighth? That too was a question that did not seem the least bit inclined to find itself an answer.

She opened the door and stepped inside. Saw that all four chairs were occupied, but Maggie Fahlén nodded to her to take a seat, it would only be a few minutes. She hung up her hat and coat, sat down in the small, tubular steel armchair and picked up a six-month-old women's weekly magazine with a summertime picture of Princess Victoria on the front cover. She was smiling broadly to reveal an abundance of shiny teeth and did not look particularly bright, noted Rosemarie Wunderlich Hermansson, but then perhaps she wasn't, poor girl?

'So, tell me honestly, how are you doing, Rosemarie dear?' started Maggie, once she was seated in the chair, glowering at her big, smooth face in the pitiless mirror. 'It was simply dreadful, what happened. Have you heard anything?'

That was two questions and one comment in the same breath, and Rosemarie stifled a sudden impulse to make her excuses and set off into the cold again. Apologize for the fact that the Hermanssons in Allvädersgatan were always causing such a commotion – first one thing and then another, television and newspapers and all that – but Maggie was ahead of her; she had been talking away since first thing in the morning, an inexhaustible and tireless commentary on all things great and small, in Kymlinge and out in the world. In the present, the past and the future. The hereafter too, if the customer favoured that sort of thing.

'Who in heaven's name cut this for you last time?' she said, raising her eyebrows to Rosemarie in the mirror.

'It was . . . er, a new girl, I think,' Rosemarie tried to remember. 'She might just have been filling in for somebody who was off sick, I can't really re—'

'Almgren,' Maggie cut in. 'Jane Almgren, oh yes. My God, the state she left the customers in, it was a good job she didn't stay any longer. Well, I would have sent her packing anyway, even if Kathrine hadn't come back so quickly.'

'Oh, ah, right,' said Rosemarie Hermansson. 'Well, I'm not sure – this one was a sort of dark blonde, I think.'

'That was her,' confirmed Maggie, snipping the air angrily with her scissors a couple of times. 'Claimed she was a trained hairdresser and everything . . . and maybe she was, what do I know, I mean they let all sorts of people through these days. And Kathrine had rung in that morning to say it was appendicitis, so what's a poor girl from Hudiksvall supposed to do, with only two weeks to go to Christmas Eve?'

Hudiksvall, thought Rosemarie in confusion. Wasn't Maggie born and bred . . . wasn't she the daughter of the old caretaker Underström over at . . . ?

'It's just a saying,' came the explanation, before she had time to ask. 'I don't know where it comes from . . . well, from Hudik I suppose, when you come to think about it. But she only lasted three days, that Jane, then Kathrine came back – to think that they don't let you stay in for a couple of days even for an appendix any more, but I was jolly glad of it, of course. Anyway, I'm going to give you a hundred kronor discount today, Rosemarie, don't let anybody say Maggie doesn't take care of her customers. How would you like it?'

'However you like,' said Rosemarie, shutting her eyes. 'Just a trim, you know.'

'Though she lives here in town, apparently,' Maggie went on as she inserted her comb into Rosemarie's greying locks. 'I'd never come across her before, but the other day she was in Gunder's buying herring – maybe she's got a cat. I couldn't care less if she's got a cat or not, as long as she never sets foot in here again to take her scissors to my customers.'

'I remember chatting to her . . .' said Rosemarie, so as not to seem impolite. 'She was pleasant enough. God, I'm so tired, does it matter if I doze off while you're doing me?'

'You sleep, my dear,' replied Maggie. 'And just close your ears if you think I'm nattering on too much. My Arne says I'll natter myself to death one day. Would you like me to wash it first?'

'Yes please,' Rosemarie sighed drowsily. 'That would be rather nice, actually.'

24

You could get two human bodies in a freezer.

She would never have thought it. And there was still room for a couple of packets of ice cream and bags of frozen berries on the top shelf.

One body, certainly, but two? It almost seemed a bit odd. She had tried her hand at many professions, and she suddenly remembered she had also spent a couple of weeks standing in for a maths teacher at an upper-secondary school. She lied and said she had a degree, and nobody checked, as usual. Eight or ten years ago, a suburb to the west of Stockholm; she couldn't remember the name and it hadn't gone particularly well. One afternoon the teaching team had got together to set a common test, and she'd sat there feeling embarrassed and stupid because she couldn't contribute anything; now she knew exactly which problem she would ask the pupils to solve.

You have two dead bodies. They weigh x and y kilos. You have a freezer with a capacity of 250 litres. How many pieces must you cut the bodies into for them to fit into it?

She sat at the kitchen table, looking out into the street. It was evening, a raw, grey, windy January evening, and the people out and about were huddled over their supermarket bags and dogs. But there weren't many of them; most were sensible enough to stay inside. She had cleaned the whole flat. There wasn't a speck of dust left, and she had even wiped the skirting boards with a damp cloth soaked in Ajax. She had showered and washed her hair. She had spoken to her mother on the phone, focused on all the positive things in life that she liked to hear about.

Everything was in brilliant balance.

Her mother had been admitted again, but she herself was still out. Signed off sick for a month at a time, that was how it had been since the summer. They were always changing doctors up at the hospital, and each new one gave her a month, the same old medication and sessions with this or that therapist attached to the care in the community programme. The therapists came and went, too.

It worked well for her. Nobody was really in control, she lived on the margins and got by on her social security payments. The inactivity gave her time to think and plan.

Consider whether she needed one more. Whether she should tackle Germund, too.

Or would Mahmot be satisfied that she had already achieved atonement? It wasn't easy to know, he didn't always make things as plain as one might have wished, Mahmot.

The first one had been an easy decision. He was a pig. She hadn't hesitated for a moment. No balance was possible in the world while he remained alive.

The second had come to her in a sudden and rather funny way. She'd had no idea what a force of evil he represented, not before he was suddenly there, like a thorn in her flesh. Mahmot had only had to whisper the word in her ear: *kill*, and she had realized that this, this was just the right way to untie the knot.

I want my children back, she had been bold enough to demand. *All in good time,* Mahmot whispered. *All in good time you will get everything back. I have big plans for you, Jane, and have I ever disappointed you?*

No, o great Mahmot, she mumbled as she caught sight of a little mark and started to give the oak-veneer tabletop an extra polish with the palms of her hands, soft, circling movements, but I haven't got room for another one in the freezer. I've got to be practical, too, not just indulge in the lovely, passionate things all the time. I've got to find Germund and my children, they've taken my children away from me, Mahmot. They're hiding from me, I don't know where they are.

That is good, my girl, whispered Mahmot. *Do not think about it now. Close your eyes, and I shall step forward and kiss your brow and make my home in your fingers. You know what I can do when I reside there?*

Thank you, great Mahmot, she whispered in her arousal. Thank you, o thank you! I wish all men were dead and there was only You. Do you want me to . . . ?

He did not answer, but she still knew how she should proceed.

THREE

AUGUST

25

Ebba Hermansson Grundt is dreaming.

She dreams she is carrying her son Henrik. She has had the same dream on a number of nights all through the summer, and it is so painful.

He is heavy, her son. He is hanging from her collarbone, dangling inside her body; between her heart and her stomach is a big empty space that she never knew she had inside her.

He is hanging in two Co-op carrier bags, green-and-white plastic, and he has been chopped into little pieces, her son Henrik.

It isn't easy carrying your adult child in pieces in the dog days of summer, and when Ebba wakes in a cold sweat at dawn, she clasps her hands and prays to God. She never believed in God, all her life, but she still asks for his help after these dreams. There is really nothing else to try.

She is no longer working. For the first few months without Henrik, she stuck to her usual timetable. All through January and February, and a little way into March. Her hospital colleagues were astonished. How can a woman who has lost her son – or whose son is missing, at any rate – just carry on as normal? Operation after operation, ward round after ward round, case conference after case conference, and ten to fifteen hours' overtime every week. As if nothing had happened. How is it possible? What kind of person must it take?

But then she met Benita Ormson, her old friend from university, who had been possessed of the same capacities and brilliant prospects as Ebba when they were medical students in Uppsala; her only real rival, in fact. They had taken it in turns to come top and second in every single exam: anatomy, cell biology, internal medicine, surgery, infection, gynaecology – but Benita chose psychiatry as her specialism after their compulsory stint as general doctors, surprising many by her choice of this low-status option. Perhaps there had been depths and dimensions to that quiet, dark-haired young woman from Tornedalen that no one had really grasped. Not even Ebba; when they found themselves at the same weekend conference in Dalarna in the middle of March, it was the first time they had met for six . . . no, seven years.

And in Benita's arms, Ebba Hermansson Grundt finally crumbled. On the eighty-third day after her son disappeared, she broke down, and it felt like a parachute jump without a parachute.

It has been five months now. Since 12 March she has not worked a single day. Not a single hour. Every morning, Leif goes off to the Co-op and Kristoffer to school, just as usual, but Ebba is in internal exile. Twice a week she sees a therapist, twice a month a psychiatrist. The latter is not Benita Ormson, which is a disadvantage; in Benita Ormson's care she could recover and move on with what she now needs to move on with – under the somnolent guidance of Erik Segerbjörk, she will get nowhere at best. You're a lemur, Erik, she confided in him during one of their sessions, but it was just water off the back of the foolish duck he was, and he smiled kindly beneath his beard and gave a few lazy blinks.

Although to be honest, she has no desire to move on. Or at least not in the direction envisaged by psychiatric science.

But she gets on better with the therapist, a hatchet-faced woman of around sixty. She is intelligent, listens in moderation, and has a sense of humour. Moreover, she has no children of her own which, Ebba discovered almost immediately, is a distinct advantage. It puts the emotional side on a firmer footing; she's not sure why it should be so – but she does not under any circumstances want to sit and talk to another woman with a son or a daughter who, in principle, could disappear. It would be improper.

Benita Ormson has no children, either. They talk on the phone once a week, on average. Ebba Hermansson Grundt can't complain about lack of backup. She is getting all the support one could reasonably expect from those around her and from the hospital system. She has a network, a word she secretly detests.

But none of it brings her a millimetre closer to getting better, because that is not what is at stake here. Ebba doesn't want to get better.

She wants her son back. If he is dead, she wants his body back so she can bury him in the cemetery.

If someone has killed him, she also wants to get hold of that person.

It is as simple as that. She could not care less about anything else.

Not Leif, not Kristoffer.

Make no demands of me, she thinks. She does not say it, but she thinks it. You keep to yourselves, Henrik and I will keep to ourselves; please respect the rules of the game. It is not Ebba who wrote these rules; they are a fundamental base that she will not and cannot depart from by the force of her own strength and will; it is not a question of priorities, not a question of putting one child before the other, not at all. Leif and Kristoffer belong together in the same self-evident way. That's how it has always been. Whenever they played partnership whist or Monopoly in teams of two, when they were cooking or doing a pile of washing up. Whenever they went out on a family ski trip. Ebba and Henrik, Leif and Kristoffer, and that – that is why this lost son has left a hole so much, so infinitely larger in his mother's soul than in his father's or brother's. Leif and Kristoffer know it as well as she does. They do not talk about it, there is no need.

But it is so painful to dream about those Co-op carrier bags dangling from her collarbone, swinging from side to side in that space filled with absence inside her, which just seems to get bigger and more desolate with every passing hour. Every day and week and month; this Monday in the dog days it is 244 days since her fortieth birthday, and every day, each and every one of those unbearable days and nights that has passed, is so immutably like all the rest.

I know I'm insane, she sometimes thinks, but that is a label of no interest whatsoever. Leif and Kristoffer treat her with a different sort of attention from the way they used to; she can see it, register it, but it is of no importance. Only one thing is of any importance, one single thing. She must get her son back. She must – if nothing else, she must find out what has happened to him. The uncertainty is the worst thing of all.

The uncertainty and the lack of action.

Take the matter into one's own hands, then, thinks Ebba

Hermansson Grundt, and this is at least a fairly new thought; not something that has been with her through all those days, through all that darkness.

The idea that she must do her share. That here lies the only solution which can stop the empty space from growing.

For God helps those who help themselves. This truth has certainly been pulsating through her for a number of days, and on this particular morning, when she gets up to a pale August day with a sparse covering of cloud, she knows it is time to get started. A mother looking for her lost son, that's what this is all about. A mother and a son. Nothing else.

During the morning, she makes a phone call to that policeman. She remembers him quite clearly from Kymlinge. A man of young middle age with a slightly melancholy expression. Tall and thin, he made a positive impression on her; perhaps he was intelligent, in fact, but it was hard to tell with quiet people.

At any event, he hadn't much to report. The investigation is continuing, but he makes no secret of the fact that not a great deal of energy is going into it. There is something in his voice that inspires confidence, all the same. We've looked into everything we can reasonably be expected to, he says, but we've got nowhere. He personally has spoken to over a hundred people with some kind of link to Henrik or Robert – but the mystery of what happened in those December days is still as unsolved as it was at the start. This is a matter of regret of course, a matter of *great* regret, but that's the way things look. Sometimes one finds oneself in situations like that, but it doesn't mean one should give up hope. Wheels grind slowly, and he has been involved in cases in which crucial evidence came to light two or five or ten years after the cases were essentially shelved.

Does that mean you've shelved Henrik's case? Ebba wants to know. Are you just sitting around waiting? Not at all, Inspector Barbarotti assures her. In no way.

Ebba thanks him and hangs up. She sits very still for a while, looking out of the window. The lawn needs cutting – Kristoffer promised to do it at the weekend but something got in the way. Something always gets in the way when Kristoffer's involved. But she doesn't care about that, either. Their plot of land faces onto a narrow strip of forest, and she recalls that Henrik used to be afraid of the trees when he was really little. When he was two or three, the trees and the dark; it's a memory that pops up all of a sudden, and not particularly representative. Henrik was a plucky little boy, never really afraid the trolls would come and get him; Kristoffer had been the more timid one. The Co-op carrier bags are swinging inside her, it hurts desperately, but she can't just sit here any longer, a good mother doesn't sit and wait for her lost son, a good mother sets out and leaves no stone unturned until she finds her son. That's just the way it is.

But where to set out to? Where should Ebba Hermansson Grundt go and start her search?

Kymlinge? Well that would be the most natural starting point of course, if her parental home were still there. But it is not. Karl-Erik and Rosemarie left Allvädersgatan on the first of March and started their new life in Spain; they actually did it. They turned to a new page, in the autumn of their lives. Ebba receives postcards and phone calls once a week, the cards from her mother, the calls from her father. The sun is always shining, they are always sitting on the terrace looking out over the mountains and a strip of sea, they are drinking sweet wine from Málaga with ice in it, yes, they really have embarked on a whole new existence. Were it not for the matter of Robert and Henrik, they would truly be in paradise, Karl-Erik thinks. Whether Rosemarie is of the same opinion is harder for Ebba to fathom, but nor does she care very much. Her mother and her father are sitting down there in the sunshine, sipping wine and trying to forget their children and their Kymlinge and their old lives, that is how it is, but it is certainly a remarkable turn of events. Who could have imagined a year ago that this was how the Hermansson family would look? Last August, everything was still normal, and now . . . now? Ebba asks herself. That's how fragile life is, that's how little we know about what can happen from one day to the next. One year to the next.

Like an egg that falls out of the fridge and smashes on the kitchen floor, that's how breakable our children are.

No, she can't go back and start poking around in Kymlinge, that much is obvious. It would be pointless. And yet, that is what she wants to recreate, when they were all together just before the birthday, when everyone was still there. Because if it really is true, thinks Ebba, if it really is true that things are interconnected, if there is a functioning chain of cause and effect in life, then the germ of what happened afterwards – whatever it was – must have been there that first evening. Perhaps on the second, too, when Robert was already gone, of course, but Henrik was still with them. There must have been something in the air, something you could have seen, if only you'd had any notion of the currents and thoughts and motives in those rooms on those days in December. An attentive observer would have been able to understand it.

Or would they? What really happened? Did Henrik already

know, when they were in the car on their way down to Kymlinge, that he was going to go out that night? Did Robert? Was there a plan? Was there a link? Who was that curious girlfriend Jenny, whom the police had proved unable to locate? Was she just an invention? And if so, why? What was Henrik concealing from his mother; there must have been things in his life that she did not know about. What was it that had happened during his first term in Uppsala? There must have been . . .

The same questions, the same sterile fumbling, it's remarkable how easily and rapidly the synapses of her brain have been drugged into disintegration by this virus; this must be how it feels when the end is near, thinks Ebba Hermansson Grundt, exactly how it feels. Futile, bewildered questions and no answers. This is how susceptible we are when our consciousness finally overcooks and falls apart, when our own eggshell also smashes – but it is not *her* consciousness that matters here. So enough of them, enough of these self-indulgent reflections, it's Henrik who matters, the Henrik screaming inside her, cut into pieces or not, hanging from— No, stop, her thoughts are running out of control again. Where did she start? What had she made up her mind to do, just now? She looks out over the shaggy lawn again; over the garden, the crumbling sundial that the previous owner of the house, Mr Stefansson, was so mightily proud of, the dark trees, the approaching autumn, and tries to recapture that optimistic train of thought that was hers just a short time ago. What was it?

Matter in own hands, that was it. Recreate the evening before it happened. Act, do something, act. Yes, that was it. She gets up and goes to the kitchen. The phone rings but she lets it ring. Kristina, she thinks. It's my sister I must talk to.

Kristina, Robert and Henrik sat up talking that evening. Perhaps Kristina detected something . . . No, she would already have told the police, of course, in that case. And the rest of us. But there could have been things that – no, not things, *signs* – signs that that gifted or maybe merely quiet policeman didn't manage to unearth . . . signs that only a mother can understand and read, a word, something he said, something in his manner . . . something between Robert and Henrik, even, that might float up to the surface in retrospect – in a conversation between two sisters, two afflicted sisters, why not?

She must speak to her sister, it was no harder than that. One has to start somewhere and one should start in the simplest, most natural place. That's how it is.

Things have never been simple and natural between Ebba and Kristina, but she's going to overlook that this time.

Within twenty minutes, she has ordered her train tickets and a hotel room in Stockholm for three nights. The train leaves that afternoon, and of course she would be able to sleep at Kristina and Jakob's if she asked them, but she doesn't want it to be like that. She wants to approach Kristina cautiously. They've been far too distant, ever since they were little; perhaps this is an opportunity for reconciliation – but best take it gently. Caution is a virtue. She does not phone to let them know she's coming, either; ringing from the hotel tomorrow morning will be enough. She doesn't want Kristina to have to go round thinking and planning and choosing her words in advance. If the memory is subjected to too much pressure, those quick flashes of recollection can get locked.

Finally, thinks Ebba Hermansson Grundt, and goes for a shower. Finally, something.

Inside her, a voice is calling to tell her nothing good will come of this trip. She and Kristina have never been able to talk to each other, they've always been like oil and water, but Ebba turns a deaf ear. She doesn't listen to just any old voice; it is the trip and the action that make it worth the effort. Of course a pair of sisters must be able to come together in an hour of need. The Co-op carrier bags hang without moving in her internal darkness as she packs a bag, writes a note to Leif and Kristoffer.

Nothing about her intentions and so on, they wouldn't understand anyway. Just that she has gone to Stockholm to see her sister.

An unwelcome shower of autumn rain comes driving in just as she is about to leave for the station. She orders a taxi. It feels as though she will never be coming back.

26

About an hour after his conversation with Ebba Hermansson Grundt, Gunnar Barbarotti goes down to the police station cafeteria for two cups of black coffee and a think about life.

It is his third day back at work after four weeks' leave, and he cannot remember ever finding it so hard to get going again after a break. He is already caught up in various cases, amongst them a sorry tale involving a Turkish pizzeria owner who got tired of being harassed by a gang of xenophobic youths and killed a nineteen-year-old with a golf club. Two well-aimed blows, one to each temple, a four-iron; as Gunnar Barbarotti understood it, he was going to plead self-defence.

Stupid to hit him twice when once would have done, reckons Eva Backman. That's going to mean an extra six years. But it's good that the immigrants have started playing golf. It's the quickest route into mercenary Swedish society.

For his part, Gunnar Barbarotti has never held a golf club, but he has seen fifteen photographs of the youth's smashed-in skull and he doesn't know what to think.

And it's hot. High summer is as boiling as a forgotten steam iron despite the fact they will soon be past the middle of August, and it feels . . . it just feels unnatural to be at work. Barbarotti spent the first half of his holiday with his three children in a borrowed cottage at Fiskebäckskil on the west coast, the second fortnight in Greece. In Kavala and on the island of Thasos, to be precise, where admittedly it was hotter still, but there was also a vivid blue sea and a woman called Marianne. He met the latter at a taverna on his second evening; she was running away from the ruins of a relationship with a manic-depressive physics teacher, or so she claimed, and for once Gunnar Barbarotti thought yes, why not? It was hard to think that it was only six days since they parted at the airport in Thessaloniki, with an agreement not to get in touch with each other for a month. Then they would see.

In Kymlinge there is no sea and no Marianne.

But there is a Chief Inspector Asunander, who is in a particularly foul mood, possibly because his false teeth are an even worse fit in hot weather. He is more curt and angry than ever in this unhealthily sweltering season, and there are those who say his dog had four stillborn puppies during the holidays, too, but nobody dares to ask.

'Hermanssons!' he snaps, for example, rolling his eyes when Gunnar Barbarotti cautiously brings up the subject. 'Find a body pronto! Or two! Do it or change job. Lost property needs staff.'

'I just wanted to know whether anything happened while I was on holiday,' says Gunnar Barbarotti.

'Enough for you not to stick nose in half-cold cas – es!' bawled the police chief. 'Two school fires, four rapes, eight ass – aults and hold-up at a mark – damn it! – et garden. And Turk kills man with golf clubs!'

'Thanks,' said Gunnar Barbarotti. 'I get the picture.'

Why would anybody hold up a market garden? he wonders in the lift on the way down. Have the banks run out of money? And it's a bit rich to dismiss a double disappearance as a cold case after eight months.

So the Hermansson–Grundt case stands as it ever did. Making his choice between a cinnamon bun and an almond tart, he takes the bun and instantly regrets it. When he thinks about it, the case that is, not the bun – Christ, inserts another voice into his stream of consciousness, there must be something wrong with the canteen air conditioning, it's like a sauna down here – and he has been thinking about it quite a lot this spring and summer – he reckons the whole thing feels like some notorious brainteaser nobody can solve. Gunnar Barbarotti had a teacher in upper secondary who loved serving up puzzles like that to his pupils, particularly on Friday afternoons, so you had the whole weekend to brood on them. Barbarotti can't recall ever successfully solving a single one of those ingenious problems; it was always the teacher himself – wasn't he called Klevefjell? – who would present the elegant solution on the Monday. Not that you always understood it, even then.

So the brainteaser ran as follows: We have two individuals, an uncle and a nephew. Along with a number of other relatives, they gather a few days before Christmas for a special occasion. The first night, the uncle vanishes into thin air. The second night, the nephew vanishes into thin air. Explain!

Bloody hell, thinks Gunnar Barbarotti, mopping the sweat from his brow and biting into his cinnamon bun. Asunander's right, there's no point putting any more time into this. I've never experienced a case in which so many working hours have been poured into achieving such meagre results. But isn't there . . . yes, there must be, it wouldn't surprise me if there was styrofoam in this bun. He can feel the dough squeaking against his teeth.

For some reason, this suspicion throws a bridge over to his ex-wife Helena. By contrast, plenty has happened there. When he went to collect the children for their holiday on the west coast, she informed him of two things. The first was that she had found a new man. The second was that she was moving to Copenhagen with him. He was a yoga instructor there, she said. For various reasons, she hadn't yet told the boys, Lars and Martin, about the change of direction in their lives, and she made Gunnar promise not to mention it while they were at Fiskebäckskil.

He kept his promise, and he hasn't heard a word more on the subject since. Maybe the removal van is already en route. Lars and Martin, wonders Gunnar Barbarotti. How are you going to get on? Will you be talking Danish to me in five years' time?

He takes another bite of his styrofoam. When sons no longer speak the same language as their fathers, where are we heading?

It's a notion he finds hard to assess. Perhaps it's just his prejudice, and this sort of thing is a matter of course for a lot of people. Nothing to trouble himself about on a day like this, anyway. It must be over thirty degrees in the canteen. He is just on his way to get cup number two and a glass of water when Inspector Backman comes tearing in.

'So this is where you are!' she declares, putting her hands on her hips. 'We've just had a report of two bodies in a freezer. Do you want to come?'

Gunnar Barbarotti considers this for half a second. Thinking about life can wait for another time, and to be quite honest, a freezer is pretty much what he needs on a day like this.

*

Ebba resisted the temptation to get off the train at Uppsala, and carried on to Stockholm. A young man and a young woman boarded and sat down opposite her. They both had short dark hair and glasses; clearly they were students, and they immediately set about studying their course material, muttering and underlining. She watched them surreptitiously and could not help toying with the idea that they were actually fellow students of Henrik's. Of course, term would not be starting for a week or so yet, but still. She closed her eyes and tried to conjure up Henrik in her mind. Expose him to her maternal eye, but it didn't really work as she had hoped, he appeared momentarily but then vanished; when she tried again he came back, but only for that rapidly fading second. It was exasperating, but that was how it had been of late. Henrik had grown evasive. Ever more elusive. Am I starting to forget my son? she thought in dismay. Why can't you stay with me any longer, Henrik? Why is it only in this jointed state in the Co-op bags that you actually seem real? A shudder ran through her and she understood that she had got away on this trip in the nick of time. There was no doubt about it.

She had rung Leif from her mobile, but had only talked to him for half a minute because she lost the signal. He did not sound particularly surprised, but then he never did, in actual fact. He confined himself to saying they were both fine, he and Kristoffer, and asking how long she planned to be away.

A few days, she said, but she couldn't be sure whether he had heard that bit. Oh well, she thought. He'll have to ring me if he's interested.

The train stopped at Knivsta. It came back to her that she had once done supply teaching in a school there for a couple of weeks. It was in the January of the second – or possibly fourth? – term of her medical degree and she had passed one of the modules early and taken the chance to earn a bit of money; maths and biology, but what she remembered most vividly was the menacing number of hostile young people and the sense of being at the mercy of forces she could not control. She had really had to psyche herself up to get through each lesson, and when it was all over – it couldn't have amounted to more than eight or ten days all told – and she could go back to her medical studies, she had felt a wave of gratitude that she had not followed in her father's footsteps and chosen teaching as a profession.

She must only have been twenty or twenty-one at the time; good grief, there had been pupils who were only five years younger than she was.

Though what struck her as strange now was that the school must be there, somewhere beyond the train window. Those classrooms she had taught in, that pine-coloured staff room with its rigid leather sofas and dusty, wilting pot plants – and those teachers, or at any rate the younger ones . . . and all of that still existed, and had existed the whole time, all those days and all those hours of those almost twenty years since then, while she had been entirely absorbed in her life, her family and her career. For some reason she found this insight utterly appalling, almost obscene, and told herself that if she scrambled off the train and located that school and went in – if she were able to find her way to that classroom with the big damp patch on the ceiling, for example, and the unimaginably foul green blackout curtains, then in fact her life would change track and she would have a chance of starting from back then. The mid-eighties, twenty years ago, yes, it must have been 1985, the year Leif Grundt would turn up in her life, before she had had her children, before things had embarked on that implacable course which led to the terrible events of her fortieth birthday . . . but if she leapt off the train this very moment and rushed out into the town of Knivsta, then time would turn on its own axis like a Möbius strip, and she would get the chance to restart her life and steer it in an entirely different direction, where she would never have to lose her beloved son and have him hanging in the black void in two green and white—

There's something about my thoughts, she interrupted herself, just as the train jolted into motion again. There's something seriously wrong. Anything whatsoever seems able to demand entry to my head. And be granted it. I must find my barriers. I must put a stop to this. I must . . . I don't recognize my own consciousness, and what . . . what sort of 'I' is going to be left? *Who* am I, and *what* is it I'm not recognizing?

She picked up a discarded copy of *Metro* as an antidote; started turning the pages but read not a word. She remained within her own terrified mind instead, and turned to that god she did not believe in.

Please help me, she prayed. Let me not lose my mind. Let my talk with my sister at least be a small step in the right direction. Don't punish me for my arrogance.

This last thought was one that had been creeping over her in recent days. Arrogance. That the loss of Henrik – or his absence – was a kind of payback for having valued the wrong things in her life. That she had been egotistical, that she had let her career affect her family, that she should have had different priorities altogether. Purely clinically and purely intellectually, she could naturally dismiss this as an automatic and obsessive thought: this was how people thought in situations like this –

but in the darkness of her heart it felt like an equation that was gaining greater validity, the more time passed. This was how the balance sheet looked. This was the punishment for her neglect.

It was just past seven thirty when she checked in at the Hotel Terminus opposite Central station. Her room was on the fifth floor, from which she could look out over the network of tracks, the City Hall and Kungsholmen – over stretches of water, bridges and buildings whose names she did not know. I could move to Stockholm, the thought struck her. If I don't find my son, I might as well leave everything else as well; find a job at a hospital here, Danderyd or Karolinska, and retreat into absolute anonymity.

She drew the curtains, turned back into the room and clenched her teeth so she would not start to cry. What the hell was the point of such illusions and delusions, she thought. Why imagine it would be possible to carry on living? Why imagine Kristina would be able to cast even the slightest light on anything?

In the minibar she found two whisky miniatures. Better than nothing, she thought, unscrewing the cap of one of them.

Fortified by this small amount of alcohol, she rang her sister twenty minutes later. She told her simply that she had been signed off work for some time now and was not feeling great; this was certainly news to Kristina, but she kept her comments to a minimum. Said it was only natural in the circumstances. Or something equally trivial. Ebba told her she was in Stockholm on other business for a few days, and asked if Kristina would mind if they met and talked.

'What about?' asked Kristina.

'About Robert and Henrik,' said Ebba.

'What would that achieve?' asked Kristina.

Ebba was suddenly finding it hard to breathe. As if the oxygen in the small room had run out in an instant. 'Because – because you seemed to be getting along with Henrik when we were there,' she forced out. 'You've always got on well with him. It occurred to me that he might – that he might have said something to you, the evening he went missing.'

It was quiet at the other end of the line for a few seconds before Kristina answered. No, she said, Henrik had not done that. Of course not, she would have said something if he had. Told Ebba and the police and anybody who asked, what was Ebba thinking? But if she dropped in the following afternoon, they could still have a cup of tea and a chat. Between one and three would be the best time to guarantee there would be neither husband nor child to disturb them.

But she shouldn't get her hopes up that Kristina could be of any help.

Ebba thanked her – as if she had been granted some sort of favour – and hung up. She just sat there for a while, not knowing what to do. Turned on the TV and watched the news for a bit. Felt herself shrinking. Switched it off, had a shower and went to bed. It was only half past nine. She turned out the light and took five deep breaths, as she always did to banish the worries and trials of the day.

But sleep did not come to meet her in the way she had expected. Instead, a memory emerged. It crystallized out of the dense darkness of her own mind and of the hotel room, and its intention was not to heal.

One summer, quite a few years ago. The boys must have been twelve and seven. They had rented a house on Jutland for the whole summer. She had arranged it; a colleague at the hospital was in the USA to do some research and did not want their place standing empty. Leif and the boys went down as soon as school finished, while she worked until the end of the first week in July. But the plan was for her to go down there for four or five days over midsummer, too.

Leif had Kristina to help him. Not that he needed help, it was more a case of Kristina needing a bit of stability for a few weeks, having nowhere to live after the break-up of a love affair; this was long before Jakob Willnius came onto the scene.

Ebba drove all the way down from Sundsvall for that mid-summer visit. She took the night ferry across the Skagerrak from Varberg to Grenaa. She reached the house, right down on the North Sea coast, just north of Sønderborg, early in the morning. They were all asleep, it was still only about six o'clock. It was a big house in a beautiful setting between the dunes; she had only heard it described by the doctor who owned it, and then by Leif on the phone, and it took her a while to orientate herself. She tiptoed round from room to room, up and down stairs, and finally she found her whole family asleep in a huge double bed under a wide skylight in the loft. All four of them: her husband Leif, her sister Kristina, her sons Henrik and Kristoffer. The boys were in the middle, Kristina and Leif on either side, and there was something about that picture, that grouping, which made her heart beat out of time. They were all facing the same way, like teaspoons in a kitchen drawer, with Leif at the back. The quilt was bunched up at their feet, she could see their sleeping bodies, the boys in shorts, her Co-op manager in pyjamas, Kristina in briefs and a T-shirt, all lightly, just lightly touching the one in front of them in their sleep – and it all exuded such deep harmony and such security that something started to swell in her throat. It was like a picture, just like an idyllic painting of a happy family.

She swallowed and swallowed, but the questions she was trying to force back down in the process kept bubbling up. *Why aren't I lying there with them? How come Leif and I have never – never ever – slept like that with the boys? Why am I standing here?*

Or: *Why am I the one standing here?*

She did not wake them. She crept back down the stairs, found a bed in another room and slipped under a blanket. She was woken four hours later by Leif, bringing her a cup of coffee and a Danish pastry. He looked at her in some surprise and asked whether she'd had an allergic reaction to something; she admitted that there must have been some variety of pollen in the air, and she had got through a whole packet of tissues on the way down.

No, this was certainly not a memory designed to heal.

27

The woman was small and slightly ruddy-faced.

Gunnar Barbarotti was fleetingly put in mind of a female marathon runner. Thin as a rake, not an excess gram on her body, she sat very upright in her seat with her hands folded on the table in front of her. The look in those green eyes was open and alert.

Thirty-five, he judged. Strong-willed, had undoubtedly been through a lot.

He nodded to her. She stood up and shook hands. First with him, then with Eva Backman. Tillgren, officer in training, shut the door behind them.

They sat down. Eva Backman started the tape recorder and went through the formalities. Indicated to the woman that she could start.

'My name is Linda Eriksson. I live in Gothenburg.'

Eva Backman stuck one thumb in the air to indicate the player was recording properly.

'I work as a physiotherapist at Sahlgrenska hospital. I'm thirty-two years old, married with two children . . . will that do?'

'That'll do,' confirmed Gunnar Barbarotti. 'Can you tell us why you're here?'

She cleared her throat and launched in.

'I'm here because I have a sister,' she said. 'Or rather, *had* a sister. Jane, her name was Jane . . . our surname was Andersson as children, but she became Almgren when she got married. I don't really know how to . . . hrrm. I'm sorry.'

'Have a drink of water,' said Eva Backman.

'Thanks.'

She poured some mineral water into a glass and took a gulp. Sighed and clasped her hands again. 'Well the thing is, my sister died a few weeks ago. She was run over by a bus in Oslo, I don't – I don't know what she was doing there. She'd been living here in Kymlinge for a couple of years. My sister wasn't . . . exactly well.'

'Wasn't exactly well?' queried Barbarotti.

'No. She had a personality disorder, as they say, and she'd been that way for quite a long time.'

'How old was your sister?' asked Eva Backman.

'Thirty-four. Two years older than me. I don't really know where to start, it's such a long story.'

'We've got plenty of time,' Gunnar Barbarotti assured her. 'Why not take it from the beginning?'

Linda Eriksson nodded and drank a bit more water.

'All right,' she said. 'I suppose you could say I come from a problem family.'

She attempted an apologetic smile, as if she wanted to say sorry for the fact that they even existed. Barbarotti felt washed by a wave of sympathy for this woman, delicate but strong. He decided, without really being conscious of it, not to question anything she said.

'But this is the price, of course,' she went on. 'There are three of us, and I'm the youngest. My mother's been in a mental hospital for some years now, my brother Henry, he's the eldest, has at least two years of his prison sentence left to serve . . . and then there was Jane. I've never seen my father; Henry and Jane had a different one, but he's dead. So they're my half-brother and sister. My dad was apparently English . . . I don't know if it's true, but my mother used to say he was.'

'But you all grew up together?' put in Eva Backman. 'You and your half-siblings?'

'On and off.'

'Where?' asked Gunnar Barbarotti.

'All over. I think I lived in ten different places in my first fifteen years,' said Linda Eriksson with a quick smile. 'Including two years here in Kymlinge. Henry's eight years older than me, and he left home pretty early. But Jane and I . . . well yes, we grew up as sisters. We only had each other, you might say.'

'If we concentrate on Jane,' suggested Barbarotti. 'Did you stay in regular contact with each other as adults, too?'

Linda Eriksson shook her head. 'No, I'm afraid not. It just didn't work. Keeping in touch with Jane would have been like . . . well, like being dragged down by someone who was drowning.'

'Why?' said Eva Backman.

'Because she was the way she was. It started when she was still at secondary school, she was already trying out drugs – all sorts. Permanently obsessed with herself and her problems, it's all part of the clinical picture, they say. She spent time in various treatment centres after she turned eighteen, and that was when we started falling out of touch. Though in the end there was one treatment that seemed to work, or she got out of the drug habit, at any rate, and found a man . . . and the other part of the story is that our mother was in a very bad way as well. I moved out when I was in the first year of upper secondary – social services and a school psychologist arranged somewhere for me to live independently.'

'And Jane?' said Gunnar Barbarotti.

'Well, she got together with this Germund. They got married and had two children. Moved to Kalmar. I thought they were doing fine, but when I went to visit them a couple of years later, I realized I'd been wrong. Neither of them had a proper job, he was a recovering alcoholic, of course, and they'd joined some kind of sect and were up to all sorts of weird things. I only went to see them the once, and six months later I heard it had all come crashing down. Jane had tried to kill her husband and children, there was some kind of jealousy motive behind it, and in the end she was sentenced to secure psychiatric care and lost the right to see her children.'

'And her husband got custody?'

'Yes. He was considered capable, evidently. But I don't know, there was a lot of trouble even after . . . though it was probably mainly Jane's fault.'

'Were you in touch with her – or with them – during this period?' asked Eva Backman.

'Hardly at all. The information came through my mother. And she wasn't always the most reliable of sources. Anyway, Germund moved abroad with the children about . . . let me see, it must be two years ago now, and I don't think Jane ever managed to find out where they lived. She was in and out of residential care, but about a year ago she was discharged, and she seems to have coped, somehow. Not declared fit for work, of course, but as far as I know – or as far as I knew, perhaps I should say – she was coping on her own. Naturally I had no idea about – about this.'

She threw her arms wide and her apologetic expression

returned. As if she were the irresponsible one, and it was her negligence that had led to the catastrophe.

'How long has it been since you were last in touch with your sister?' asked Barbarotti.

'I haven't seen her for over a year. But I talked to her on the phone. The last time was in March.'

'What did you talk about?'

'She wanted to borrow money. I said no and she slammed down the phone.'

'When did you find out she was dead?'

'The day she died. They rang from the hospital in Oslo. She had my number on a scrap of paper in her purse, apparently.'

'The twenty-fifth of July?'

'Yes. We were just back from a two-week holiday in Germany. My husband's from there.'

'Tell us what happened after that,' prompted Eva Backman.

'Well, it was me who dealt with the practical side. I went to Oslo to identify the body. I contacted the undertaker and arranged the funeral and the inventory of her estate and all that. I didn't bother trying to get any help from my brother and mother, but they did come to the funeral. Three mourners plus two prison guards and a psychiatric nurse – not exactly a cheery occasion.'

'What date was the funeral?'

'The fourth of August.'

'Here in Kymlinge?'

'Yes. She lived here these past few years, like I said.'

'And then?'

'Well, then there was her flat to see to. I managed to get the landlord to agree to half the month's rent as long as I got everything cleared out by the fifteenth, and it was last Monday I came up here and started to sort it out.'

Eva Backman looked in her notebook. 'Fabriksgatan 26, is that right?'

'That's right. I'd set aside three days, not that she owned much stuff, of course, but it still takes time. I decided to get rid of everything. I arranged with a firm of hauliers that they would come and fetch the things and take them to various charities, or direct to the tip – I know she was my sister, but I simply couldn't face poking about in her dismal life. She hadn't kept anything memorable either. No photo albums or anything like that.'

'Her children and former husband?'

'I discussed it with the police and a couple of social workers and we all more or less agreed it would be best to leave them in peace. There was nothing to gain by dragging Jane into their lives again. It may sound a bit cynical, but that was what we decided.'

'How old are the children, did you say?' asked Eva Backman.

'Ten and eight.'

'Sounds like a sensible decision,' observed Gunnar Barbarotti. 'So you were clearing out her flat, and it was then that . . .'

Linda Eriksson closed her eyes for a moment. She took a deep breath as if to steel herself. The thin shoulders in the green cotton dress rose and fell. Gunnar Barbarotti thought again that this was a woman he admired. Her life had the worst possible starting point, but she had come through. He exchanged a glance with Eva Backman, and thought he could detect she was feeling the same.

'Yes. I started with the other rooms, left the kitchen till last.

It was this morning, and . . . well, when I started emptying the freezer, it was then I caught sight of those . . . fingers. Sorry . . .'

A shudder ran through her thin body, and for a second Barbarotti thought she was going to throw up on the table. But she recovered. Shook her head and drank some of her water. Eva Backman put a hand on her arm.

'Thank you. Sorry, I think I must still be in shock. It was so awful when I realized what was in that plastic bag . . .'

Gunnar Barbarotti waited, and gestured to his colleague to say nothing either.

'It was an arm. Cut off at the elbow. A supermarket bag, from ICA, one of those red-and-white ones, and I must have just sat there staring at it for ten minutes before I was able to do anything. I'd started dumping everything from the freezer in a bin bag, ready to throw it in the refuse room, and if those fingers hadn't been sticking out, I might not have noticed anything . . . but then I opened another bag. At first I couldn't work out what it was, but then I saw it was part of a pelvis.'

She stopped. A few seconds passed.

'A man?' said Eva Backman.

'Yes, a man.'

A movement outside the window caught Gunnar Barbarotti's attention for a moment. He turned his head and caught sight of a magpie as it came flying in and settled on the windowsill. Why are you landing there? he thought in bewilderment. Are you a spy sent by the Devil, or what?

Gunnar Barbarotti had never been in any doubt about the existence of the Devil. It was only the potential presence of God that was the problem.

'Hrrm, right,' Eva Backman cleared her throat. 'So what

did you do? I can understand it must have been traumatic for you.'

'It certainly was traumatic,' admitted Linda Eriksson. 'I ran to the loo to be sick, then I pulled myself together and rang the police. And while I was waiting for them, I opened another bag – I don't know why I did it, maybe because I suspected what it might be and wanted to confirm it. Anyway, it was a head. I rushed back to the loo and threw up again, and then I stayed there until the police came.'

Gunnar Barbarotti sat up straighter in his chair. 'And you stayed in the flat while they unpacked the rest?'

'I waited in another room while they did it. With a police-woman.'

'And you heard that there were two bodies?'

'Yes.'

'Which your sister was storing in her freezer for some reason?'

'Yes.'

'Have you any idea why she did it?'

'No.'

'Did you get to see them?'

'Yes. The police asked if I was prepared to look and I said I'd try . . . that is, I looked at the heads.'

'And?'

'I didn't recognize either of them. They were in a pretty bad state, but I could see they were both men.'

'I see,' said Gunnar Barbarotti, glancing back at the magpie, which had clearly seen and heard enough, because it flapped its wings and flew off. He felt pretty much the same way. He had heard enough. He wished for a moment that he, too, had wings. Eva Backman had leant forward and put a hand on Linda Eriksson's arm again.

'Had your sister shown any violent tendencies while she was alive?'

Lina Eriksson hesitated. They let her hesitate.

'I don't quite know how to answer,' she said finally. 'As I told you, she did try to kill her family, and I think – I think people . . .'

'Yes?'

'I think people have to understand Jane was really ill. She ought not to have been allowed out – for her own good and everybody else's. But you know how it is with mental health provision in this country, I assume? Let all the loonies out onto the streets. They cause a bit of harm and suffering, but they don't live long. Cheaper for society in the long run.'

Gunnar Barbarotti agreed with this damning verdict pretty much one hundred per cent, and he knew Eva Backman did, too, but he chose not to make any comment on Linda Eriksson's analysis.

'It is what it is,' was all he said. 'And there are a lot of things that should be organized differently – I mean in healthcare in this country. But for our purposes, we have to focus on getting some clear view of what's actually happened. We'll be needing to talk to you a few more times. Where can we reach you?'

Linda Eriksson started to cry for the first time. Eva Backman passed her a pile of tissues, and she blew her nose and wiped her eyes.

'I'd like to go home to my family in Gothenburg,' she said faintly. 'If that's all right.'

Barbarotti exchanged another look with Backman and her thumb went up in reply. 'That's fine,' he said. 'We've got your address and phone number. I'm sure we'll be back in touch with you tomorrow. How will you get to Gothenburg?'

'My husband will come and fetch me if I ask him. It only takes an hour . . . well, two, for him to drive here and back.'

Gunnar Barbarotti nodded. Eva Backman nodded.

'There's a rest room next door. You can lie down there and wait for him.'

'Thanks,' said Linda Eriksson and followed Eva Backman out of the door.

Poor devil, thought Gunnar Barbarotti. And . . . and if only she'd started with the kitchen, she'd have been saved the bother of clearing the rest of the flat.

'So what do you say about this?' asked Eva Backman half an hour later, sinking down in the visitor's armchair in his office.

'What do *you* say?' asked Gunnar Barbarotti.

'Grotesque,' said Eva Backman. 'Utterly grotesque.'

'Do you think she cut them up in the kitchen?'

'In the bathroom, Wilhelmsson said. There were clear traces.'

'In the bath?'

'On the tiled floor, more likely. The sister had given it all a good scrub, maybe Jane as well. But blood is blood.'

'How long ago?'

'He couldn't say. But clearly it's been a while.'

'And we're pretty sure about one of them?'

'You saw yourself, didn't you?'

Gunnar Barbarotti nodded. Even though the face was not in great shape, there was little doubt. One of the heads was that of Robert Hermansson, who had been missing since 20 December the previous year. Eight months, all but a few days.

'And you don't think we ought to ask her if she knows of any link?'

'Between her sister and the Hermansson family?'

'Yes.'

'No, I don't. Not until we're a hundred per cent sure. But if the identity is confirmed before she leaves, I'll go in and ask a couple more questions. What do you think about the other one?'

Eva Backman shrugged. 'We'll know about that in a couple of hours, too. I've no idea. Could be Henrik Grundt, could be somebody else. Wilhelmsson says the body was in a worse state. Especially the head. It seems to have been left to rot for a few days before she packed him up and put him in the freezer.'

Inspector Barbarotti leant back and clasped his hands at the back of his neck. All at once he felt immense fatigue descend on him. And powerlessness. He took a deep breath to improve his oxygen supply.

'And if it isn't Henrik Grundt we're dealing with,' he said with a kind of understated and perverse thoroughness, 'then it's some other poor wretch that has had the pleasure of being killed and cut up by our little friend Jane Almgren. Is that what you're saying?'

'No, that's what you're saying,' observed Eva Backman in roughly the same tone. 'But basically I agree with you. Either it is Henrik Grundt or it isn't. In the latter case, we've got yet another question to straighten out.'

Gunnar Barbarotti looked at the time and pondered.

'Borgsen's started drawing up a list,' he said. 'Of people we ought to talk to. Neighbours and social workers and therapists and all sorts . . .'

'The husband?'

'Him too. Assuming we can find him. And the mother and brother. Borgsen was up to fifty-two names an hour ago. Exactly a deck of cards. I wonder . . .'

'Yes.'

'I wonder whether you fancy sneaking out to the Elk for a beer and a sandwich before it all kicks off? We'll be working late tonight.'

Eva Backman sighed. 'A cold beer before the war,' she said. 'Yep, not a bad idea. Better just call home and tell the family first.'

'Good,' said Barbarotti. 'I ought to have a quick word with Sara, too.'

Eva Backman got to her feet to leave, but then stood in the middle of the room for a few moments, looking out of the window with a slightly absent expression. Then she turned her cornflower-blue eyes on her colleague.

'You know what I think, Gunnar?'

Gunnar Barbarotti made a 'search me' gesture with his hands.

'I think this feels totally sick. Good God, imagine how the papers are going to feel when they get hold of a story like this. TV celeb found dead in freezer! Jointed and packaged! Bloody hell, Gunnar, I should have done exactly what they told me. Taken over Dad's shoe shop and married Rojne Walltin.'

'Who the hell is Rojne Walltin?'

'Haven't I told you about Rojne?'

'Never.'

'He's got a chain of shoe shops in Borås and Vänersborg. If we'd paired off we'd have had a virtual monopoly. And he did propose, in fact.'

'Are you and Willy having problems?'

'Not at all. Well, no more than usual.'

'Ah, OK. Go and ring him and say you're on the late shift tonight. At least you won't have to play unihockey.'

Eva Backman nodded and left the room. Gunnar Barbarotti sat there a bit longer with his feet up on the desk, wondering whether he ought to put together an existential prayer to Our Lord. But neither the right words nor the right odds presented themselves, so he left it. For now, God was well above the line, largely thanks to Marianne and Greece – on the basis of which He had made great advances – and deep inside, Gunnar Barbarotti had started to hear a voice, expressing at regular intervals the seductive truth that it was easier to be at ease in this world if there actually was a benevolently inclined higher power.

And that suggested the aforementioned power perhaps didn't – in the long run – much appreciate having His existence called into question all the time.

Content with this bargain-basement analysis, he rang home to have a word with his daughter. She did not answer, but he left a message to say he had to put in some overtime at work and would be late home.

Like the considerate father he was, he omitted to mention that the work involved a jigsaw puzzle of two people's frozen body parts.

28

Ebba Hermansson Grundt got off the metro at the Skog-skyrkogården stop. She went through the underpass beneath Nynäsvägen, following the directions she had been given, and came into Old Enskede. She had never been to visit her younger sister before and was immediately taken aback by the classiness of the area. Leif and the boys had been here once, a couple of years since, but she had had to opt out. Probably a colleague calling in sick, but she couldn't remember.

The old wooden villas were larger and more charming than she had imagined, with big gardens and trees weighed down with fruit. Involuntarily comparing all this with her own standard at home in Sundsvall, she registered that Kristina must be several rungs above her on the ladder of social success.

But it was simply an automatic reaction, not anything that worried or barbed her. There was no room for further barbs after Henrik's disappearance. As far as she was concerned, she would be prepared to live out the rest of her days in a tiny flat in some suburb, if only her son came back. Or to cut short her own life – why not? – in return for Henrik being able to live.

But there was a problem with equations like that, of course. They didn't really exist.

She turned into Musseronvägen and it struck her that she should have bought flowers. It couldn't hurt, and hadn't she passed a florist's a few minutes ago? At that little square of shops. She stopped and looked at her watch, realized she was early and turned back.

It struck her then that for one short and terrifying moment, she had forgotten why she had come.

'Thank you,' said Kristina, somehow contriving to sound genuinely surprised. 'You needn't have. And I'm so useless with pot plants.'

'It's an orchid. It only needs watering once a month.'

'Excellent,' said Kristina. 'It'll survive for a month then, at least.'

'Apparently, there are three thousand different kinds,' said Ebba.

'Really, that many?' said Kristina.

It's a good thing I bought it, thought Ebba. It gave us something to talk about when I got here.

Kristina went ahead of her to a glazed-in verandah looking out over the garden. Coffee and some kind of cake were waiting on the table; she indicated that Ebba should take a seat in one of the basket chairs. No tour of the house, no ceremony. Nor had she expected anything like that. Only once the coffee had been poured and sampled did Ebba notice her sister was pregnant. She had no bump yet, but there was something about the way she was sitting; her legs somewhat parted and her back straight.

'You're expecting?'

Kristina nodded.

'Congratulations. How far gone are you?'

'Twelve weeks.'

There's something else as well, thought Ebba suddenly. Her eyes don't look the way they normally do. She's anxious about something. And her jaw is tense, she looks as though she's finding this disagreeable.

It surprised her that she was in a position to make these observations when she was so wrapped up in her own concerns. But perhaps that's how it is with sisters, she thought. We read each other with no more than a look. Whether we like it or not, it's quite natural.

Though on the other hand it perhaps wasn't that odd for Kristina to be unenthusiastic about the visit. Ebba could understand that. All her life she had been inferior to her elder sister, or that must have been how it felt, particularly when she was a teenager – but at least she'd had a good relationship with the children. Ebba's children, that was to say. Henrik's disappearance had been a blow to her, too. And Robert's. Kristina and Robert had always been close, Ebba suddenly remembered; *she* was the one who had distanced herself from the other two. She was the one who had created a boundary line and made sure to maintain it. As she sat there waiting for them to find their way into some kind of conversation, these irrefutable facts ran through her head, and she felt a lump in her throat. Get a grip, she thought with a mixture of irritation and fear, don't start blubbing, anything but that!

Perhaps Kristina picked up on how brittle her sister was – read her with that sisterly reflex – because suddenly she did something unusual. Ebba could not remember anything like that happening before. Kristina leant forward in her chair and stroked her arm.

Simply that.

It was a gesture that only took a second but it bore witness to . . . something beyond words, thought Ebba. She felt a sudden light-headedness. Blinked it away and looked into Kristina's eyes. Saw that anxiety there again, that tense look, which did not fit at all with the stroking of her arm. Got to start now, she thought. Got to start talking, silence has its limitations.

'I don't know why I'm here,' she said. 'Not really.'

'Nor do I,' said Kristina.

'Maybe it's just because I can't stand doing nothing.'

'You've never been good at doing nothing,' said Kristina.

Ebba cleared her throat. Whatever that constriction was, it didn't want to shift.

'I'm finding it so difficult to bear, Kristina. I thought I might gradually get used to it, but I'm not. It's just getting worse and worse.'

Kristina made no reply. She chewed her lower lip, her eyes fixed on some point above and behind Ebba's head.

'It gets worse every day. I've got to find out what happened to Henrik.'

Kristina raised her eyebrows a millimetre. 'I don't quite understand.'

'What don't you understand?'

'What it would achieve.'

'I don't know what it would achieve, either, but all this hanging about waiting is driving me crazy.'

'Crazy?'

'Yes, it really is. The doing nothing is turning me crazy. There must . . .'

'Yes?'

'There must have been something about Henrik, those days we were there. Something that . . . well, that I didn't notice.'

'What do you mean?'

'I mean he did actually make the decision to go out that night.'

'Yes, it seems that way.'

'Perhaps he decided a long time in advance. And – and since you talked to him a fair bit, well, perhaps you noticed something? That was what I was wondering.'

'I didn't notice anything special, Ebba,' said Kristina, with her eyes still fixed on that point. 'And I've told you so a hundred times already.'

'I know you have. But looking back on it now, is there really nothing that comes to mind?'

'No.'

'But there ought—'

'Ebba, please, do you think I haven't thought about this? I've done scarcely anything else since it happened. I've asked myself about it day and night.'

'I understand that. But what did you talk about?'

'Pardon?'

'What did you and Henrik talk about?'

'We talked about all sorts of things.'

'All sorts of things?'

'Yes.'

'Like what?'

'Like Uppsala. I don't like you interrogating me, Ebba.'

The lump in her throat was suddenly threatening to burst. 'Yes, but what am I supposed to do then, Kristina? Tell me that. You're not helping.'

Kristina hesitated for a moment. Lowered her gaze and

looked her sister in the eyes. 'I'm not helping, because I can't help,' she said slowly, almost as if she were addressing a child. 'There really is nothing Henrik said or did that could explain what happened. Why would I keep anything quiet, Ebba, please can you tell me that?'

'I don't know,' said Ebba. 'No, of course you're not keeping anything quiet. Did you talk about – about me?'

'About you?'

'Yes. Or family relations in general? Maybe you touched on things that you think might be too sensitive for me to hear? In that case I beg you, Kristina, to stop making allowances of that sort. It's totally immaterial what—'

'We didn't talk about you, Ebba. Nor about the family.'

Ebba briefly fumbled with her coffee cup. She put it back on its saucer without drinking any.

'Uppsala? What did the two of you say about Uppsala, then?'

'Henrik told me a bit about his course. And his accommodation and so on.'

'And Jenny?'

'Yes, he mentioned her.'

'And?'

'I didn't get the impression it was anything all that serious.'

'Do you know the police never tracked her down?'

'Yes . . . no . . . what do you mean?'

'They haven't located that Jenny.'

'Oh?'

'It's a bit odd, isn't it?'

'Why should it be odd?'

'He hadn't even got her phone number written down.'

'What are you driving at, Ebba?'

'I'm not driving at anything. I'm just saying I think it seems odd.'

'Do you think Jenny's got something to do with Henrik's disappearance?'

Ebba gave a dejected shrug. 'I don't know. It's all so horribly weird, the whole thing. And where does Robert come into the picture?'

Kristina sighed. 'Ebba, please, this is getting us nowhere. As you say, what happened is incomprehensible. It was incomprehensible then, and it's just as incomprehensible now. There's no point rooting around in it any more, can't you see? We've got to move on with what's left, concentrate on other things – if we ever find out what happened to Robert and Henrik, it won't be because of anything we've done or not done. You've got to put your energy into going forwards, Ebba, not backwards.'

'So what you're saying is that you don't want to help?'

'I *can't* help, that's what I'm saying.'

'But what do *you* think then, Kristina? You can confide that much in me, surely? What do you really think happened to Robert and Henrik?'

Kristina leant back in her basket chair and regarded her sister with a look of . . . well, what, Ebba wondered. Pity? Rejection? Boredom?

'I don't think anything, Ebba, dear. I don't think anything at all.'

'Are they alive? Can't you at least tell me if you think either of them is still alive?'

Her voice scarcely held, it was little more than a whisper. Kristina once again had that look in her eyes that was so hard to interpret, and now she was holding on hard to the arms of her chair, too; for a few seconds, it looked as though she couldn't make her mind up.

Whether to get to her feet or not. Whether to answer or not. In the end, she took a deep breath, relaxed and let her shoulders go slack.

'I think they're dead, Ebba. It would just be stupid to go round imagining anything else.'

There were ten seconds of silence.

'Thank you,' said Ebba. 'Thank you for letting me talk to you, anyway.'

Kristina stood at the window, watching as her sister went out of the gate. Even once Ebba had disappeared out of sight along Musseronvägen, she did not feel able to move. An icy paralysis spread from the soles of her feet all the way to the top of her head, and soon her field of vision started to contract too; she was conveyed backwards through a rapidly shrinking tunnel, and the second before she fainted, she managed to soften the fall a little by bending her knees and leaning forwards.

She came round on the hall floor some time later, crawled on hands and knees to the toilet and threw up. Went on vomiting as if it were not just the contents of her stomach that had to be ejected, but everything else as well. Her guts, her internal organs, life itself.

Her unborn child.

But she did not crack. She found unexpected strength from somewhere, the child clung on, she splashed her face with cold water, pulled a brush through her hair, stood up straighter, looked at herself in the mirror. I pulled it off, she thought in surprise. I did it.

Then she returned to the verandah. Cleared away the coffee pot, cups and cake.

She threw the slender orchid in the rubbish bag and took it out to the bin. All traces eradicated.

29

The evening tabloids were having a field day.

TV STAR KILLED AND DISMEMBERED

said the front page of one.

WANKER ROB BODY PARTS FOUND IN FREEZER

shouted the other. A total of sixteen pages was devoted to the story, and if the reality TV show *Fucking Island* had started to fade from popular memory, it was now fished up to became the focus of renewed attention. To the delight of some and the horror of others, presumably. The coverage – in both papers – also featured the sad news that Miss Hälsingland 1995, who almost precisely nine months earlier and together with ice hockey stud 'Gherkin' Johansson had hit the jackpot of 3.1 million kronor and should have been giving birth just about now to the fruit of the couple's happy union, had miscarried in February, and at the same time had left Gherkin for a singer in a Goth hard rock band from Skene, just twenty and covered in tattoos.

While he was snatching a belated, quarter-hour lunch – comprising a cheese and ham roll, a banana and a small apple juice – Gunnar Barbarotti flicked through both newspapers and then threw them into the wastepaper basket in frustration.

'Well we're not being overlooked, that's for sure,' observed Eva Backman, coming through the door at that moment. 'What time is the press conference?'

'In fifteen minutes. Have you had time to look at the interviews?'

Eva gave a shrug. 'Just a quick glance. There doesn't seem to be anything.'

'Nothing?'

'Not at first sight, at any rate.'

'What do the doctors say?'

Eva Backman sat down. 'We've talked to three, but there are two more who might have something relevant to say. There's evidently quite a high staff turnover. At any event, these three think a greater level of institutional care would have been desirable for Jane Almgren.'

'Really?' said Gunnar Barbarotti. 'Well I believe I would have come to the same conclusion.'

'But with the politicians having reformed all psychiatric care out of existence, there was nothing to be done, they claim. On the other hand, there's nothing in Jane Almgren's pathology that indicated . . . well, her being this insane.'

'Not particularly unexpected opinions, then?'

'Hardly. The fact that she had previously tried to kill her family was of no great relevance, one of them thought. Excellent medication had brought all that under control.'

'Aha? And if she didn't take her medication . . . ?'

'Well it's nothing anyone else can be blamed for, in that case. Anyway, the way I see it is that we'll get nowhere if we start looking for scapegoats and attacking the care system. Actually . . .'

'Yes?'

'Actually, I don't have much clue what we ought to focus our attention on. We've found the murderer, after all. But what do you think, Mr Inspector? The case is solved.'

Gunnar Barbarotti shuffled a drift of paperwork off the edge of the desk to make room for his elbows. He put his head in his hands. 'Not exactly solved, perhaps,' he pointed out. 'You're forgetting we have an unidentified victim.'

'Thanks for reminding me,' said Eva Backman, popping two bits of chewing gum into her mouth and starting to chew thoughtfully. 'Who do you think he is? Or was?'

'Good question,' said Gunnar Barbarotti, picking up a piece of paper that had escaped the desk clearance. He glanced through it swiftly. 'According to Wilhelmsson, what we have is a male individual aged thirty-five to forty. Presumably a pretty rootless character. Lousy teeth, signs of needle use . . .'

'Yes, I heard. A junkie, basically. How long had he been in the freezer?'

'A long time. Maybe even longer than our friend Robert. It'll take a few days for us to get an answer on that little detail.'

'Do you think there's a link?'

'How do you mean, a link?'

'Between him and Robert.'

Gunnar Barbarotti scratched his head. 'How the hell should I know? They both knew Jane Almgren, I suppose. There's one link for you, at least.'

Eva Backman gave a quick smile. 'Now, now, constable, no need to be petty. Let's just be glad that at least we have a murderer. Even if she's dead. It feels a bit back-to-front, don't you think? The jigsaw is finished even though it's missing a piece.'

'Finished?' snorted Gunnar Barbarotti. 'What the hell are

you on about? We have – listen up now – we have good grounds for assuming that Jane Almgren killed Robert Hermansson. On equally good grounds, we can assume she dismembered him and put him in the freezer. Along with some other guy, who was presumably already there. As far as I understand it, that's all we know with any certainty. We've got a thousand questions and only one answer, namely that the murderer's name was Jane Almgren. And we're not even sure of that, incidentally, so if you think—'

'Calm down,' interrupted Backman. 'I just mean that it's unusual for us to know the perpetrator's name before we know the victim's. It's usually the other way round. But I'm absolutely clear on the fact that Henrik Grundt still has to be considered missing.'

'Good,' said Gunnar Barbarotti. 'On that point, we're in agreement.'

'And we will find out who Robert's roommate was, I'm convinced of that. There are a few hundred people reported missing who are awaiting our attention . . . but you must still agree that we've come a bit further along the road, thanks to Jane Almgren?'

'Yeah, yeah,' sighed Gunnar Barbarotti. 'But the road to where? To hell, or what?'

Eva Backman threw her chewing gum into his bin and stood up.

'Just trying to cheer you up a bit,' she said. 'But it's a waste of time, I can tell. Good luck with the press conference. I think you ought to toddle off now. Remember not to gnash your teeth, it makes a bad impression.'

Gunnar Barbarotti struggled into his jacket and accompanied her through the door.

'If that bald idiot from *GT* turns up, I'll throttle him,' he declared grimly.

'Fine by me, supercop,' said Eva Backman. 'I can chop him up and freeze him for you if you're too busy.'

A woman shouldn't really be talking like that, thought Gunnar Barbarotti, but he didn't say it out loud.

By the time he got home that evening it was ten thirty and Sara was sitting in the kitchen with a Frenchman. His name was Yann and he had stopped off in Kymlinge on his way back from the North Cape to Paris. They were travelling in a revamped old Volkswagen camper van, Sara told him, four young men from Paris – they had met at the outdoor cafe of the city hotel, where Sara had been with a few other girls, friends of hers, in this final refrain of the summer holidays, and she had invited Yann home for a cup of tea because she liked him.

Gunnar Barbarotti, who had about twenty words of French and a thirteen-hour working day to his name, muttered an inspired 'Bon soir', and tried to smile at the young Adonis. He could see Sara appreciated his discomfort, but she didn't do anything to mitigate it.

Instead, she said, 'A woman rang.'

'A woman?'

'Yes. She said her name was Marianne and that you knew each other. She was ringing from Helsingborg. She sounded nice. You must have forgotten to tell me about her, Daddyo.'

'No, I . . .'

'I told her you were still at work, and she said she might ring back later.'

The French boy said something he didn't catch and Sara

laughed. Gunnar Barbarotti ventured a cautious 'Salut!' and left the kitchen.

If he's still there in half an hour I'll throw him out, he decided as he stood in the shower. Coming here on the prowl in his Frenchy way.

And she did ring. He had just crawled into bed and she apologized for ringing so late.

'It doesn't matter,' Gunnar Barbarotti assured her. 'I hadn't managed to get to bed.'

'I thought as much. I saw you on TV. You looked so good that I started missing you. And you come across as really intelligent, did you know that? How are you?'

Gunnar Barbarotti swallowed. A warm Mediterranean night beneath a clear and starlit sky came washing over him without warning. A terrace with mattresses on the ground – and ouzo glasses and olives and a naked woman with pendulous breasts riding him . . . oh God!

'Fine,' he croaked. 'How about you?'

'Good. But I'm missing you, as I said.'

We had an agreement not to be in touch for a month, he thought. It's been barely two weeks.

But it seemed a bit petty to point it out. Eva Backman had called him petty.

'Wouldn't mind seeing you, either,' he heard himself say. 'Though I've got a lot on at work at the moment.'

'Yes, I realize,' she said. 'I just wanted to call and wish you good night. And remind you of my existence.'

'I remember, I remember,' he assured her, a little poetically.

'So if I were to ring you on Saturday and suggest a date, you wouldn't say no?'

'Wouldn't dream of it,' said Gunnar Barbarotti. 'Sleep well, Marianne.'

An hour and a half later, he still hadn't got to sleep. As far as he could judge, the French boy had left, and what was preying on Gunnar Barbarotti's mind was the possibility that Sara had gone with him. But he didn't want to go and check; there hadn't been a sound from either the kitchen or her bedroom for the last twenty minutes – but then nor had he registered the front door opening and closing. Bloody hell, he thought. What if his own daughter were at this very minute being seduced in her bed by a pretty-boy frog!

It was more than he could bear. He was well aware that Sara was in fact eighteen, and that he had made his own sexual debut at sixteen. But that was irrelevant, and his own experience was not one he would have wished on his beloved daughter.

On the other hand, nor did he want to subject her to him sticking his head round the door as she lay naked in the arms of a French . . . Christ, he thought. This is driving me crazy. I'm as primitive as a male gorilla and as bigoted as I don't know what. Who am I to go interfering in her life? Just now I was watching a film in my mind of a naked woman sitting astride me. It would be nothing but totally normal if—

Ponytail! He had a ponytail, that Yann. If there was one thing Gunnar Barbarotti couldn't stand, it was men with ponytails. It was simply—

You're talking crap, protested his superego. You're a jealous, overprotective father! Don't interfere in your daughter's life, she's not a minor any more!

And so it went on. Half-formed and mildly hysterical thoughts ran riot in his head, but in the midst of this desperate mental wrestling, he suddenly heard that click, the front door. He sat up in bed and strained his ears . . . it was . . . it was Sara coming in. Just one person? He listened even more intently, trying to evaluate the sounds from the hall.

Yes, just one.

Good. He gave a sigh of relief. Sara had gone with the Frenchman, for a little walk. They had parted outside his camper van and she had allowed him to kiss her on the cheek. They had promised to keep in touch, exchanged email addresses, and by tomorrow morning he would be on the motorway down through Denmark and Germany. Excellent.

Gunnar Barbarotti looked at the time. Twenty to one. Now I'm going to lie on my back with my hands folded and think about the Jane Almgren case until I fall asleep, he decided.

That took another forty-five minutes, and there were still just as many question marks when he dozed off as when he started. But at least he had listed them in his mind, which was something.

And counted them. There were four. Hundreds of smaller ones of course, but really only four big ones.

The first was to do with the connection between Jane Almgren and Robert Hermansson. Although it was now a day and a half since Linda Eriksson had made her macabre discovery in her sister's flat in Fabriksgatan, they hadn't identified any link.

Always assuming there was one. Perhaps they'd merely run into each other in the town that night and Jane had picked him up and taken him home. Killed and dismembered him. There were indications that this could be the case, and he had a sense that Eva Backman was thinking along the same lines. Jane had certainly lived in Kymlinge in an earlier phase of her life. That was some years ago – while Robert Hermansson was still living at home with his parents in Allvädersgatan. But they were never at the same school, and moreover, Robert was two years older – and of the people they had talked to so far, nobody could think of anything to connect them.

Perhaps, thought Gunnar Barbarotti as he lay there staring up into the darkness, listening to a shower of rain that was passing over and tapping on the metal windowsill, perhaps she simply recognized him from TV? Could it be as vile as that? Could that be what had landed him in hot water?

Assuming she had deliberately selected him, that is. Perhaps it was entirely random that he was the one; he had already explored the thought. One had to bear in mind that she wasn't normal.

Anyhow, question number two. *The other man?* Who was he? Was there any connection between him and Robert Hermansson? Between him and Jane? And when had he died? It seemed reasonable to assume that Robert had ended his days some time around 20 December – but what about his equally deep-frozen companion in misfortune? How long had he been there? That would take a few days to investigate, but in a week or so they ought to be able to determine it.

A junkie? Had Robert Hermansson been in such a bad state that he, too, came into that category? Barbarotti didn't think so; there was nothing to indicate that he had used drugs to any great extent, and it would have been pretty astonishing if they had managed to miss anything like that after eight months of digging around in his life.

Assuming there was any point at all in looking for things the freezer chums had in common, that is.

Number three – Gunnar Barbarotti had always liked making

lists; in his younger days he had kept exercise books full of notes on all manner of things: players in the Swedish football league, Italian cities, astronauts, African animals, the world's tallest buildings, assassinated heads of state – so now, number three: *Why?*

That was an extraordinarily important question – but he wondered whether they would ever get an intelligible answer to it. An answer to why anyone murdered two men, chopped them up and kept them in a freezer. Well, the motive must presumably be pretty well hidden in the perpetrator's darkest inner recesses. As usual. It was nothing a simple detective inspector had any chance of understanding and taking in. And when she also happened to be dead, as in this case, there was no option of questioning her – and probably, thought Gunnar Barbarotti, probably it was just as well not to know.

There was of course a very small possibility of Jane Almgren not being the perpetrator. As he had said to Backman. That she had just put her freezer at someone else's disposal, as it were – but for the time being he did not want to give that solution any serious thought. It would only complicate the picture still further, and it was bad enough as things stood. Quite bad enough.

So fourthly, then? Well of course, when it came down to it, this was the most crucial question of all. The one that was preying constantly on his mind. There was no doubt about it.

Henrik Grundt. When they received the notification this morning that the other body in the freezer was not that of Robert Hermansson's nephew, Gunnar Barbarotti had felt a dubious mixture of frustration and relief.

Frustration that they still had that mystery to solve. Relief that there was still a small chance of the boy being alive.

But it was not large, this chance, and he was the first to admit it. He had discussed the likelihood of Henrik Grundt being alive very thoroughly with Eva Backman, and they had agreed that it was probably around one per cent. At most. People went missing to start new lives, that did happen – they created new identities for themselves for one reason or another – but the idea that Henrik Grundt, at the age of nineteen, would have had such a reason, and made such a choice . . . well, it seemed pretty far-fetched. Admittedly he had been keeping his sexual orientation secret. They still hadn't revealed this to his mother and father – it was slightly unclear why they had taken that decision, but perhaps it was just so as not to further increase the burden on them.

But for this secret to have made Henrik take such a drastic step as running away from everything – leaving his parents and brother in the limbo of despair where they were undoubtedly marooned – seemed absurd, and for various good reasons. They had made that judgement call eight months ago, and they made the same call today, on learning what a terrible fate had befallen Henrik's uncle.

And last but not least, question five, or 4B, to be more precise. Was there really no link? Could it actually be pure coincidence for two people to disappear from the same family at the same address in the space of twenty-four hours? And for the one to have absolutely nothing to do with the other? What were the odds of that happening?

This was yet another probability problem he and Eva Backman had been trying to thrash out between them for several months, not continuously of course, but at regular intervals – and just before he fell asleep on that protracted Thursday, Gunnar Barbarotti decided that if there were one scientific theory that did *not* apply to events at Allvädersgatan in Kymlinge, it was this one: probability calculus. Tomorrow he was going to tell that to Eva Backman.

Satisfied with these observations and this decision, he turned over his pillow and started dreaming of a warm nighttime terrace in the Greek town of Helsingborg.

30

Karl-Erik had booked a hire car from the airport, and once they were on the motorway, Rosemarie Wunderlich Hermansson started hoping they would collide with an elk.

She had not been back home since their move to Spain on 1 March. Almost six months, but it felt like six years. Or perhaps only six seconds. Sweden seemed simultaneously alien and oppressively familiar; like – while Karl-Erik fiddled with the ventilation system and disparaged the make of car, whatever it was, she tried to find a passable comparison – like a boil that had been surgically removed but then came back, she decided. Or a cancer.

My old life a cancer, she wondered. Was that really the case? And why did these strange things come into her mind? Elks and cancerous tumours? On the way to her son's funeral. Though maybe it wasn't that strange. Suffocating dog days seemed to hang over the landscape they were driving through; the promised time of Canada geese and flowering algae on the lakes of the clay flatlands. Perhaps this was what people's thoughts turned to when they could not bring themselves to look truth in the eye. Find the cherries in the cake.

Coffin or urn, they had been asked. What would you prefer?

Could you put a dismembered body in a coffin? Did they reassemble it, if so, or what? Had they already put Robert back together again? Dressed him somehow? Fixed his head to his neck and his . . . every time she approached these thoughts and questions, it felt as though her own guts were about to dissolve.

Distractions, the tanned therapist in Nerja had told her. What you need, Mrs Hermansson, are distractions. Something to keep you busy, it's actually a pretty common problem amongst my patients here. Lack of activity. It's easy for black thoughts to come crowding in when you've nothing purposeful to spend your time on.

Purposeful distractions, she had thought. No thank you. It had been May when she went there. She had given up after the second session. Sweet Málaga wine worked better in every way, and for the price of a single consultation she could buy eight bottles. And far from the cheapest brand, at that.

She had grown used to it and developed a regular habit. Always two ice cubes. A glass first thing. Number two in the 'garden' sometime in the morning, while Karl-Erik was out on one of his ploys. On the bedroom wall they had a map of Andalusia, and by means of pins with little blue and yellow heads, he was marking every town and village he visited. Frigiliana. Medosa Pinto. Servaga. And the bigger places of course. Ronda. Granada. Córdoba. When he was at home, he was often writing, she didn't know what. They spoke to each other less and less often, never sought physical contact, but she had no objections to this state of affairs. None at all.

The third with dessert at lunch.

Then it was time for the best part of the day, the three-hour-long siesta. And then three glasses in the course of the evening, the last just before bed. If anyone had told her a year ago – in that former, aborted cancerous tumour – that she would be drinking at least a bottle of wine a day, she would not have taken them seriously.

But that was what it had come to. Sometimes, when the woman next door, a certain Deirdre Henderson from Hull, was there – on either their terrace or hers – it was even more. Especially when Mr Henderson and Karl-Erik were playing twenty-seven holes of golf. It was so much easier to speak English with a couple of glasses inside you, and Deirdre had even been known to switch into German.

I'm a drunken old needlework teacher, she would think as she tumbled into bed at the end of evenings like that.

And nobody cares. I've put on five kilos in less than six months, what's more.

But here she was now, sitting in the car without a drop of Málaga wine in her veins. Just a couple of tablets, tranquillizers – which should have been making her sleepy but weren't. She assumed that must be why she was wishing for that elk. It was only quarter past eleven in the morning, and she dared not think how she was going to get through the day. The funeral was at three o'clock. Followed by coffee and cake for the mourners, in the church hall. Then a little family dinner, nothing fancy, at the hotel – and somewhere, somewhere at the end of that endless succession of seconds and minutes and hours and unbearable thoughts waited the breakdown, she knew it. It seemed as inevitable as – as a thunderstorm after a hot day at Lake Tisaren in Närke, where she had spent a couple of the best summers of her childhood, wherever *that* memory had popped up from.

Tisaren? How funny, she thought, that my life peaked so early. Eleven or twelve years old, and all the rest had been a downward slope. Was it that way for everybody? Was loss of childhood the real moment of our death?

Those peculiar thoughts again. *The real moment of our death?* Perhaps it was the effect of the tablets? Opening all those doors and windows of the soul that should by rights have remained closed.

She was to take another two in the middle of the day; those were the orders of the old Swedish doctor she had consulted, the one who had lived in Torremolinos for the past forty years of his life, and who reminded her a little of an elderly Gregory Peck – or was it Cary Grant, she had always found it hard to separate those two greats in her mind – but they hadn't helped so far, the tablets that is, and her hopes of them ever doing so were minimal.

So, while Karl-Erik hunched forward over the steering wheel, muttering and trying to get the only serious channel on the car radio, she decided she would double her dose. Come what may, he was not going to be pleased with her if she broke down, Karl-Erik.

But best of all would be the aforementioned elk. Bang, straight into the windscreen, and then down with the curtain forever. To die on the way to your dismembered son's funeral, that was just the sort of thing you could pray for to the god you didn't believe in.

The young man at reception sported a tie and a head of hair in the same shade. Light carrot. She thought she recognized him; perhaps he was a former pupil. They were always popping up, and she wondered if he had bought the tie to go with the hair or vice versa: dyed the latter. Seven out of ten young men had dyed their hair at some point, according to the magazine she had found in the pocket in front of her air-line seat. She wondered if it was true.

'Please accept my condolences,' he said, at any event, and it sounded like something out of an old film. It occurred to her that it would suit her wonderfully well for all this to be just an old film that you could choose to stop watching at any moment. Get up from your uncomfortable seat and leave the auditorium.

She did not reply. Karl-Erik was dragging a suitcase about behind her back. He seemed to be trying to keep out of sight of the young man; maybe it was in fact one of *his* former pupils and maybe, it suddenly struck her, Karl-Erik was feeling as self-conscious as she was. It wasn't like him to let her handle – what was it called now? – the check-in.

Not that they had devoted a particularly large part of their lives to checking in.

'Just one night?'

'Yes.'

'You'll be in the same room, in fact.'

'Pardon?'

'You'll be in the same room that Kristina and family had in December,' clarified the receptionist, and gave an uncertain smile.

'Oh yes?' replied Rosemarie, wondering if that was the explanation. Perhaps he had been at school with Kristina. But he looked a bit young for that; Kristina was thirty-two, after all.

'Yes, I was working that week before Christmas, it's – it's a dreadful business. And for you to have to . . .'

He fumbled for words for a while and evidently found none

that felt suitable, because he cleared his throat and gave her a form to fill in instead.

'Life isn't a bed of roses,' she said. 'So you know Kristina and Jakob, then?'

'Not her husband,' he said firmly. 'Only saw him very briefly when he came back during the night.'

'Came back during the night?'

'Yes, I wasn't expecting it. Three o'clock. And then they all left just before eight.'

What is he talking about? she thought in confusion as she tried to focus on what she was meant to write on the form. He saw her bafflement and indicated two boxes. Name and signature, that was all.

'We were in the same class,' he said. 'They haven't arrived yet.'

So that was the explanation, after all. And of course Kristina and Jakob were going to stay at the hotel, too. And Ebba and her family, what was left of it. She remembered that Allvädersgatan didn't exist any more. She had done that a hundred times since this morning. That particular time and grief and malignant tumour was past; today, as they gathered to bury what remained of Robert, Kymlinge Hotel was where they had to be. It felt as makeshift and arbitrary as life itself.

And death itself. If I have to stand at this counter for ten seconds more I shall start to cry, she realized, and held out an imploring hand for the room key. Or scream. Or sink to the floor as if I'd been shot.

'There you are. Number one hundred and twelve. First floor. I'm really sorry it had to be in these circumstances.'

'Thank you.'

'And if there's anything you need, don't hesitate to ask.'

He slid a small paper wallet with two plastic cards across the counter. Oh yes, of course, you don't get hotel keys any more. Not even that. She gave him a nod; Karl-Erik was already over by the lift with the cases. Four tablets, she remembered, I've got to take four tablets as soon as we get into the room. Then I'll tell Karl-Erik I need to sleep for an hour.

Olle Rimborg, wasn't that his name, that carroty receptionist?

Reaching the lake, Hornborgasjön, she stopped in an empty parking area and threw up. It had almost become a habit. Throwing up. A faint mist floated above the flat, dreary landscape; the sun was scarcely coming through and the heat felt sticky. Dog days, she thought, and I've a child in my belly, it's hardly surprising I feel sick. If anybody comes, that'll do fine as an explanation.

It was three hours until the funeral, but the drive would only take an hour and a half. She knew she had to get to the church at just the right time – only ten or fifteen minutes in advance, because if she got there too early it could all very easily run out of control. She had a limited number of ready-made things to say that she had prepared in her mind, and she did not think she would be capable of uttering anything over and above those.

No, I'm afraid Jakob isn't here, he couldn't get away. Something to do with an American company. Millions of kronor.

No, I didn't want to bring Kelvin all this way in the car.

Yes, I've got to get straight back afterwards.

Darling Robert, I've hardly slept, all these nights. Darling Robert, why?

No sorry, Mum, I simply can't bear to stay. It's all so awful.

Like the threadbare lines of dialogue in one of those soaps she used to write. And not eye to eye with Ebba. She must remember that. Preferably not eye to eye with anyone else, either. Exploit your bereavement, Jakob had instructed her. If you absolutely must go. But (switching language) *don't fuck it up*, whatever the hell you do, *don't fuck it up*.

She knew what it meant when he started speaking English. This is my brother, she replied. Robert was my brother.

His eyes took on that fake look of indulgence. He said he knew that, just as he knew Henrik had been her nephew. Yes, he was familiar with those strong family feelings amongst the Hermanssons. He surely did not need to remind her of how things stood?

No, he did not. If there was one thing Kristina did not need to be reminded of, it was how things stood.

If I die, she had asked him once the shockwaves of the first few weeks had begun to subside, in about mid-January, will you tell them?

It hadn't taken him more than a couple of seconds to think about it.

We're both going to live until we die a natural death, you and I, Kristina, he had explained in an almost kindly way. If it happens any other way, I'll make sure they find out.

She threw up again. Nothing but bile this time. It was painful. She leant her cold and sweaty forehead against the peeling, rusty top of the rubbish bin and thought she believed him. That's just the way he was, Jakob Alexander Willnius, and nowhere in the world was there any compassion to be found.

She looked at her watch. It was ten past one. She got back in the car, reclined the seat and shut her eyes.

*

Kristoffer Grundt had only been to one other funeral in his fifteen-year-old life. This time last year, a boy in the parallel form in his own year had hanged himself the day before the start of the autumn term, and half the school had sat in the church, sobbing. They all knew Benny Bjurling had been the victim of bullying ever since lower secondary, but now he was suddenly some kind of inverted hero.

'Those whom the gods love die young,' Mr Hovelius the headmaster had said, and Kristoffer had thought that if there really was a god, then this would presumably be his most important task.

To love those that nobody else loves. As he had sat there in the hard church pew, he had felt this to be a great and just thought, something from which you really could squeeze a little consolation – and now, in the equally hard pew in Kymlinge church and faced with the closed coffin, placed at the front on the little raised platform, and containing, as far as he could judge, the dismembered body of his uncle Robert, he tried to find his way back to that feeling.

But he couldn't. True, he was more or less certain Robert had been pretty unloved in the course of his thirty-five years on earth, but Kristoffer found it hard to imagine that any special favours awaited him on the other side. Benny Bjurling had been a victim and that was a plus, of course, but Uncle Robert had been . . . well, what, wondered Kristoffer. A real goddamned loser? You weren't supposed to speak ill of the dead, and he had nothing to complain of personally, but if you got pissed and then wanked in full view on TV, and went on to get yourself murdered and chopped into little bits, well, your life probably hadn't been up to much. He remembered thinking

Uncle Robert was a bit cool, back then, at Christmas when he went missing, but he didn't think that any more.

The vicar, who was tall and thin – couldn't have been much under two metres – contrived to make something out of it, even so. *It does not become us to judge. What do we know of what is at work within a person's heart and within the eye of God? Robert Hermansson may perhaps have burned his candle at both ends, but many are they who now see for the first time what an empty space he leaves behind him.*

Kristoffer couldn't help finding that impressive. He heard his mother snuffling on his right-hand side, and from Granny to his left came something partway between a hiccup and a belch. He wondered whether Granny was quite with it. She'd seemed a bit odd when she got out of the car in front of the church. Her mouth was half open and she looked cross-eyed. Granddad had to prop her up, or that was how it looked, to stop her falling over and to keep her moving at the same time, so she didn't just grind to a halt. 'How are you Mummy?' Auntie Kristina asked, and Granny said something along the lines of: 'He always made more Easter witch cards than anybody else. He had such cute knees.' Assuming Kristoffer had heard right.

Well, Granny had probably slightly overdone the tranquillizers, but that was only to be expected. *Cute knees?*

He tried to hold onto those thoughts of Granny and the vicar and Benny Bjurling as long as he could – and of Uncle Robert, of course – but eventually he couldn't do it any longer. Henrik slipped into his head through his right ear, and once he had ensconced himself there, he filled every nook and cranny. It was just the same as usual.

Hi, said Henrik. Here I am in your skull again.

Thanks, I noticed, replied Kristoffer.

You've no objection, I hope?

No, no, why would I?

I'm your brother, after all.

Yes, you're my brother, after all.

Brothers have to stick together.

Exactly, Henrik.

In life and in death.

I know, but tell me one thing, Henrik.

Sure thing, brother.

Are you dead or alive?

That's a good question.

Well, answer it then.

A good question, but a hard one. Not easy to find out.

Surely you must know if you're alive or dead, though?

You might think so. How are you doing yourself, Kristoffer?

I don't give a damn how I'm doing. But if you force your way into my skull and I let you stay there, then I want to know the state of play.

State of play?

Whether you're alive or dead.

I realize that's what you're asking. But I'm afraid I'm prevented from answering your question.

But why? Mum's losing her marbles, and Dad can't go on much longer, either. If they at least knew where they stood, then maybe—

I get what you're saying, Kristoffer, Henrik broke in, and it hurts me that things are like this for you all. But as I've tried to explain, I've got no say in the conditions that apply in current circumstances—

Current circumstances? Kristoffer's mild irritation turned to anger. What sort of rubbish is that, the circumstances have been the same for ages now! And if you really want to know, I'm on the slippery slope now as well. Going right down. My school marks are dropping like a stone in a well, I'm drinking every week, and I'm actually pretty tired and fed up of you occupying me the whole time. I can't put up with it for much—

I'm sorry, dear brother, but I've nowhere else to stay for the moment.

Eh?

Henrik sighed.

Because Mum's so tied up with Robert. Granny's one big tangle, there's scarcely room for a postage stamp in there. Dad's trying to swim through a whirlpool, you should keep an eye on him, Kristoffer, and at Kristina's, everything's closed up, as usual. Granddad, well, let's leave him out of it, he's gabbling something in Spanish.

Why is it closed at Kristina's?

How should I know?

I thought you knew everything.

. . .

Wait, don't go . . . no, you're right, Dad really doesn't look his normal self, what did you say he was trying to do?

Leif Grundt never noticed when he started to cry, but he became aware of it when the tears had been dripping onto his clasped hands for a while. At about the same time, he also felt himself slowly but surely being dragged down into bottomless despair. Yes, it really was just that – a sucking, bottomless whirlpool of despair – and for the first time in eight months he gave in and realized his son was dead. Of course, it was his black-sheep brother-in-law Robert lying up front in the oak veneer coffin of the second cheapest design, but it could just as well have been Henrik. His son was dead. Ebba's and his firstborn son, Kristoffer's brother. Dead, dead, dead – and it was no longer fitting for him, Co-op manager Leif Grundt, to believe anything else. To maintain the opposite. Not to his increasingly crazy wife, nor to God, nor to anyone else.

It was not fitting for Leif Grundt to be optimistic and strong any longer – to continue this wretched, desolate life day after day, hour after hour in some kind of absurd normality, as if there was still some kind of thread on which to fasten some kind of hope and meaning. Go to work every day, encourage the employees, joke with Kristoffer morning and evening, listen to how he had got on at school. Not let on that he knew the boy was secretly smoking and drinking beer . . . make sure there was food on the table, clothes were washed, bills were paid; all those little practical details and unbearably minute duties that were required to keep a family that had lost a son afloat – on an ever-shrinking, ever-thinning ice floe, until everything ultimately sank to the bottom and was reduced to nothing after all. He had not made love to his wife for nine months, had stopped even thinking about it. Life was at an end, it was as simple as that. It was over. They might just as well all go and lie down with Robert at the front.

Death. Why put it off? What was the point?

But then things went into reverse. In some remarkable way, they actually did. As inexorably as a cork, Leif Grundt floated up out of the whirlpool, drew the handkerchief out of his breast pocket and blew his nose with a resolute trumpeting that made the vicar at the front take an unplanned pause for thought. Because the one who first lays claim to madness as their domain, thought Co-op manager Leif Grundt – and Ebba had indubitably done that – then has the right to it for all time. The sole right.

When one grows weak, the other has to grow strong.

It was an incontrovertible truth and it was bloody unfair, thought Leif Grundt, but then he found himself thinking of what he had heard Bishop Tutu say on television once.

Or was it Mandela himself?

Those who have the strength have a duty to go on finding it.

Because that was exactly it. *To go on finding the strength.*

But he had been swept round in the whirlpool for the first time.

He blew his nose again, a little more discreetly, and this time the vicar was prepared.

'That Olle Rimborg,' said Rosemarie Wunderlich Hermansson.

'Yes,' said Kristoffer Grundt. 'Who?'

'Olle Rimborg, I took him for German, I remember now.'

'We'd better be moving,' said Karl-Erik. 'We've got to get over to the church hall now.'

'Wait a minute,' said Rosemarie. 'I'm talking to Henrik – I mean Kristoffer – yes, that was his name, and he was a red-head even back then, now I come to think of it. Rimborg. Lively boy, on the whole.'

'Er, yes?' said Kristoffer.

'He works at the hotel now.'

'Oh?'

'There's so much going on with all sorts of things now-adays, but he said he came back in the night.'

'What?'

'Right then, off we go,' said Karl-Erik.

'He came back in the night. Jakob, that is. Do you hear that, Kristoffer? That dreadful night when your brother disappeared – it wasn't him we just buried, it was Robert, but Henrik is missing. He said it when we were there to what's it called? Check in? Olle Rimborg, that is. Kristina's husband came back at three o'clock, he said. They were in the same class, he and Kristina, but I didn't teach Kristina at school of course, she didn't do German and you shouldn't teach your own children anyway . . .'

'Look, it's raining now as well,' said Karl-Erik impatiently. 'What in the world are you going on about? You'll have to excuse Granny, Kristoffer, she's a bit confused.'

'It doesn't matter,' said Kristoffer.

'I should ask Kristina about it, definitely,' Rosemarie went on. 'I don't know why he said it. Don't interrupt me all the time, Karl-Erik. And you ought to trim your nose hair, too, couldn't you have thought of that with this being a funeral and everything? And there really was far too much of that vicar. He must have been . . . Well, how tall was he? What do you think, Kristoffer?'

'A hundred and ninety-eight centimetres,' said Kristoffer.

'Here comes Ebba to chivvy us along,' said Rosemarie Wunderlich Hermansson. 'Blistering barnacles, we'd better step on it. Where are we going?'

'We're going to the church hall for coffee, Mummy,' said Ebba Hermansson Grundt. 'Whatever that's supposed to achieve.'

'Of course, I know we're going to the church hall, Karl-Erik keeps rabbiting on about it,' her mother declared firmly. 'Those pills I've got are really something. I feel as bright as a button. So, you reckon a hundred and ninety-eight, Henrik, well, I think you've hit the nail on the head there . . . I mean Kristoffer. Olle Rimborg, that was it, I remember that, too. Don't you go forgetting it, Kristoffer! But where's Kristina got to?'

31

'All right then,' said Gunnar Barbarotti. 'What have you come up with? Take it slowly, please, so you don't have to go through it again. I've just come from a funeral and I'm even more dull-witted than usual.'

Gerald Borgsen stretched the right-hand corner of his mouth a centimetre, to show he'd appreciated the self-deprecation. He blinked a couple of times behind his lightly tinted glasses and started.

'Quite a lot, actually,' he said. 'The most important thing first, maybe?'

Gunnar Barbarotti nodded.

'Hrrm. It *was* Jane Almgren's phone Robert Hermansson called the night he disappeared. And he had called her once before, a few days previously. We had that number, right back in December, but . . .'

'Pay as you go,' supplied Gunnar Barbarotti.

'Spot on. And we didn't get any further with it. Or we didn't put sufficient resources into it, is probably how I should express it . . .'

It was a well-known fact that Sorrysen thought he was under-resourced. Gunnar Barbarotti tilted his head to one side, like that Finnish skier he still couldn't remember the name of, and tried to look sympathetic.

'There are over thirty million calls made every day in this country,' Sorrysen went on. 'From Robert Hermansson's mobile, for example, at that point, if we focus on December, we had sixty-four different numbers to investigate. Jane Almgren's was only one of those. Every number then generates a hundred to a hundred and fifty more, but if we'd really made sure to—'

'I know, Gerald, for Christ's sake,' interrupted Gunnar Barbarotti. 'It's completely crazy, of course, that you have to deal with all this yourself, but tell me about this particular phone. Jane Almgren's, that is. Not all that many calls were made to it in December, if I remember rightly?'

'Only six,' said Sorrysen. 'Two to a pizzeria, one to a ladies' hairdresser's, one other, and two from Robert Hermansson.'

'I remember that,' said Barbarotti. 'But how about earlier on? In November, say?'

'Around twenty-five different numbers,' Sorrysen told him patiently. 'Mostly to other pay-as-you-go accounts and withheld numbers, but not all of them. It also seems, in fact, that she did some temp work at that hairdresser's for a few days in December. Our friend Jane, that is. But after Robert's disappearance, not a single call – that was the reason we couldn't get any further.'

'Even if we'd had the staff?'

'I didn't hear that. But there are a few calls to landlines, too.'

'In November?'

'Yes.'

'How many?'

'Four. I've looked into them all. Three to private individuals, one to a car-hire firm. Two of the individuals live in Stockholm, they're both men, I've got their names and addresses of course, and they both say they've no idea who Jane Almgren is. The third individual doesn't know anybody of that name, either, but in my view she's still of interest to our investigation.'

'Oh yes?'

'Her name's Sylvia Karlsson. She's seventy and lives in Kristinehamn. On twenty-second November last year she received a phone call from her son – from this number, that is – and since then she hasn't heard from him.'

Aha, thought Gunnar Barbarotti, feeling concentration slip away from him. He turned his eyes from Sorrysen and looked out of the window instead. Noted that it was raining. Allowed several seconds to pass as he tracked the meanders of two water drops down the window pane.

'Don't forget those dull wits of mine,' he reminded his colleague. 'So, what you're telling me is . . . ?'

'Exactly,' observed Sorrysen. 'I can see you're keeping up. It's worth pointing out that we were in touch with this woman back in December – or possibly a few days into January – but at that point, she didn't know she had a missing son, of course. They don't have much to do with each other, evidently. But she turned seventy in June and he usually gave her a call on her birthday.'

'Hmm,' said Gunnar Barbarotti. 'Was he a bad lot?'

'You could put it that way, if you wanted to be a bit old-fashioned.'

'Nothing wrong with being old-fashioned,' observed Gunnar Barbarotti. 'What's his name? Have we got him on record?'

'Sören Karlsson. I did a search on his name and he's got a nice little portfolio.'

'Such as?'

'A bit of everything. Narcotics offences. Assault and battery. Accomplice in a bank robbery. Various stretches in prison, twenty-two months in total. The last time was three years ago.'

'Connection to Jane Almgren?'

'We haven't established one yet. But he was registered in Kalmar at the time she was living there. So it's possible there's a link. Not to say likely.'

Gunnar Barbarotti put his hands together and pondered.

'Good,' he said. 'And since he's in our records, I assume we're busy comparing?'

'You bet,' said Gerald Borgsen with unusual emphasis. 'If he turns out to be Robert Hermansson's roommate in the freezer, you'll know within four hours. I should—'

'Hang on,' cut in Barbarotti. 'I want to get this clear in my mind. So it could be the case that Jane Almgren killed this Sören Karlsson sometime before she turned her attention to Robert Hermansson? Then she kept his mobile and used it for a week or two, but suddenly stopped using it?'

Sorrysen nodded. 'More or less, yes. Maybe the battery ran out. Or the money on the card. The last call is actually the one Robert made to her, the night he disappeared.'

'And all this is thanks to . . .'

'. . . thanks to mobile phone monitoring,' supplied Sorrysen. 'Correct again.'

Couldn't you have worked all this out in December? thought Gunnar Barbarotti, but he did not ask the question out loud. Instead he said 'Thanks Gerald,' and got to his feet. 'Will you be staying tonight until word comes through?'

Sorrysen cleared his throat and gestured in the direction of his loaded desk. 'Got plenty to be getting on with, as you see. Yep, I'll be here. I'll ring you when I know.'

'You do that,' said Gunnar Barbarotti, and left his colleague's office. He checked the time. It was ten past six. Some people claimed Gerald Borgsen did an average of twenty hours' overtime a week, but Barbarotti had never gone to the trouble of checking if that was actually the case. It could easily have been an underestimate.

For his part, he wasn't going to put in any overtime. No more than he already had today. He was going to swim a thousand metres and then take a sauna for an hour. It was Friday evening and Sara had promised to cook a pasta dinner for half past eight. As long as he didn't trip over any corpses on his way to the sports centre, he should fit it all in nicely.

Perhaps put a call through to Helsingborg later on, too.

They had to wait until Saturday morning for the identification. Gunnar Barbarotti had no idea why it had taken so long, and he didn't bother trying to find out.

'I've put a sheet of paper on your desk,' said Sorrysen's weary voice on the phone. 'Now you can read all about our friend Sören Karlsson. He was about thirty-nine. We don't really know if he made it to that last birthday in November, because we can't say exactly when he died. And I didn't ring his mother to tell her, I thought I'd leave that to you. I'm a bit tired of telephones. Bye.'

Despite that last comment, he called again two minutes later.

'I can add,' he said with a heavy sigh, 'I can add that the reason Jane Almgren started using the victim's phone was very likely because Telia shut down her landline account on 25 November. That was all.'

'Thanks Gerald,' said Gunnar Barbarotti, and hung up.

An hour later, he was in his office holding Sören Karlsson's past in his hand. In Sorrysen's minimal handwriting – he was one of the last people alive who still liked writing things by hand – it covered just over half the sheet of paper and told him that SK was born in Karlstad in 1965, and that he had left home and moved to Stockholm after finishing a basic course at upper secondary in 1984. That he had lived in about ten different places in Sweden, had some twenty different ways of making a living, and that his first documented criminal act was an assault on a seventy-six-year-old woman in the course of snatching her bag on Västerlånggatan in Stockholm's Old Town. That was in the summer of 1988. He had never been married and had no children that they were aware of. For a period of eighteen months in the late 1990s, he had lived at an address in Kalmar while working for a smallish cleaning firm, and there was a reliable witness statement to confirm that he had at this time briefly kept company with a certain Jane Almgren – who was at that point still married, had two children and worked for the same cleaning firm.

Right then, thought Gunnar Barbarotti, and gave a deep sigh. That's the lot.

At the bottom of the sheet, Sorrysen had written a telephone number and a name. Barbarotti closed his eyes and took a few deep breaths through his nose. Time to ring Mrs Sylvia Karlsson in Kristinehamn, no doubt about it. To ring her and explain that it had nothing to do with negligence, the fact that her only son had omitted to ring and wish her a happy seventieth birthday.

Hope she isn't in, he thought, and started dialling the number.

But he didn't enter into any kind of bet with God, and Sylvia Karlsson answered gruffly after the second ring.

'How was the funeral?' asked Eva Backman.

It was Monday morning. And raining. Gunnar Barbarotti had spent most of Sunday in Helsingborg and across the water at Helsingør (and the Louisiana Museum of Modern Art), and had not got home until nearly midnight. A total of almost ten hours in the car, but what wouldn't one do?

'Very nice,' he said. 'Shame you missed it. And Sören Karlsson's apparently going to be buried in Karlstad, so perhaps you're not free for that one, either?'

'I'll have to think it over,' said Eva Backman. 'You seem pretty chipper, anyway. Rainy Monday and eleven months to your next holiday – are you on Valium or helium or what?'

Gunnar Barbarotti shook his head.

'Hmm,' said Eva Backman. 'Well, it's none of my business. Shall we agree this is all clear now, then?'

'Apart from the minor detail of Henrik Grundt, it's crystal clear,' concurred Gunnar Barbarotti. 'But do tell me the rest of the Jane Almgren Story, if you feel like it. How did it go with this new witness? We were able to fill a few gaps, I gather?'

'A few,' said Eva Backman, draining the last drop of coffee from her mug. 'So a woman turned up yesterday and told us that Jane might possibly have had a little affair with Robert Hermansson when they were in their teens. Well, affair isn't the right word. There was a gang of them, evidently, and

Robert had switched to – well, to this witness, in the middle of the night.'

'Ouch.'

'You might say so. And in the middle of the sleeping bag.'

'Eh?'

'Yes, that was her phrase. They were camping somewhere out Kymmen way, and I don't know if this is significant, but the witness, who was a friend of Jane's, right, claimed that Jane went really wild and started threatening to kill Robert. Actually tried to do it, too, apparently.'

'That far back?'

'That far back. She was sixteen; as the twig is bent, so shall the tree . . . Anyway, there's clearly a link to Robert going back a long way. Perhaps it's like you said: she remembered his betrayal when she saw him on TV twenty years later. Sören Karlsson was the direct cause of the break-up of her marriage in Kalmar, wasn't he, so I think we can probably assume there's a revenge motive in the picture. In both victims' cases.'

'Some old business in a tent?'

'Things just lie there smouldering, you know. They can flare up after twenty or thirty years, especially in minds that aren't in proper working order.'

'Yes thanks, I know. But what about her husband – ex-ditto, I should say?'

'What indeed? He must have been a potential victim as well. But he and the kids were given some kind of protected identity. They live in Drammen in Norway; what do you think Jane Almgren was doing in Oslo? If she hadn't been run over and killed, she might have got on *his* trail, too.'

Gunnar Barbarotti chewed on his lower lip and thought about this for a while.

'Jesus Christ,' he said.

'Yes,' said Eva Backman. 'That sums it up pretty well. But you and I can shelve her for now, I think. Don't you?'

Barbarotti nodded. 'I reckon so. Berggren and Toivonen can fill in the missing bits. The main thing left to do is the mental profile and Toivonen's brilliant at that sort of thing.'

Eva Backman gave a fleeting smile.

'And what are you brilliant at?' she asked. 'When it comes to the crunch?'

Gunnar Barbarotti drew himself up and avoided meeting her eye. He pulled a face and thought about it. 'I'm glad you brought that up,' he said. 'I've wondered about it quite a bit myself.'

'And what conclusion did you reach?'

'I think – I think I'm a right devil for stubborn persistence.'

'Really?'

'Yes. Once, when I was at school, I spent two whole weeks solving the Königsberg Bridge Problem. We had a teacher who liked setting us that kind of puzzle. You know the Königsberg Bridges?'

'I thought that one was insoluble.'

'Yes, it is. And he told us that. But I didn't care, and tried to solve it anyway.'

Eva Backman nodded and bit the nail of her index finger. 'I see,' she said. 'And Henrik Grundt, since I assume that's where this is leading.'

'Far from insoluble,' said Gunnar Barbarotti. 'Just give me a bit of time.'

Eva Backman said nothing for a while.

'How much time?'

He shrugged. 'It doesn't really matter. A few months or a few years. Though actually, it feels pretty urgent. They looked as if they were in shreds.'

'Shreds? Who?'

'The family. The whole lot of them, at the funeral. Hard to say who was suffering worst. But one thing's for sure, it wasn't Robert they were grieving for in that church. Poor devil, he didn't even manage to be the main character at his own funeral. You have to admit that's rock bottom.'

'Drew a losing ticket in the lottery of life,' said Eva Backman. 'But it wouldn't by any chance be the case that you think Henrik Grundt is still alive?'

'I find it hard to imagine he is,' said Gunnar Barbarotti. 'Very hard.'

'And just as hard to imagine he died a natural death?'

'Almost as hard,' sighed Barbarotti. 'But if I can convince Asunander to sanction it, I'd like to sit down for three days and go over the entire case one more time. Everything we've got. All the interviews, the whole lot, turn every word inside out and question every damn person.'

'Wouldn't it be better to do the opposite?'

'What?'

'Question every word and turn every damn person inside out?'

'You can be very irritating, Mrs Backman, do you know that?'

'My husband often tells me so,' said Eva Backman. 'But you go ahead and talk to the boss. I saw him this morning.'

'Asunander? How did he seem?'

'Gloomy. Very.'

'Then I'll wait until tomorrow,' decided Gunnar Barbarotti. 'The Lord did not create the concept of haste.'

'Are you acquainted with the Lord?' asked Eva Backman. 'I would never have thought it.'

'Only a little,' admitted Inspector Barbarotti. 'Only a little.'

FOUR

NOVEMBER

32

Kristina got off the tube at Gullmarsplan because that particular train was heading for Farsta Strand. She leant into the squally gusts of wind, and battled her way across the deserted square and through the piss-drenched underpass up towards the Globe complex. The rain came driving in frosty cascades and she asked herself why she hadn't followed Jakob's advice, done her shopping in the market hall at Östermalm, and taken a taxi home to Enskede.

But maybe that was how it worked – that it was in these trifling acts of disobedience she had her pockets of resistance. There, and there only. Why not? She had to find the oxygen for her survival somewhere.

They were having guests. Two Danish film producers and their wives, an unaccompanied Swedish TV boss and a Finnish director, a lesbian. The cooking and drinking were to be fit for a prince. There was a pan-Nordic project at stake. Blinis and whitefish roe with schnapps. Venison and Barolo. Caramelized figs and chèvre cheese and coffee and Calvados and the whole shebang.

She was tired to the bone. But she had decided to do her shopping at the Globe arcade; if she was obliged, in spite of everything, to play the young, perfect – and becomingly pregnant – wife, she surely at least had the right to decide where the raw ingredients were to be purchased? Those ingredients that in the course of the afternoon would be prepared and processed, to be ready towards evening for stuffing in the mouths of the ravenous media moguls and their heavily made-up wives. Plus the TV boss and the Finnish dyke.

Simulated resistance, she thought again. It was only eleven in the morning. There was plenty of time, five to six hours having been set aside for gourmet preparations. Jakob had even promised to pick up Kelvin from the childminder; let nobody say he didn't show his pregnant wife due appreciation and consideration.

She went into the shopping arcade via McDonald's. It was rammed full and she had to elbow her way through, but not a second more than necessary was spent out in the cold, persistent rain. She felt the need to sit down and rest for a short while before she made a start on the provisioning. She found a decent coffee place, took off her raincoat and ordered a cappuccino. She perched on a high stool at a tiny table amidst the crush. She had got her taste for coffee back last week. In the middle of the seventh month, just like last time.

Last time, she thought, and as she absent-mindedly stirred the foam with the sad wooden stick, she tried to remember how she had felt when she was expecting her first child. The uncommunicative and introverted Kelvin. She tried to recall that feeling of unspecified expectation and naive optimism, to find its tone at least, but it was futile. Everything was so dreadfully changed. The terms of her life so fundamentally restructured that she sometimes asked herself if there was any point believing she was still the same person. Was it the same brain thinking these thoughts, giving her hand the order to raise the cup, and her mouth the instruction to explore the frothed milk that was still far too hot? A good question. She had been living in a perpetual and continuing nightmare for almost a year now, and there was no sign of it ever stopping. No sign at all.

'You don't look happy,' Marika at the antenatal clinic had said. That was where she had spent the morning so far. Well half an hour of it, at any rate. By rights she should have been attending an antenatal clinic in Old Enskede, but she had taken to Marika when she was expecting Kelvin, and Marika was based in the centre of town, at Artillerigatan. Jakob had suggested Enskede, but she had chosen Marika. Resistance.

'You're right, I'm not happy,' she had replied. 'I don't want this baby.'

She didn't know what had got into her. She had never owned up to anything like that before. But that was what Marika was good at, she supposed. One of the things she was good at, drawing the truth out of people.

She put her rough hand on Kristina's arm and looked her deep in the eyes from just twenty centimetres away.

'You'll find a way,' she said, in her ringing Finnish accent. 'Believe me, when the time comes, you'll find a way. Don't you worry, dear.'

Then she asked if there was any problem with the paternity. In any way. Kristina shook her head and thought that this wasn't about the paternity, but the father himself. That was where the madness lay. She happened to be married to a murderer and it was the murderer's child she was now carrying under her heart. But she was in this crazed murderer-husband's power, there was simply nothing to be done about that; it was the punishment of the gods for having played a forbidden game, and for the rest of her life she would never escape its terms and conditions.

But she had not confided any of this to Marika. That was another of the conditions – the silence.

She sipped her coffee again and shook her head in the present, too. She swallowed both the hot liquid and the lump in her throat, as she had accustomed herself to doing. For a few moments, she watched two young women engaged in cheerful, lively conversation at the next table, and thought that if she had been born ten years later, one of them could have been her. The one with dark hair, if she'd been able to choose; she had such an attractive face. Carefree somehow, her future stretching ahead and no heavy baggage.

Then a bare second passed and the plan came back into her head.

Or *The Plan*; in recent days it had started presenting itself with initial capitals and italics, whatever that might signify. Like a sign suddenly flashing on in her head, its seven letters written in vivid, blood-red script.

It had not been like that from the start. On the contrary, when it first showed itself it had been a mere thief in the night, tiptoeing discreetly, not intending to be spotted or taken notice of. But then it had, by some strange means, acquired a backbone, suddenly not allowing itself to be rebuffed so easily, hanging around and demanding precedence; it was certainly a remarkable thing, like a . . . well, like a beau at the ball who kept asking her to dance, and she couldn't decide whether to send him packing or not.

I'm your only option, he kept saying. Your only way out of this, Kristina. You know that, you can choose whether to admit it now or in ten years' time. But sooner or later you're going to take me in your arms. Your cowardice determines the length of time, nothing else; it's your decision how many more days you want to spend under his tyranny.

Murder, she thought. Kill him. That's what he's telling me, my beau.

But none of these words spelling out her situation were ever italicized or lit up by a flash in her mind's eye. It was more the opposite; as soon as she thought them, they faded and vanished into their own absurdity.

Or the fog of her own timidity, or whatever it was.

But that was still what *The Plan* amounted to. That and nothing else.

The dream, on the other hand, never faded. It was replayed three or four nights a month and each time, every detail was uncompromisingly in place. Nothing changed, it was all still there: Jakob's entry; Henrik's terrified intake of breath; those protracted seconds of total silence and frozen motion; Jakob's hands grabbing the boy from the bed, tossing him brutally onto the floor; his knee on his chest; her own stifled scream.

Jakob's three or four hard blows with his fist; his hands round Henrik's neck; those eyes that seemed on the verge of popping out of their sockets; her own inability to do anything at all; the clenched teeth of her powerlessness and Jakob's final words: 'There, he's dead now.'

His stinging blow to the side of her head and his spittle in her face.

Like a documentary. It wasn't a dream, strictly speaking. It was an authentic – completely authentic and minutely accurate – memory sequence of that night. Wrapping Henrik's dead body in the sheet. Heaving it off the fire-escape balcony down into the bushes. Dragging it to the car. No one had seen them. No one had heard them. It was four-thirty by the time they were done. Then he slapped her face again and raped her. By seven they were sitting in the hotel restaurant having breakfast. Kelvin too, inserted into the red-lacquer high chair after sleeping like a log all night. It was quarter to eight when they left Kymlinge.

He had dealt with burying the body by himself. She still didn't know where Henrik's grave was. He had been gone all the following night, so she knew he had made a serious job of it. Maybe the sea, maybe some stretch of forest near Nynäshamn – he knew his way round there. She never asked, and he would never have told her.

And when he explained the framework for the continuation of their life, she had already known what it would be.

If you expose me, I expose you.

A few weeks later he had added that other thing.

If you kill me, it's all there in my will.

If you kill me, it's all there in my will.

For a long time, she had believed it. For a long time, she had had dreams of that document, too. Believed in its authenticity.

Believed he had really written that. Gone to a lawyer and handed over a sealed envelope: *To be opened after my death.* Or: *To be opened in the event of my death in unclear circumstances.*

Now she had her doubts. She had been suspecting for a while that there was no such document. What interest could Jakob possibly have in being exposed as a murderer after his own death? Was there really any reason to leave himself with that legacy?

It was a terribly difficult question. She had spent days and weeks turning it over in her mind. And there were other questions that followed from it.

For example: did he really hate her so much? So much that he wanted to punish her even when he was no longer alive?

In that case, why had he opted to bind her so closely to him at all? To trap her like this. Was it really as simple as that? He wanted a wife who would never deny him anything? Whom he had given himself the moral right to rape night after night, whenever he felt the urge.

Perhaps? Perhaps *that* was it? Perhaps Jakob Willnius was constituted that way, and was so sick that he could – and wanted to – live like that. There were indications that it might be so. Some men were like that, deep down.

There was a more interesting supplementary question. Gradually, having turned it over in her mind countless times, brooded on it for several weeks, she almost dared to reclassify it as a statement.

The important, really crucial part – from Jakob Willnius's point of view – was of course not actually writing a document of that kind, but *convincing his wife that such a document existed*. The latter was what enabled him to tie her hands behind her back and provided him with life insurance, not the former. That was the fact of the matter.

Surely, Kristina asked herself. Surely? Surely? Surely?

And it was by means of the cautiously uttered, barely audible answer of 'yes' to this half-rhetorical, half-desperate question that the plan was hatched. *The Plan*.

She took a mouthful of coffee and checked the time. It was twenty to twelve. The chatty friends at the next table had been replaced by a tired man with a pile of shopping bags at his feet. The arcade was bustling with people. Young, old. Dry, rain-drenched. Men, women. I'd swap, thought Kristina Hermansson, distractedly stroking her taut belly, I'd swap identities with any of these people, without a second's hesitation.

Then she got to her feet, leaving her cardboard cup of coffee half-drunk on the table, and went off to the supermarket to commence her wifely duties.

But how, she thought. *How?*

Leif Grundt parked the Volvo on the drive and turned off the engine. He just sat there with his hands on the steering wheel, unable to bring himself to get out. It was half past nine in the evening. It was a Thursday in November. It was raining.

The house lay in darkness, apart from Kristoffer's room, where a bluish flicker revealed that the television was on. Leif Grundt was tired, tired to the bone. He had left home before seven this morning, got away from the shop eleven hours later and then spent another two sitting with Ebba at Vassrogga.

She spent her weekdays there and her weekends with the family. A private clinic; some form of intensive therapy, he wasn't sure what it actually entailed. Twelve to fifteen kilometres inland along the Indalsälven river, anyway; it had been three weeks so far, and would continue for another three. Every Thursday evening there was a family conversation session, and he went along and tried to be nice and understanding. He managed the nice bit OK, he supposed, but the understanding was harder. He didn't think his wife seemed to be making any discernible progress.

When he tentatively put this to the therapist, the answer from this extremely gentle and extremely bearded man of about sixty was that Mrs Grundt had lost a son and it was going to take time.

Leif Grundt felt like answering that, always assuming the son *was* lost, he was his son as well. But he knew this was not the sort of thing one said.

Tomorrow evening, Ebba would come home, and it struck him that he was feeling uncomfortably ambivalent about this. As if it placed an instant demand on him and Kristoffer. The demand that they keep Ebba in a good mood. Or keep her going, or however you wanted to see it. For a while now he had had a line ringing in his head: *Sometimes I get so bloody tired of you, Ebba, can't you understand that?* And he knew that if these words actually slipped out of his mouth at some point, nothing could ever be mended again. It would be the final nail in their marital coffin. The final nail in the Grundt family.

Though maybe, he thought, his fingers half-heartedly massaging the rigid steering wheel, maybe it was already past saving.

Some families can withstand a catastrophe, he had read somewhere, while others just can't.

And all the indications were that the Hermansson-Grundt family came into the latter category. It had taken eleven months – a year ago everything had radiated well-being and harmony, at least by any normal measure and his own modest appreciation of these things. A senior consultant wife, a Co-op manager, a student at Uppsala and a reasonably promising upper-secondary pupil. Today, the student was missing, very probably dead, the senior consultant was on her way into her own darkness, and as for him, he was incapable of getting out of his own car.

That was how it was. That was what they were reduced to. And Kristoffer?

He dared not think about Kristoffer, not really. It was clear the boy had started smoking and was keeping pretty undesirable company, and the level of effort he was putting in at school left plenty to be desired. No doubt he was drinking beer and other things from time to time; Leif knew about it and Kristoffer knew that he knew, but they both preferred to pretend this wasn't the case. Or at any rate not to comment on it. Things were bad enough already; no more problems on the agenda, please. He still managed to give the boy a hug and some words of encouragement sometimes, and hoped that would be enough in the long run. They had a sort of gentleman's agreement, which basically consisted of not talking about anything unpleasant and pretending life was normal.

And in this new normal, it was raining. Leif could see the drops bouncing off the bonnet and condensing into a thin haze, which in turn instantly dissolved into nothing. The engine still had not cooled. Why am I sitting here? he thought. In my forty-third year, I am sitting in my own car on my own drive, staring at the rain. As down-in-the-mouth as a captive lobster. So why? Why am I sitting here? And what – what have lobsters got to do with it? But of course, he realized, it was those frozen ones from Argentina that he'd had to chuck out after the complaints from those pesky women at . . . wait, he was losing the thread again. What had he been thinking about?

Oh, yes. Kristoffer. He was goggling at the TV again, that boy, the bluish gleam from his window was unmistakable. Apart from putting away a bit of food now and then, and going outside for a crafty smoke, that was pretty much the only thing he did when he was at home.

What he got up to when he wasn't at home, most of the weekend for example, was something Leif Grundt preferred not to think too much about.

And it was as if their eyes never really met. Not like they used to. Though that was just the way of these things, he supposed. Avoiding seeing each other. Everything had its price.

Soon, I'm not going to have the strength to keep finding the strength, thought Leif Grundt, opening the car door and climbing out into the rain. Bloody hell.

He dashed the few steps to the front door and let himself into the darkened hall. He took off his coat and hung it up without putting the light on and then went into the kitchen. He put on the light over the sink and saw that Kristoffer had left the butter, cheese and tube of fish roe out of the fridge, and that the dishwasher must be full, because there was an unwashed pasta saucepan and colander in the sink.

It took him fifteen minutes to get everything cleared up, and then he went in to see his son. As expected, he found him lying there watching a film, but at least it was Swedish. One of the actors said 'Go to hell, you fucking whore,' just as Leif Grundt opened the door. Well that's something, anyway, he thought, wondering at the same time why it should be reassuring that the film was Swedish.

'Mum says hi,' he said.

'OK,' said Kristoffer.

'She's coming home tomorrow evening.'

'Don't know if I'll be in when she gets here,' said Kristoffer.

'I see,' said Leif Grundt. 'Well, I think I'll hit the hay. What time do you start tomorrow?'

'I can lie in. Don't start until ten.'

'Shall I wake you when I go?'

'No need. I can get myself up.'

'All right. See you sometime tomorrow evening, then?'

'I expect so,' said Kristoffer Grundt.

I wish you a good night's sleep, my beloved son, thought Leif Grundt. May you, at least, be delivered from evil.

But he didn't say it. He just yawned and left the room.

He must have dozed off at some stage in the last third of the film, because he woke to the music that accompanied the final shot of a burning house, as the credits rolled. It seemed a bit stupid to run the credits against a background like that, thought Kristoffer, because you could hardly read some of the names. But then, it had been a pretty stupid film all round. Typical Swedish B-movie.

And maybe that – the fact that you couldn't really make out all the names of those actors and cameramen and assistant directors and sound technicians – was why he carried on lying there, and tried to do so. Something he certainly didn't usually waste any of his concentration on. Name after name after name . . . imagine it taking that bloody many of them to make such a useless film, thought Kristoffer. He hadn't ever realized before. That it took so many people. Film editors and casting teams and continuity girls and costume people . . . As he lay there, staring lazily at all those unknown individuals, those otherwise anonymous underlings of the film world, a name that he recognized suddenly popped up.

Rimborg. Olle Rimborg.

Hang on, thought Kristoffer. Where have I seen that before? Or heard it?

Before he had time to look and see what function this Olle Rimborg had fulfilled in the strange world of film, the name had rolled off the screen. *Rimborg?*

He dug out the remote control from under the pillow and

switched off the TV. Wished he had a fresh film to watch, but he hadn't got any in. Just old rubbish he'd watched until he was sick of it. It was only quarter to eleven, just the right time for a decent film to fall asleep to, if he'd had one.

Rimborg?

He got out of bed. Decided to have one last smoke out of the window, and then he supposed he might as well try to go to sleep anyway. It was Friday tomorrow. Double PE first thing, but he planned on skipping that. OK, he'd had an official warning after the mid-term review that he was likely to fail the subject, but two hours in a crappy indoor swimming pool were no way to start a Friday. Not according to Kristoffer's worldview.

His current worldview, perhaps one should add. He was well aware that, for the time being, he was not really living the way he wanted to live. That he was *going through a phase*, as the counsellor had tried to explain to his form teacher, Mr Stahke, after that mid-term review. How the hell could anyone be called Stahke?

He leant out into the November gale and got his cigarette to light. Luckily, the balcony upstairs was just above his window, so at least his cig didn't get wet.

Olle Rimborg?

It was after two drags he got the first lead (there, see, the beneficial effects of nicotine on the ability to think). It was something to do with Granny. Something she said . . . but when? At the funeral? Yes of course, that was it. They'd been standing there outside the church – and as it happened, that was the only time he'd seen her all year, so it wasn't very hard to work out – and she'd been babbling on about somebody called Rimborg.

And then she said that he came back.

He came back. Who the heck was *he*? Admittedly Granny hadn't really been all there at Robert's funeral, but she'd really gone on about that Olle Rimborg, and about someone who came back during the night. Someone *else*, who wasn't Olle Rimborg. She'd been really insistent, Granny, so there must be something in it, he assumed. In spite of her being gaga.

Kristoffer Grundt took a deep drag on his cigarette. What else had she said? Not that it mattered, but since he hadn't got a film to watch, since he hadn't got anything to do besides having a crafty smoke out of the window on a forlorn and rainy November evening, he might as well exert his mental machinery a bit . . . Yes, exactly! Now he had it! Olle Rimborg was a receptionist at the hotel in Kymlinge. That was it – at least if Granny was to be believed – and he was the one who had said someone came back, and there was something important about it all. Granny had tried to explain it to him, but she'd been so confused that he hadn't really bothered to listen to her, it had all been a bit embarrassing, poor Granny.

And then . . . then the name crops up on his television screen two or three months later, isn't that odd? As if it had been lying there waiting for him. Olle Rimborg didn't only have the one job, evidently, he was a receptionist but also did some kind of film work, it was as if . . .

The next drag was a bit too deep and made his head spin, and then all of a sudden he had Henrik with him again.

Hi, brother, said Henrik.

Hi yourself, said Kristoffer.

It's bad for you, smoking.

Thanks. I know.

How are you?

Fine thanks.

Are you sure?

Mm . . .

Henrik was settling in, and went quiet for a while.

OK, little brother, he said at last. I don't give a damn about your lifestyle. Maybe it's just a phase, like you say. But I'd quite like you to show a bit of interest in this Olle Rimborg.

You what? asked Kristoffer.

Check it out, said Henrik. Can't do any harm.

Why?

You know there are some things I can't tell you, we've talked about this before.

Yeah, I know, but—

No buts. If you want something useful to do instead of smoking and drinking beer and messing about at school, you can check on Olle Rimborg. You've already worked out who he is, right?

Sure, but— began Kristoffer.

Right then, that's settled, concluded Henrik. Stub out that damn cigarette now, you need to pull your socks up a bit, brother.

Kristoffer Grundt sighed and took one last drag. Chucked the butt out into the rain; the lawn mowing was over for this year and his dad wouldn't find it. He closed the window and crawled into bed.

Go and have a wash and clean your teeth while you're at it, Henrik added. Just because Linda Granberg's moved to Norway it doesn't mean you need to go around smelling like a skunk, right?

Kristoffer sighed again, kicked off the quilt and got back on his feet. Brothers, he thought.

33

Gunnar Barbarotti woke up, and didn't know where he was.

He felt a warm hand on his stomach. It wasn't his.

The hand, that is. It was a woman's hand. For a fraction of a second, all the women he had ever woken up with in the course of his forty-six-year life flashed through his morning-fuddled mind. It stopped at the right one.

Marianne.

Quite right. The route to Marianne was not particularly long. Apart from his ex-wife he had only ever made love to a dozen women at most; half of them only once or twice, almost all of them over twenty years ago. His student years in Lund.

But now here he was, lying beside Marianne. Just so. She was still asleep, breathing in through her nose with a little snuffle, and he wondered how on earth such a beautiful woman could fall for an oaf like him.

Though he supposed this too was all part of the feminine mystique, of course. Thank goodness.

Malmö. He looked cautiously around the room and realized they were at Hotel Baltzar in Malmö. A big corner room on the fourth floor. Those student years were no more than ten kilometres away, when he came to think of it. *That* was where he was, and now he had established that, the rest of the jigsaw fell swiftly into place.

It was morning. It was Saturday. It was mid-November. They had arrived last night and would be staying until Sunday. For a wedding.

Not their own, that would have been a bit quick off the mark. It was still less than four months since they had met, those magical weeks on Thasos, and rushing was the last thing they needed to do. On the contrary, let's suck each other like a couple of delicious sweets, she had said, and then we'll see. Gunnar Barbarotti had certainly not objected, though he found it a bit difficult to imagine himself as a delicious sweet, but what the hell. And there was no denying that their taste for sweets had intensified considerably in the course of the autumn. They had met at least ten times, he had introduced Marianne to Sara, and he had met Marianne's children – a boy of fourteen and a girl of twelve – on two occasions. There had been no friction to speak of. O great God, he had thought just the other day, I concede I hadn't asked for her, but I'm almost ready to dish out ten existence points for you having sent her my way.

Our Lord had replied that if people only had the sense to ask for things they really needed, it would be simpler to keep them supplied – and Gunnar Barbarotti had defended himself by saying he had imagined it was the extant god's responsibility to equip the human race with precisely such sense.

On this point, Our Lord had asked to get back to him once He had the right answer.

But now there was to be a wedding. Marianne's sister Clara, a twenty-eight-year-old art director – Gunnar wasn't entirely sure he knew what that involved – had finally found her prince, a Danish architect called Palle. Marianne herself worked as a midwife – a profession with much more obvious content. She was twelve years older than her sister the bride (there were no fewer than four sisters and three brothers in the family, most of them half-siblings), and Gunnar Barbarotti had initially been alarmed at the thought of attending a youthful wedding party and meeting 138 people of whom he knew precisely one. But turning down the invitation seemed even worse, and with proceedings now extended to a whole weekend in Malmö – private accommodation at a hotel, just him and Marianne – it had all appeared in a much less threatening light.

'Of course you've got to go, you old goat,' Sara had exhorted him. 'You need to see the good side of life sometimes, too.'

My dearest daughter, thought Gunnar Barbarotti, and gave a happy yawn. If only you knew.

The ceremony was held in Sankt Petri church, the bride and the bridegroom both said yes, and the party afterwards was in the church's own function room just a minute's walk away. (And only three or four back to Hotel Baltzar, a fact that Marianne had not forgotten to point out.)

The wedding breakfast turned out to be a long one. They took their places just after six, and five hours later they were still sitting there. Gunnar Barbarotti had counted twenty-four speeches and performances, and according to the toastmaster – a well-fleshed young man in a light-blue dinner jacket who did not begrudge himself the pleasure of adding his own running commentary – there were at least half a dozen more before the dancing and whiskies and soda could start.

But that was fine, Inspector Barbarotti was doing all right, he had to admit. He had found himself seated in a lively and unsophisticated corner of the large venue, a corner where drinking and noisy talk and laughter were the order of the evening – and he had Marianne in his sight and almost within hearing distance, diagonally across a beautiful table centre-piece of yellow leaves, heather and rowan berries. Sitting to his right was his official table partner, a cousin of the bride-groom's, who was from a little village in Jylland and spoke an impenetrable Danish that become no easier to understand, even after seven glasses of wine. On his left side, he had a den-tist from Uddevalla, a girlfriend of the bride's and gifted with a singing voice that brought him out in goosebumps when she performed her own composition, a love song to the young couple. Entirely a cappella and verging on the erotic; quite possibly some of the goosebumps resulted from the fact that he made sure to have eye contact with Marianne throughout the performance.

As expected, there was a lot of chat about his profession. A real live detective inspector was a real someone in any setting, and particularly at a wedding party. Before they got to the ice cream, all the most spectacular criminal cases in Sweden, from the murder of Olof Palme to the present day, had been discussed, in no particular order. Catrine da Costa. Fadime Şahindal. Åmsele and Knutby. Thomas Quick. An increasingly tipsy EU secretary sitting beside Marianne insisted more and more doggedly as the evening went on that he had met the Hörby murderer on a cycle tour of Österlen in the mid-nineties. And that his name was most definitely not Olsson. The woman sitting beside him – they evidently knew each other a little already – gradually tired of his line of talk and suggested he go out for a dip in the nearby canal to sober up a little. To underline how seriously she meant it, this being between the twenty-fifth and twenty-sixth speech, she promptly drank up his dessert wine, which had just been served – to the great amusement of those sitting around them.

Gunnar Barbarotti had not caught the name of this self-willed woman, who was long-necked and red-haired and looked only a few years younger than himself, but he discovered that her place card was lying between them on the table and took a quick look at it.

Annica Willnius.

Willnius? That rang a bell, somewhere deep in his mildly intoxicated brain.

It took another two speeches and a glass of wine to come to the surface.

Jakob Willnius. That was his name, Kristina Hermansson's husband. He still had a few functioning synapses.

But it was now – he had to work it out – just over ten months since he had talked to the man in that beautiful home in Old Enskede. Surely the name Willnius couldn't be coincidence? No, it seemed far too unusual, they must be related in some way.

And in just a few seconds, as he leant back and cautiously sipped the sweet wine – and gave up concentrating on the twenty-seventh speech of the evening – the whole case came sailing into the harbour of his mind. Or to be more precise, half the case. Robert Hermansson's grim story was now definitively closed.

That left Henrik Grundt. That left the need to get somewhere, anywhere at all, with his disappearance. Gunnar Barbarotti sighed and took another sip of wine. Officially, the investigation was still going on, but the currently extant god knew that it was running at half speed. Or a quarter. Or an eighth. Since August, not a single thing had happened, and all that was going on in terms of police work was basically that inspectors Barbarotti and Backman discussed the situation once or twice a week, expressing their frustration and noting that there had been no new developments.

But as Eva was fond of observing, how the hell can anything happen in an investigation when no one's doing anything? Are we waiting for somebody else to get run over by a bus in Oslo, or what?

He registered that thinking about the case was making his spirits sink. It was always the same. Racking his brains over insoluble problems might have appealed to him as a schoolboy, but it was no pastime for a grown-up detective. He knocked back his wine. Thought of the golden rule that inebriation has a positive effect as long as the alcohol levels in the blood are rising, a negative one as soon as they start to fall. The speeches were still going on; this one was a jovial childhood friend of the groom's, who spoke a Danish almost as incomprehensible as Barbarotti's table partner – but eventually he proposed a toast. Gunnar raised his empty glass, looked to right and left and straight ahead, as he had been taught, and just as he simulated the act of drinking, he found he had eye contact with the redhead opposite. She winked at him and smiled.

I'll have to ask her, he thought. That's the least I can do.

But I think I'll get her on her own first.

'Nice to get a drop of fresh air.'

She invalidated her own statement somewhat by taking a

deep drag on her cigarette at that very moment. They were standing out on the big balcony, and it was just before twelve. Everyone had left the table and furniture moving was in full swing in the hall, ready for the dancing. The rain had stopped, and he rested his elbows on the chest-high stone balustrade, looked out over wet, glistening streets, the streaks of mist and dots of golden light, and thought to himself that November evenings could be rather attractive. Tender-hearted, in some strange way. Marianne had left him to queue for the powder room, and he had got himself a bottle of beer from the newly opened bar.

'Definitely. But it was very pleasant in there.'

She nodded.

'I've got to ask you about your name.'

'My name?'

'Yes. It's Annica Willnius, isn't it?'

'Detective inspector again?'

'No, no. But I came across a Jakob Willnius a while back. You must be related?'

She took another deep pull on her cigarette. Seemed to be considering something.

'My former husband.'

'Oh yes?'

'What's he done?'

Gunnar Barbarotti gave a laugh. 'Nothing. He cropped up in an investigation, that's all. You meet a terrific number of people in my job.'

'I can imagine. Well, anyway, we divorced five years ago. I don't have anything to do with him. I suppose he still lives in Stockholm, with his new partner presumably, and I live with mine in London. That's life, isn't it?'

'In the twenty-first century,' added Gunnar Barbarotti. 'Yes, in fact, I'm heading for a similar thing myself.'

That was bold of him, and he realized it was the alcohol helping him along. She nodded and looked thoughtful for a moment. 'Though I kept his name, as you said. I was a common-or-garden Pettersson as a girl and my new hook-up's called Czerniewski. What do you reckon to Annica Czerniewski?'

'Well, I'm a Gunnar Barbarotti myself,' said Gunnar Barbarotti.

She laughed. He laughed. It's great when people have had a few drinks, he thought. Why do our inhibitions always have to get in the way? She had brought a wine glass outside with her, and now she raised it.

'Cheers. You seem a nice cop.'

'You too . . . though you're not a cop, of course.'

He drank some beer from his bottle.

'Not exactly. The theatre's where I make my living. But only behind the scenes.'

'I see.'

'But let me confess one thing.'

'And what's that?'

'It wouldn't surprise me in the least if Jakob had crossed the line. Not in the slightest.'

'What do you mean?'

She took another drag on her cigarette and hesitated. Blew out smoke in a thin, reflective stream. He was struck by the thought that she looked like some actress in a French film. But then she worked in that field – maybe it rubbed off onto everyday life sometimes.

'I only mean that Jakob Willnius is a total shit. A really

nasty piece of work. You can't see it on the surface, but I was married to him for eight years, so then you know.'

'Been having a nice time?'

Marianne inserted her arm in his and kissed him lightly on the cheek.

'Oops. Lipstick.'

She licked her finger and rubbed it off.

'Yes thanks. And you?'

'Great. Who was the woman in red?'

'Don't know. I just happened to recognize her name, that's all. I was sitting opposite her.'

'OK. It's the bridal waltz now, and then you've got to dance with your table partner. But after that, you're only allowed to dance with me.'

'I wouldn't dream of dancing with anyone else,' Gunnar Barbarotti assured her. 'Hmm.'

'What does "hmm" mean?'

'Pardon?'

'You said "hmm". It sounded as if you were brooding about something.'

'Can't think what that could have been,' said Gunnar Barbarotti. He put his arm round his lover's waist and steered her gently into the ballroom.

'Hi,' said Kristoffer Grundt. 'Am I speaking to Olle Rimborg?'

'The very same.'

'Sorry?'

'Yes, I'm Olle Rimborg.'

'Er . . . good. My name's Kristoffer Grundt. I'm calling from Sundsvall. You're the one who works at the hotel in Kymlinge, right?'

'Yes, I do reception work there now and then. What is it you want?'

'It's just this thing,' said Kristoffer. 'Though I don't really know . . .'

'Yes?'

'So, my name's Kristoffer Grundt. Our family was visiting Granny and Granddad in Kymlinge in December last year, and then . . . well, then my brother Henrik disappeared. My uncle too, and he was found—'

'I know who you are,' Olle Rimborg interrupted with sudden enthusiasm. 'Of course I do. I know the whole story. Wank— I mean your uncle was found in August, dismembered. So you're the brother of . . . ?'

'Henrik Grundt, yes. The other one who went missing.'

'He hasn't turned up, I don't suppose?'

'No . . . no, he's still missing.'

'Didn't you stay at the hotel in August? At the time of Robert's funeral. With your mum and your—'

'Yes.'

'Thought so. I was working then, as well. Maybe we saw each other.'

'Maybe,' said Kristoffer.

The line briefly went quiet.

'Er . . . so what was it you wanted?'

Kristoffer cleared his throat.

'It was just this thing Granny said . . . and I thought I ought to check it with you. It probably isn't anything important, but we're going through a bit of a family crisis up here, actually, and I . . .'

'I can well imagine,' Olle Rimborg put in.

'. . . and it would be good to, like, know for sure, even if it meant . . .'

'Yes?'

'. . . even if it meant my brother really is dead.'

'Got you,' said Olle Rimborg. 'So what was it your granny said?'

'She said she'd been talking to you . . . and you told her someone had come back.'

Olle Rimborg said nothing for a moment, but Kristoffer could hear his sharp intake of breath.

'That's right,' he said once he had let the air out again. 'Now I understand. Yes, I did talk to Mrs Hermansson a bit when they were staying here for the funeral, and I did refer to something . . . well, something I'd been wondering about a bit.'

'Oh yes?' said Kristoffer Grundt.

'Yes, that's how it is, isn't it, you start thinking about things when something like this happens. It isn't exactly every day two people disappear from Kymlinge. Not in – not in circumstances like these, at any rate.'

'I can see that,' said Kristoffer Grundt. 'So who was it that came back, that is . . . I didn't really understand all that much of what Granny was saying, to be honest. I'm sure it's nothing important, but I decided I ought to call and ask you about it, just in case.'

'It was her husband,' Olle Rimborg told him. 'I mean Kristina Hermansson's husband. They stayed at the hotel here in December, as you know. Kristina and I were in the same year

at school, actually, so we go back a long way, as you might say
. . . so she's your aunt, right?'

'Right,' said Kristoffer Grundt.

'Well, what I've been wondering about – and what I mentioned to your granny – is the fact that he came back in the
middle of the night, Kristina's husband. We understood he'd
be driving back to Stockholm late that evening, and so he did.
Left about midnight. And she and the little boy stayed here,
asleep in the room. But then he came back, just before
three—'

'Wait a minute, which night are we talking about?' Kristoffer asked him. 'Was it . . . ?'

'The night your brother disappeared,' clarified Olle Rimborg. 'I kept up with everything in the papers about it – you
find you can't help yourself. Your uncle disappeared on the
night of Monday into Tuesday, and your brother the following
night. From Tuesday into Wednesday, in other words. That's
right, isn't it? The week before Christmas, it was.'

'Quite right,' confirmed Kristoffer, and felt his heart start
beating a little harder. 'So what you're saying –' he tried to
find the words – 'is that Jakob . . . whatshisname? . . . Jakob
Willnius initially drove off around midnight . . . that must
have been just after the party ended at Granny and Granddad's . . . but that he came back at three o'clock. Is that it?'

'Precisely,' said Olle Rimborg.

'And what happened then?'

'Then? Well, they went off early the next morning, the
whole family. Kristina and . . . what did you say his name
was?'

'Jakob Willnius.'

'Jakob Willnius, and their kid. Yeah, they left early the next morning. Had breakfast at seven and checked out around quarter to eight.'

The line went quiet again.

'And?' said Kristoffer Grundt.

'Well, that was it,' said Olle Rimborg. 'Nothing that remarkable really, but I've thought about it a bit. I meant to ask Kristina at the funeral in August, but she looked so miserable I didn't like to intrude. Sure, we were in the same school year, but I didn't really know her. You know how it is, you can be in the same year right the way through, yet hardly ever talk to each other.'

'I know,' said Kristoffer Grundt.

'So this is what you were ringing about?'

'Yes, I guess so,' said Kristoffer.

'It wasn't really anything worth mentioning. But not much ever happens here in Kymlinge . . . if you get what I mean.'

'I get it,' said Kristoffer Grundt. 'Thanks anyway.'

But after he had hung up, he wondered whether he really did get it. If indeed there was anything there to get. It didn't seem like it. Jakob Willnius had come back to the hotel that night. He drove off and returned later. So what? Kristoffer looked to see what time it was. 9.40 a.m. Time to get himself to school if he didn't want to miss yet another lesson. Oh well, he thought, at least I've done what my brother wanted.

He almost expected Henrik to pop into his head and say thank you very much. That was surely the least you could ask?

But no brother turned up.

It was as silent as the grave from that direction.

34

'Who is she then?' asked Eva Backman. 'I think it's about time you came out with it.'

Gunnar Barbarotti bit into a carrot and tried to look inscrutable. They were at King's Grill, a stone's throw from the police station. Its speciality was traditional Swedish fare; forgotten dishes from days gone by, like root mash and pork knuckle, herring balls with currant sauce, stuffed cabbage leaves, horseradish pike with melted butter. Today, smoked sausage and potatoes in white sauce, served with carrots, was on the menu for both Barbarotti and Backman, and they ordered tomato salad and beetroot on the side. It was Wednesday; they usually went to King's Grill once or twice a week, and Gunnar Barbarotti realized Backman had restrained herself from asking for longer than he had any right to expect. Considerably longer, but at King's Grill, questions of a sensitive nature did tend to surface rather rapidly. He chewed on a piece of sausage.

'Marianne. Her name's Marianne.'

Eva Backman regarded him critically.

'I know she's called Marianne,' she observed. 'You mentioned it yesterday. Is that all you've got to say about her? Is your view of women that they're only distinguishable from each other by their names?'

'What now?' said Gunnar Barbarotti. 'I thought we were going to talk about work. Not my supposed love life. But all right, she's just over forty. Divorced midwife from Helsingborg with two teenage kids.'

Eva Backman sighed.

'Excellent. Thank you for that. You really are a romantic to the core, my dear Detective Inseminator. Is she attractive?'

'Never seen anything prettier.'

'White teeth?'

'Yes.'

'Violet-blue eyes?'

'Yes.'

'Nice tits?'

'Oh yes. A pair of those.'

Eva Backman laughed. 'And she's got a soul?'

'Yes, a hundred per cent proof,' said Gunnar Barbarotti. 'But I think that's enough information for now. After all, she hasn't proposed yet, and what's so odd about me starting to go out with someone again?'

'It's odder than you think,' said Eva Backman with a mysterious smile.

'Indeed? Well, anyway, I expect you'll get to meet her in due course . . . if we carry on, that is.'

'Is that a promise?'

'More like an inescapable fact. But forget that now. There's something work-related I want to talk to you about. If I treat you to posh sausages, it's only fair that you play ball.'

'I see,' said Eva Backman. 'You need help as usual. There's no such thing as a free sausage. What's up?'

'Henrik Grundt.'

'Aha.'

'What does "Aha" mean?'

'I don't know. That I'm a bit surprised, I suppose. You haven't brought the case up for over two weeks now.'

'That doesn't mean I'm not still thinking about it.'

'I'm thinking about it too. Well?'

'Hrrm. Well, there was this woman at the wedding.'

'The bride?'

'No, not the bride. There were at least seventy other women there.'

'I see.'

'I was sitting opposite her at the reception.'

'Oh?'

'We talked a bit afterwards. It turned out her surname was Willnius.'

'Willnius?'

'Yes. Annica Willnius.'

Eva Backman raised a quizzical eyebrow.

'She's Jakob Willnius's first wife. Jakob Willnius is now married to Kristina Hermansson. And Kristina Hermansson is—'

'Thanks. I know who Kristina Hermansson is. So you met the ex-wife of – let me get this right – Henrik Grundt's aunt's husband? Is that what you're telling me?'

'Yes.'

'Impressive. How did you manage that?'

'Shut up, Inspector Backman. If you just get on with your sausage, I'll explain.'

'Deal.'

'You watch too many third-rate police dramas. But that's your problem. *My* problem is something she said about Jakob Willnius.'

'Mhm?'

'She said he was a nasty bit of work. And it wouldn't surprise her if he'd killed somebody.'

Eva Backman swallowed a mouthful of potato and took a gulp of her Ramlösa mineral water. 'Did she now?'

'Or words to that effect.'

'And?'

'That was all. It might not mean anything, but I can't help wondering about it.'

'Wondering about what, exactly?'

Gunnar Barbarotti paused and leant back in his chair.

'I don't really know. About whether we ruled out the so-called family aspect a bit too readily in this case, for example?'

Eva Backman put down her knife and fork and wiped the corners of her mouth thoroughly with a serviette. She regarded him even more critically than before and sighed.

'So what you're basing this on,' she said slowly – and not without an irritating undertone of ridicule, thought Inspector Barbarotti, 'is a comment from a former wife at a wedding. Former wives tend to not always love their former husbands, perhaps that's news to you, but—'

'For Christ's sake,' he cut in with a sudden anger that felt surprisingly genuine. 'I'm only saying it made me think a bit. It's nearly a year since Henrik Grundt disappeared from Allvädersgatan, and we don't know any more about what happened than – than Asunander's sausage dog knows about the emancipation of women. If you've got anything better to go on, you're more than welcome to put it forward.'

'Interesting comparison,' said Eva Backman. 'And sorry, sorry. I trod on your sensitive toe there. Of course the family angle is interesting.'

'Thank you.'

'Though to be honest, we've never forgotten it. Have we? I thought we were in agreement that it was a dead end, that's all. What motives could any of them have for killing Henrik? What would Jakob Willnius's be? Had they ever even met before, Henrik and the nasty ex-husband?'

Gunnar Barbarotti threw up his hands disconsolately.

'No idea. No, it was an over-optimistic thought. But I just wanted to mention it to you.'

'Thanks for sharing it.'

'You're welcome. But it's daft to let all the flashes of inspiration stay in one pitiful head. Presumably you can agree with me on that?'

'Daft indeed,' said Eva Backman. 'Especially a head like yours. I promise to think about it. Is dessert included in this glamorous lunch invitation?'

'Coffee's included,' Gunnar Barbarotti said firmly. 'That's all.'

In the first days – even the first weeks – after she decided to kill her husband, Kristina Hermansson felt the presence of a sort of mild euphoria. It wasn't much, no more than a thin ray of hope really, but it cut through the darkness and she felt in her robotic existence a streak of . . . of something human. Her consciousness found direction. The convulsive state in which she had grown used to living, those slowly rotating fists – one in her stomach, one in her throat – perhaps wouldn't inevitably be with her for the remainder of her days.

With Jakob out of the way, she would be able to start her own penance and begin to tackle her own grief. Perhaps.

But the new state proved transient. The fists clenched

again. As she sat there with two-and-a-half-year-old Kelvin on her lap and looked into his cold, empty eyes, it felt as though she was being filled with all the darkness and despair of existence. It was terrifying and devoid of all hope. Life was a wretched joke. A cynical melodrama, she thought, cobbled together by some bitter failure of a TV dramatist in the inebriation of the dismal hour before dawn, to be avenged on their own lack of success. Yes, she could actually believe in a god like that, a peevish clown who intended the whole of creation as a farce and scorned it as some black joke.

She had not worked for over a year now. Perhaps it was because of Kelvin. He wasn't like other children; this was a truth she had pushed away from her for so long, but it was becoming increasingly impossible to keep it at a distance. He had not started walking until he was two and now, a good six months later, he still wasn't saying anything – except for the occasional disconnected and incomprehensible word, which could escape him at the most unexpected times. He did not play with the other children, not even with Emma and Julius and Kasper, whom he saw every day at his childminder's, three doors down in Musseronvägen. He scarcely even played on his own; he could spend short periods on Lego bricks or finger-painting, but was considerably more interested in demolishing than in building. He spent most of his time staring emptily in front of him, his fingers twining mechanically and aimlessly. As if he was brooding on something, she would think, as if he bore some black secret within him that he was unable to get proper sight of. A bit like herself, she thought. We're both stuck where we are, my son and I.

And then there was the sleeping. Kelvin could sleep fourteen to fifteen hours a day, which wasn't normal.

Perhaps she could have loved him, all the same. Kelvin wouldn't harm a fly, and if only everything else had not been reduced to ash and ruins, perhaps she could have been content with his quiet ways. If it had only been him and her.

Perhaps.

But he did not absorb her. What absorbed her most through those dark days of mid-November was the possibility of recapturing that thin ray of euphoria.

The possibility of killing Jakob.

Daring to believe in it, at least. Thinking of it as an actual possibility, for the time being, that was enough. Because somewhere along the way, at some point on one of those dispiriting November mornings, her thoughts had achieved a certain clarity. A lucid state in which she told herself that it really would be possible. This chink that let the light cut through the darkness soon closed, to be sure, but she remembered it. And knew that this was precisely the step she had to take, sooner or later, if she were to pull through this.

To kill.

For there was no document, she had made up her mind about that. Jakob had not deposited anything, neither with a lawyer, nor anywhere else. If he died, nothing would come to light and reveal the background of the Henrik tragedy. He would not identify himself as a murderer, not even after his own death. Not even to take revenge on her.

She was not entirely convinced that this line of reasoning really held good, but she decided to stick to it anyway. If she were to find the strength to make progress in any direction at all, she had to follow it.

Kill him, then.

But how?

And when?

And how to evade suspicion? Suspicion of her and suspicion linking Jakob's death to events in Kymlinge. If he died and it all came out, the battle would have been in vain, anyway.

Jakob's death was the only road to take, but how should she embark on it without taking any false steps?

She brooded on the problem for days and nights and seemed not to come a centimetre closer to a solution, but all at once – or so she persuaded herself – an option opened up.

Or perhaps she was just imagining things. Perhaps it was all a question of distance. Of pushing things into the future and believing everything is easier to achieve somewhere else. Forgetting that you always, wherever you are, have to drag yourself around – your own presence and your own uncertainty.

Thailand. It was Jakob's idea. Two weeks in December. Just him and her; Kelvin left with the childminder. It had worked before; the boy was no trouble, after all, and the money they paid her always came in useful.

Kristina had said neither yes nor no, but the next day he booked the trip: two nights in Bangkok, twelve on the islands off the Krabi coast. It was a few years since the tsunami and it could be interesting to see how they had coped with building things up again, thought Jakob. He had not travelled in Thailand for twelve years; Kristina's experience of the country amounted to two weeks in Phuket back in 1996 or possibly 1997.

They were to leave on the fifth of December, anyway, and come home on the twentieth, and that very evening she saw her opportunity.

Swedish tourists had disappeared in Thailand before. Not only at the time of the tidal wave disaster. She had read about such things in the papers, and it wasn't hard to visualize herself in tears, telling a local policeman with exceedingly poor English that her husband *had gone missing*. That she had not seen him for over twenty-four hours and that she was afraid something might have happened to him.

She could see – very clearly – in her mind's eye the helpless but kindly Thai people failing in all their efforts to get to the bottom of anything, and herself tearfully boarding a plane home to Sweden, five days earlier than anticipated. The tabloids back home would devote a headline or two to the case, not more. Shocked friends would ring to express their condolences.

What would she need?

A knife and a shovel, she thought. Both could undoubtedly be purchased pretty much anywhere in Thailand, and the ground in the jungle was no doubt loose-textured and easy to dig, she was convinced of it.

She could see the deed itself, too. The knife-thrust to the back on their night-time walk, perhaps she would lure him out with the promise of sex under the stars . . . his groans, the surprised (hopefully terrified) look in his eyes and the blood gurgling out of him; a couple more stabs of the knife, then an hour's digging and finally a purifying bathe in the sea.

So simple. So liberating.

When Leif Grundt arranged a work experience placement for Kristoffer in a Co-op store in Uppsala, he himself thought it was a very good idea. The week fell at the very end of

November and a few days into December, and if there was one thing the lad needed this miserable autumn it was to get away from home for a while. His form teacher and his study advisor had both agreed on that. Kristoffer, too, in his usual slightly listless fashion.

But once he had put the boy on the train on Saturday 27 November – and put himself in the car for the drive back to Stockrosvägen – he felt a sudden lump in his throat. It was late afternoon. Dingy twilight and thin, driving rain. The house would be entirely empty. No Kristoffer. No Henrik. Not even any Ebba; his wife had – on her bearded therapist's advice – decided not to leave the Vassrogga clinic for the last two weekends of her treatment. Being at home was evidently considered bad for her. Leif Grundt had little insight into what actually went on at Vassrogga, but in some obscure way he still felt they had made the right judgement where the weekends were concerned. Ebba had not displayed any pleasure when she had come back to him and Kristoffer on previous Friday evenings, and when he drove off with her on Sunday afternoons she seemed to have no hesitation in leaving them again. Just the opposite: though she did not express herself one way or the other, there were signs to indicate that she thought it was nice to go back.

Or, at any rate, Leif Grundt thought he could detect such signs.

Perhaps three weeks' total separation would foster a change of mind? Perhaps twenty days without her wounded and mangled family were what it would take to shake something up inside Ebba Hermansson Grundt?

But probably not. Leif Grundt was under no illusions. For the past few days, that embroidered sampler hanging above his own grandmother's nursing-home bed – which he had sat and spelled his way through as a five-year old – had kept coming into Leif's mind at ever shorter intervals.

Sufficient unto the day is the evil thereof.

Wise words to rely on in one's hour of need, thought Leif Grundt. Though not particularly optimistic ones.

But anyway, things were as they were. He would be alone at home for a whole week. As he drove along the familiar streets up to Hemmanshöjden, through intensifying grey rain, he tried to remember when anything like that had last happened.

It must have been a very long time ago, he concluded. And he had never been completely on his own at Stockrosvägen, he knew that for certain. A few hours maybe, an afternoon, but a whole week? Never.

Hence the lump in his throat. And of course, there was nothing very odd about that. Leif Grundt had always had problems with people who saw themselves as victims. Who blamed circumstances and gave themselves the right to be bitter. But just now, he felt he was on the verge of it himself; it wasn't easy to find any benign angle of approach from which to view this state of affairs. He was *stricken*. No doubt about it. His family lay in ruins; it had started with Henrik's disappearance and things had been unravelling ever since. Barely a year had gone by, and Leif Grundt had simply not been able to imagine that anything like this could happen – that it would lie within the realm of possibility. Sometimes, he couldn't help asking himself how things would look in another year's time, if it all continued at this pace. How would the Grundt family look by December next year? And the year after that?

But at the same time, he felt guilty. He couldn't really understand why; surely it was hardly his fault that Henrik had gone missing? Or that his wife was going out of her mind? Or that Kristoffer was going astray?

But there it was, something pricking his conscience. Perhaps it was just that phrase Bishop Tutu had used, or whoever it was.

Those who have the strength have a duty to go on finding it.

But what if he no longer had the strength?

He parked the car in front of the garage, as usual. As he had done a thousand times before. He climbed out and hurried the few steps through the rain to the front door, thinking that he ought at least to have left the light on to mark the desolation. *Mark the desolation?* Where did expressions like that come from? Was there something amiss with his own thoughts too, with the words that cropped up in his head? They seemed to come from some secret store inside him that he had never glanced into before. Never needed to.

But he had not put a light on. He did so now, instead, going round upstairs and downstairs and switching on all the lights; then he picked up the phone and called Berit in Uppsala to let her know Kristoffer had departed on schedule.

Kristoffer was going to stay at Berit's while he did his work experience. Leif Grundt had no brothers or sisters, but he had two cousins he was close to. Berit in Uppsala and her twin brother Jörgen in Kristianstad. Henrik, too, had spent a couple of weeks at Berit's, last autumn while he was waiting to move into his student room in the Triangle. She was divorced, but still lived with her ten-year-old daughter out in Bergsbrunna, in a house that was far too big for her. She was more than happy to take in Kristoffer, just as she had taken in Henrik last year.

So how are you doing? she had asked, and Leif Grundt had not known what to answer.

After the call, he sank down at the kitchen table and wondered how to make the time pass this Saturday evening. Not to mention Sunday.

And how he could deal with that gnawing feeling of negligence. Of having not done enough for his wife and his son.

I ought not to have sent him away, he thought suddenly. I only did it to be left in peace for a week. If I were a good father, I wouldn't have pushed the problem away like that.

He looked at the time. It was twenty to five. He put his head in his hands and started to weep.

35

Kristina took the underground to Fridhemsplan and walked the few blocks to Inedalsgatan. It was Sunday afternoon. The Sunday before Advent, with its text on the Last Judgement. In three days' time it would be 1 December and that was the date by which Robert's flat had to be cleared out. That was what she had agreed with the landlord; or rather with the tenant who sublet the flat to Robert. Erik Renstierna.

She had put it off twice. She had promised to empty the flat by 1 October, and then by 1 November, but it had not happened. Jakob had shown a certain amount of understanding – or indifference, at any rate – the first time, but the second time he was furious.

'Are we supposed to pay the rent on Wanker Tarzan's hole for the rest of our lives?' he demanded to know.

But now she had sorted it all out. Tomorrow, Monday, a removal company would come and decant all her brother's possessions into a Shurgard self-storage unit; on Tuesday, two highly qualified cleaners would arrive. If she wanted to go through anything or pick up some form of memento, today was her last chance. When the formal arrangements were made after Robert's death, this was the scenario they had all agreed on. His daughter Lena-Sofie had expressed no immediate claims, either directly or through her mother, and the other potential beneficiaries – his parents Rosemarie and Karl-Erik – had shown the same lack of interest, so Brundin the lawyer had made do with dividing Robert's financial assets of just over four thousand kronor into two equal parts (after first subtracting his own fee of three thousand six hundred) and distributing them amongst the direct heirs.

And Kristina had undertaken to arrange the emptying of the flat.

Robert had already been carved up once. In a way, it would have felt hard to carve up his property as well.

There was a drift of junk mail on the hall floor. The flat had a stuffy, shut-up smell. She had never set foot here before, even though it had been Robert's home for eighteen months and she lived in the same city. She could not prevent a feeling of shame creeping over her as she thought of this, and she did her best to nip it in the bud. She walked round the flat for a while, switching on all the lights she could find. Two small rooms plus a tiny kitchen, that was all. It had stood untouched – apart from a couple of police visits – for eleven months; she decided against opening the fridge door. The melancholy was palpable, which was what she had expected. Dirt and mess. Cheap furniture, tatty art posters on the walls, nothing of value. Naturally, there were reasons why no visits had been paid in his lifetime, she thought. Good reasons. She had liked her brother, considerably better than most of the others had, but that did not mean she wanted to be involved in his exist-ence. *Would have wanted to be involved*; she had not imagined him alive for a long time, but just for a moment there, she actually had done. It suddenly struck her hard, the realization that he was dead. That he had been for almost a year. Robert, that stupid oaf.

What am I doing here, she thought, biting her lip to stop herself crying. What sort of meaningless ritual do I think I'm performing by tramping round in this squalid place? Duty? Scarcely. Robert was never the dutiful type; quite the opposite. Nor was she. Burn all that crap, Kristina, he would presumably have urged her if she had ever bothered to ask him. Don't go poking around in this garbage heap, the shit will just rub off on you!

There was a fairly well-arranged bookcase in the living room, at any rate. Robert had been quite a keen reader, and perhaps she could take a few books with her? But why? What would the point of that be? She turned her eyes to the desk. It was large, and cluttered with junk, but on the right-hand end, beside the computer, there were two piles of paper, one on its stomach, as it were – lying face-down – the other on its back. Could it be . . . ? She suddenly remembered that Robert had talked about a novel. It surely couldn't be . . . ? She turned the stomach pile over so the text was uppermost. She put the two piles together and looked at the front page.

Man Without Dog, it said.

A novel by Robert Hermansson.

Of course, she thought, and something rather akin to joy gave a jump inside her. Yes, he said he was working on it. That Christmas, he mentioned it.

This, she muttered as she carefully aligned the edges of the sheets in the pile, this, lying here, is your soul, Robert. You laid it out here for me to come and get. Thank you, now I know why I came here.

She put the manuscript in the shoulder bag she had brought with her, and then paused for a moment to consider whether she needed to look round any further. Whether it would take more than this one simple thing. *Man Without Dog*, her brother's spiritual will and testament; for her to look after and hold in trust for posterity? It was strange, very strange, or so she felt.

And as she stood there in her dead brother's seedy living room with his posthumous novel in her bag, the mobile phone rang in her coat pocket out in the hall. She hesitated for a moment and then decided to answer it.

It was Kristoffer.

Her nephew, Kristoffer Grundt.

'Hi there, Kristoffer,' she said in surprise. 'How nice of you to ring. What's on your mind?'

'Hi,' said Kristoffer. 'Well, there's something I wanted to ask you about.'

'Oh yes? What's that?'

'It's about that night.'

'Which night?'

'The night Henrik disappeared.'

Something happened inside her head. A tone began to ring, sharp and persistent. It was like the sound of a distant saw-blade, and she wondered why. It must have been twenty years since she last heard a sawblade.

'Yes?'

'There's someone who claims your husband came back.'

'What?'

'The receptionist at the hotel in Kymlinge. He says your husband came back in the middle of the night. I just thought I ought to check with you.'

Presumably she lost consciousness for a second or two, but she didn't fall. She just felt her field of vision shrink as she herself was swiftly sucked into a long, dark, contracting tunnel. To emerge into the light on the other side. The saw-blade died away.

'Hello?'

'Yes, I'm still here . . .'

Am I, she wondered in bewilderment. Am I really still here?

'So, er, it was just that, really,' Kristoffer went on, with a nervous cough down the line. 'I thought I ought to just ask.'

The blood came rushing back into her temples, she could hear it. 'I see,' she said. 'You're ringing from Sundsvall, are you?'

'No,' said Kristoffer. 'I'm in Uppsala. I'm doing work experience this week, so I'm staying with Berit, Dad's cousin—'

'Uppsala?'

'Yes.'

She took a deep breath. 'Kristoffer, do you – do you think we could meet, you and I? Sometime this week. You could take the train to Stockholm one evening, or I could—'

'I'll come,' said Kristoffer.

'Good. Then we can go out and eat somewhere and talk a bit. OK?'

'OK,' said Kristoffer. 'When?'

She thought about it. 'Tuesday?'

'Tuesday,' said Kristoffer. 'Shall I call you when I know what time . . . I mean when I finish work and so on?'

'Yes, do. Then I'll meet you at Central station.'

'Thanks. Bye then,' said Kristoffer.

'Bye.'

She sank down onto her dead brother's hall rug feeling as though she weighed a ton. For a whole minute, her consciousness was as blank as a turned-off screen. Why is this happening just now, she asked herself when thought returned. Seven days before Thailand?

Judgement Sunday?

As if the vengeful arch-manipulator and clown god had suddenly woken up and decided to pull a couple more strings.

There was an old rule. Gunnar Barbarotti didn't know where he had first come across it, not that it mattered.

If you can't stop thinking about it, then do something about it.

That was true, of course. And if he did not have to go to too much trouble, he usually put this principle into practice. For his own peace of mind, if nothing else.

Some would cost too much, of course. There were plenty of things Gunnar Barbarotti tended to brood about, but actually getting to grips with them would have required dizzying amounts of effort.

The nature of love, for example.

Or the murder of Olof Palme.

Or the concept of democracy. Was it really reasonable that people who swallowed absolutely any stupid advertising slogan should decide the fate of a country? People who elected presidents on the basis of eye colour and members of parliament because they could tell a smutty joke?

All of them good questions, probably, but hardly worth the trouble of brooding over. It was like that old serenity prayer, really. Gunnar Barbarotti had never been a member of Alcoholics Anonymous, but he had two friends who had been.

Who still were, as far as he knew, but neither of them lived in Kymlinge any more and he wasn't in touch with them these days.

> God grant me the serenity to accept the things I
>   cannot change,
> Courage to change the things I can,
> And wisdom to know the difference.

A real ten-pointer in fact, when he came to think about it, and having not bothered Our Lord with any existential prayers for almost three works, he fired one off now.

O Lord, make me as wise as a recovering alcoholic, he prayed. Grant me the wisdom to determine whether it's worth my while to delve any further into this blessed Jakob Willnius or not.

He realized that there was a certain lack of clarity in both these simple formulations, but it was Sunday evening and he was tired. Really whacked; it was presumably as a result of having run seven kilometres that afternoon, after neglecting his training recently. To make sure the terms and conditions were completely clear, he added:

The way I see it, dear God, is that if I do decide to follow up his ex-wife's base insinuations, then You get three points if it leads anywhere, but You lose two if it's a blind alley. OK?

Our Lord made no reply, despite being currently eleven points over the boundary line, but presumptuous leaders had suffered from hubris and gone down the pan in world history before, it was nothing new. There was no particularly complicated psychology lurking behind such shortcomings.

So thought Detective Inspector Barbarotti, as he put out his bedside light and turned his pillow over.

36

In the course of Monday and Tuesday, Kristoffer didn't actually feel real.

Or rather, everything around him was unreal. Alien. In the mornings, he woke up in a big, light room with a piano, a stuffed elk's head and strange green plants. After breakfast with Berit and Ingegerd (how the hell could you christen a child Ingegerd?) he took the bus into the centre of Uppsala. Got off at the bus station, lit a cigarette and crossed a street that was busy with traffic. Stubbed out his cigarette, cut through one shopping mall and into another. He found the Co-op store, his place of work. He started by putting on a green jacket and shifting frozen foods about, then chilled foods, and then tinned goods until it was time for lunch; then he went out into the mall and got himself something to eat from the Thai takeaway. He walked round the town for a while, smoked and watched people he didn't know. At one o'clock he went back to the store, donned the green jacket and shifted some more stock about until five. The bus to Bergsbrunna went at quarter past.

The thought that he could just as well have been another person entirely kept gnawing at him. Someone else entirely. Nobody would have noticed the difference. Probably not even Berit and Ingegerd; they hadn't seen him for several years and would doubtless have accepted anybody who turned up and claimed their name was Kristoffer Grundt.

But on Tuesday afternoon, he didn't take the bus back to Bergsbrunna. He got onto the commuter train to Stockholm instead – and that felt even more unreal. As he sat staring out of the grubby window at the dark landscape that went racing by (surprisingly little settlement considering they were heading into Stockholm, he thought; it looked almost like the expanses of Norrland), he wished Henrik would pop into his head. Talk to him and offer him a word or two on his way. That would have been useful, not because Henrik had anything much to do with reality any more, but it would have felt good. There was something about Henrik's voice – Henrik's *imagined* voice – that had a calming effect on him. But he was unable to summon it just now, and closing his eyes and concentrating as hard as he could did not help. Henrik was gone, and had been for the past two weeks. Was he starting to disappear for good? It stung Kristoffer inside to think of it; he gave up and tried to focus on the future instead. The concrete and immediate future.

Going out for dinner with Auntie Kristina in Stockholm! Why? Why had she suggested they meet in that way? It was by way of not making a lot of sense, as their aged neighbour in Stockrosvägen, Mr Månsson, would have said. Kristoffer had never met Kristina on his own before. If she wanted to talk to him about Henrik and Robert and all that – now that he happened to be close by in Uppsala – then surely it would have been more natural to have invited him round to her place? To Musseronvägen out in Enskede; he had paid a visit there with his dad and Henrik a few years back and could remember what it looked like. His mum had to cry off at the last minute; some operation, he supposed, it usually was. Back then.

But instead, Kristina was going to meet him at Central station and they would go to some restaurant nearby and sit there and talk.

What on earth would they talk about? What good would it do Kristina to go out for a meal with a scruffy, timid fifteen-year-old?

And all because he had told her that thing the night porter had said. Olle Rimborg. Wasn't that why?

Yes, that was definitely why. They hadn't talked on the phone for more than a minute, he and Kristina. As soon as he mentioned Olle Rimborg's observation, Kristina had suggested meeting up. If he had rung her about anything else (he couldn't think what), she wouldn't have suggested any such thing, he felt pretty sure of that for some reason.

What am I imagining?

And he was aware that the sense of unreality enveloping him like a dark cloud had less to do with Uppsala, the Co-op, Berit and Ingegerd than it did with the conceivable answer to that specific question.

He had forgotten that she was pregnant.

Or perhaps he hadn't known. At the funeral in August nothing had showed and he couldn't recall his mum or dad saying anything about it.

But he'd probably just forgotten. In any case, she had a substantial bump now. He almost didn't recognize her at first, but it was nothing to do with her stomach. She was wearing a red duffle coat and a red beret and there was something different about her hair.

'Kristoffer.'

Something about her face, too. She looked – she looked older. Or worn out, somehow.

'Hi,' he said, holding out his hand. She ignored it and gave him a hug instead.

'Great to see you, Kristoffer.'

She didn't sound as if she meant it. If there was one thing she didn't think, it was that this was great.

'Yes . ... thanks . . . you too.'

He found it hard to get out. He felt the words stick in his throat and was forced to prise them out, one by one. Pity I never learnt how to vanish into thin air, he thought gloomily. Because if I had, I could do it right now.

But then he realized, looking at her carefully, that she was even more uncomfortable than he was. It was true. Kristoffer might be finding the situation awkward, but it was nothing compared to what Kristina was experiencing. A series of tiny nervous twitches passed across her face and she kept on blinking. Ill at ease would be putting it mildly.

And she didn't say anything, either, and after the perfunctory hug they both stood there as if rooted to their own spot, staring at each other. With a metre between them. It felt extremely peculiar, but she was the worst afflicted, there could be no doubt about it.

'How are you?' he said, entirely automatically.

She swallowed elaborately. Then she put one hand on his arm.

'Come on, I know a place we can go.'

She didn't exactly say it. Her voice wouldn't hold, and it came out as no more than a whisper.

The restaurant was called Il Forno, and it only took them a couple of minutes to get there on foot. Neither of them said a word as they walked. It was only about six in the evening and they had no trouble getting an alcove to themselves, tucked away at the back of the large restaurant. Kristoffer registered that it was Italian, with red, green and white flags hanging up here and there and a Juventus banner on display. But not just pizza, and it didn't seem to be a particularly cheap place.

'Let's order first. I expect you're hungry?'

They ordered – two lasagnes, a Loka mineral water and a Coke – and then Kristina excused herself and went to the toilet.

She was gone for at least ten minutes and the food arrived in the meantime. 'I'm sorry,' she said when she got back. 'Forgive me, Kristoffer.'

He mumbled something in reply and sneaked a glance at her. Her face looked red and swollen. What on earth is up with her, he wondered. She must have been blubbing in the toilets. She cleared her throat and took a deep breath. Looked straight at him with her bright, glassy eyes.

'Kristoffer, I can't take this any more.'

'Um, oh . . . ?' he said.

'When you rang . . .'

'Yes?'

'When you rang, the day before yesterday, it felt to me like being shot.'

'What?'

'Or as if I was waking up from a bad dream.'

'I don't think I understand . . .'

'No, you can't understand. But I've been living in Hell for eleven months, Kristoffer. I still am, but last night I realized I can't go on like this any longer.'

He didn't answer. He couldn't understand what she was talking about, yet at the same time it felt as if . . . well, he didn't really know what it felt like, but suddenly everything seemed like something else. Something very familiar, like when – like when someone finally tells you the answer to a riddle, and you can see how easy it would have been to work it out for yourself.

Though not quite that moment, but the moment just *before*.

'What are you talking about?' he said.

Kristina shook her head and sat in silence for a few seconds. She wasn't looking at him. She was staring at her untouched lasagne instead, and had hunched her shoulders as if she was really cold.

She stayed like that for a while, completely motionless, then cleared her throat and seemed to find fresh strength. A scrap of it, at any rate.

'What was it you wanted to ask when you called on Sunday?'

'It was . . . but I already told you,' said Kristoffer.

'Tell me again,' Kristina asked.

'OK. It started at Robert's funeral – in August, that is. When we came out of the church, Granny was talking to me about someone called Olle Rimborg . . . and something he'd told her.'

'Granny?'

'Yes. Olle Rimborg works at the hotel in Kymlinge and he'd told Granny that your husband – Jakob, that is – that he'd come back to the hotel in the middle of the night . . . that night Henrik disappeared.'

He stopped, but Kristina gestured to him to carry on.

'I suppose I didn't really think about it much, and I really don't know why Granny brought it up. She wasn't entirely with it . . . so, no, I didn't take much notice, but about a week ago I was watching this film on TV—'

'A film?'

'Yes, and Olle Rimborg's name came up in – what are they called – the end credits? And that made me remember. So I rang that Olle Rimborg; it was – it was just on a whim, really.'

'And?' said Kristina, and although it was only a very little word, her voice broke again.

'And he said I was right. That your husband came back to the hotel at three o'clock and he'd wondered why . . .'

'Oh yes?' whispered Kristina.

'That was all. Plus, I started thinking about it a bit myself.'

'About why Jakob came back to the hotel at three in the morning?'

'Yes.'

Kristina pushed her plate away and clasped her hands in front of her on the table. Five seconds of silence passed.

'Why?' she said at last.

'Sorry?' said Kristoffer.

'Why have you been going round thinking about this, Kristoffer?'

'I – I don't know.'

'Oh Kristoffer, I think you *do* know.'

He felt the blood rushing to his head. His temples started to throb.

'I haven't had all that much to think about lately,' he said.

'I got kind of hung up on it. And I mean, it was . . .'

'Yes?'

'It was the night Henrik went missing.'

'Go on.'

'I thought maybe there . . . could be a connection.'

On those last four words, it was suddenly his voice that couldn't hold together. *Could be a connection*, he croaked, and at the instant he did so, he knew it to be true. *That* was the answer to the riddle. That was the terrible solution which was banging on the door all of a sudden, and it was Kristina holding the handle down on the inside, but now she was opening it . . . no, that was a weird image, it was Kristina herself who was in possession of the truth, he could tell by looking at her now, and she was staring at him with a look brimming over with . . . well, he didn't really know what, except that it was something appallingly terrible and naked and vulnerable, and now, at this hopeless, irrevocable second, she leant across the table right up close to him, her desperate eyes held there just fifteen or twenty centimetres from his own and then – then she said it, the thing he suddenly realized he already knew. No, not *said*, she *whispered*, because she had no voice left in her either.

'Kristoffer, it was Jakob who killed your brother.'

Time passed. Long, short, he couldn't tell. She did not move, he did not move. A party of diners, two women and two men, came into the restaurant and sat down at a nearby table – but it was a table in another world and the people, too, were part of that separate, entirely alien world. Beneath the glass dome it was just him and Kristina – his aunt who had shattered reality with her whispered, unsparing sledgehammer of truth. These were the strange words that went

fluttering through his head, trying to make themselves understood, like unfamiliar birds of passage which had flown off
course. *Glass dome? Sledgehammer of truth?*

Birds of passage?

And questions. Just as the words had stuck in his throat an
hour before, the questions did now, like another, different
throng of strange and restless birds, and all at once he found
it hard to breathe and was aware of something ticking inside
his chest, something that threatened to blow him up from
inside if he did not break free of the paralysis that was swiftly
growing under the glass dome. Finally, the most obvious of
questions floated to the surface.

'Why?'

She stared at him.

'Because . . .'

She stopped herself. Tried to look into his eyes for some
kind of reassurance, presumably. Reassurance that he was . . .
old enough. Yes, that was exactly how her green eyes felt as
they bored into him; she was looking for some sign that it was
possible for him to understand. And he realized he had to live
up to it; what else could he do? Match her unspoken question.
I'm prepared, he tried to say without speaking. Tell me how it
was, Kristina.

She took a deep breath, exhaled air in a slow, thin stream
and, at the very end of the stream, just before the air ran out,
it came.

'Because he caught us, Kristoffer.'

'What?'

'Me and Henrik.'

'You and . . . ?'

'Yes. Jakob came back and he found me and your brother in bed.'

Once it had been said it was impossible for him to decide whether he had suspected it or not. Perhaps he had carried the solution to the riddle inside him in some sort of bubble that was just lying there – *had* just been lying there – waiting to burst. At any event, it was not surprise that he felt, no, more like . . . confirmation? Was that it? Had he, in actual fact, in some dark meander of his desperate heart, known all along?

No, he thought. Surely even in my wildest imagination I couldn't have . . .

But he was back to those strange word-birds again. Kristina interrupted their uncontrolled flight by leaning even closer to him over the table. She took hold of both his hands.

'I feel so guilty, Kristoffer. I don't deserve to go on living. And yet I have had to live with this for almost a year. I don't ask for forgiveness or understanding, it's my fault that Henrik died, I have – I have all your lives on my conscience. I'm the one who is to blame for all your grief. If you want to know what depths of despair a human being can be in, then look at me, Kristoffer.'

He looked at her and could see that it was true.

'I couldn't tell anyone about it. It would have been too much for Ebba . . . your mother . . . to bear. I don't know if you will be able to either, Kristoffer, but when you called and asked, well . . . My thinking was that the best solution – the only solution – would be for no one ever to find out what happened. It wasn't cowardice, Kristoffer, think about it, it was out of consideration for – for you all. I've been feeling – been feeling so awful.'

She released his hands and slumped forwards over the

table, but straightened up again almost instantly. 'Forgive me, Kristoffer, I'm being pathetic.'

'No,' said Kristoffer quietly. 'You're not being pathetic.'

He didn't know whether he meant it. All at once he could see the whole thing very clearly in front of him, a picture of ghastly intensity: Kristina and Henrik fucking like bunnies in a strange hotel bed, and then the door is wrenched open, and there stands Jakob, just like in a film where the two lovers are exposed by the jealous, deranged husband who arrives home unexpectedly.

'How?' he asked. 'How did he kill Henrik?'

She turned that searching look on him again. Three seconds went by.

'With his bare hands, Kristoffer. With his bare hands.'

Kristoffer stared at her. He felt a wave of nausea rising inside him. 'Bloody hell,' he said.

'Yes,' said Kristina. 'I would give my life for it never to have happened. I hope you realize that, Kristoffer. If I could exchange my life for Henrik's, I would do it without hesitating for a second. But it feels as though – as though I've been sentenced to live. I don't know if you can understand that?'

'Why are you still with him? With Jakob, I mean . . .'

'Because he's forcing me to.'

'Forcing you?'

'Yes.'

'I don't understand.'

'He killed Henrik, but the guilt is still mine. If a husband finds his wife in bed with another man, he has some kind of right to . . . well, to kill the other man. Defending his honour, there's something ancient in that, and in some cultures it's not even punishable by law.'

'Honour killing?'

She nodded. 'Something like that. And the fact that I did it with my own nephew . . . No, if I leave my husband, he's going to expose me. He knows his guilt is less severe than mine. For as long as he wants me, I'm trapped in his vice.'

'But what you really want is . . . ?' His eyes went involuntarily to her stomach. He was embarrassed, and lost his thread.

'I hate him, Kristoffer. Jakob is a brute.'

He waited.

'A calculating brute. I knew there was something wrong even before this happened. Our marriage was falling apart all through last year, but now – but now . . .'

She fell silent. Looked at him with those terrible, naked eyes again. A few seconds elapsed.

'Why did you do it?' asked Kristoffer. 'You and Henrik?'

She shook her head. 'It was like a game. A forbidden game . . . We went too far.'

'Too far? I see.'

'I'm so sorry. But a few times in life we do cross lines that we know we shouldn't cross. Some people get away with it, others are cruelly punished. We didn't intend it to happen, but of course there's no point in my sitting here making excuses. It started when Henrik told me something.'

'Yes?'

'No, I can't say this.'

An idea suddenly struck him. 'He told you he was gay?'

She raised her eyebrows in surprise.

'You knew?'

'No. Not really. But I thought he might be.'

'I see. Well, Henrik told me, anyway, and I didn't believe him. You remember we had a fair bit to drink that evening?'

'The first one?'

'The evening before the party, yes. It doesn't excuse anything, but I got a bit drunk, and . . . and I took it into my head to try to prove to Henrik that he was wrong. That women could turn him on, too . . . No, sorry Kristoffer, I've already said enough. Quite enough.'

Kristoffer nodded. She was right. That was enough, and he felt he didn't need to know any more.

And suddenly, as they sat there in renewed silence, looking at each other, two thoughts sailed into the harbour of his sluggish mind.

I understand him, said one of them. I understand you, brother.

The second thought was blacker than mourning.

And I understand you too, Jakob Willnius. But that doesn't help, you've got to die.

You've got to die. The words repeated themselves quietly inside his head.

Then all was emptiness and silence for a long time, and he became aware of a terrible craving for a cigarette.

But there were good reasons why smoking in front of Kristina was not an option. And anyway, there was presumably no smoking in this restaurant, as in all the others.

'Shall we go?' he said. 'I don't fancy anything to eat.'

She looked at him in surprise.

'Kristoffer . . .'

'Thank you for telling me,' he said, realizing there was suddenly a grown man talking out of his mouth. 'I promise not to reveal what you said to anyone else. You can rely on me.'

She tried to say something, but he forestalled her. He felt he ought to make the most of this adult voice while he had it.

'I must get back to Uppsala. Can I call you when I've had a bit of time to think about it?'

'What? Well, of course, Kristoffer, you can call me whenever you like. Of course you can.'

'Good. I – I've got to think about it a bit, like I said.'

'I understand.'

So they left Il Forno and went out into the November darkness. Neither of them had touched their food. Neither of them said a word on the way back to Central station.

'No, she isn't in,' said Jakob Willnius. 'She was meeting someone in town. Expect she'll be back in an hour or so, who shall I say called?'

'Just a colleague. It's nothing important. I'll call back.'

The line went dead. He looked at the caller display. *Unknown.* No surprise there, thought Jakob Willnius.

Colleague?

Kristina hadn't worked for over a year now.

And if there was one thing he could boast, it was an exceptionally good memory for voices.

He put out the light and stared at the knotted black silhouettes of the fruit trees outside the window. He felt something harden within him.

Gunnar Barbarotti sat there with the phone in his hand, looking out into the darkness.

Shouldn't have spoken to him at all, he thought. That was stupid.

FIVE

DECEMBER

37

Ebba Hermansson Grundt is dreaming.

It is early in the morning, long before dawn, it is the first of December and the snow is falling heavily outside her window – but she knows nothing of that, for the blind has been carefully lowered and time does not interest her. She is lying in her bed in the entirely white room in the Vassrogga clinic, dreaming of her son.

He is dangling inside her body, he has been chopped into pieces and packed into two green-and-white Co-op carrier bags, he hangs from her collarbone, swinging to and fro like the heavy, rusted tongues of a forgotten set of church bells. You dream what you dream, and no one can reproach her for it, but this morning there is something that is not quite right. A distorting hint of unease runs through her sleeping body, a gust of icy wind makes her skin creep, she feels around with her hands on her breast and stomach, used as she is to bearing her son through the nights in this way. She has done it month after month. But there is something about Henrik this morning, something other and different that she does not recognize.

It *isn't* Henrik. It's Kristoffer. He, her younger son, is the one who has invaded the emptiness inside her this morning, and what can that mean?

Within a few seconds, she is wide awake. She swings her

legs over the edge of the bed and sits up, her feet on the cold floor. What is going on? Why has Kristoffer taken Henrik's place?

It must mean something, because dreams are keys. That is always the case, and it's just a matter of finding which lock they fit.

To lock in, or to unlock. Ebba Hermansson Grundt would prefer to lock in, indeed that is what she has been persistently engaged in all summer and all autumn. Shutting everything out, keeping open only that tiny, innermost room where time does not exist, but where the most important things can be accommodated. Old summers, a sailing boat, a blue tricycle, a grazed knee being tended, sticky little child fingers combing her hair, and his beautiful eyes.

That room which her therapists expend so much effort on locking up, but which she herself opens with a firm but gentle hand every night.

But Kristoffer? How has he been able to find his way in here? What has allowed him over the threshold? Why is he now chopped up and dangling in a Co-op bag from her collarbone? Two of them, wasn't it, two bags? Whatever can it be that he wants to tell her at this dark hour, long before dawn?

She gets to her feet, lets up the blind and looks out of the window. It is pitch black out there, but the snow is falling, thickly and heavily.

Kristoffer, she thinks. Not you, too?

Kristina Hermansson is reading. Getting away from the torments of this world, into others that she does not know. It is the first of December and the snow is falling. Has been falling all night, or so it seems, and is continuing far into the morning. The apple trees outside her window are assuming entirely new forms and characteristics, the currant bushes are huge, woolly musk oxen.

Jakob has gone to the TV centre at Värtahamnen and Kelvin is with the childminder. She is waiting for Kristoffer to contact her, waiting for the ultimate rupture of her existence, but while she does so, she is reading Robert's book.

In the shadows beneath my hands there was a yearning, he writes. *My fifteen-year-old cowardice harboured a hope. Where did it go?*

She does not always understand what her brother writes, but she finds it beautiful. He speaks to her from the other side of the grave; she can hear his voice behind the words. She has only got to page 40 of 651, yet it feels as though he is here in the room with her. As if she could talk to him, ask him the questions that occur to her in the course of reading.

What do you mean, brother Robert? What sort of yearning? What sort of hope was it that you lost along the way?

He does not answer, but perhaps he has hidden the answers further on in the book.

I was born a loser and have laboriously kept this fact buried in oblivion all my life, he writes on page forty-two. *But when knowledge and truth raise their ugly heads, I instantly recognize them. We are only who we are.*

She is still unsure whether Robert is talking about himself. Perhaps it is actually somebody else. The book is written in the first person, at least initially; the main protagonist is called Mihail Barin, a strange, itinerant character, drifting not only in space but also in time, or so it seems. Russian, as far as one can tell, and he pops up in the present but also way back in the nineteenth century, so perhaps he is not a real person after all. Perhaps he is just an idea.

But she reads on in fascination, and Robert's voice comes through more intensely with every page she turns.

If I go to prison, she thinks, it will be Robert's book that keeps me occupied and alive.

But perhaps there will be no need for existence to rupture. Perhaps it is not an utter necessity. Today is Wednesday. The flight to Bangkok leaves on Sunday, and that is only four days away. Four miserable days; if only that short period could flow by without incident, then the matter would be in her own hands again. Once she is sitting on the plane with her husband, she will know how to proceed. All obstacles will have been overcome, and everything will resolve itself as planned.

But they feel so long, these few days. Kristoffer will ring, something will happen; she knows it the minute she lifts her eyes and her thoughts from Robert's book – but for now, in this lingering moment, it is only the snow falling.

Kristoffer Grundt holds the solution in his hand.

It is Wednesday evening. The first of December, a day when the snow has been falling from morning to night; the bus out to Bergsbrunna took half an hour longer than usual and almost skidded into the ditch several times. Luthman, the manager at his Co-op store, announced at the afternoon break that the whole country was in chaos, especially down south in Skåne, where they barely had any roads left open, and in Dalsland, where five thousand households were cut off. The state things might be in towards the coast in Roslagen did not bear thinking about. There had not been such volumes of snow in living memory and it was sixteen hours since it had started.

But none of this worries Kristoffer Grundt, who is standing in the basement in his father's cousin's house in Bergsbrunna, holding the solution in his hand.

It is flat and cold and he guesses it must weigh about half a kilo. The manufacturer's name, Pinchmann, is engraved on the butt, where you also load it by slotting in a magazine from below. Each magazine has space for twelve cartridges, he has already tried it, and he sends a grateful thought to Ingegerd, who showed him the gun and its hiding place when they visited four years before. She did it to impress Henrik and Kristoffer, no doubt, her big boy cousins from Sundsvall. The licence must be in the name of Berit's husband Knut, whom she divorced when Ingegerd was just three; he used to go hunting for this and that, but if there are only two solitary women in a house outside town, you need a weapon to defend yourself with. Just in case, of course.

But once Kristoffer has finished, he intends throwing the Pinchmann in a lake or burying it, so no one will ever be able to trace it, and no one will suspect him. He doesn't think Berit and Ingegerd are in the habit of getting their old gun out; it was covered in a thick layer of dust in the drawer where he found it, in the little storeroom in the basement. He's been mulling over his plan all day, ever since the idea came to him on the bus into town this morning. There are no catches, and this afternoon he has been hearing something that sounds like Henrik's laugh, deep inside him, and though he hasn't really been able to pin it down, because unfortunately it wasn't clear enough, it still feels like something warm and good and strong, and he knows that the solution he has found is exactly the right one. That he has Henrik's full support. To be honest, nothing seems particularly less unreal than it did before his conversation with Kristina yesterday, but as he runs his finger-tips over the cold steel, he feels as though the whole thing is actually a film. He is an actor who has to perform what is written in the definitive script; that's how it is, precisely like that. He is under the director's orders. Or the choreographer's. When he looks at things in that light, it all seems clear and comprehensible. Sometimes life is so huge that you need that sort of help.

And he isn't the least bit worried. He wraps the pistol and the box of cartridges in a towel and puts the bundle in a Co-op plastic bag. Takes it back up to his room and hides his solution in the wardrobe. Berit and Ingegerd are at a parents' evening and won't be back until after nine – assuming they can get home at all in this snowstorm, which shows no signs of abating. No, he doesn't feel the least hint of anxiety churning up his insides; he's going to kill his dead brother's murderer, there's nothing to be afraid of. For someone carrying out their duty, everything is simple and easy.

Albeit not actually real. The snow is still falling as he moves about the kitchen getting himself some tea and sandwiches. The time is ten past nine and there isn't any sign of Berit and Ingegerd yet.

Gunnar Barbarotti is stuck in a snowdrift, and while he waits for help that is taking its time to arrive, he makes up his mind. Beside him in the car is his daughter Sara, and when she tells him she is going away with some friends for the weekend, that clinches it. It gives him the necessary room for manoeuvre. To hell with Backman, he thinks. A man's gotta do what a man's gotta do. I needn't even tell anybody I'm making the trip. To hell with rhyme and reason, I've got to talk to her again.

But not a word to him. There's only a fraction of a suspicion; a fraction of a fraction. If it were false it would be disastrous.

If it were true it would be doubly disastrous.

'What are you thinking about, Dad?' said Sara. 'Is it work again?'

He laughs. 'Not at all, sweetheart. I'm wondering whether it wouldn't be best for you to get yourself home on foot. You should be there in ten minutes, and all you'll do here is freeze your backside off.'

She laughs too. 'What, leave my dad in a car in a snowdrift? What sort of daughter would that make me?'

He switches the engine on and sets the windscreen wipers going. It's quarter to ten in the evening. 'Tell me what you want to be when you grow up,' he says.

Leif Grundt has dropped off in front of the television but is woken by the ring of the phone.

Initially he mistakes the remote control for the cordless phone. But he just about gets out into the hall in time to answer.

It's Ebba.

His wife Ebba. They haven't spoken to each other for more than a week.

'I want to talk to Kristoffer,' she says.

'Kristoffer isn't here,' says Leif Grundt.

'Where is he then?' asks Ebba.

'He's down in Uppsala at Berit's,' explains Leif. 'I did tell you about it. They've got work experience week at school, and he's working in one of our shops down there—'

'I'm worried about him.'

'You needn't be.'

'I've been worrying about him all day. You've got to look after Kristoffer, Leif. You mustn't forget him.'

I mustn't, thinks Leif Grundt in suddenly flaring anger. *I* mustn't forget Kristoffer? This is going too far. It'll end in—

'I don't like you sending him to Uppsala.'

'Ebba, please . . .'

'You know what happens when we send our children there.'

'Ebba, he's staying at Berit's. He's working in a Co-op store for a week, nothing's going to happen to him.'

There's a long silence at the other end of the line. Then a click. She has hung up. Leif Grundt puts the phone back on its hook on the wall. He stands there in indecision for thirty seconds while irritation and sorrow change places inside him.

Then he goes out to dig the snow off the drive again. It is past ten, and the snow must have been falling for almost twenty-four hours.

'That policeman, what was his name?'

'Who?'

Jakob Willnius comes in from the bathroom. Yellow towel round his waist. Kristina is already lying in bed. It is around twelve and he has been out to dinner with a Danish producer. Or was it German? Or maybe just a Swedish one? There is a haze of alcohol in the air around him but it is only a thin one. He definitely isn't drunk. Perhaps he's just randy, yes, that's probably it – the towel is bulging. She takes a deep breath and steels herself, running one hand over her taut belly. From behind, he'll take her from behind, that's how it has been these last months, in view of the current state of things.

'From Kymlinge.'

'What – what are you talking about?

'Barotti? Wasn't that it? Italian name? The one who came here.'

She shakes her head, not understanding.

'Oh, him? Yes, it was something like that. Why have you brought him up?'

He sweeps aside the towel to reveal his splendid erection. 'You don't happen to have heard from him?'

'No, why would he . . . ?'

He slips under the quilt and puts a hand on her hip.

'A man called yesterday and asked for you. It sounded like him. You know I'm good at recognizing voices.'

'Why would he ring here? I mean, it's been a year now . . .'

'I don't know,' says Jakob Willnius. 'I don't know what reason he could have for calling us. But it was you he wanted to speak to, not me.'

'Me?'

'Yes.'

'And he didn't give his name?'

'No, he didn't.'

'I don't get it. Perhaps something's happened that . . .'

'That what?'

He is kneading her buttocks now. Kneading and parting.

'That changes things. Do you want me to put out the light?'

'No, I want to see you, you know that. He didn't ring back then, this Inspector Barbotti, or whatever the hell his name is?'

'No.'

'I want you to tell me if he does.'

'Of course.'

'And I don't want you to forget that.'

'I promise not to forget that.'

'There we are then. I've changed my mind. Put out the light.'

And as he penetrates her from behind, she sees through the window that it has finally stopped snowing.

38

Just as Kristoffer boarded the bus out in Bergsbrunna on Thursday morning, his mobile phone rang.

It was his father Leif.

'How's the snow?' he wanted to know.

'There's lots of it,' said Kristoffer.

Then they talked about the job for a while. If Kristoffer might possibly consider following in his father's footsteps, it was just as well to start with the basics, Leif said. So he knew what he was getting into.

But perhaps he hadn't any plans along those lines?

Kristoffer conceded that for the immediate future he had no such plans, and then his dad asked him when he was planning to come home.

'Saturday,' declared Kristoffer. 'I'll take a morning train I expect. I'll ring and let you know when I'm due to arrive.'

'And you've got enough money left for your ticket?'

'Yes.'

'And on your mobile top-up card?'

'A bit.'

'All right. If you let me know, I'll come and pick you up at the station. Saturday afternoon, right?'

'Saturday afternoon,' confirmed Kristoffer.

'Regards to Berit and Ingegerd.'

Kristoffer promised to pass on the message and rang off.

Reality, he wondered. What is it in actual fact, reality? That was the first question to come into his head after the phone call. For some reason. He tried to see out of the misted bus window. The snow had evidently stopped falling during the night and the snowploughs had pushed it into piles that were metres high. It felt as if all this snowing had something to do with what was going on. With *the plan* and *the solution*. The white world was an alternative reality, and it was in an alternative reality that he would carry out his deed. Then, when it was over, things would be more normal again. Go back to how they usually were. Finally. Once he had well and truly avenged his brother, he would reach a point from which it was possible to look forward. He had lived for almost a year in this strange state, where everything seemed to consist of nothing but obscurity and question marks. A dogged waking dream that held him captive in some peculiar way. He had lost contact with his old life, it was no exaggeration to say that; he couldn't care less about school, nothing was important to him any more, his friends from Years 7 and 8 had drifted away and his family was in ruins. He smoked like a chimney and got pissed at least once a week – but he could see an end to this whole desperate business. An end and a far boundary, he realized that now. Once he had killed his brother's murderer he would reach that boundary. It was – it was, thought Kristoffer Grundt, as if there was a hand steering developments . . . or a director; a fixer who made sure everything that had to happen really did happen.

Someone who arranged for Granny to say those words at Robert's funeral, for example. Specifically to him. And who then made sure that he watched that useless TV film right through to the end so he would see Olle Rimborg's name. And that he plucked up the courage to ring his aunt.

And that his dad got the idea of sending him to Uppsala for his work experience week.

As he thought like this, as his thoughts ran along these well-worn paths, it suddenly made his head spin. True, he was sitting on a bus crammed full of unfamiliar, sleep-fuddled, slightly grumpy people, rumbling through an alien landscape, wintery and white – but at the same time, at the same time, he was part of something else. A completely different story, so much larger and so much more important. A long chain of events, in which one thing led to another and it was impossible to stop and go into reverse once one had decided on the first step to be taken. Because there was no way of redoing and correcting any mistakes – and he suddenly realized, as the bus slowly manoeuvred its way along clogged Kungsgatan in Uppsala, this winter morning at the start of December, that this was exactly what life looked like. This was the model for it all. What happens, happens, and it was a question of understanding what you had to do.

And accepting it.

And when finally, more than twenty minutes late, he elbowed his way off the bus at the station and set off on his tramp to the first shopping mall, he could hear Henrik's voice deep inside him for the first time in ages.

Well done, brother, he said, sounding both a little distant and unusually serious. *Very* serious.

Good, you're learning, Kristoffer.

*

'I'm in Stockholm on other business so I thought I'd make the most of the opportunity.'

He had decided on that opening gambit; it was important to find the right balance between earnest and casual.

Not too serious. But still with a certain weight to it.

He could hear her swallowing, or at least imagined he could. A sort of hesitation, wasn't there?

'I don't understand. Are the police still working on this?'

'Of course. Until we've established what happened, we keep the investigation open.'

'But . . . ?'

'Yes?'

'Has something new come up?'

'Hard to say. But in any case, I'd appreciate a quick chat. Friday or Saturday, and it should only take about an hour.'

'But what . . . I mean, can't we do it now, over the phone?'

'I'd rather not.'

There is something, he thought, feeling the excitement start to pound through his head. She's afraid of something. Well I'll be damned.

She was silent for a few seconds. 'I think . . . yes, I think I could see you sometime tomorrow afternoon. Where shall we . . . ?'

He realized this was not a time for visiting her in Enskede again and was grateful she hadn't suggested it. 'The lobby of the Royal Viking,' he suggested. 'By Central station. We can talk undisturbed there. How about two o'clock?'

'Two o'clock,' she repeated. 'Yes, I expect that will be all right. But I still don't really see the point. You and your colleagues haven't – you haven't got a new lead or anything?'

'It would be a bit much to call it a lead,' he said. 'Let's just say a little idea.'

'An idea?'

'Yes, but I'll explain everything tomorrow. Two o'clock at the Royal Viking, then?'

'Yes, all right, I'll come,' she said, and her voice sounded as fragile to him as old porcelain. Almost like the voice of a schoolgirl who has been caught smoking or bunking off PE or something, and has now been summoned in to see the head for a telling-off.

I'm imagining things, he thought after he had hung up and found himself staring at his messy desk for ten seconds. I want this to be an opening, so I'm interpreting all the signs as though they support my hypothesis. I'm an absolutely worthless detective.

Then he lifted the receiver again to book his train ticket and hotel room.

On the Thursday evening – after Berit's showpiece dinner of potatoes au gratin with strips of beef fillet and Béarnaise sauce – Kristoffer lay on his bed in the room with the big green plants and honed his plan.

Tomorrow. The night from Friday into Saturday, that was when it had to happen. He had told Berit he was going to sleep over at a mate's in Uppsala for his last night, and then take the train home to Sundsvall on Saturday morning. A mate? Berit had queried. Yeah, there was this really nice guy who worked on the checkout, he was nineteen, Kristoffer told her. They were going to see a film in the city centre, and then home to the guy's parents' place at Vaksala torg. His name was Oskar and he was in the Almtuna ice hockey team.

He knew Berit wouldn't bother to check up on him, and it was highly unlikely she would say anything to Leif, either. Not that it mattered – he'd just have to spin his dad the same yarn if need be. They would be going straight from work, he and Oskar, so it would be best for him to take his bag with him from Bergsbrunna on Friday morning. He was packed and ready to go.

But there was no Oskar. Or at any rate, no Oskar who worked on the checkout at the Co-op and was a mate of Kristoffer's. Instead . . . instead he would get on the train to Stockholm tomorrow evening, leave his bag at the station (he knew where the luggage lockers were), wait a few hours in the city centre, maybe go to the cinema if he felt like it. He had plenty of money, enough for a film and a couple of hamburgers.

And an underground ticket out to Enskede a bit later on. Around ten or eleven. As he remembered it, you had to get off at Sandsborg or at Skogskyrkogården, where the famous woodland cemetery was. The green line. He had been travelling with Henrik and Dad last time. But he would get a map at Central station to be on the safe side. The address was 5 Musseronvägen, he had checked.

It would be dark when he got there. He would wait until midnight, or preferably a little later, before approaching the house. He would take a walk round, do a recce of the surrounding area. Check that no one was out and about and that Kristina and her family were at home. Perhaps, if he dared, he would already have rung Jakob Willnius earlier in the evening.

Hung up as soon as he answered. Or if Kristina answered, disguised his voice and asked to speak to her husband.

But only if he dared; there would undoubtedly be other ways of assuring himself the victim was at home. Perhaps he would simply catch sight of him through a window. It didn't feel like a major problem.

In actual fact, none of it felt particularly difficult as he lay there in the big, quiet room, digesting his dinner and trying to visualize the operation. That sense of carrying out an assignment, of following a pattern he had to follow, still hung inside him. It had been hanging there all day, there was no space inside him for hesitation and cowardice. He really was going to take the train to Stockholm, make his way out to the expensive wooden villas of Old Enskede, and there, at 5 Musseronvägen, he would shoot and kill Jakob Willnius. He would murder his brother's murderer; it was no less than his duty. A sort of honour killing, in fact.

And it was because it was a matter of duty that he would be able to carry it through. Exactly how he would achieve it was impossible to foresee, at least in detail. He would have to rely on his judgement and his – what was it called? – intuition? He would have to make it seem like a break-in, of course. Presumably he would have to smash a window to get in. He would wait a long time from when the last light went out in the house, give them plenty of time to fall asleep, but making too much noise as he went in might prove unavoidable. Perhaps he would encounter Jakob Willnius without even needing to go upstairs. He would have to be ready with the gun the whole time; as soon as he was inside the house he would be prepared to fire. He knew their bedroom was upstairs, and it was quite likely Jakob would come rushing, or creeping, down the stairs. He wouldn't give him a second. If he turned up there, he would shoot him instantly. Two shots straight in the chest, to bring him down. Then another in the head, to make totally sure.

And then get out of there. Perhaps, if there was time, he could snatch something or other to make it look like a break-in. A burglar who had been caught red-handed and had fled.

If Jakob didn't come downstairs, Kristoffer would go up to the bedroom and shoot him there. In bed; that was actually a more attractive prospect, since bed was where Jakob had killed Henrik. If he had interpreted Kristina correctly.

But he would have to get Kristina out of the way first. He wasn't going to let her obstruct him, not on any account. Though he didn't think she would try. She wanted Jakob dead as well, there could be little doubt about that. Perhaps she would be shocked when Kristoffer turned up, but that wasn't important. He would not get into any kind of discussion, it was important to remember that, not with Kristina and not with Jakob either. He would not start talking.

Just shoot him, plain and simple. No mercy, not for a single bloody second.

And finally, when it was done, waste no time leaving the house and getting away from Old Enskede.

No more underground. He would make his way into the city centre again by slow backstreets. Dispose of the pistol by throwing it into the water somewhere. Stockholm was full of stretches of water and it was simplicity itself to drop your gun from some bridge or quay. The only thing he had to watch out for was police patrols. A solitary fifteen-year-old walking the streets at three or four in the morning might arouse suspicion. Although, what did he know, maybe nobody would raise an eyebrow in Stockholm. Maybe the whole city was crawling with young people at that time of the night. But anyway, he would be careful, and gradually make his way to Central station, which opened about five or six in the morning, he thought. Possibly have a bite of breakfast – and then jump aboard the first available train to Sundsvall.

He wouldn't turn his mobile on until he'd covered some distance, when the train reached Gävle, say. He would call Leif and say he was on his way. And when he expected to arrive.

If Leif – contrary to all expectations – had heard anything about a murder in Enskede the previous night, and if he brought it up, Kristoffer could just play the innocent. If Leif said it was Kristina's husband who had been shot, well, then he would play even more dumb.

That's it, thought Kristoffer Grundt. You'll soon be able to rest in peace, brother. This is going to be as easy as pie.

He lay there for a bit longer, searching for any lingering doubts and anxieties inside him, but however hard he tried, he found nothing of that kind.

It really was rather remarkable, and a feeling of elation that almost felt like delight was filling him more and more. It had to fight for space with the beef fillet, Béarnaise sauce and potatoes au gratin.

He checked the time. Quarter to ten. Perhaps a cup of tea and a few ginger snaps would slip down quite nicely, after all. Perhaps a full stomach was the best way to go.

Because there was one other detail. One little detail. He had a bit of shooting practice to do tonight. He had to be sure his gun was working. But it would be easy enough to do. He had set his alarm for three. Up out of his bed, throw on his clothes, tramp out into the snow and fire a shot. Maybe two, in swift succession. A few hundred metres from the house – no one would notice a couple of distant shots in the middle of the night. It would be easy as anything.

But he had to do it. No skimping on the details.

39

On Friday, 3 December, it started to snow again. Not with quite the same intensity as the snowfall that had created nationwide chaos earlier in the week, but still enough to cause problems. Amongst other things, public transport in southern and western Sweden suffered significant disruption. Gunnar Barbarotti was glad he had had the foresight to book himself onto a train that left Kymlinge at six in the morning. In normal circumstances, he would have reached Stockholm around ten; in fact he arrived around twelve, and with his previous escapades on domestic flights also still very much in mind, he could not help asking himself if he would just have to give in and drive everywhere in future.

Though on the other hand, the roads were almost certainly impassable this morning, too – and he still had two hours in hand until his meeting with Kristina Hermansson. He crossed the area in front of the station, then Vasagatan, and checked in at Hotel Terminus – his room was not ready, so he had to leave his bag at reception – before going another hundred metres through the swirling snow to Jensens Bøfhus. His lunch was a Danish take on meat patties with onions.

As he sat over his meal, he began to feel a growing sense of anticipation for the coming encounter. His scalp was itching, something it generally only did when something out of the ordinary was brewing.

Either that or his dandruff was coming back. It had been a recurring problem while he was going through the divorce; once he and Helena had separated and were living apart – once all the papers were signed and all the open wounds had started to scab over – his scalp had decided to behave again. His hairdresser, a young lady with an impressive array of perfect teeth and eyes like deep wells, had reckoned it was psychosomatic. She stumbled over the pronunciation of the word, but still. People who felt OK simply didn't get dandruff, her two and a half years in the profession had taught her that.

But I do feel OK, thought Gunnar Barbarotti, ordering a double espresso and a slice of cake. I haven't felt this good since I made out with Veronica at upper secondary.

So that meant it wasn't dandruff. It was the impending meeting that was making him itch. It was the anticipation. He looked at the time. Still forty-five minutes to go, but with the Royal Viking diagonally across the street, he could stay where he was if he liked and watch Kristina Hermansson arrive. If she came from the right direction, that was. Though it might be better to sit and wait for her inside the hotel; perhaps it would put him at more of an advantage?

It was high time to decide on his tactics, at any rate. What on earth was he going to say?

Er, the thing is, I've heard your husband's a pretty nasty piece of work. Is that correct?

Not quite like that, he decided. Presumably the situation called for a slightly more subtle attack. Straws you were grasping at could so easily break; his considerably more than two and a half years in the profession had taught him that.

On the other hand – on the other hand there were those who said Gunnar Barbarotti was one of the best interrogators the country (or west Sweden, anyway) had to offer. He had heard this from a number of different, usually well-informed sources, but there were times when he couldn't help wondering if they were confusing him with somebody else.

O Lord, thought Gunnar Barbarotti. Permit me to suggest a little deal.

And Our Lord listened, albeit a little distractedly.

'What do you mean?' said Jakob Willnius. 'Why haven't you got time?'

'I'm meeting someone,' said Kristina.

'But I told you Zimmerman was in town and would want to have lunch with us.'

'I'm sorry. I forgot.'

'Who are you meeting?'

'A girlfriend.'

'A girlfriend? Which one?'

'Her name's Henriette. You don't know her. She's from before you and I got together.'

'You know how much Zimmerman means? What time are you seeing this Henriette?'

'Two o'clock.'

'And where?'

'At – at the Royal Viking.'

'Well, there we are then. We'll have lunch with Zimmerman at Rydbergs at twelve-thirty. You'll have time to get to the Viking; it's only five minutes from there. And I'm sure she won't mind waiting half an hour, if we happen to run on a bit?'

'I don't know . . .'

'I'm off now. Make sure you're there at half twelve at the latest. And put on something low cut, you know what he's like.'

'Good grief, I'm seven months pregnant, Jakob.'

'So your breasts haven't shrunk, have they? Half twelve at Rydbergs, Kristina. I've had enough of this messing about.'

As she watched this thorn in her flesh get into the taxi, she felt nausea welling up inside her.

He had clearly made a good impression, because when it got to two o'clock on Friday afternoon his supervisor Greger Flodberg – whom he had not seen since Monday – came and said he could finish for the day. He also gave him a plastic carrier bag, the standard green-and-white Co-op variety, and told him that since he had worked all week without pay, he was welcome to fill the whole bag with pick 'n' mix sweets.

Greger Flodberg had a brother who was a dentist up in Sundsvall, and he was running a bit low on customers.

He guffawed with laughter, which echoed round the store, and slapped Kristoffer on the back – and Kristoffer did his best to laugh uproariously, too. Then he dutifully filled the carrier with five kilos of loose sweets, said his goodbyes to Urban and Lena and Margareta, who had been his mentors for the week, and handed back his green Co-op jacket.

He took his bag and his carrier of pick 'n' mix, and set off.

He just caught the three o'clock train from Uppsala (it was supposed to have departed twenty minutes earlier, but the morning's persistent snow had left its mark on the timetable), and within the hour he had stowed all his stuff in a locker at

Stockholm Central station – with the exception of his gun, his ammunition and half a kilo of the sweets, which he put in the roomy pockets of his coat. He felt slightly uneasy about the pistol. But only slightly. Things had not gone to plan where the test shooting was concerned; he must have done something wrong when he set the alarm on his mobile. It had failed to go off in the middle of the night – or perhaps he had switched it off in his sleep. It had happened before. Anyway, the upshot was that he had not yet actually fired the Pinchmann, only pulled the trigger a couple of times with an empty magazine, but for heaven's sake, he thought, it was bound to work just the same when it was loaded. He didn't think he would get the chance to test-fire it out at Old Enskede before the real event. The risk of discovery was simply too great – almost a million people lived in this city, after all.

He bought a packet of Prince cigarettes at the newsagent's kiosk in the station and went out into the cold, raw December dusk. The snow had eased off, but it was still falling.

OK, he thought. Time to kill some time before I do the real killing.

It was a few minutes past three when Kristina Hermansson left the Royal Viking, and she really didn't know what to think.

But she was acutely aware of one thing. Her own mental collapse was not far away. What was the name of that Almodóvar film that had been on at the cinema a few years ago? *Women on the Verge of a Nervous Breakdown*? She had never seen it, but that was how she was feeling now. *On the Verge*. She climbed into a taxi at Centralplan, gave her address in Old

Enskede and started to cry. The driver, a fifty-something immigrant from Iraq, regarded her sympathetically in the rear-view mirror for a moment, but said nothing. He just gave a kindly nod and concentrated on the driving.

Her tears lasted only half a minute. She fished a couple of tissues out of her handbag, blew her nose on one of them and dried her eyes with the other. She leant her head against the cool headrest and tried to think back over the conversation – and understand what had really been said.

On the surface and between the lines.

He had started tactfully. Almost apologetically.

'I didn't mean to sound brusque on the phone.'

She had assured him that it didn't matter. She had had to come into the city centre anyway. For one vertiginously short second she imagined his not actually being a policeman at all, but her secret lover. Imagined them having a drink and then taking the lift up to their room on the eighth floor, where they would lock the door and make love for two whole days. Or two hours, at any rate. Then she caught sight of her belly and her chapped hands and was brought abruptly back to real life.

'I'm finding it hard to let go of this case,' he said. 'That's the way it is in my profession, sometimes.'

She said she could understand that. A waiter came past and they each ordered a Loka mineral water.

'I thought it was strange from the word go,' he explained. 'We spent a long time working on the assumption that the disappearances of Robert Hermansson and Henrik Grundt were linked.'

'It sounds reasonable. Your assumption, I mean.'

'Yes indeed. But when that proved not to be the case, it was a different matter, of course.'

She cleared her throat cautiously.

'Are you really sure that's right?'

'What do you mean?'

'That Robert's death and Henrik's disappearance aren't linked?'

At this point their bottles of mineral water arrived at the table and he took his time answering. He poured some water and took a drink. Set down his glass. Folded his hands in front of him and regarded her with an expression she could not interpret. But it was not the expression of a lover by any stretch of the imagination. A shiver of distaste ran through her.

'Yes,' he said eventually. 'We're pretty sure about it. Why do you ask, do you take a different view?'

'Me?' She noted that her voice came out at rather too high a pitch. 'I've no view on the matter at all.'

He just sat there for a few seconds, as if weighing up her answer.

'Another angle that came and went,' he continued, 'was what we might call the family aspect.'

'Family . . . ?'

'Well, call it what you like. It naturally came up for discussion in the various phases of the investigation, but you might say it's taken on . . . well, renewed topicality, since your brother's murder was solved in August.'

'Oh yes?'

Those were the only words she could get out. He drank some more of his Loka and took a pen from the breast pocket of his jacket. He twirled the pen for a moment as he pondered, squinting into thin air through half-closed eyes.

'If the case of Henrik's disappearance happens to have an

'. . . internal solution, so to speak, then that's inevitably going to have certain consequences for the investigation.'

'Internal solution?'

'Yes.'

'I don't think I understand.'

'Apologies for not expressing myself clearly enough. What I'm trying to say is that if Henrik's been murdered, for example, and it has something to do with the situation in your family, then it could be that someone . . . or several people . . . apart from the murderer . . . are concealing information.'

Barbarotti's delivery of this final, choppy statement was exaggeratedly slow, its staccato sound accentuated by little taps of his pen on the table edge. She couldn't help wondering whether he had practised the whole thing.

And whether the aim was to break her on the spot. Whether he was sitting there waiting for her to give up and confess. I assume so, she thought, I assume that's what this is all about. He thinks I'm hiding something, and he thinks he can break me with his perfectly measured insinuations.

In some strange way, they infused her with strength, these thoughts, and the fact that he appeared to underestimate her; it all provoked her. She sat up straighter and then leant towards him slightly over the table.

'Inspector Barbarotti, I have to admit something.'

'Yes?'

'I have no idea what you're talking about. And I don't know why you wanted to see me today. I got the impression there was some new development in Henrik's case, and that was why I came. But so far—'

He interrupted her by raising one hand.

'Apologies again. But you have to understand the rules of the game.'

'The rules of the game?'

'Yes. Don't forget I am a policeman and I am investigating the circumstances of your nephew's disappearance. I may not want to – or be able to – reveal to you everything that has emerged in the course of the investigation. My job is to get at the truth and the truth is not necessarily served by putting all my cards on the table.'

She caught herself staring at him. What was he saying? Was he just drivelling or did he really know something? Was he bluffing? Was that why he had happened to use the card game metaphor?

'What on earth are you driving at?' she said. 'And what contribution are you expecting from me?'

'Your husband,' he said, and it felt as if he were suddenly forcing her head under water. All her strength and will to resist suddenly washed away.

'My husband?' The sense of asphyxiation was very real.

'What's he actually like?'

If the electrodes of a lie detector had been attached to her at that moment, she would have given herself away. She could feel her pulse galloping and her temples burning. Why wasn't I prepared for this? she thought. This particular attack was the only thing I had to fear, after all. Why do I suddenly feel so defenceless?

'I love Jakob,' she hissed. 'Why the hell are you asking me about him?'

She could not determine whether her anger masked her panic adequately. Maybe, maybe not. He was giving her an appraising look.

'Because certain information has reached me,' he said. 'Information that I'm afraid I can't disclose.'

'About Jakob?'

'Yes.'

'And that's all you've got to say?'

'Not entirely. But I have to ask you whether you think your husband would be capable of killing someone?'

'What the hell . . . ?'

'Purely hypothetically. If it came to the crunch? What do you think?'

She gave no answer. Merely shook her head and drank the last of her water. Asked whether he had any more insinuations to offer her, or whether she was free to go.

He made it clear that she was at liberty to go, but that he was sorry she had interpreted things the wrong way. She thanked him for his time, stood up and left.

Interpreted things the wrong way? She thought about this as the taxi passed the Johanneshov ice stadium. How in heaven's name had he expected her to interpret them?

And most crucially of all, how would she have reacted if she really had not understood what he was talking about? Exactly as she just had, or in a completely different way?

The question was impossible to answer, but she knew it was between these lines he was racking his brains for an answer, still sitting in the lobby of the Royal Viking. At any event, the threat of a nervous breakdown seemed to have receded for now. It had merely been swept under the carpet, of course, but presumably that was the best she could hope for. She checked the time and realized that in less than forty-eight hours she would be on the plane to Bangkok. It felt . . . it didn't really feel real.

It was only when she had paid the gentle, dark-eyed taxi driver and stepped into the hall in Musseronvägen that the other question surfaced.

Where on earth had he got that information about Jakob? Surely he hadn't just invented it?

40

Kristoffer Grundt wandered aimlessly round Stockholm city centre. It was half past six in the evening. He had forty-five minutes before the film started at the Rigoletto. *The Usual Suspects*, he had heard it was good. Or read that it was. Time passed slowly. He had already had a burger at McDonald's and hung around the shops. The Åhléns and PUB department stores and various shopping malls. He had eaten pick 'n' mix until he felt sick, and ended up chucking the last few in a bin. If he fancied any later, there were always the other four and a half kilos in the locker at Central station.

It had stopped snowing and the streets and pavements were a slushy mess. Lots of people and lots of traffic. He suddenly came to a place he recognized. *Kreatima?* Hadn't it been called something else when it happened? He thought it had. But anyway, it was a big DIY shop; that certainly tallied. This was where Olof Palme had been shot. Kristoffer stopped. It had happened a few years before he was born, but the location had been pointed out to him at least three times before. Virtually every time he had been in Stockholm.

The murderer then fled into Tunnelgatan. That was right, wasn't it? He stared into the narrow passageway. Up the steps, that had been the escape route.

Back then. And now he was the one about to become a

murderer. He lit a cigarette and looked around him. People were scurrying past in all directions. They all seemed to be in a hurry. They all seemed to be on their way somewhere important. Cars sent up a spray of slush. Nobody cared. Nobody spared a thought for the fact that this was where the Swedish prime minister had been murdered. But after all, it was over twenty years ago now. Kristoffer gripped the gun in his jacket pocket. And here am I, he thought, here am I with a pistol in my pocket. If the current prime minister came walking by, I could shoot him, too. I could actually do that. What uproar that would cause.

It was so damn easy to kill. He had never thought about it before. All he had to do was raise his gun and fire. He took a drag on his cigarette and laughed to himself. You didn't have to be sick in the head or a terrorist or a drug addict to go out and commit murder; all it took was for you to raise your gun and pull the trigger. A second was all it took to deprive a person of their life, that was the grim truth of it. Just one measly second to put an end to that succession of days and evenings and nights. And it made no difference who was in the bullet's path. King or beggar. The pressure of an index finger. Then it was over, and it was no help at all if you had a hundred million or were the most famous film star in the world. Or just some poor tramp.

It was a giddying thought. And pretty unjust, in fact. If I got out my gun and shot that woman in the red jacket and then ran away exactly like Olof Palme's murderer, thought Kristoffer, nobody would fucking catch me. I'd run like hell for twenty or thirty metres, go up the steps, turn the corner and then just act normal and walk away. He stared into the alleyway again; it would be as easy as anything.

The woman in the red jacket was slowly approaching and she didn't look as stressed as most of the others, far from it. She was talking on a mobile phone and laughing. She wasn't particularly good-looking, thought Kristoffer. Must be getting on for forty though she was trying to look younger. High-heeled boots and tight black jeans. Dyed blonde hair. Maybe she was a prostitute. Why not? Stockholm was teeming with them, everybody knew that. She came towards him and he found himself clutching the pistol in his pocket.

Now, he thought. I'm going to do it. Right now. A test run on the very spot where Palme was shot, fucking hell!

'Hi there, Gittan!'

A man came dashing over the crossing. A car braked and gave an angry toot of its horn. The woman stopped.

'Jörgen? What the hell are . . . ?'

They hugged. Laughed and hugged again. Kristoffer swallowed hard and started walking. Christ, he thought. What the hell is up with me? What am I doing? For a moment there, I almost . . .

Or maybe he hadn't come that close after all. Thoughts were one thing, actions another. Maybe there was some sort of barrier inside him. Maybe there was more than one, there might even be a whole bank of barriers that made sure you – you didn't go through with such acts of madness. Made your finger refuse to obey the order from your brain, for example. Refuse to pull the trigger at the vital moment.

He went cold all over. What if that was true? He took a drag on his cigarette and tossed it away, although he had only smoked half of it. He started walking again. What if he couldn't fire when he had Jakob Willnius there in front of him!

What if his courage failed him? For a few seconds, he felt his fear of such an outcome threatening to smother him, he felt everything going black before his eyes and the sweets and nicotine embraced one another in his stomach – but then, at the critical moment, he heard Henrik's calm voice deep inside him.

Take it easy Kristoffer, he said. It's going to be all right. I'm with you, don't forget.

And that was enough. His worries evaporated in a second. Henrik was the important thing, nothing else, and as long as he always kept that in the front of his mind, nothing could go wrong.

Henrik, his big brother and guiding star. He suddenly found himself thinking of the Brothers Lionheart. Jonathan and Rusty. Well, he hadn't expected that!

And here was the Rigoletto, too. He checked his watch. Seven on the dot. *The Usual Suspects* would be starting in fifteen minutes. He pushed open the glass door and slipped into the warm foyer.

Detective Inspector Barbarotti felt frustrated.

He had been lying on his hotel bed and staring up at the ceiling for over an hour. This is how it feels, he thought. This is exactly how it feels, I remember now.

What he remembered was the problem somebody had dubbed the Detective's Dilemma – it had doubtless originated on the other side of the Atlantic. One of that hard-boiled generation of writers in the 1940s, probably. Gunnar Barbarotti was not acquainted with a wide variety of detective fiction, but he had read Hammett and Chandler, at any rate. And a Crumley or two.

The crux of the dilemma lay in two factors.

First, being in possession of knowledge that was the key to the case one was working on.

Second, the fact that there was no way of using this knowledge.

Incompatible, as they said these days.

Though knowledge was possibly slightly too strong a word, seen in context. In *this* context. Perhaps it wasn't such a pure and simple dilemma, when it came to it. For if he had really dared to trust his feeling that there was something suspicious about Kristina Hermansson – something really suspicious – then surely he would have found some way to get to her? Wouldn't he?

If only he had put more faith in his intuition.

There was something up with her, that much was clear. No sane person with nothing to hide would have behaved the way she did during their conversation at the Royal Viking. She had viewed him as . . . well, as an opponent; the conversation had been a sort of trial of strength, and that had been the clincher for him. Why had she been so nervous? Why hadn't she wanted to help, if it did so happen that there was a new lead in the investigation of her nephew's case? Wouldn't the natural thing have been for her, too, to want the murderer caught – if the boy had indeed been murdered? Why was she stalling? *Why?*

But here he had to stop and examine himself a little. Perhaps it was his own fault things had gone the way they did. He had brought up the family aspect almost straight away, and an attack directed at the Hermansson-Grundt family was perhaps automatically also perceived as an attack on her. On Kristina. And on her husband. In actual fact, it was perhaps the most natural thing in the world for her to react defensively.

Because what had he been claiming, after all? What allegation must she have discerned behind his smokescreens?

That her husband Jakob Willnius had something to do with the disappearance? Wasn't that exactly what he had been insinuating? Was there any scope whatsoever for alternative interpretations?

And wasn't that what he believed, at heart – but was doing his utmost to pretend he didn't believe?

Bloody hell, thought Gunnar Barbarotti, getting up from the bed. If I can't even assess my own motives and reasoning, how can I ever decide what some other person is thinking?

And what possible reason could Jakob Willnius have had for doing away with the lad? He didn't even know him, after all.

A crucial point, undoubtedly. Barbarotti heaved himself into his coat and left the room. It was past seven, and a walk in the slushy snow plus a dinner at some reasonably empty restaurant might clear some of the dross out of his skull. He ought at any event to try to dispel that mental image of Klampenberg the prosecutor laughing in his face when he came to present the facts of the case.

'So what have you got for me on this Willnius?'

'His ex-wife alleges he's most unpleasant, Mr Prosecutor.'

For God's sake, no, thought Gunnar Barbarotti, thrusting his hands into his coat pockets as he came out onto the street. This isn't going anywhere.

He didn't feel remotely hungry, and decided to go for a half-hour walk first. He took the route past the Åhléns store and the square at Sergels torg, and continued northwards. He had just crossed Sveavägen by the concert hall when a film poster caught his eye. *The Usual Suspects*. It was the Rigoletto cinema.

He checked his watch. Half past seven. Shame, he thought, it's been going for quarter of an hour. Wouldn't have minded seeing that again.

He shrugged and continued down Kungsgatan to Stureplan. He was starting to feel very cold and realized he had left his gloves and scarf back at his hotel room.

And the frustration continued to gnaw away at him.

'You're late,' she said. 'I thought—'

'Of course I'm late,' said Jakob Willnius, hanging up his coat. 'Zimmerman rejected the whole translation. I don't know what I pay those wretched scriptwriters for. And it was pretty vital to get it all sorted today, wasn't it now?'

'What do you mean?'

'Have you forgotten we're off to Thailand on Sunday? You don't suppose I want to leave this in Törnlund or Wessing's hands, do you?'

'No, I suppose not. Do you want to eat straight away?'

'No, I want a bloody large Laphroaig first. And I suggest you have one, too.'

'Jakob, I'm seven months pregnant.'

'I know that. I just thought you might need it for your nerves.'

'What do you mean, for my nerves?'

He went over to the drinks cabinet and took out a bottle. 'Yes, you heard me right. For your nerves. To help you . . .'

'Yes?'

'To help you watch your step.'

'I don't really follow.'

'You don't? Come on, I think you do, really. The thing is, I came past the Royal Viking this afternoon. Zimmerman's staying there while he's in town and he needed something from his room. So it must have been about quarter past three, when you were sitting chatting to your girlfriend in there . . . what was she called again?'

'Henriette.'

Suddenly she wasn't sure whether that was the right name. Had she said Henriette or Josefin? Both of them existed in real life; she was so bad at lying that she had to rely on old friends even in a situation like this.

'Henriette, right. The funny thing is . . . well, can you guess what the funny thing is?'

'No, I don't understand. What are you talking about, Jakob?'

He poured a large whisky before he answered. He put the cork back in with great care and took a gulp. 'The funny thing is,' he said, 'that while I was sitting there in the car waiting for Zimmerman, I saw someone I knew coming out of the hotel. I assume you can't hazard a guess, even now?'

She shook her head. She dug her nails into the palms of her hands and wished it were a way of killing yourself. Or making yourself invisible.

'That goddamn policeman. The one who rang the other day. Are you sure you wouldn't like a small whisky? I think we'll have quite a lot to talk about this evening.'

41

Time was really dragging.

As Kristoffer boarded a train on the green line at T-Centralen metro station, he remembered the strange wish that had come into his mind almost a year ago. When they were all in the car on their way down to Kymlinge and nothing had happened yet.

His wish to skip a bit of his life.

If he remembered rightly, he'd fancied skipping three or four days on that occasion. Just so he could get home to Sundsvall and Linda Granberg. Linda Granberg, who had then thrown him over for one of the Niskanen brothers from Liden before moving to Drammen.

How ridiculously immature he had been back then. And yet it was less than a year ago. But a good deal had happened since, thought Kristoffer Grundt. That was undeniable.

But right now, on this dark and fateful December evening, at this very moment as the train gave a jolt and moved off again, here he was with the same wish in his head. To be able to skip time. Though this evening, he wasn't asking so much. Not four days, he could make do with . . . well, two hours, in fact.

So he was spared the darkness and the cold.

And the waiting. He was bound to be at the Skogskyrkogården stop by half past nine or ten. Damn, it was way too early. Just think if it had been possible to manipulate the hours a bit, so the time moved on to quarter to twelve instead. That would have been just right, thought Kristoffer. As things stood, he couldn't go direct to Musseronvägen. Not before midnight. Not even to check the lie of the land, it was too risky. Somebody might see him and remember what he looked like. He couldn't start the actual break-in until one at the earliest, he had decided. Or maybe not even then, if it turned out that Jakob and Kristina stayed up late. At least an hour from when they put the light out, he had decided. It was important to stick to the plan. As long as you remembered to do that, you didn't risk making a load of wrong decisions along the way.

But that meant at least two hours to while away before it was time. It felt like an eternity. He could have spent the whole time on the underground, of course, travelling to and fro between various stations, getting off and on again a few times – but he wasn't very happy on the underground. He never felt at home. There was an atmosphere of fear and hostility down here, and he didn't like it.

Something was hanging in the air that felt as if it might explode at any second. A loud-mouthed gang of kids was making a racket further along the carriage and the guy who had just sat down opposite him was clearly drugged up: a cross-eyed weirdo who kept chewing his lower lip and scratching his wrists. He must have weighed a hundred and fifty kilos, and if the wrong thought happened to pop into his short-cropped head he'd very likely decide to land a punch on Kristoffer. Just for looking cocky or something. Or for obviously being from Norrland.

I'll shoot the fucker if he tries it, thought Kristoffer, and a desperate laugh was about to escape his lips.

He managed to stop it, and decided to pretend to be asleep instead. Presumably nobody could take exception to that? He closed his eyes and rested his head against the window. The train braked. A metallic voice announced they had reached Skanstull. Five stations to go, thought Kristoffer. He had memorized them all. Gullmarsplan. Skärmarbrink. Blåsut. Sandsborg. Then Skogskyrkogården. That was where he would get off. Perhaps he could take a stroll round the woodland cemetery itself? Wander amongst the graves for a while? It was a big place, he had heard. Perhaps that was a good way for a murderer to psyche himself up? Test his weapon, even?

No, that was too much. You don't go round cemeteries using them for target practice. An amble round while he collected himself, that would have to do. He'd smoke a few cigarettes, buy a hot dog and a chocolate milk somewhere, a bit later on – he had the money – and focus properly. Try to stay warm.

And then the underpass beneath Nynäsvägen when it got to twelve. Into Old Enskede and then to Musseronvägen. Do you think that's a good plan Henrik, he asked, directing the question deep inside himself.

The train began slowing again, another squeal of its brakes, and Henrik replied that it was a bloody good plan.

There were no official visiting times at the Vassrogga clinic, and social calls were not generally recommended anyway. Unplanned visits from the outside world were considered disruptive to treatment programmes, but in the case of Benita

Ormson they made an exception on a Friday afternoon. Benita Ormson was not only a good and long-standing friend of Ebba Hermansson Grundt, she was also a practising psychiatrist herself. Though a little too far to the cognitive side for their taste, she was a far from unknown name – and it was judged that there would be no appreciable negative impact on the patient if they were allowed to spend an hour together. It was Friday and, after all, the original intention had been for Mrs Hermansson Grundt to spend weekends with her family.

Benita Ormson brought two presents for her old friend and fellow student, and once they were alone in the room, she produced them. One was a bag of Marianne chocolate-filled mint sweets and the other was a Bible.

'I'm not religious,' declared Ebba.

'Nor am I,' said Benita Ormson. 'Wouldn't dream of it. But the Bible is something else entirely, you see.'

'Hmm,' said Ebba.

'How are you?' Benita Ormson asked. 'Really?'

'What do you mean by "really"?'

'I mean I can see that you like being here, and are sufficiently intelligent to furnish yourself with a justification for it.'

Ebba sat in silence and thought about this for a while.

'A sharp intellect is certainly overestimated as a companion.'

'Couldn't agree more,' said Benita Ormson. 'The heart has its reasons, of which reason knows nothing.'

'So I've heard,' said Ebba. 'But I think my problem is that I can't see one single little reason to go on living.'

'So why do you?'

'Go on living?'

'Yes.'

'I really don't know. Perhaps I see even that as some sort of duty. A feeling that you ought to live your life to its end once you've been given it.'

Benita Ormson nodded. 'And these are insights that came to you after your son went missing?'

'Yes. I realize they're insights that must afflict everybody – to a greater or lesser degree – and that most people can work through them and carry on. But that just doesn't work for me. The fall was . . . well, I think it was just a bit too brutal.'

'You're assuming Henrik's dead?'

'Yes, I think I probably am.'

'And why was it Henrik, in particular, who meant everything to you?'

'That's something else I've no control over. Is it all right if I have a Marianne?'

'Please do.'

'You know what, I don't think I've had one of these since we were revising for our exams.'

'Nor me. But why Henrik specifically? When we have children, it's part of the deal that they can die before we do. There are no guarantees, you know that as well as all other parents.'

'I – I think I'd forgotten.'

Benita Ormson gave a laugh. 'Yes, I think you had, Ebba dear. I'm sure there are a few other things you've forgotten along the way, too. But of course, we all do that and it generally works until we get to about forty. You're in good company.'

'I've no desire to be in that sort of company.'

'I know that. You're not a social person, Ebba, but in

some situations, we just can't cope on our own. That's why I brought you the Bible.'

'Good God, Benita, you know I . . .'

'We all need some company, Ebba. We all need someone to talk to. You've been your own company for forty years and now you're tired of it. You've got to choose, either other people or Our Lord.'

'No thanks, that kind of thing isn't—'

Benita Ormson raised a hand and Ebba broke off. She took another sweet and regarded her friend with eyes brimful of scepticism. A few seconds went by.

'I do understand,' said Benita Ormson. 'You prefer to keep all the doors shut. To shut me out, too. But it's your choice, Ebba, and you're the one this is all about. I'm not the least bit religious, you know that. I'm pretty much an agnostic. But this book represents ten thousand years of collected experience. It's not propaganda, it's wisdom. What you need is to be comforted. You need consolation and love and a decent dose of compassion, nothing else can help you. All other questions simply pale into insignificance, and I think you're discerning enough to understand that. But you're not wise. You're stunted, Ebba, you've chosen to trap yourself with Henrik in a closed room, a dark and claustrophobic space. At least try to expand it a little, let in a bit of light. But again, it's up to you, and I . . .'

'And you?'

'And I'm only the messenger. Don't shoot the messenger, Ebba.'

'I know, I know.'

'Right then.'

'Mm, they're really nice, these Mariannes. Imagine it being so long ago . . . and them still being around.'

'Of course they're still around, Ebba.'

Silence. A long silence. A nurse opened the door a crack. He closed it again when he saw the two women sitting on the edge of the bed, one on either side.

'What are you thinking about, Ebba?'

'I'm thinking . . . I'm thinking about Kristoffer. Please excuse me Benita, but I believe I need to call my husband.'

'You know best what you need to do, Ebba. Today as on every other day.'

'Thank you, Benita. Thank you for coming, but I think I ought to get on with it right away.'

'Of course, Ebba. Of course. I'll leave you with the Bible and the Mariannes, and come back to see you another day.'

Somehow she held out.

It amazed her that she was capable of it. That she could persevere despite Jakob's more or less single-minded attacks. Perhaps it was because she was sober, perhaps it was as simple as that. Jakob was drinking Laphroaig, glass after glass, his voice sounding airier and airier, but he never flared up and lost his temper. That calm was still in him, lying there in wait like a cobra in the sunlight. That's what his problem is, she thought, the whole problem with his life. The fact that he can go on storing up more and more emotions until he is finally full of them and explodes.

But it struck her that the explosions, too, were strangely cold. Calculated. He never lost his self-control, not entirely.

Even when he killed Henrik he was in control of what he was doing.

Even then. When she came to think of it, this was probably the most horrible thing of all.

The control. The inhuman composure.

'What did you think of him?' he said.

'Who?'

'That cop. When he was here in January?'

It was quarter past eleven. They were sitting in the armchairs in front of the open fire. Kelvin had been asleep upstairs in his bed for the past two hours. Jakob lit a thin black cigar. Barrinque, which was the only make he smoked. They were specially imported for him by a small shop on Hornsgatan.

'I scarcely remember him. Jakob, can we talk about something else?'

'Such as?'

'Thailand, maybe? We'd better go into town and buy a couple of guide books tomorrow, hadn't we?'

'Done that. Popped into Hedengrens and picked up three. It's all sorted. So, what did you think of him?'

'I don't remember, Jakob. For God's sake, I told you I don't remember him. What are you so suspicious about?'

'Suspicious?'

'Yes.'

'Is there any reason why I should be suspicious?'

'No, but you sound as if you are.'

'I find it a bit hard to believe in coincidences, that's all. In some situations.'

'I don't understand.'

'Oh yes you do.'

'No Jakob, I don't. What is it you're trying to get me to say? I've nothing to hide.'

He took another gulp of whisky and another drag on his cigar. He was filing his arguments to a sharp point.

'Listen to me,' he said. 'That cop rings here at the start of the week and asks for you. He lives down in Kymlinge, four hundred kilometres from here. Three days later I see him coming out of the Royal Viking, at the very time my wife claims to be in there having a chat with a girlfriend I've never heard of . . .'

'How many of my girlfriends do you know, Jakob?'

'A few.'

'No you don't. Can we go to bed now, I'm tired . . .'

'I want to sit here for a while and talk to you, Kristina. But OK, I'll leave the cop for now. You can switch the light out, and we'll sit on the sofa. Shall we have a bit of Coltrane?'

He's getting horny, she thought. There was even more air in his voice now. But that was just as well, of course. She sighed. Cautiously, without making a sound. Two days to go, perhaps she could pull it off.

Inspector Barbarotti got back to his hotel around eleven. Even though he had had two glasses of red wine and a large brandy, he was perishing cold. Stockholm was in the grip of a raw and biting winter, with a northerly wind sweeping through its streets and whirling up any snow that had not been melted by the under-road heating. Christ, thought Gunnar Barbarotti. I'm glad I don't live here. How do the rough sleepers cope? They must freeze to death every single night.

Once he got up to his room, he called Marianne. The

weather wasn't much better in Helsingborg, she told him. Three degrees above zero, rain and a fierce westerly wind.

It would be nice to have a man and a glass of red wine to warm me up, she added.

Gunnar Barbarotti asked her whether there might possibly be a night train from Skåne up to Stockholm in, say, about half an hour. He'd be happy to meet her at Central station early tomorrow morning and his hotel room was booked for another night.

'I thought you were working?' said Marianne.

'Well, off and on,' declared Inspector Barbarotti.

'I'm afraid my children need me all weekend,' said Marianne. 'How about planning things a bit further in advance?'

Gunnar Barbarotti promised to sharpen up his act in future and then they cooed nonsense at each other for a while before hanging up.

Working, he thought, and then went to the window to look out over the railway station and the tracks. Well yes, that was the idea. *Had been* the idea. But things had gone somewhat awry.

Or had they? Perhaps his usual, naturally depressive evening tendencies were just playing tricks on him? What had he really expected from his session with Kristina Hermansson? That she would break down and admit something, God only knows what?

Scarcely. But in fact – he thought with a wave of optimism that was as sudden as it was unexpected as he unscrewed the top of the small bottle of red wine from the minibar – hadn't she rather confirmed his suspicions, when it came to it? As they sat there in the Royal Viking lobby, she'd definitely been keeping a lid on all manner of things, hadn't she?

Hadn't she? And wasn't that exactly what he'd wanted confirmed? The fact that there was something very wrong with the Hermansson-Willnius marital idyll in Old Enskede. Something that just didn't tally and that he couldn't simply ignore, now he'd come this far.

He took a drink from the plastic bottle and poured the rest down the washbasin in the bathroom. What rotgut, he thought. And I shall have to pay 65 kronor for that crap when I leave.

But to get back to Jakob Willnius. Wouldn't it be just as well to take the bull by the horns?

He undressed and got under the shower. Turned on the hot water and decided to stay there until he had come to a decision.

It took twenty minutes, and when he climbed into bed he was still far from convinced he had made the right choice – but at least he had made it, and he felt in rather better spirits than he had when he was struggling through the biting wind on the streets and squares of the capital an hour before. That was a fact.

42

Kristoffer Grundt was freezing cold.

It was twenty past twelve. Finally. He walked slowly past the house, 5 Musseronvägen. This was the second time; a quarter of an hour before, he had gone past in the other direction, on the opposite pavement. All the windows were dark, the only light coming from a little orange lamp above the front door. It had looked just the same fifteen minutes ago. They were asleep; every indication was that Kristina and Jakob were asleep in bed, like all their neighbours. Kristoffer knew this was not the sort of area where people lived it up, late into the night. Not entirely unlike his own neighbourhood up in Sundsvall, in fact. If you happened to get home after midnight, you generally found every house in total darkness. Not a sign of life.

While he was wandering round the woodland cemetery area and the streets on either side of Nynäsvägen, he had been struck by a sudden worry that he wouldn't be able to find the right house in Musseronvägen – but once he saw it he knew straight away. He realized it was being cold and alone that had made him imagine things. Going in and shooting the wrong guy, well, that would have been quite something!

But as it was, there was no doubt. There were various things he recognized. The path leading to the front steps, where he and Henrik had mucked about with a ball, two and a half years ago. The little summer house in the middle of the lawn, now completely covered in snow. The terrace where they had drunk squash and eaten buns. Oh yes, this was where they lived all right, Auntie Kristina and her husband – the man he was going to kill. He carried on walking, right past the house, and the mere thought seemed almost to warm him.

The thought of killing. It was strange, but perhaps that was how it was. Perhaps the blood started to flow more quickly through your veins when you thought about certain things? And not only girls.

He had felt freezing cold for so long. He'd bought a hot dog and a coffee from a burger stand about an hour ago, but that was all he'd had. You could warm up a bit if you kept on the move, but it didn't work indefinitely.

And it was still a bit too early to get started. He decided he would do one more circuit of the entire area, and if everything looked peaceful when he got back to the house, he would strike.

OK bro? He had to ask the question.

OK, answered Henrik.

Five to one. He hadn't met a soul. The house was as dark as it had been half an hour ago. He was not quite as cold any more, for some reason. Perhaps it was the tension, just as he'd thought.

Right then, he told himself. Let's go, it's now or never. He looked all round, right and left, then pushed his way through the hedge and into the garden. He'd decided on the French windows facing onto the terrace. No point having to hoist yourself over windowsills, if you could just walk straight in. He might be able to force open the French windows just by applying some pressure with his shoulder, like you could back home in Stockrosvägen.

He tramped through the snow, which lay half a metre deep in some parts of the garden, whereas out in the street, most of it had melted. Or the snowplough had cleared it. Coming up onto the terrace, he saw a pair of French windows, just as expected, and crept over to them. There was wooden decking beneath his feet and no snow, because this area was under cover. It creaked, but only slightly. Nothing to worry about, thought Kristoffer. He screwed up his eyes and peered through the panes of glass, but he could scarcely make out anything in there. The French windows had no handles on the outside, but the doors seemed to open inwards. He stood stock still for five seconds, then tried applying a measured dose of shoulder pressure.

Nothing happened. He cupped his hands together, leant forward and tried to see what the handles inside looked like. An ordinary lever latch handle on one of the doors, as far as he could see. He pressed his shoulder to the doors again, a bit harder. Thought he felt them give a little. But it was going to take a lot of force to make the wood yield.

And it would make quite a lot of noise. He decided to go for the alternative solution. Make a little hole with his pistol butt and then enlarge it by breaking off more glass, bit by bit. He wasn't entirely sure it would work, but he had seen some-one do it in a film a few months ago, as smoothly as anything. The important thing was not to let big chunks of glass drop down, otherwise there'd be a terrible racket as they smashed.

But a single, brief crunch wouldn't wake anybody. Not if they were asleep in bed upstairs. And if they did happen to wake, they would decide it must have been a cat and go back to sleep. So it was important to leave a bit of time before starting to enlarge the hole. And important not to make any more noise.

He took the pistol out of his pocket. Counted to five and then hit the glass. There was a tinkling as the bits fell to the ground. He went down on one knee by the wall so as not to be seen if anyone put the light on. He had the gun raised, ready to fire; if Jakob Willnius opened the door and came out, he would mow him down instantly.

There was no sound from inside. Nobody switched on a light. He waited nearly two minutes before getting up to look. He studied the hole in the glass, which was big enough to put his hand through, and only then did he realize the door was double glazed, meaning he would have to break the other pane of glass, too. That film he'd seen had presumably been set in a warmer country.

But it was as silent as the grave in there, and after a little while he had picked away the whole outer layer of glass without dropping a single bit. It worked. Time to knock another hole, he thought. He raised the gun and struck.

At virtually the same moment as the fragments of glass hit the floor, the light went on inside. Jakob Willnius was standing there in the doorway to the hall, stark naked and staring straight at him. Kristoffer hesitated for half a second. Then he hurled himself at the doors, leading with his left shoulder. He heard wood splintering as shards of glass went flying around him. He got inside the room and stopped dead; Jakob Willnius wasn't moving, and Kristoffer saw that he had something in his hand. A poker. He felt wild triumph bubble up inside his head, just as he saw Kristina coming up behind her husband. She wasn't naked but wrapped in a red bath towel and she, too, had something in her hand, though he couldn't see what.

A poker against a pistol! It was laughable! Kristoffer raised his weapon. Kristina screamed and Jakob Willnius finally moved; he put up his hands – still with a firm grip on the poker – a stupid sort of gesture, presumably meaning . . . well, that he gave up. Kristoffer gave a laugh. Aimed at his chest and pulled the trigger.

The pistol clicked.

He fired again.

Another click. Jakob Willnius lowered his hands and took a step forward.

A third try. Not even a click. The mechanism had jammed. Kristoffer stared at his gun – and at his hand holding the gun – and at his aunt Kristina, clutching the red bath towel to her protruding belly, holding something in her other hand and looking utterly terrified. Suddenly he heard someone give a howl.

It was him. It sounded barely human. Jakob Willnius was only a metre away from him now.

43

His mobile rang while he was at breakfast.

It was Eva Backman.

'Where are you?' she asked. 'Did you go up to Stockholm in the end?'

He hesitated for a moment. Then he admitted that her surmise was correct.

'Good,' said Eva Backman. 'Because it turns out you could be right after all.'

'How do you mean?'

'I spoke to Sorrysen this morning. That is, he rang me. Apparently tried to get through to you first, but you didn't answer.'

Gunnar Barbarotti now registered that his display had said *New Message* when he answered Backman's call. 'Must have been in the shower,' he said.

'Right. Anyway, a certain Olle Rimborg rang the Kymlinge police . . . er, about an hour ago.'

He checked the time. It was quarter to ten.

'Olle Rimborg?'

'Yes. You don't happen to know who he is?'

'Not a clue,' said Gunnar Barbarotti.

Eva Backman cleared her throat. 'He's – amongst other things – the night porter at Kymlinge Hotel. He thought about ringing the police earlier. He actually did ring on one occasion, but got cut off, which is too bloody bad of course, but we'll have to look into that later.'

'What did he want?' said Gunnar Barbarotti. 'I've got an egg going cold here.'

'Boiled?'

'Yes, boiled. Get to the point, Mrs Backman.'

'Boiled eggs shouldn't be eaten hot. But maybe we can look into that later, too. At any rate, this Olle Rimborg was working the night Henrik Grundt went missing. The night between the twentieth and twenty-first of December.'

'I know which night Henrik Grundt went missing.'

'Good. Olle Rimborg was on the reception desk that night and he claims Jakob Willnius came back to the hotel at three o'clock.'

'What?'

'I'll repeat that. Olle Rimborg, night porter at Kymlinge Hotel, claimed in a phone call to Gerald Borgsen earlier this morning that Jakob Willnius, who had set off for Stockholm just before midnight, came back to the hotel about three hours later . . . that same night.'

'What the hell are you saying?'

'Exactly. What the hell am I saying? Or rather: what is Olle Rimborg saying?'

Gunnar Barbarotti sat in silence for five seconds.

'It doesn't necessarily mean anything,' he said.

'I'm entirely aware of that,' retorted Eva Backman. 'But if it *does* mean something, then what does that something amount to? That's the question I was asking.'

'Thanks, I heard,' said Gunnar Barbarotti. 'And then – then

the two of them went back to Stockholm early the next morning?'

'The three of them. You're forgetting little Kelvin, inspector. But you're right, they left the hotel around quarter to eight.'

Inspector Barbarotti contemplated his egg. I wish I had a couple fewer glasses of red wine in my bloodstream, he thought. Where is this leading?

'Where is this leading?' he asked. 'How long have you had to think it over?'

'Fifteen minutes,' said Eva Backman. 'Just over fifteen minutes. But the analysis isn't complete yet.'

'Did he say anything else, this Olle Rimborg?'

'Not much, evidently.'

'But you didn't speak to him yourself?'

'No, only to Sorrysen.'

'So why did he bother ringing us at all? Was Jakob Willnius behaving strangely that night?'

Eva Backman gave this a moment's thought before she replied.

'I don't think so.'

'Don't *think* so?'

'No. But the very fact that he sets off at twelve, comes back at three and then leaves again before eight – the same night as his sister-in-law's son vanishes – well, I reckon I'd have reported it, too. Though a little more promptly. Anyhow, the way I see it, this has come rather conveniently, what with you being in Stockholm and all. But maybe you've already had a word with Mr TV Producer Willnius?'

'Only with his wife,' conceded Gunnar Barbarotti.

'Oh? Well then, perhaps you should have a word with him

too? There could be something in what his ex-wife told you, after all.'

'I'm going to pounce this afternoon,' said Gunnar Barbarotti. 'You can be sure of that. Have you got a phone number for this Rimborg?'

She gave him the number and they ended the call.

Strange, thought Gunnar Barbarotti, decapitating his luke-warm egg. I'd already decided to do that very thing. But I'm still wondering: what the hell does this mean?

What?

Leif Grundt was in a state of agitation.

'What do you mean, you don't know where he is?' he shouted into the phone.

'I expect he's on the train,' said Berit Spaak. 'Take it easy. Or maybe he's still asleep at his friend's house. It still isn't ten o'clock.'

'Quarter past,' said Leif Grundt. 'Up here in Sundsvall, at any rate. Have you got this friend's number?'

'No, sorry. But it was someone he worked with at the shop. I think his name was Oskar.'

'You think his name was Oskar! Are you out of your mind, Berit? You have to damn well make sure you know whose place he's sleeping over at. I've been trying to get him on his mobile for over an hour now.'

'It needs recharging, probably. Why are you making such a fuss, Leif? If he's that precious to you, he'd better just stay in Sundsvall from now on. Kristoffer's fifteen years old and he asked if he could spend his last night at a friend's in the centre of Uppsala. That's nothing to get worked up about, is it?'

'He didn't tell me about these plans of his.'

'Didn't he? Well if he didn't, that's your problem. Not mine.'

'Thanks. But surely you understand why I get worried? I only want – I only want to know what time he's arriving this afternoon, so I can pick him up from the station.'

'He might already be on the train. As I said. And I'm sure you know how tricky it can be to make calls from trains? How's Ebba, by the way?'

Leif Grundt told her Ebba was more or less the same as before, and hung up. He rose from his desk chair, but then just stood there. Was that true? he thought. Was Ebba really the same as before?

Good question. Another good question.

Was there anything at all, in fact, that was the same as before?

At any rate, it was Ebba's doing that he had called Berit and asked about Kristoffer, and he knew, too, that his irritation was mainly directed at himself. He knew it very well, just as Berit had told him.

Because strictly speaking – strictly speaking – things were not really as he had led his cousin to believe. In fact, they were just the opposite. He *hadn't* been worried about Kristoffer, that was the problem. He hadn't got the strength to worry any more. The sense of responsibility for continuing to find the strength was leaking out of him like water from a defrosting turkey. Just leaking away. Everything was crashing down, or that was how it felt; suddenly it seemed impossible to hold things together any longer, to make his thoughts run in their normal channels, to get things done – to carry on living in this unbearable, grating ordinariness – not with a son missing and a wife on her way into the darkness.

But then, yesterday evening, this dark wife had called him and said she was worried about Kristoffer and wanted to speak to him. Leif had explained that the boy was currently on a week's work experience down in Uppsala, and Ebba had asked him to get the boy back home straight away. He had argued with her about it for a long time and finally given her a semi-promise to . . . well, he didn't quite know what. Ring Kristoffer and talk to him, at least. Check up on him a bit.

And that was what he had tried to do for the rest of the previous evening. At regular intervals and without result. He had also rung cousin Berit repeatedly, both her landline and her mobile, but there had been no answer from her, either.

In the latter case, it was because she and Ingegerd had been invited to an American supper round at a neighbour's house, as he had discovered this morning. They hadn't got home until after twelve.

Her mobile? Why would she have needed her mobile for dinner at a neighbour's? Ingegerd had been sitting beside her all evening.

Leif had not slept well. He stood in the study a while longer, looking at his reflection in the mirror and seeing the telltale signs. I'm forty-two, he thought. That flabby, grey-faced bloke looks at least fifty-two.

He shrugged his shoulders and rang Kristoffer's mobile number again.

No answer.

Gunnar Barbarotti decided not to use the telephone.

At least not if he could avoid it. He also decided not to contact his colleagues in the Stockholm police force. He was sure they had enough on their plates already, and the role of ham-fisted country cousin asking for assistance in a matter like this was not a very tempting one.

But he rang Backman and told her what he intended to do. Go out to Old Enskede. Go to Musseronvägen, ring at the door of number five and ask for answers to one or two questions. That was all.

He hoped he'd be home. It was a Saturday, after all.

'Brilliant plan,' said Eva Backman. 'Are you sure she won't have told him the two of you had that little talk?'

'As sure as I can be,' said Gunnar Barbarotti. 'Can you stay within reach of your phone in case I need some sound advice?'

Backman promised she would. She wasn't busy, it being a Saturday, as previously mentioned. There were at least three different unihockey matches on the day's agenda, but she had decided to stay at home. The four men of the family were already champing at the bit in the hall.

'Good,' said Gunnar Barbarotti. 'I sense we're getting close now.'

'Be careful,' said Eva Backman.

He took the underground to Old Enskede. Got off at Skogskyrkogården, made his way under Nynäsvägen and got to 5 Musseronvägen just before half past twelve. He stood outside on the pavement for a while, contemplating the lovely old wooden villa with the mansard roof, as he tried to control the nerves he could feel ticking away inside him. The weather had turned a little milder; the streets were full of slush but in the garden in front of him there was still a thick layer of snow covering the trees and ground. There was no sign of life in the house; there was no car on the drive. Perhaps they were out shopping? Buying food and wine and other requisites for the evening. At some foodie heaven like Östermalmshallen. He remembered finding himself prey to a sense of class consciousness last time he had been in the district. But also feeling that Kristina Hermansson did not really belong here, either.

He went through the gate, up the three steps to the front door, and rang the bell.

Waited thirty seconds or so and rang again.

No reaction. I'm stupid, thought Gunnar Barbarotti. Of course they're not at home. It's common knowledge everyone's out shopping at half past twelve on a Saturday.

He went out into the street again. Plan B, he decided. A bite of lunch, then another try.

And if Plan B didn't work, either, he could always resort to Plan C. The telephone. It might prove unavoidable. He had their home number and he had Jakob Willnius's work number. He also had his mobile number and his wife's mobile number.

But anyway, that was Plan C. There was a clear advantage to confronting Jakob Willnius face to face. That was the main idea. To ask those questions and observe the reaction, without giving him a chance to prepare himself first.

It was imperative, really. The phone had its disadvantages, thought Inspector Barbarotti. You couldn't see the person you were talking to. Not on ordinary phones as yet, at any rate, and of course one had to be grateful for that. Most of the calls going on were hopefully not of the kind he anticipated his conversation with Jakob Willnius would be. Anticipated and hoped. He nodded grimly to himself and set off back to the little square of shops at Nynäsvägen, where by all the usual conventions of town planning there ought also to be a local pub or restaurant.

It was called the Red Lantern and he spent a bare hour

there in the company of hash with boiled beetroot, washed down by a low-alcohol beer. Coffee and a gooey macaroon. Eva Backman rang once to ask how he was getting on, and he replied that it was only a matter of time.

It was five to two when he rang the doorbell at 5 Musseronvägen for the second time, and by his third attempt it was already three thirty. Dusk was falling, bringing with it showers of fierce, diagonal rain.

What the hell am I doing, thought Detective Inspector Gunnar Barbarotti as he headed despondently back to the tube station. And why haven't I even got an umbrella?

Forty-five minutes later he was back in his room at Hotel Terminus, implementing Plan C.

'My goodness,' said Eva Backman. 'Are things that bad?'

It was half past seven in the evening. Gunnar Barbarotti was slumped in the room's sole armchair, staring glumly at his trousers. There were two unmistakable beetroot stains, one on each leg. The only result of his day's work, you might well say.

'Yes,' he said. 'Things are that bad.'

'You sound tired.'

'That's because I am.'

'Shit happens. They've probably gone off for a weekend's sailing or something.'

'In December? Are you mad?'

'Only trying to console a colleague, but see what thanks I get for it. We'll just have to deal with this character when he turns up. There's no actual law to say you have to answer your phone . . . or be at home.'

'Thank you, I'm aware of that,' said Gunnar Barbarotti.

'I'm just saying it's a cussed nuisance. People do generally answer their mobiles, you know. The ones I ring do, anyway.'

'Did you leave a message?'

'Of course not. I don't want to give him the advantage.'

'You sound pretty sure he's involved in some way.'

'Do I?'

'Yes, actually.'

'Really? No, I'm not at all sure he's involved, though I certainly am bloody keen to grab a chat with him. But seeing as it's been a year already, maybe there isn't any great hurry.'

'That's exactly what I'm trying to tell you,' said Eva Backman. 'Calm down. Go out for a beer or ring Maria or something.'

'Marianne.'

'Eh?'

'Marianne. Her name's Marianne.'

'All right. Call her for a bit of lovey-dovey stuff, and put that shady producer out of your mind for now. He isn't worth our attention. We'll have to carry on working on this when you're back on Monday.'

Gunnar Barbarotti sighed. 'You're balm for the soul, let me tell you, Mrs Backman.'

'That's what my husband says, too,' said Eva Backman. 'In his better moments. Kiss kiss, have a nice time.'

I can't be bothered to go out, he thought once Eva Backman's voice had gone. Not in this foul weather. He tried to see out of the window, but there was very little to make out. The rain was still falling, the wind driving it against his window in cascades so it looked like a storm in an aquarium. Presumably Central station was still out there somewhere. And City Hall. Not that he gave a damn. The dejection hung in him like lingering heartburn. What the hell did I expect, he thought. What did I think I was doing here?

Bloody good thing he hadn't asked the Stockholm police for assistance, anyway. At least that was something; they'd have laughed their arses off.

He decided to heed his inner voices and the weather gods, and stay in his room. He browsed through the information folder on the diminutive desk and then rang down to order a Caesar salad and a dark beer from room service.

He had watched the news and two thirds of an old American gangster film when his phone rang.

Marianne, he thought hopefully, muting the sound on the television.

But it wasn't Marianne. It was Leif Grundt, ringing from up in Sundsvall.

44

She switched off the light and closed her eyes.

Double darkness, she thought. Just what I need. What I deserve.

And all at once, the unfamiliar room felt like an embrace. A cocoon of safety or a womb where she could rest, beyond reach of all danger. Hidden. Saved. Yes, it was really true; she listened, and the only sound to be heard was the faint hum of the ventilation system – and Kelvin's breathing, fainter still.

My poor, sleeping child, she thought. She gently ran her hands over her taut belly and rephrased herself. *My poor, sleeping children.*

What is to become of you?

What was to become of her was less important; here in this anonymous capsule of the hotel it was so clear that they were the ones who mattered. Kelvin and his unborn sibling. They were the ones she had to get to safety. The innocents.

Safety, she asked herself. What do I mean, safety? What are these spurious solutions my mind is laying out for me? What are these figments of my imagination?

And yet: *the innocents*? Well yes, that was how it felt to her. It was a justified thought, that they were the ones she had to protect. Why else should she go on living? Why care about struggling on for even another second?

But where shall I find the strength, she thought. How in the world shall I find the strength?

And once again she wished it were possible simply to switch everything off. Stop it all. Perhaps that would be the best outcome, even for the innocents? The finality of nothingness. She lay there for a while, listening to the ventilation and to Kelvin. If the universe is going to collapse, it will do it now, she thought. Now.

But nothing happened. She opened her eyes and turned her head. The little red numbers on the TV set were just changing from 23.59 to 00.00. Midnight, she thought. Can it ever possibly be more like midnight in any person's life than this?

Presumably not. Hopefully not.

And yet . . . here she was. She had got herself all the way here. It was a fact that could not be ignored. They were *here*. Right *now*. When she thought back over the previous twenty-four hours it seemed almost inconceivable. Yet here she was, lying with her children in the illusory womb of the night, and she still had the game in her hands. Wasn't that so?

Why yes. There was still everything to play for. The luggage was by the door, ready to go; she hadn't thought it worth unpacking. She had a change of underwear for herself and Kelvin in her shoulder bag. Tickets, passports and money.

A sponge bag and Robert's book. That was all she needed. And courage to carry on finding strength for a little longer. Extend this moment, she thought. Let us stay here for a long time, let these hours pass slowly; I need time to gather my strength, ready for tomorrow. Sleep and more sleep.

Yet she felt that this was the one thing she was not going to be allowed. Her body was like a nervous, ticking bomb; she presumed it was utterly futile to believe she could sleep in this state.

She sat up. Padded over to the desk and switched on the lamp. Kelvin didn't react. Kelvin hardly ever reacted to anything and at that moment, she was glad of it.

She dug Robert's manuscript out of her bag. Robert, my brother, she thought, I wish – I wish we were children again and you were here beside me. It could have been so different. It *should have been* so different. Things weren't meant to go like this for us.

In life and all that. You lost yours because you once abandoned a girl in your youth, a moment's thoughtlessness. She came back many years later and killed you, if things really happened the way the police described it.

Action and consequence, anyway. Cause and effect. She was still hanging on to her own life, for now, and the ultimate consequences of her own thoughtlessness could not be calculated. But things looked black, very black.

Be with me tonight Robert, please, she begged. Help me through these hours and give me some words to help me along the way. Robert, my brother.

To her surprise, she found she had her hands clasped together and was mumbling out loud.

But there was no answer to be heard, neither from within her nor from the night beyond. She bent over the small circle of light, opened the pile of manuscript pages at random and started to read.

For it is with life as it is with our tongue, he wrote. *In childhood we love sweetness, but it is bitterness we have to learn to accept. Otherwise we will never become fully formed people and our taste buds will remain undeveloped.*

She leant back and pondered this for a while. What odd words he used. She had never heard him speak like that. And the title: why was the book called *Man Without Dog*? She had read a good hundred pages and had yet to encounter a dog. But perhaps that was the point? That no dog ever appeared. She turned to another page.

Maria and John (they were evidently main characters of some kind, she had come across them before) *decided not to speak to one another for a whole year, and that was how they cracked the shell of their despair. Human speech is the most imperfect of all the soul's instruments, it is a whore and a usurer and a fairground quack, and when John silently observed his wife from behind, it did not take many months for her to know that look.*

Odder still. Robert, my poor brother, she thought. What is it you have been through? If we were children again tonight, would we be able to find different paths?

She shook her head. Her own words sounded alien, too. *Whores and fairground quacks?* Well yes, maybe that was so. Her thoughts went coiling like disorientated snakes inside her, and now the baby was kicking as well.

I shall have to give them up, she suddenly thought. That's what will happen. They'll take my children from me.

Unless I hide them far away in foreign lands.

Panic began to dance inside her again. How am I to get through this night? she thought. Am I supposed to sit here and stay awake until dawn? Why haven't I at least got a sleeping tablet in my sponge bag?

Dawn, really? There would be no dawn. The plane was due to take off at half past seven, so it would still be pitch-dark winter until they rose above the clouds. Check-in by six at the latest. She went on reading:

When John was a child, he thought for a long time that he had been misplaced. That he had been swapped somehow, and his mother wasn't his mother and his father wasn't his father. There had been a mix-up at the hospital and one day the mistake would be discovered, and John would be taken to where he really belonged. That was a dark, damp place with no real people; it was a region populated by some creatures with long fur and horns but faces that looked quite human. And they were capable of human speech. John often dreamt about them and he loved them. One day, he asked his mother when they would finally come and collect him. Yes, he asked his mother the question, but his father happened to be there and it was he who delivered the box on the ears. It smarted for a long time, and even in adulthood he occasionally felt its slight after-effects in his cheek, especially on dark, damp days.

She pushed the sheets of paper aside, feeling that this was too much for her on top of everything else. Robert's words were providing no support. On the contrary, they were causing her to feel a shortness of breath. Something claustrophobic, like a . . . well, like a womb within a womb. Darkness within the darkness.

She glanced towards the television. The digital numbers informed her that in the real world, the time had advanced to 00.32. Her eyes were feeling tired now, too. She checked she had set the alarm on her mobile for 05.00, then switched off the lamp and went back to bed. She put a gentle hand on Kelvin's chest.

Oh God, please grant me a little sleep, she prayed. Let me dream about my brother. Just lie here in my cocoon with my children and dream about Robert for a hundred years. But not about his words.

Perhaps about Henrik, too. A nice dream about Henrik.

She had little hope of her prayer being answered, but ten minutes later she was asleep, in spite of everything.

Gunnar Barbarotti gulped down some more of the lukewarm coffee and stared at his colleague.

The latter went by the name of Hellgren, or it might have been Hellberg, he had forgotten which; but he had one blue eye and one brown, which meant Barbarotti would have been able to pick him out amongst fifty thousand policemen. If that should ever prove necessary for any reason.

Right now, it didn't feel necessary at all. It was five to three in the morning, the setting was Stockholm police headquarters on Kungsholmen, and it was a question of sorting the wheat from the chaff.

'What the hell are you saying?' he asked.

'What I'm saying,' said Hellgrenberg, 'is that she's got a ticket to Bangkok for tomorrow.'

'Bangkok? Well I'll be damned. So you think . . . ?'

'What do you think yourself?' said Hellgrenberg with a yawn.

'She and the child, I assume?'

'Nix. She and the husband.'

'Aha? What time?'

'Eleven in the evening.'

'From Arlanda?'

'Yeah, where the hell do you think? Where have *you* come from?'

'Sorry,' said Gunnar Barbarotti. 'I grew up in Manhattan and Rio de Janeiro. Which suburb did you say you lived in?'

Hellgrenberg didn't bother to reply. He just scratched the back of his neck and glowered at him.

'But at any rate,' said Gunnar Barbarotti, 'er, at any rate, this has to be considered a red-hot lead.'

'That's what I'm saying,' said Hellgrenberg. 'All you've got to do is get yourself out to the airport and nick her, I reckon.'

'The child,' said Barbarotti. 'She'll have to take the child with her.'

'It can have the husband's ticket, I expect,' said Hellgrenberg. 'You don't think he'll be going with them, then?'

'I'm presuming not,' said Barbarotti. 'But can you change a passenger name just like that?'

His colleague rubbed his brown eye with a balled fist. 'Dunno,' he admitted. 'But if it's just a little kid, surely that'd be OK?'

'We'll have to find out,' said Barbarotti.

'Who's "we"?' asked Hellgrenberg.

'All right, I'll handle it,' said Gunnar Barbarotti. 'Have you got the flight number and so on?'

His colleague handed over a piece of paper. 'Thai Air,' he said. '23.10. So perhaps I can turn in now?'

'Go ahead,' said Gunnar Barbarotti. 'But I'd be grateful if you could get a car to take me back to my hotel first.'

'If I have to,' said Hellgrenberg.

It was getting on for half past four when he rang off after his conversation with Arlanda airport. He was so tired it was making him feel ill; he had a buzzing in his temples and eight cups of dreadful coffee were burning his stomach and his gullet – but just as he had put his head on the pillow, a random thought popped into his mind.

An idea that initially weighed no more than the wingtip of a butterfly – but its fluttering flight through his overexcited head still turned the weathervane just enough to keep him awake.

Or however one cared to express it.

Well I'm damned, he muttered, sitting up in bed. I'd never behave like that. Never in my life.

He grabbed the phone again. He could still remember the number.

45

An image went through her mind as she emerged into the departure hall.

If the hotel room had been a womb, then this was a chicken farm. This must be just what it felt like to hatch out of an egg.

She was pushing Kelvin's buggy ahead of her with one hand and pulling her suitcase along with the other. It was almost impossible to weave their way through the crowds of people and luggage. It's six in the morning, she thought. Is this when all the planes leave?

Ten minutes later she had orientated herself and found the right check-in desk and the right queue. There were at least a dozen passengers in front of her, but at least she was there now. Kelvin was awake but sat there placidly in his buggy, making no fuss as usual. The baby inside her seemed to be asleep. This is going to work, she thought.

I'm going to get away.

She instantly feared the presumptuousness of the thought. Don't count those chickens, she told herself. For God's sake, don't count those chickens before they've hatched.

But as she waited there, shuffling slowly towards the spruce young women in uniform, a sense of calm descended on her nonetheless. What could go wrong? she thought. What could actually go wrong? Why should anybody have discovered what had happened?

There was no reason to fear that they had. There really wasn't. And nobody would see anything strange in her being out of touch for the next two weeks. They were going to Thailand, everyone knew that. The fact that she was actually going to Málaga, and half a day earlier, well, who would suspect that? She had even pulled off the conversation with the childminder. Explained that they had decided to take Kelvin with them. At the last minute, yes, but there had been space on the plane.

So she could certainly count on a fortnight's grace, and after that . . . well, she had coped so far, so she would be sure to think of something.

Cometh the hour, cometh the inspiration.

Assuming there was a need to carry on living, that is. The main thing was for the children to get away. Her nocturnal thoughts were still with her, and of course she would have to give birth to the new baby, too. She had at least six weeks to go, so the fortnight would have to be extended somewhat, of course, when she came to think about it . . . How had she overlooked that in her calculations? Why did she find herself forgetting her as yet unborn child every now and then? How could you ignore something like that?

To be fair, she had scarcely had time for any calculations at all, and the fear of her own presumption returned, waving its red flag. It was so easy to imagine the whole tunnel was illuminated, just because you had glimpsed a candle flame at the far end. Yes, it was all too easy to count your chickens.

No more plans until we're in the air, she decided. No plans

then either, in fact. Thinking a couple of hours ahead, a day at most, was definitely sufficient . . . definitely enough.

In front of her there was an old couple, standing hand in hand. Well-tanned, even in mid-December. They must be Swedish expats, she thought. They'd probably been home for a week to visit the family, and now they were on the way back to their paradise on the Costa del Sol. The man was wearing a slightly crumpled cream-coloured linen suit and the woman was in trousers and a sea-green tunic. She felt a stab of envy. Just think of being that old, they must have been approaching eighty, but still standing lovingly hand in hand at an airport. That will never be me, she thought. And I can't look at them without feeling envious, I haven't even learnt that much.

The snake thoughts began to writhe inside her again, and suddenly she remembered what she had been dreaming. It had not been about Robert, her first choice, but about Henrik. Not the pleasant dream she had asked for, but a dream of that night, those first hours – no, that single hour, that was all it had amounted to – when they were able to be together, before everything was shattered.

She had dreamt of his shyness. Of his awkwardness and his young, unused body. The dream had actually played out in that hotel room, but she had not been Kristina. That was the strange thing. Instead she had been someone else, standing outside the window, seeing them in bed in there, watching as they made love – and it took a very long time for her to understand that she was Jakob. She stood there staring at herself and Henrik through Jakob's eyes, and when she finally realized, she let out a howl and threw herself through the window to tear the two lovers apart and . . . but before reaching the bed, she had woken up.

Woken up and not remembered a single thing about the dream. Not until now, an hour and a half later. It was remarkable. Could sunken dreams suddenly resurface like that? Why? What did it mean? She felt a droplet of sweat leave her armpit and trickle down the side of her body – and at the same moment, a note began to sound inside her head. A low, barely audible note, more like a vibration. What's up with me, she thought in dismay. What's happening to me? Am I losing control after all?

It was the old couple's turn to check in. She stepped forward to the yellow line. Took a deep breath and clenched her hands.

She kept it together. Once again, she kept it together. Ten minutes later, the buggy and the case had been safely checked in. All that remained was security control and an hour's wait at gate 15. She hoisted Kelvin onto her arm and headed for the entrance to the security area. Showed her boarding pass to a short-haired young man in a white shirt and dark tie. He gave her an accommodating nod but did not return her pass.

'Just a moment please,' he said, and nodded to a fellow staff member.

His colleague emerged from the shadows and looked at the boarding passes, both hers and Kelvin's. Then smiled at them both and asked them to come with him a different way, through a door.

'But why?' she asked.

'It's to do with your pregnancy,' he explained kindly, showing her into a little room in which there were two small tables, each with two chairs. 'As I'm sure you know, flying in pregnancy does involve certain risks, and we need you to fill in a couple of forms. It's just a formality. Please have a seat.'

She sat down at one of the tables and put Kelvin on her knee.

'Why didn't they say anything at check-in?' she asked. 'Or when I bought my ticket?'

He didn't answer. Instead, another door opened.

She didn't recognize him immediately. She couldn't – for the first fractions of the first second – understand what he was doing there.

But then she understood. Everything.

He cleared his throat.

'Kristina Hermansson,' he said. 'Your husband was found dead yesterday in your home at 5 Musseronvägen in Old Enskede. I have to inform you that you are under arrest on suspicion of his murder.'

She closed her eyes for a second. Opened them again.

'I see,' she said. 'And yes, you are quite correct. I'm sorry I had to lie to you.'

'No need to apologize,' he said.

46

Ebba Hermansson Grundt leant forward over the kitchen table. She gravely regarded her son and then her husband, one after the other.

'I've realized something these past few days,' she said.

'It's been hard,' said Leif Grundt. 'For us all.'

'I've realized we have to consider Henrik dead. He *is* dead. We can't go on living if we keep imagining anything else.'

'I've been thinking about that, too,' said Leif. 'I reckon you're absolutely right.'

'I think the same,' said Kristoffer.

Ebba Hermansson Grundt clasped her hands round the teacup in front of her and carried on looking at them a while longer. 'It's been a horrible year. But from now on, we must try to remember the brightest and best things about Henrik.'

'That sounds good,' said Leif Grundt. 'What do you think, Kristoffer?'

'Yes, that sounds good,' said Kristoffer, pushing his long fringe aside so he could look at both his mother and his father. A few silent seconds passed. Leif Grundt gave a sigh.

'Well that's decided then,' said Ebba. 'You need a haircut, Kristoffer. So, you enjoyed your work experience down in Uppsala, did you?'

Kristoffer gave his father a look. 'Yes, thanks. But it's nice to be back home, actually.'

'I think so too,' said Ebba. 'We've got to try to look forward a bit now.'

'I reckon that would do us no harm at all,' said Leif Grundt.

'By all means go into a bit more detail,' suggested Eva Backman.

'I know you think I should,' said Gunnar Barbarotti. 'But I haven't slept for over twenty-four hours, so unless you've anything—'

'Knife, you said?'

'Knife, yes. Stabbed him nine times in the back, the last six when he was already on the ground.'

'And she confessed straight away?'

'Didn't even have to ask her any questions.'

'And he . . . ?'

'Killed Henrik Grundt, yes.'

'Did she tell you why?'

'I've got to think it over.'

'Eh?'

'I said I've got to think it over.'

'I heard you. And what the hell does that mean? That you've got to think over whether he . . . ?'

'It's rather a tricky one, this. I've got all the information I need on Henrik Grundt's death and on Jakob Willnius's. But there's some excess information, too. The sort of thing there's no point making public. Or including in my final report . . . I've got to think it over. As I said.'

'I don't understand.'

'No, you don't. But let me say one thing: truth can sometimes be an overrated jewel.'

'You must have read that in . . . well, the Mickey Mouse Pocket Compendium or some of that other reading matter you like to get your nose into.'

'Bloody hell, Backman, why do you always have to be like this? Imagine if you were to congratulate me on having cleared this case up, instead.'

'Oh yes, you'd love that,' said Eva Backman, and hung up.

Before he went off to sleep he lay there thinking for a while.

It had required so little, he thought. A minute – that was as long as it had taken to dig out the overrated jewel of truth.

'But don't you see?' he had asked. 'Don't you see that I can't make do with just this? If you can't tell me why your husband killed Henrik Grundt, I might start to suspect that you killed him, too. That you did it together. You've got to give me a reason.'

She had hesitated for a moment.

'I was the reason,' she had answered.

For one second flat, he had failed to understand. Then he had understood beyond all doubt.

No, it hadn't even taken a minute.

'How did the two of you get the body out?' he had not been able to stop himself asking.

'There was a little fire-escape balcony. And a staircase. It was easy.'

He had decided not to press her on where they had buried the body. Not for now. It hadn't even felt important.

More important was deciding how to deal with that excess information he had spoken to Backman about. The dark knowledge of what had been at the root of the whole story. Kristina and Henrik. The aunt and the nephew who had crossed the boundary into a forbidden land.

If you wanted to be poetic about it. Inebriation and lust, if you preferred plain prose. A great deal had been wrecked by their actions, but was it really necessary to shatter what little was left?

Good question. The secret currently rested with four people: him and Kristina, Kristoffer Grundt and his father. Couldn't it be left at that? Did Gunnar Barbarotti – as a detective inspector and a human being – have some kind of duty to make sure everything was brought to merciless and universal light?

A crucial decision, undoubtedly, but in his present state he wasn't prepared to tackle it, as he had tried to explain to Inspector Backman. Lying on his back in the soft hotel bed, the curtains closed and the game won, he did, however, feel a certain sense of urgency about contacting the conceivably extant Almighty.

To check the balance of their account and one thing and another – but there was not time even to do that before sleep sank over him like a warm and lazy summer's day.

Rosemarie Wunderlich Hermansson was sitting in one of the bars at Málaga airport.

It was two hours since the plane Kristina and Kelvin were supposed to be on had landed. She had drunk three glasses of sweet wine and made twice that many phone calls to try to find out what was going on. She could get no answer anywhere. It was incomprehensible. Spoilt brat, she thought.

Could at least get in touch and say she was catching a later plane. That really wasn't asking too much.

Ringing with hardly any notice to say she'd left her husband and had to come down. And then not turning up. She'd thought the better of it, of course. Taken him back. And then completely forgotten a waiting mother who was worried sick.

She would have liked a bit of information from the airport staff about passenger lists and so on, but she knew how bad their English was. There were always misunderstandings. And it felt a bit off, somehow. A daughter who didn't turn up as promised. They would think she must be a bit weird for something like that to happen to her. Rosemarie Wunderlich Hermansson was sick and tired of things happening to her.

And there was another plane, due to land in an hour and a half's time. Coming via Copenhagen, admittedly, but still. Karl-Erik was out playing golf. It took between forty-five minutes and an hour by taxi to get from the airport to their *urbanización*. Depending on the traffic. She had nothing important to do. Might just as well sit here and wait for that plane, too – if Kristina really was on board, she couldn't actually get in touch at the moment.

It was what it was, and she had never really warmed to that Jakob. There was something untrustworthy about him. Coming off the phone last night, she had felt quite exhilarated at the thought of having her daughter and grandson to live with her for a while.

Rosemarie Wunderlich Hermansson sighed and ordered another glass of wine. She enjoyed using the small amount of Spanish she had learnt, in spite of everything.

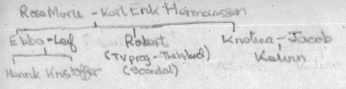